STEAMBOAT SEASONS

Dawn of a New Era

THE SEQUEL TO
STEAMBOAT SEASONS AND BACKWATER BATTLES

A HISTORICAL NOVEL

To Victor,
Happy Trails, Always!

Kendall D. Gott

ISBN 978-1-63630-078-8 (Paperback)
ISBN 978-1-63630-079-5 (Digital)

Copyright © 2020 Kendall D. Gott
All rights reserved
First Edition

Covenant Books, Inc.
11661 Hwy 707
Murrells Inlet, SC 29576
www.covenantbooks.com

Contents

Book 4

Maps

Upper Mississippi and Illinois Rivers

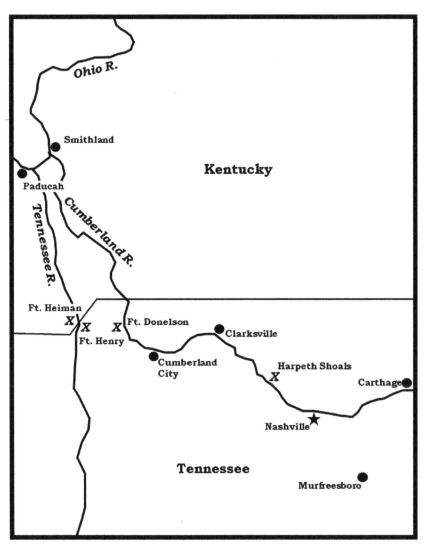

Cumberland River

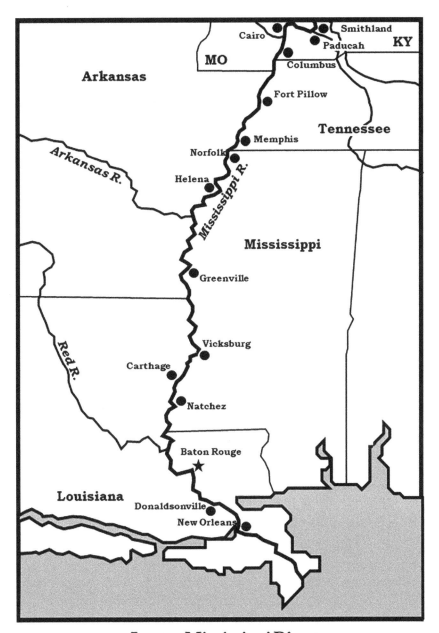

Lower Mississippi River

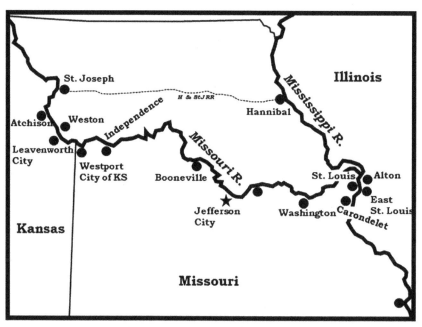

Lower Missouri River

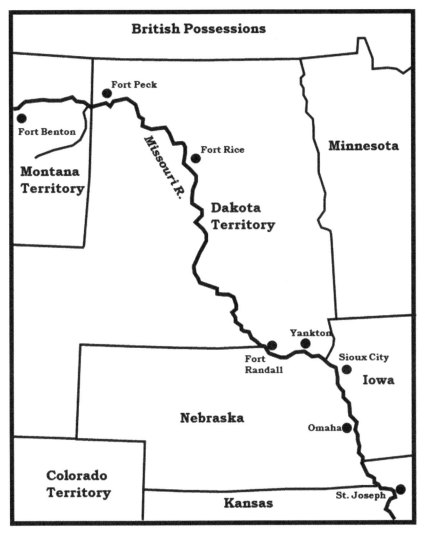

Upper Missouri River

Introduction

Change can come in forms that is quite unwelcome,
but change is how we grow. It is important to live
your life without fear of change. That is not a painless
lesson. The younger you learn that the better.
—Sylvanus Geldstein

The war was over. The Union is restored, but the Confederates had gone down fighting all the way. Some holdouts fought on for a while out west of the Mississippi, but even they finally realized the futility of it all. With four long years of conflict, the Southern Confederacy was no more. The combined tally of the dead and those who died of disease is over six hundred thousand, but the clerks are still counting. They were not even trying to calculate the thousands of civilian casualties and the millions of dollars in lost property. Over a million horses and mules were lost too. Historians will reflect upon the enormity of it—the thousands of miles marched, the number of cities captured. Accounts of the military exploits will be written for years to come.

Meanwhile, the South remains broken by war and lays prostrate under Union army occupation. It faces the daunting task of rebuilding its shattered economy and demolished infrastructure. Billions of dollars in the economic value of slaves was wiped away by their emancipation without financial compensation to the owners. The slaves were technically free, but their suffering is not yet over. Although their humanity is recognized, the political and economic forces are now battling over their status as citizens and how they will fit into American society.

Economically, the Northern states emerged from the war virtually unscathed. Industry is on the rise, and a new wave of immigrants from Europe is streaming into the country seeking a better life. Railroads are stretching their tentacles across the land, making inroads into the traditional steamboat trade. But perhaps now we could all get back to work and business. The South still had to rebuild from scratch, but the Union army still had thousands of soldiers spread across the old Confederacy in occupation. And all those men still needed their supplies.

It is still a good time to be a steamboatman in the summer of 1865.

At this time, the trials and tribulations of the nation seemed far away. I had located my childhood sweetheart, Ann. We had grown up together up along the banks of the Illinois River, but when I decided to seek my fortune on the steamboats, she was no longer interested in my affections. The lowly status of a deckhand and the periods of long absence were no doubt a great portion of her thinking.

While I served through the war as a pilot on a gunboat, Ann became a nurse at one of the five large military hospitals in Quincy, Illinois, located on the Mississippi River. Alerted to her location, the end of the spring shipping season gave me my chance to make my way there. My desire was to see her again and possibly renew our relationship that ended so badly when I left to become a riverman. Her rejection then was harsh but falling for a friend named James Simpson made it worse. His great ambition was to join some bank up in Havana, or maybe it was further up the Illinois River in Peoria. I could never remember which.

I found Ann in a ward located in the imposing five-story former German and English College on the north side of Spring Street. Our meeting was a joyous one, and she easily obtained a release from her director, Brigade Surgeon Nichols. The hospitals were being emptied anyway, and plans were for closing them all by mid-July. I brought her back to my home port of St. Louis with the intention of getting reacquainted and to show her my world. Rising from deckhand to pilot over the years, and now captain of my own boat, there was much to see, including the big city. A new era was at hand.

Book 1

Ann

The small packet *Tamaroa Band* would make a quick trip of the 144 river miles between Quincy and St. Louis. She needed to as this was the last run of the season unless heavy rains came soon. The *Tamaroa* was under the same company flag as mine but ran a regular packet line between St. Louis and Davenport. The captain is a good man and offered me a watch at the boat's wheel. I declined with thanks but told him I would only do so in a time of dire if need. Despite my uniform, I was on board as a passenger. My wardrobe was simply limited to wearing that or a barrel.

Ann had lost considerable weight over the years and looked almost sickly. She quickly showed her moods could swing from happy and content to sad and frustrated without provocation. She continued to wear her hospital dress, inferring she had no other attire or simply chose it for ease in traveling. I didn't know which, and men did not ask those questions. Those skirt hoops with "civilian" attire could be a bother, particularly on a steamboat. The builders did not have those in mind during their construction. Quickly approaching the ripe old age of thirty years, we could bend societal norms just a bit. We both thought it silly to need a chaperone, but to protect her virtue, we of course lodged in separate cabins. There was no way I would subject her to the main-deck steerage. The "deckers" there got less attention from the crew than did the cargo.

The weather was warm but not stifling. The skies were clear, and the hyacinths along the banks were in bloom. A good breeze from the northeast coyly indicated rains may be on the way. If they came in quantity, the rivers would rise enough to begin the summer season. We passed the time on the covered gangway which wrapped around the upper boiler deck. Inside the walls, men were engaged in lively game of faro in the forward saloon. No doubt there would be pairs of blacklegs working to fleece their targets. Steamboat passengers were generally well behaved but took matters in their own hands if cheating was exposed. The offenders could find their heads shaved, be beaten, tossed overboard, or a combination of all three. The women passengers were no doubt in the aft parlor seeking refuge from the smoke, liquor, and swearing.

"You have aged wonderfully, Ann."

"And you haven't aged a day. How tremendously impolite of you. You surprise me by not asking about James."

"I didn't figure the need. I'm not sure I want to know."

"You're not even a bit curious of the man who promised to sweep me off my feet and is now conspicuously absent?"

"Fine, tell me. How is James Simpson? Is he president of that bank yet?"

"Why, so nice of you to ask. With the outbreak of war, James enlisted in Company C of the Second Illinois Cavalry. He died of measles while in Camp Buter, just north of Springfield. He passed just before the elections held to choose the officers and noncommissioned officers. He had expectations to be at least a lieutenant, maybe a captain. Poor James is buried there in a common soldier's grave. I wonder if it is even marked."

She teared up but did not cry. They say time heals all wounds, but there is often a scar.

"I'm very sorry to hear of James. Remember, he had been a friend of mine at one time."

While aboard, we took our meals with the other passengers, who often mistook me for the captain of the boat. I told them to forward any complaints to the first mate. The food was certainly not lavish. It consisted mostly of various meats and sausages stacked high on platters with loaves of bread to the side. The cook sounded a dinner bell at the time of readiness and stood clear as the hungry travelers ravenously fell upon the "food pile." Men and women fought with equal aplomb for the choicest morsels. I was used to such scenes, but Ann was appalled. We held our distance until the serious tussles were over and picked through the remains, looking for something fit to eat. We were like coyotes picking through a carcass after the wolves ate their fill.

"My goodness! They were like animals. Even the well-to-do fell under the spell. Does this happen on your boat?"

"You've seen, my dear, one of the many reasons my boat would rather haul cargo than passengers. Their fare isn't worth the cost and fuss. Some of the larger boats solve this problem by hiring waiters to serve at a table. We eliminated the problem altogether by only offering main-deck steerage."

"What does that mean?"

"The passengers on the main deck below us paid for passage only. They bring their own food and drink."

"Where do those people sleep? I haven't seen any of them come up to their cabins."

"Deck-class passengers are supposed to remain on the main deck. They sleep amongst or on top of the boxes, crates, and sacks of cargo."

"That deck has no walls or shelter. What if it rains?"

"They better hope they brought a blanket. It's not inhuman in practice. They get themselves and their heavy baggage to their destination cheaper than the railroad and in more comfort than any stagecoach."

The packet did make good time but made landings at Hannibal, Louisiana, Clarksville, and Hamburg. Such dockings usually cost an hour or two of time. Fortunately for us, the stops were mostly for taking on or discharging passengers and not much handling of freight. I wondered how this boat turned a profit.

The *Tamaroa Band* plied through the night, and I tried not to worry about the boat hitting a snag or other hidden obstruction. This was not my vessel, and I had to trust the judgment of the captain and his pilot. The leadsmen up on the bow were sounding the depth of the river, and it was shallow and falling. No doubt the captain was in a race with Mother Nature to reach St. Louis before the boat was left high and dry on a sandbar. Fortunately, we scooted into the St. Louis harbor without any delay or incident.

St. Louis lies on the west bank of the Mississippi River and extends nearly seven miles and almost three miles back. The city is well laid out with sixty-foot-wide streets and, with few exceptions, intersected at right angles. Front Street ran along the landing and was made one hundred feet wide to facilitate all the handling of freight. Splendid five-story wholesale stores and warehouses were built here along the length. Front, Main, and Second streets run parallel to each other to the west. Second Street is occupied by grocery, iron, receiving and shipping houses. Fourth Street is the fashionable promenade and contains the finest retail stores. The city has made large expenditures from time to time to grade and improve the all the busier streets and alleys.

The waterfront was rather quiet, with most boats being laid up for the season two weeks or more already. Only little boats like the *Tamaroa Bend* were still active. There were at least eighty respectable steamboats packed in tightly along the waterfront and at least forty more across the river at Alton. There was just not enough water to make a safe journey anywhere with them until the river rose again. That could be tomorrow, next week, or next month. Mother Nature was queen in such matters. Responsible companies used such slack times to overhaul engines, scrub boilers, and generally clean and paint their boats. The cacophony of metal striking metal and general use of cursing and profanity meant that rivermen and mechanics were toiling away.

Coming ashore so late in the season meant we landed where we could find a space. There were few left to choose from. This meant a considerable walk to my company's designated berths and the company office just beyond. As Ann was with me, I hired a delivery boy to take the trunk and carpetbag to a carriage and its driver carried us on to our first destination.

The company office is located within a grand five-story brick edifice at the foot of Market Street. It is proudly one of the first buildings in St. Louis to have gas lighting. The ground floor contains the business of the steamboats. The second, third, and fourth stories hold the myriad of business offices that the Geldstein family owned outright or partially so. The fifth floor is reserved as the owner's residence. Most magnates built their mansions up town, but the founder, Sylvanus Geldstein, always wished to remain close to his interests. His son Thomas inherited the whole pot of gold last year upon the old man's death.

"The large sign has a gold ship wheel, the same as on your cap and lapel. I just thought it was a common nautical bauble."

"That's the company symbol. Welcome to the company office. I need to stop in briefly. If he is available, I would like to introduce you to Mr. Thomas Geldstein, the owner of the company. I owe him my life several times over and my present position as well. I must warn you about his appearance, though."

"What could possibly be so queer of his countenance that it needs a warning?"

"He was badly scalded years ago during a mishap on a steamboat. The left side of his face is rather gruesome. Normal clothing conceals the full extent of his injuries."

"I am not sure I can withstand the spectacle. I have seen enough burns and wounds."

"You can wait in the parlor then. No need for embarrassing him or yourself."

I instructed the carriage driver to deliver Ann's trunk and my carpet bag to the Barnum Hotel, just up the way. It wasn't the fanciest hotel in town, but it was convenient and comfortable. A very generous fifty-cent tip insured they would reach their destination.

The Negro doorman at the office greeted and welcomed us to St. Louis. The golden ship wheel was on his lapel too. He was a company man. He did, though, look older every time I saw him.

"Mr. Geldstein is in residence, Captain. He has a slate of visitors today, though."

As Ann remained so skittish in meeting Thomas, I left her in the company parlor. A Negro behind the bar would provide her refreshments until my return. I found Mr. Geldstein's next appointment was late, and he could spare some time.

"Ah, my good captain. Welcome home. Did you find your Ann?"

"Indeed, I did. She is in good health, although I believe her service in the hospital may have deeply affected her."

"No surprise there. She must have witnessed many a horrible scene."

"I brought her here to St. Louis for the dry season to show her around, get reacquainted."

"I would like to meet her. Where is she?"

"I'm afraid that she is rather timid in meeting you. I warned her of the extent of your injuries, and she is now waiting for me in the parlor. I am so sorry, Thomas. She has seen enough burns and wounds. Her words, not mine. She does extend her warmest regards."

Thomas looked crestfallen. This was certainly not the first time such a thing occurred.

"She tolerates your ugly mug but may be repulsed by mine?" It was the humor of a hurt man.

"Come now, Thomas, I know I am no Winfield Scott Hancock. She is just woefully uneducated of your comely attributes. Perhaps next time."

"No, you're more the John Owens type, but at least he seems to improve with age. Perhaps you will too. Maybe you should grow a beard. Yes, it is regretfully understandable with your Ann. Please give her my best. By the way, we have a wire from Keokuk that the river is on the rise there. Heavy rains are reported up north. The rivers should be finally navigable here in the next few days. Have your Mr. Bemis meet with the contracting officer here if he has not done so already. Implore him also to drum up any additional business at the landing. He knows the routine. How is he doing?"

"He certainly isn't his old self. He has just returned from his recuperation from his wounds three weeks ago. He gets around fair enough on crutches, but without a large flock of passengers to fleece at his faro table or selling concessions, there is little money to be made on the side. That conniving spark required of all pursers seems to be gone. He is rounding up consignments from the shipping agents just fine, but I fear not with the same aplomb. We'll see."

"Six months ago, the man lost a leg when the Rebs ambushed and demolished our old boat beyond economic repair. He is lucky to be alive, although he may not fully agree. We three served together on that gunboat for almost the whole war. Although Bemis is taking large amounts of morphine sulfates, he has a job at this company as long as he can hold a pencil. We'll strap him to a chair if need be. It might, though, be time for a little reorganization on your boat."

"What do you mean, Thomas? The boat is running along fine."

"The steamboat inspectors are enforcing the regulations with more precision, and more of both are surely coming. Some of their findings relate to mere terminology, but there are some real changes in order. Your boat has cut costs by combining two jobs into one or underpaying those men in position. You have overworked yourself since becoming a pilot and captain, and you expect the same of all others. That can't continue. Promote Bemis to chief clerk and instruct him to hire a mud clerk to do all the dirty work. No more talk of 'pursers.' His position is now *chief clerk*. Be sure to call him 'captain' too. The navy thought highly enough to give him command of a vessel without a master's certificate. He has earned that title in my book. Also, promote your foreman, Mr. Voight, if I recall his name correctly, to first mate. Designate one or two men as second and third."

"That will cut down on our profit margin, Thomas. The hike in salaries is substantial."

"That may be true, but it will keep the inspectors off our backs an' keep our licenses and certifications in order. Good for morale too. You're running a tramper boat, and they examine them in finer detail than the lead-line packet boats. It's the cost of doing business. I won't keep you from Ann and your boat any longer. No doubt there is an appointment waiting outside for me."

"Aye, Mr. Geldstein. All will all be in place by this next run."

I had not hired a mate to keep costs down, fifty dollars a month in fact. A foreman was adequate to manage the deck crew below. The engineer and his gang toiled at the boilers and engines. Chief pilot Swanson was in the wheelhouse, and I was there much of the time as well. But with no mate, there was always a need for me to leave the pilothouse to strut about the boat, checking this and that. These changes might be good.

Thomas and I shook hands as he saw me to the door. Seated outside was a well-dressed elderly man waiting patiently, holding a plump chicken on his lap. I could not resist speaking to him.

"Um, good day, sir. I don't know much about yardbirds beyond the leghorns, but that is quite a handsome bird you have there."

"This, good sir, is a Brahma. A superior winter layer and fine roaster. It is the future of poultry production in the New West."

"Good luck with that, sir, and good day. Good day to you too, Mr. Geldstein."

I beat a hasty retreat before I could bust a gut laughing and perhaps ruin whatever Thomas was cooking up. Literally.

I made my way down the long corridor to the company parlor. It was here the captains and pilots loitered about to exchange notes on the river conditions and generally kill the time between runs. Large maps of the river hung on the walls with colored pins marking various snags or other hazards to navigation. The number on the pins corresponded to a pilot report posted off to the side. No doubt my pilot, Mr. Swanson, would pay a visit and benefit from the experience of a fellow pilot who had just completed a run.

At a set of padded chairs, Ann was in deep conversation with my old mentor Captain Sulloway. This hard-drinking man is a legend on the rivers, perhaps only second to Horace Bixby or maybe James Eads. He had survived the cholera epidemic and the great fire back in '49 but lost his family to the calamities. Mostly retired from river service, he spends most of his time overseeing the steamboats of the company. Although still early in the day, he was drinking in earnest, with two fingers of brown liquor in his glass. He had lost weight and reduced his consumption during the war, but he was back to his habits and old beefy self.

"Ah, good day, lad. Good to see you. I hope you don't mind if I was keeping this lovely creature entertained in your absence."

"Not at all. I hope he wasn't boring you to tears with fanciful tales of his exploits, Miss Ann."

"Oh, Captain Sulloway here is quite incorrigible. Beyond all hope," she said with a smile and a pat of the hand to his knee. It was the first big smile I had seen from her since our reuniting.

"She has the fire of a filly, my boy. You should take her on your next run and show her the life on the river."

The thought had not occurred to me. Would she even consider it? It could be considered quite scandalous, if not handled properly. A strict set of rules and etiquette that governed almost all aspects of everyday life in well-to-do society. Even the daily life of a middle-class lady like Ann was directed by rule after rule, from the time she rose in the morning until the time she went to bed at night. Women are so hard on themselves and one another. On a steamboat, unmarried couples pretending to be otherwise were generally put ashore at the nearest town if discovered. Ann's reputation could be ruined if an improper word were spread.

"Uh, that is something we will have to discuss, sir. The matter could be a delicate one."

"Oh, what a simply scandalous idea! When will we depart?"

"Um, are you quite certain, Miss Ann?"

"Oh my, yes!"

"I'm not sure it is the best of ideas, but all right. When we ship out, you may have my cabin, and I will take up residence further aft. Good day, Captain Sulloway. We need to get settled, and then I must get the boat ready for her next run. Looks as though high water is coming down from the north."

"No other place it could come from, my boy. Bon voyage, if I do not see you before departure. Au revoir, mademoiselle."

"Merci, mon capitaine. Le plaisir était pour moi," Ann replied in a most mischievous tone and a perfect French accent.

We checked into the Barnum Hotel with no fuss. It helped that we asked for separate rooms. At the arranged time, Ann emerged from her room looking remarkable. She had changed from her hospital dress and back into hoops. It was a simple and somewhat plain day dress but a vast improvement over her previous dour attire. She even carried a fan. A fan is one of the only means free expression for women by their use of coded messages using the art of "fan language." Where a woman placed or carried a fan sent more messages than a Coston light signal. When she carried a fan in her left hand, for example, meant that she wished to make your acquaintance, but drawing the fan across her forehead meant that she and you were being watched by someone. All women communicated such things even though most men were oblivious to the code cipher they used. The message I was most familiar with was the drawing the fan through the hand, meaning the lass had grown tired of the conversation and was signaling for rescue. Someone someday should write a book exposing all the female mysteries and secrets. Such a tome would probably contain several volumes.

Using the Case and Wells omnibus, I showed her my usual off-season haunts in St. Louis, such as the Mercantile Library and the opera house on Market Street, and the nice park setting at Lindell Grove. I steered clear of the faro dens, taverns, and the waterfront. Those were no places for a respectable lady. Ann seemed to enjoy the day, but by suppertime, even I could tell she was running out of steam. We dined at the Barnum and adjourned to the parlor. She had wine while I nursed a brandy a cigar. The tobacco was a good blend and did not produce clouds of smoke like my usual brand. A good choice. A well-dressed Negro softly played the piano in the corner.

"What do you think of the fair city of St. Louis?"

"Oh, Quincy has everything St. Louis does, just not as many or as big."

"That is a very astute observation. Any others?"

"Captain Sulloway told me of your injury to your hand while trying to save your friend in the wheelhouse. He says it was quite a freak shot to damage the whistle pedal and flood the whole structure with steam as it did. Is that why you always wear gloves? I thought you were just being gentlemanly in your role as captain."

"Yes, I wear gloves in public so as not to frighten the women and children on the streets. Only the left hand was injured, though, up about halfway to the elbow."

"I would like to see it. Please."

That was a strange request as earlier today she balked at meeting Mr. Geldstein on account of his fearful injuries. I gingerly removed the glove for her inspection. Although the injury occurred several months ago, the skin was still fiery red and pulled taut over the bones and muscle. It looked as if it were conjured from a Beadle's dime novel.

The sight made her recoil in disgust and revulsion, as if it brought forth visions of nightmares past. I knew instantly that she would never look at me the same again. In the steamboat trade, I would be called "damaged goods."

We retired early and remained in our separate rooms throughout the evening. After a continental breakfast, we returned to the company office. I wanted to make sure a notice for departure was posted and to arrange provision for coaling and attend to some manning issues. My hope was to find Mr. Bemis with good news in securing contracts and cargo for a profitable trip. My old friend was exiting the contracting office as we rounded the corner. He was still struggling with adapting to the crutches. It was a sad sight. The loss of his leg was complete, all the way up to hip and beyond. How he even survived the wound and surgeries was a miracle, and his pain was obvious. He froze in shock when he saw us, which surprised me. I was more prepared for a friendly quip about finally having a woman on my arm than what happened.

"Anna! What are you doing here?"

I turned to see she was as shocked as he. I was certainly confused.

"Lieutenant Bemis! Why, I should be asking that of you!"

"Um, you two know each other?"

"Yes, indeed we do, Captain. Miss Anna here was an attending nurse while I convalesced at the hospital in Quincy. Is this your Ann you spoke of during your times on the farm?"

"Indeed. Upon hearing of her location, I took a steamer upriver and returned here."

"Well, ah, ahem, it is good to see you again, Miss Anna." Bemis slightly bowed his head in formality.

So she wants to be called Anna now. I probably won't ever break the habit.

There was clearly something amiss that I couldn't put my finger on. Ann—or Anna, as she was apparently being called now—went deathly quiet. Mr. Bemis broke the awkward silence.

"Um, Captain, we have a consignment of army rations and quartermaster supplies bound for Nashville that should fill the hold and the main deck. Assorted commercial sundries and food products will take up most of the boiler deck. We may have a handful of deck passengers but won't know that for sure until we are about to shove off. That will be in the morning unless the engineer has objections. I have arranged a telegraph sent to the shipping agents announcing our travels and intention to return to St. Louis. Hopefully, we will not return with an empty boat."

"Thank you, *Captain* Bemis. Good work and welcome back to the boat. Just like old times. I have the pleasure, though, to tell you that you are promoted to chief clerk, and your wages will be correspondingly raised. Hire a mud clerk to assist in your duties. Our friend and boss Thomas Geldstein insisted."

Normally such news would be received with more cheer. Instead, Bemis's gaze was locked onto Ann, Anna, whatever.

"Oh well, thank you, Captain. The additional funds come at a good time. I can't think of a capable mud clerk right now but will keep my eyes open. That's a fine new boat you have, and it even bears the name of our old gunboat."

"You know how sentimental Thomas is. I suspect there will be a boat of that name in the fleet for the duration of his ownership. Too bad we don't have the old bell to put on display with all the others in the company parlor."

"Oh, it's on its way here. Couldn't let it be left behind on the old gal to end up as scrap."

"Well, I'll be. How did you manage that?"

My question was answered with a sly smile. That was our old Bemis at work. Maybe all was well.

Ann finally spoke. "Why did you call him 'captain'? His shoulder straps while at the hospital were those of a navy lieutenant."

"Navy men who command a boat or ship are called captain regardless of rank. 'Captain' Bemis here was placed in command of our gunboat a few weeks before my departure and return here. He has earned the right to be called that honorific by rivermen forevermore."

The silence now exceeded awkward. It was time to go our separate ways, and with such an early departure, there was much a boat captain needed to do.

"Miss Ann—uh, Anna—it appears as though we need to depart the Barnum Hotel and move onto the boat. I should already be there to oversee things anyway. See you on board, Captain Bemis."

This would be the first run of the new season. High waters should bless our travels until the late autumn dry spell.

The omnibus ride to the hotel took but a few minutes, and shortly we were packed, and the bill was paid. I arranged for the delivery of her trunk and my carpetbag, and we made our way down Market Street to the riverfront. Along the way we stopped for cigars, horehound candy, and Necco wafers for me. The bottle of whiskey in my other trunk on board was more than plenty for the run to Nashville. At a druggist store, Ann stocked up for the voyage. Along with various female items and medicines, she procured a handful of packets containing opium powders. Opium was considered a wonder drug and was found in all sorts of foods and pharmacies. I had yet to have any need of it, and my trust in the medical profession was very low. Doctors prescribed opium in various forms too often out of ignorance of a cure. To their little credit, they confessed it didn't cure anything, but it gave relief to everything. For me, whiskey did the same thing for my few ailments.

The St. Louis levee was teeming with activity as all the boats prepared to renew their seasons. The dockmaster will have his hands full as each boat vied to depart first. Collisions were bound to happen in the morning. Gangs of roustabouts heaved various boxes, crates, and barrels aboard, and the deckmen stowed them in the holds and on deck. The mates and foremen made sure the loads were distributed evenly to keep the boats on a level trim. The process called for much yelling and of course a liberal application of cussing. It was no place for a lady, but Ann said she had heard it all before and had used such colorful language occasionally herself when the need arose.

"Wait, that's your boat? It's surely big enough, but not much to look at."

"It doesn't have the fancy gingerbread-house trimming and feathers on her stacks because it is workhorse freighter-packet, not a glitzy showboat. I apologize if I gave you the wrong impression."

"I suppose it floats, I guess."

Those would be fighting words from anyone else, but I let it go. My boat was a proud and respected vessel. I was seriously having second thoughts about this whole idea of bringing her along. Catching sight of the foreman, Mr. Voight, I beckoned him over. He has been with the company for at least five years and was assigned to the boat when I made captain. Remarkably, he ably motivates the men of the deck crew without much of the yelling and cursing. I suppose it was his deadly-looking eyes and chiseled face that intimidated them. After introductions, I told him of the plan to place Ann in my cabin and told him to have a man place my carpetbag in a cabin further aft. He gave no indication there was anything scandalous with this arrangement.

"Captain, the coal bunkers are full, and the army rations are in the holds. Additional rations are stored on the main deck, as well as the quartermaster supplies. The boiler deck has what weight it can stand of general cargo. Mister—I mean *Captain*—Bemis has the list of scheduled stops. Our engineer, Mr. Weatherby, reports all his machinery is in readiness. He has a full crew, and I have twenty deckhands. There are some Irishmen mixed in, but that couldn't be helped. The cook says he has a good supply of food on hand but may sortie ashore for more produce along the way. Welcome aboard, Miss Anna."

"Just a moment, Mr. Voight. I have the pleasure to promote you to first mate with the commensurate pay and benefits. I am remiss about not having your cap and frock coat in hand, but a company man will bring them over shortly. Also, name a second and third mate to assist you. I want to meet with all the boat officers after supper as we usually do. In the meantime, let's get the boat ready to depart. I would like to get underway in the morning."

"Aye, Captain, and thank you. I was going to talk to you about my status and pay. She'll be ready to steam at your command. Oh, Mr. Swanson is up in the pilothouse. He has a brand spanky new cub pilot up there, and he is showing him the ropes."

I led Anna across the gangway and up the main ramp to the next deck. Almost all other boats used a grand stairway to go up to the boiler deck. As this was a freighter, the builders installed a heavy ramp for ease of loading cargo. The company men and the roustabouts from ashore politely gave Anna a wide berth. But one lad, apparently with some navy background, whistled the "Turn to Call" signal. Anna was apparently oblivious or uncaring of the improper use of the navy gesture. Whistling like that at a woman was poor behavior even for the docks. The young man was not wearing the company ship's wheel on his vest, so he must be one of the journeymen from ashore. My glare and sharp point of my finger silenced the errant roustabout instantly. If I saw him again, I might think to cast him overboard, or worse.

"Love, I don't understand what your Mr. Voight was saying. He pointed to the first deck we were on as the main deck but referred to this second deck as the boiler deck. From what I saw, the boilers are below us on what he called the main deck."

Ann called me "love." I found that odd since although generally friendly, she had not shown any real affection. She must be toying with me. With a brief stammer, I answered her question.

"Th—that's true. The boilers and machinery are on the main deck below us. This one is called the boiler deck. No one really knows why, but every boat does so. We are going above to the third deck, which is called the hurricane deck as it gets very windy up there. The long cabin that sits on it is called the 'Texas cabin' on some boats, but we often just say 'go to up to the hurricane deck.' On top of the Texas is the pilothouse."

We ascended to the hurricane deck and entered the long cabin there.

"The off-duty crewmen berth here while any passengers we have make do amongst the cargo on the main deck. If the weather is foul, I allow them on the boiler deck, but they usually get their dirty paws into the cargo. As you may have noticed, we don't have cabins or a grand saloon on the boiler deck like most other boats."

I showed her to my cabin, which took up almost a third forward space of the Texas. It had a wonderful view to the front and sides, almost as good as the pilothouse directly above.

"Oh my, this pretty luxurious in size but sparse in décor. Why are there two beds in here? Whose trunks are those? Oh my, there is a sword on the wall."

"Married captains sometimes bring their wives aboard. I use this one. Take the other. It has not yet been occupied. Those trunks are mine. I only needed a carpet bag to retrieve you in Quincy and left them here. The saber on the wall is a just a memento of the war. The flag on the wall there came from my last boat. Oh, our toiletry facilities are located on the deck below us just forward of the paddle-wheel boxes. Just like on the *Tamaroa Band* from Quincy. Feel free to walk about the boat while I perform my duties. I will see you in a just a bit. You are welcome to come up to the pilothouse anytime."

A walk through the boat showed that everything was in order. The boilers were glowing hot, and the soft rumble meant the draught was strong with the smoke rising up and out of the stacks. Mr. Weatherby's men were applying oil and grease to the moving mechanical parts. That is a nearly constant job when underway. I was pleased with the new petroleum lubricants. They were of a far superior quality to the animal fats used before. They had a queer smell, but it was preferable than burning bear grease.

Mr. Weatherby was by his throttles and waved to say all was in readiness. He was in his midtwenties, and the company had assigned him to the boat when I was appointed captain some months back. He sometimes had a devil-may-care attitude that did not sit well with me when it came to the machinery. I took a moment to chat with the man.

"What does the Bourdon gauge say, Mr. Weatherby?"

"Boiler system pressure is 120 pounds, Captain. I will get it to 150 once on the river."

"Fine, but not one pound more. We want to live to tell the tale. Be sure to have the men check those gauge cocks often and not solely rely on the Bourdon gauge. As you know, it becomes useless when a little river mud gets into it."

Some men could tell the water level in the boiler by its sound. Mr. Weatherby claimed he could. For the mere mortals, each boiler had three levered valves, called gauge cocks, to determine the water level within. Normally, the top valve cock will vent steam if the boiler is not overfilled. The middle valve should release mostly water. More water must be added quickly if this one vents pure steam. If the bottom valve vents steam at all, then there is but little water left in the boiler, and catastrophe is at hand. Water introduced into the boiler at this juncture would contact the red-hot metal and create superheated steam. This could easily overwhelm the boiler and cause an explosion. The best course of action would be to add water very slowly or even shut down the boiler and let it cool. That, of course, meant slowing or stopping the boat. That costs time, and time is money, so the job at the gauges required a man of diligence and a spark of intelligence.

I was gratified to see several crewmen wearing their old army bummer caps or kepis. Some of them still wore their issued light-blue uniform trousers. Most all of those were faded and worn by years of service. The men may have worn them for pride in service or because they were short of cash for new duds. Men who had served together should have a good bond between them, which might keep the level of general tomfoolery among the men to a minimum. I was glad to have them aboard.

I found Ann had taken my suggestion to ascend to the pilot-house. Mr. Swanson was showing her the bell pull ropes to signal the engineer. A system of signals told the men at the engines to go forward, astern, and cut power, and so forth. As this was a side-wheeled boat, one paddle wheel could be reversed independently and spin the boat about almost in place. A rope dangled above the wheel that rang the main bell. Treadle pedals on the floor operated the two steam whistles mounted on the roof of the pilothouse. The boat's unique signal consisted of two short peals followed by a long one and resulted in "Hip, hip, hooray!" when the treadle was pressed just right.

Swanson introduced his new apprentice, Mr. Olsson. He was a young lad of maybe twenty years, and he and his kin hailed from Jacksonville, Illinois. He had the lanky frame found on the farm, and there was a spark of intelligence in his eyes. His company frock coat was too wide for his shoulders, but his cap fit well enough. When he earned enough wages, he should visit a tailor.

"Welcome aboard, Mr. Olsson. Has Mr. Swanson instructed you on your most important duties on this boat?"

"Yes, Captain. I am to have the coffee ready and never to sit in your chair. Just curious, sir. How much coffee do you drink in a day? I just want to be prepared is all."

There was hint of an accent I couldn't identify. Swedish perhaps? It was reminiscent of the few Scandinavians I had met in the past.

"It's do one's business how much coffee a man drinks in a day. I drink more than some people know and less than others believe. The way to make it is to put four handfuls of coffee in that one-gallon pot of boiling water and let it boil over twice. Pull the pot off the fire and dump a cup of cold water to settle the grounds. If you learn your duties quickly, we'll make you into a pilot in no time."

Ann was most impressed with the great wheel. It was almost eight feet in diameter and sunk about a third of its circumference into the floor. It was made of a beautiful cherrywood, and the boat's name was engraved in relief. The wheel was the most beautiful object on the boat, but few people ever got to see it.

"Mr. Swanson, why is this spoke larger than the others? It even has a coin embedded in it."

"That's called the king spoke, Miss Anna. When it is straight up and down at the top like that, it tells you that the rudder is straight and not turned. That old Spanish-dollar piece is for good luck for a profitable run."

Ann had changed back into her hospital dress for ease of movement while on board. Traversing the narrow causeway up to the pilot house in hoops would undoubtedly cause embarrassment. It was good to see her smile.

"Care for some coffee, Captain?"

"You know I do, Mr. Swanson. Mr. Weatherby reports we have steam up and all is in readiness. Once we pull off, no doubt Mr. Voight will have his men shift some cargo to produce an even keel. Our turn to depart is coming up. Let's keep on our toes. With all these boats leaving at once, it will be a mess of beans."

Boats were generally departing the landing as directed by the dockmaster, but some of them paid him no mind. At present, there was no set penalty for such behavior. If a boat caused an accident, though, the dockmaster would gleefully tell the insurance underwriters what had transpired. If a boat made the practice a habit, the owners could be told not to land here again.

I took my old faithful spyglass out of my possibles bag hanging from a hook for a better look. It extended to just over a foot in length, and the image was sharp and clear. Good Germanic workmanship. Field glasses were more useful at night, though. I would let Ann look, though, it in a moment. I quickly spotted trouble.

"Tarnation. Keep an eye over yonder for the *Cahokia*. She must have started her run early today and is approaching from upstream. Amid all these boats trying to clear of the landing, she can make a real mess of this."

Young Mr. Olsson asked, "What is the *Cahokia*, Captain?"

Swanson was quick with the answer. The cub pilot traditionally was instructed by the pilot he paid his fee to. In this case, it was Mr. Swanson and five hundred dollars. Any other pilots on board and even the captain was to serve only as stalwart examples and not interfere unless it endangered the boat.

"She's is a center-wheel boat of the Wiggins Ferry Company that runs between St. Louis and the village of East St. Louis there across the river. She has a regular schedule to keep but could have easily delayed just a bit for a clear river. Coming in now places her running in the opposite direction of the dozens of boats plying north from the landing about to swing around and head downstream. Sometimes common sense is in short supply on the river. It certainly is today."

The Wiggins Ferry Company not only operates a ferry business for individuals wanting to cross the Mississippi, but it also maintains train yards and warehouses on what was once Bloody Island on the east bank of the river. For years, it was more noted as a place for duelists to meet. The Wiggins company yards are becoming a major connecting point for the many railroads terminating at the river over there. Without a bridge, the Alton and Terre Haute and the Ohio and Mississippi railroads depend on old man Wiggins to ferry the train cars over to the west bank. If engineers ever figure out how to make a bridge long enough to span the Mississippi, then Wiggins may be put out of business. In the meantime, he is making a handsome sum of money.

"I see her now. Not much to look at."

"All right, gentlemen. The dockmaster is waving his green flag at us. Ring the bells for casting lines and engines astern and let's get out of here. Hopefully, we won't blow up in the process."

"What do you mean by that, Captain?"

"Well, young man, while at the landing, the boat has been riding high at the bow and low in the stern. The water in the boilers has flowed to the rear, leaving parts of the metal air flues running through them high and dry. When the boat becomes level, the water will slosh onto the red-hot metal, creating superhot steam that can overwhelm the boilers. Many accidents occur at such times."

"How can a pilot mitigate the chance of such an occurrence?"

"Don't run your bow high up onto a landing if you can help it, and once you build up steam, back off the shore as quickly as you can. Oh, and pray a whole heap. Now pay attention to Mr. Swanson here. The dance of the bells and whistles is about to begin. It is probably the most complicated and nerve-wracking maneuver there is, and you have to get it right every time."

The mass of boats leaving the landing vied for position as jockeys do at a racetrack. We were not on a strict schedule and had the luxury of time. Several boats bumped into one another, but apparently there was no major damage. A sternwheeler from the North Western Packet Company did have her wheel stove in by a boat from behind. That was one of the troubles with the sternwheelers with their wheel so exposed. Sidewheel boats were still superior in my mind as they were more maneuverable. The damage was bad, but she could limp back to the landing. The story probably would not even make mention in the *Alton National Democrat.*

While touring the boat, I saw we had a couple dozen or so passengers on board, including a handful of women. The men had rearranged some of the cargo to create makeshift walls and shelter. If the weather turned exceptionally awful, I was prepared to allow them up onto the covered boiler deck until it passed. Thank God there were no small children or animals. Both tend to break things, get in the way, and foul the deck.

About halfway between Ste. Genevieve, there is a place on the river known as the Chain of Rocks. It is a dangerous place at certain stages of water for steamboat navigation. On this fine day, nature cooperated at least.

We did not make good time down the river as the large number of boats created a logjam. The sand bars at Ste. Genevieve delayed the long procession even more. Ste. Genevieve is known as the first town in Missouri and is also known as a steamboat graveyard. There had been over thirty serious mishaps on this stretch of river over the past few years, leaving a dozen or more wrecks. Just a week ago, the *Wyaconda* caught fire and burned near here, causing one death. I would be glad when we were clear of this area. It seemed cursed to me. The big New Orleans boats up front drew six feet or more of water and should have waited another day or two for higher water. The first one took considerable effort to get over the bar, but it was handy in gouging out a channel for all to follow. The powerful river assisted in making the breach wider and deeper, and each succeeding boat found it easier to transit. By the time our chance came, there was no need to even slow down. The day was clear, and we steamed south without incident.

Although we were not pressed for time, I didn't want to dawdle. On most boats, it costs over two hundred dollars a day in fuel, lubricants, and wages to operate. I cut costs by running the boat short-handed and asking more of the officers than their titles indicated. Until the mandated pay increases by Mr. Geldstein, the boat ran on about $150 a day. I offset this by treating the men well and hiring a decent cook. Although the boat still ran more cheaply than most others, there was no need to stop if we didn't have to. The moon was bright, and the winds calm, so we pushed on into the darkness. We fell behind a big steamer bound for Cincinnati and reasoned if she got through, our packet boat could as well. Our challenge was not to overtake her and crush her stern. Fortified with coffee, Swanson and I split the night and day into shifts. Mr. Olsson brought a plate of food up to the pilothouse, so I did not have to leave. The plate contained sausage, cabbage, and potatoes. We will see this dish quite often on this trip. We served the men a beer with meals, but for me, the coffee was more fitting for the occasion.

So far, Olsson is an adequate cub pilot. It initially concerned me that he was a southpaw. After some consideration, I couldn't think where that might matter in the pilothouse. If he favored his left hand was not a matter of concern. They say that sort of thing runs in the family.

The cub pilot dined below, and when he returned to the pilothouse, I asked Mr. Olsson how Ann, or Anna, was faring down below. He told me she and Captain Bemis dined with the other off-duty officers just down below in the Texas cabin at the big table. He added she planned to retire for the evening in her cabin.

Once relieved by Mr. Swanson, I went below and found Anna in my usual cabin. I needed to check in on her and retrieve a few things from a trunk. I especially needed a fresh shirt.

"Forgive me for being such a poor host. Duty called. How did you find the food this evening?"

"Oh, I learned not to complain about food. Last year our chief nurse, Mrs. Blackford, was dismissed over the issue. The food of hospital was of the poorest quality, and there was never enough. She appealed to Major Brinton, the man in charge, with no result. She then circulated a petition and took it all the way to Governor Yates in Springfield. That act brought about her dismissal. Fortunately, she could go back to her millinery shop in town and not become destitute."

"No need to worry here about that. If I put ashore everyone who complained about the food, I would have to shovel the coal myself."

First Run of the Season

In the morning, Anna and I enjoyed the view from the hurricane deck. The land was alive again. Waterfowl, deer, and leaping fish were in abundance. During the war, all of them seemed to be in hiding. I lit a fresh cigar and nursed my tankard of coffee. We watched as the sternwheeler *Messenger* overtook us on portside. She is a brand-new boat on her first season, intending to run the line between St. Louis and Pittsburg. Some weeks back, I met her captain, William Dean. Affable fellow. He must be in a big hurry to burn coal like that. Both Swanson and Weatherby had standing orders not to take up any challenge for a race. Instead they were to allow faster boats to pass without accelerating, making it more difficult. Such practices are a waste of fuel and dangerous, especially while heading downstream.

"Oh, let's have a race! You boatmen always claim to have the swiftest vessel on the waters."

"Not today, Ann. I won't burn the coal for foolishness."

Noticing the disappointment on her face, I changed the subject.

"Look up ahead. We are nearing the confluence of the Mississippi and Ohio Rivers. Beyond the bend, there is the town of Cairo. We put in there many times during the war as it has machine shops, and it was the navy's headquarters out here on the rivers. Fort Defiance was there on the point. I care not to land again if I can help it. Besides the memories of the war, the city is built on a thin strip of land between the river and a swamp. It is an unhealthy and unhappy place."

"It certainly looks dreary. Can you blow your cigar smoke somewhere else please?"

"Sorry, my dear. I will be more careful where I blow the smoke."

"You know, most gentlemen do not use tobacco in the presence of a lady."

"'Tis true. As surely you are certainly a lady, I am captain of this boat. As such, I can do just about anything I want to do, as long as it doesn't violate the Ten Commandments or the laws under local jurisdiction."

Our conversations were mostly reminiscing about back home before the war and comparing notes on the goings-on since we both left to find our futures. I was surprised to find I knew more about what had transpired back home than she. As I exchanged letters with Mother and Father about once a month, she had virtually severed contact with her family. I told her in very general terms what I did during the war but was able to tell when to stop when she took to slowly opening and closing her fan. She spoke of her time in the hospital only briefly and never in any detail. A dark pall would come across her face, and she would drift away in thought.

"Just up ahead, my dear, is Mound City. It was our home port for much of the war."

"You never said a good word about it, but it looks far more pleasant than Cairo does. It could use a good washing, though. The mosquitoes don't seem to be as bad here. Maybe that's just because of that dreadful cigar you are smoking."

"One must keep up appearances, my dear. Besides, a man is entitled to one vice. Oh, and coffee is not a vice. It is a virtue. I can choose another if you like."

"No, this one is bad enough. No telling what you would select in its stead."

Mound City was still busy and looked like it would be for some time. Trains and steamers were packed with happily discharged soldiers and sailors. Bless them while on that rickety miserable train ride north. But there was no longer an admiral's flag at the headquarters. The grand Mississippi Squadron was no more. Gunboats that been taken out of commission filled the river. The tug *Daisy* was busy shifting them around, and steam launches were shuttling prospective buyers to the boats.

"There are the gunboats, my dear. The big ironclads are already stripped and laid up there at Tow Head Chute. Oh, there is my old boat. You can see the number on the pilothouse. All of the guns and iron plate are gone."

"What will happen to it?"

"Well, Bemis says the big auction is scheduled for August 17. What isn't sold will be scrapped. Her hull took much damage, and her machinery is worn. I'm afraid she will not fare well. Bemis was able to retrieve her bell, but I don't want to know how that one-legged bandit got hold of it. All good things come to an end, my dear."

"And all good things have a beginning, my love."

I raised my hand to Mr. Swanson, and he nodded knowingly. With that, he applied his foot to the treadle. A final salute was rendered to a gallant lady who served the company and her country well.

The tune "Hip, hip, hooray!" pealed through the main whistle. It took practice to get it right, and Swanson did not fail.

"My goodness! What was that all about?"

We were probably a bit too close to the whistle, which tends to be too loud to the uninitiated. By her tone, I could tell Anna's friendly disposition was gone in an instant.

"That is our boat's greeting, Ann. Each boat has its own signature call. Our old gunboat over there used it before and during the war. We took up the signal on this boat when the ol' gal was laid up and taken out of commission. Since both boats share their name, many folks on the river think the boats are one and the same."

"I learned to hate the whistles of the steamboats while at the hospital in Quincy. They meant another boatload of wounded and sick. Uh, now I have a headache. I'm going to lie down in the cabin for a while."

This happens every time when I talk of the boats with the fairer sex. Women just don't appreciate river traditions and such.

With Anna on her way to her cabin, I went below to check on the boat. I felt the need to do something useful. Paducah was just thirty-two miles upstream and then another dozen to Smithland. There we would enter the Cumberland River and steam on to

Nashville. Not a soul was on the boiler deck, and none of the cargo there looked molested. The passengers on the main deck appeared to be of good cheer and were amusing themselves with playing music. One of the men was even playing an Alpine zither, a complicated instrument with forty-two strings. But Mr. Voight knew his duty and repeatedly told them all to keep it down so the men at the engines could hear the signal bells. Some of the passengers had started a card game known as poker, which was far quieter than the music. Soldiers during the war had picked up the amusement, and it was now quite popular. Poker had the virtue of not requiring a special table like faro. On the other hand, the pace of the game seemed agonizingly slow in comparison, and the odds of winning did not seem as good. Someday I may have to learn the rules.

The chief engineer waved for me to come over. He had something to show me.

"Good day, Captain. I need to tell you that our coal supply is getting short. As you can see, we might have enough to get to Smithland, but I recommend we make a stop at Paducah to be on the safe side."

"Very well, Mr. Weatherby. I will inform Mr. Swanson."

I walked the short distance to the voice tube, opened the brass flip cover, and ran the bell. Swanson quickly responded with "Ahoy!"

"Mr. Swanson, we will be making a landing at Paducah to take on coal. If I recall correctly, we have no consignments to offload, so make the land as near to the coal yard as possible."

"Aye, Captain. I hope this gaggle on the river doesn't have the same idea. We might get stuck there for a while."

Boats of the past used wood for its primary fuel, but those days are mostly gone. The banks of the river are now stripped of trees, and the consistency of wood heat is wanting. Coal burns hotter, longer, and doesn't take up as much space. Overall, coal was cheaper than wood and didn't require as many frequent stops. We now used wood only when coal was not available.

Situated at the confluence of the Ohio and Tennessee Rivers, Paducah was a major supply base during much of the war. The long occupation was bitterly felt by the largely secessionist population.

My old gunboat played a small part in repulsing Nathan Bedford Forrest's attack there in March of '64. My word, that was almost a year and a half ago but seemed like a decade. I noticed the palm of my right hand was sweating. My seared left hand didn't perspire anymore.

I went back up to the hurricane deck cabin to inform Bemis about the change in plans. He would be responsible for paying for the coal, although First Mate Voight and Engineer Weatherby would handle the loading. Bemis appeared brooding in his office, but his face lit like a lantern with the news.

"I could use a stretch of the legs—err, leg—and get off this boat for a while. While ashore, I will see if there is any cargo or passengers destined for Nashville."

"Good for you, Bemis. While you are out enjoying yourself, I am going to catch up on some sleep. Even the coffee isn't enough to keep awake."

During the war, Union troops in Paducah had dug an earthwork around the whole depot site called Fort Anderson. The Marine Hospital was within the perimeter. The hospital was built with federal funds and by the State of Kentucky to treat rivermen and was finished four years ago just in time for use by the Union army. After Forrest's raid late last year, Colonel Hicks, the local commander, razed all the buildings within musket range of the fort to prevent Confederate sharpshooters from ever occupying them again. The vast open field that had been part of downtown showed no signs of rebuilding yet. There was still an army depot here, but it was a fraction of its former glory. Small groups of white soldiers milled about too. They were probably just waiting for their discharge while guarding what was left of the supplies. Most of the soldiers still here, though, were from a colored regiment mustered in late in the war. Their terms of enlistment probably had months or a few years before expiration. No doubt their presence in town irritated the secesh locals immensely.

We were fortunate to get a good spot on the landing, but the bad news was, the coal yard was overwhelmed with the sudden arrival of a dozen steamers in need of fuel. To prevent total chaos, the owner of the yard established a first-come–first-served policy. Two boats were ahead of us. The one next to us was the *J. G. Blackford*, a common sight on the Ohio River with big coal bunkers. Our wait would be several hours. Until then, I directed Messrs. Voight and Weatherby to allow small groups of men to go ashore by watch. They would have a few hours to stretch their legs, but hopefully not enough time to get into trouble. They were warned that they were expected to return on time, ready to work and be sober enough to do so.

I retired to the small cabin up in the Texas to catch up on some rest, and sleep came on easily. I did though miss my old bed and looked forward to returning to my proper cabin.

It seemed like minutes later I awoke to knocking on the cabin door. The light streaming in from the window showed hours had gone by. The first mate was the man behind the knocking.

"Yes, Mr. Voight. How is the coal situation?"

"It was the damnedest sight I ever saw, Captain. The white journeymen were protesting they weren't being paid enough to handle coal. Captain Bemis refused to pay the increase and told them their beef was with the owner of the coal yard, not us. They still refused, so he hired a negro roustabout gang to do the job. The white boys took that badly enough, but when they found out Captain Bemis was going to pay them white wages, there was nearly a riot."

"That doesn't sound like Captain Bemis. He can squeeze pennies hard enough to make them scream. I wish you had sent for me."

"There was no time as it was over so quickly. Some colored soldiers were on hand watching the whole affair and fixed bayonets. They thought it was great fun that the Negro roustabouts were getting the better end of the deal on them former Rebs. There may have been bloodshed had it been for Miss Anna."

"Miss Anna? Why the devil was she out there?"

"She and Captain Bemis had gone into town on some errands. They couldn't have gone far as he doesn't get along too well on those crutches. Miss Anna spoke to all those men as if she were scolding an entire schoolyard. No one dared cross her. We might not be so welcome next time we visit, though."

"That must have been a sight to see."

Throughout the war, the city of Paducah was never a very welcoming community. It's strange how the Kentuckians seem even more pro-Confederate now than they were during the war. Joining the cause after the war already killed it is just foolishness and bad for business. If they keep it up, the Union army might decide to stay around for a while.

"Ah, I hear the men coming aboard with the coal. By your leave, Captain, I will get back on the job."

"Before you do, put on your new frock coat and cap. You are boat officer now, Mr. Voight."

"Is that necessary, Captain? Most boats don't make their officers wear a uniform."

"My word should be good enough, but Mr. Geldstein says we do. Put them on or go back to *foreman*."

"Uh, aye, Captain."

Coaling the boat was usually an "all-hands" operation requiring the participation of every able-bodied man. The yard here consisted of a large pile of the fuel simply dumped near the riverbank. As coal was sold by the bushel, it took two men to lift and carry the large scuttles each carrying eighty pounds of it. In more genteel yards, the coal was stacked in bags, allowing one man to carry a bushel. Bags were faster and cleaner to load but more expensive, usually two cents per bushel more. The railroads were also voracious consumers of coal and often caused shortages along the river. Nowadays, we were usually happy to get whatever was on hand. The alternative was to seek out the woodpiles farmers offered for sale along the river.

"We should be done with this chore in a few hours, Captain. There should be enough to get us to Clarksville."

"Get as much coal on board as possible, Mr. Voight. There isn't any good coal between here and there if we run short. Cut loose the engineer's men as soon as possible so they can get some rest. We don't want any of them falling asleep at the gauge cocks. Where is Captain Bemis?"

"He had a spell of fatigue and went up to his office. He said he just needed to lie down a few minutes. I don't think he is feeling well."

Up on the hurricane deck, Bemis's cabin doubles as his office and contains the boat's strongbox and papers. The door is a stout one but strong enough only to keep honest men honest. My anger was rising. He had placed Ann at a point of great danger at the coal yard. Was my anger only that, or was there something more? Was I jealous that they had gone into town together? A knock at the door produced a "Come in" from our chief clerk. He sounded tired and weak.

"Oh, don't get up, Bemis. I wanted to ask about the coal."

"The yard sold it to us at twelve cents a bushel. The north side of the pile looked wet, so I directed the men to shovel from the south side. It's mostly good bituminous coal, but the yard has mixed in some soft coal to get rid of it."

"Why would we pay twelve cents? We should be getting pure anthracite for that price. That or receive a discount. I hear too you paid the Negro gang white wages."

"With four other boats to fuel, the yard owner was not going to haggle. The other boat clerks were offering fourteen cents a bushel just to get ahead in the line. We were fortunate we shook hands on the deal before they showed up. The white roustabouts demanded 10 percent more than the going rate. They are a surly bunch. The Negroes got more than usual, but they are getting the job done and faster than the white gang would even if I had paid them what they demanded. All in all, the transaction went in our favor, as usual. You have never questioned me before. Is there something else on your mind, Captain?"

"Indeed. I wasn't there to see it, but I hear Miss Ann was amid the dispute. She could have come to harm."

"Ah, the crux of the matter. The point is you were not there, Captain. While you found time to sleep, Miss *Anna* became bored and restless. She was in need of medicines, and I escorted her to the nearest apothecary. She was going to go with or without an escort. She had a grand time. I have never seen her smile like that. The incident at the coal yard occurred when we were returning to the boat. She rushed forward only when the situation became a hostile one, and I was powerless to stop her. Anna certainly defused those hotheads. It was a sight to see."

My anger was still there, but I realized I was partially at fault.

"Medicines? We had procured a substantial supply before leaving St. Louis. There were at least three cans of hop at four dollars apiece. What on earth did she purchase?"

"We are a long way from St. Louis, Captain. As a gentleman, I did not ask of the contents of her bag. Now look, you have been burning the candle at both ends and look dog-tired. Meanwhile, I am in considerable pain. I suggest we renew the conversation in the morning before either of us say something we surely don't mean and will certainly regret."

"Very well, Bemis. We discuss this when we are more our usual ourselves."

We pushed off at first light without any further incident. The guards posted on the forecastle during the dogwatch made no notice of any disgruntled coal yardmen in the vicinity all night. Twelve additional passengers boarded with their four-dollar passage. I was in the pilothouse watching the proceedings and trying to further size up our new cub pilot. Mr. Olsson seemed bright enough, but the maneuver to back out into a moving stream seemed to perplex him. I also wondered what he did in the war. The young man was old enough for service, but did not give off any indication he had served. I made it a point not to discuss personal matters, particularly in the pilothouse. It was distracting and potentially dangerous.

"Mornin', Captain. The coffee should be ready by now. The pilot reports in Paducah say the Cumberland is in good shape all the way up to Harpeth Shoals. No mention of conditions further on. A big steamer is about a half hour ahead of us, and if she is making good time, we can follow her on up. The other boats back there in Paducah don't even have steam up. I reckon they are still taking on coal."

"Thank you, Mr. Swanson. I will relieve you as scheduled, but we will probably not push on past dark. These clouds promise a moonless night."

I pulled my chair away from the hot stove and took a seat. Mr. Voight had procured copies of the Paducah papers from a hawker at the landing. Nuggets of opportunity were often found in the local newspapers. More often, though, was found the unwelcome news of a planned railroad route. The *Federal Union* was the authorized periodical of the Union garrison here. It told of the gift of a fine carriage to the wife of Brigadier General John Cook Pope, the present commander of Cairo and Paducah. He was preparing to resign his commission and return to Indiana in a few weeks. I quickly found the *Paducah Daily Kentuckian* was not such a staunch defender of the Union. The paper was still crying out for the head of Brigadier General Eleazar Paine. The editors hated this abolitionist as during the war, he had a habit of rooting out Confederate spies and bushwhackers and executing them on the spot. That General Paine received only a verbal reprimand for his deeds had put a burr under their saddle. The war was over, but hard feelings remained.

I was midway through the papers when we came upon Smithland and started the ascent of the Cumberland River. Smithland was always a way port for me. A handful of times, we had picked up grain consigned for the B. S. Rhea and Son mills in Nashville. It was here also that downbound boats deposited their cargoes to be picked up by other steamers heading up or down the Ohio and beyond. Smithland was garrisoned during the war, but now no flags flew from the two small forts overlooking the town. Smoke still rose from the fires of the Negro contraband camp, though.

Glancing up from the papers, I was alarmed to notice Swanson was sitting on the bench lighting a cigar. I looked over to see the new cub pilot at the great wheel. He was shifting his feet nervously, but the wheel was steady. Swanson produced a roguish grin.

"Do you have a spare cigar, Mr. Swanson? I will spell you later. Oh, and if the boy wrecks the boat, it's coming out of your pay."

My tone of voice was playful, but I meant every word. Swanson understood fully.

A big steamer ahead of us was apparently in a hurry. Thick black smoke poured from her stacks. She must have six boilers at full pressure, for she was pulling ahead. The Cumberland must be free of obstructions and deep as she is making this dash with abandon. We didn't have the coal to burn to keep up with her though.

A few hours later, we came upon the wreck of the steamboat *St. Louis*. She had been ambushed, captured, and burned by the Rebs last year. She had run mostly on the Ohio until the war halted traffic, and she then was used by the army to carry troops and supplies. The *St. Louis* had been a proud boat, about three hundred feet long and 170 tons. Her engines were salvaged for use in another steamer after her demise. The boilers and burned timbers were left to mark her grave. Mr. Swanson knew her story.

"She took her chances in traveling alone up the river, not wanting to wait for a convoy. A warning shot forced her to land, and then the Confederates swarmed aboard. They took off everything they could carry and burned the rest. We found the Negroes that had been on board shot through the back of the head and left sprawled along the bank. We resolved then never to surrender as long as the boat was still underway."

"We saw such scenes too and made the same resolution, Swanson. What a horrible war. What waste it produced. I am very glad it is over."

A dozen miles up the river lay the town of Dover. It is the seat of Stewart County, Tennessee, but it was the site of two battles during the war. The old Confederate earthwork north of town called Fort Donelson lay quiet and abandoned. Grass and bramble were already reclaiming the site. The chimneys of the fort's cabins dotted the hillside, and only a few charred logs remained of the huts. This was where Ulysses S. Grant forced the unconditional surrender of the Confederates in February '62. That was his first major victory, and it eventually propelled him to the head of the Union army. Most people figure he will run for president someday and will probably win.

The town of Dover was mostly destroyed during the second battle a year later in '63. Only four buildings survived, including the ramshackle hotel at the landing. The local iron industry was also shattered during the war with the demolishing of the furnaces in the surrounding area. There were few people in sight and no sign yet of rebuilding.

"Mr. Swanson, it is getting dark, but I would rather not come to here. Can we make Clarksville? At least coal will be waiting there for us."

"Aye, Captain, but I can use a relief, though."

"Go on ahead and take Mr. Olsson with you after he makes more coffee. Tell Mr. Voight to have the men light the running lamps. I will be fine until your return."

Being alone in the pilothouse brought back many memories, good and bad. It was here I felt most at home. Behind the great wheel, a gentle turn or a pull of a bell rope set this great mass of wood and machinery in any direction I chose. Captains traditionally allowed the pilot to steer and navigate the boat, only giving general guidance on where to land and such. Where to land was most often determined by the clerk's schedule or need for fuel. The engineer ran his crew as he saw fit, and the first mate saw to the daily activities of the deck crew. The job of captain often seemed to be a simple figurehead. At times like these, I yearned to be relieved of the administrative burdens and be a full-time pilot once again.

Upriver, we passed the hamlet of Cumberland City. We had shot it up pretty good back in the war and burned the tobacco warehouses. Unlike Dover, there was signs of rebuilding here.

Swanson and Olsson returned promptly at one hour. They already had their supper and informed me it would be served to the officers upon my arrival at the great table. Well, the table wasn't that great. It was simply large enough to seat all of us. It is located in the aft section of the Texas cabin. The space was designed to berth Negro crewmen and was called the "coon pen" on the boats. As we currently had no Negroes on board, I used the space to meet with the boat officers after supper. It was a practice I adopted from the navy. Each officer gave an update on his realm, and I gave the orders for the next day. The men chafed at the formality of it, but it did serve its purpose.

My place was at the head of the table and Ann sat to my left. Once again, our meal was sausage, potatoes, and cabbage. This time, the cook had baked bread and provided cherry preserves. That was about as close as we ever came to dessert. We normally ate with the men down below at our own convenience, but with Miss Ann aboard the cook and his two stewards were rolling out the red carpet.

"Thank you for your reports, gentlemen. We will come to in Clarksville tonight, probably around midnight. We will coal up in the morning and back off at the earliest."

The river narrows in its final approach to Clarksville but generally deepens. Without the big steamer somewhere up ahead in view, the leadsmen had been kept busy all day sounding the river. These men were good at using the weighted ropes, but in my day, I preferred the pole. For me it was faster, less tiring, and I could instantly tell the composition of the bottom. When Linwood Landing and old Fort Sevier came in sight, the river was deep enough the rest of the way to Clarksville to give them a rest.

Clarksville was a city of some twenty thousand souls before the war. Some of the white population had left but was replaced by former slaves in search of life beyond the plantation. The city and nearby forts Sevier and Clark were all captured without a fight a few days after the fall of Fort Donelson. My old gunboat paid a visit to help recapture Clarksville months later, and although many of the buildings were damaged, there were obvious efforts at repair and rebuilding.

The tobacco industry is still king here and produces a dark-fired tobacco the locals call *black patch*. Before the war, steamboats carried hogsheads of it to St. Louis and beyond. Perhaps Bemis can arrange a shipment on our downbound trip. The Memphis, Clarksville, and Louisville Railroad runs across the eastern side of town and connects with other railroads all the way to Nashville. The railroad bridge spans the river but fortunately does not obstruct passage of the boats.

As it was past midnight, we did not use the whistle to announce our arrival but quietly nudged onto the landing and secured the boat with hawsers to the bollards. The dogwatch was posted to keep any vagabonds from boarding during the rest of the night. Some of the passengers we picked up in Paducah departed the boat, and that was fine by me. The fewer the better. The rest of the boat's company turned in for the night.

A rap on the cabin door awakened me hours later. The sun was just coming up.

"Mornin', Captain. There's a feller at the landing that wants to talk with you. Says he is from the sheriff's office."

"Thank you, Mr. Voight. I will be along directly."

I donned my frock coat and hat and made my way below. A tankard of coffee would be good right now. I found the man easily enough as there was no one else at the landing yet. He was carrying a short double-barreled shotgun, and a Colt revolver was stuck in his belt. A roll of fat conveniently kept it in place better than any leather flap. He sported no badge but spoke with authority.

"Captain. I'm just here to tell you that you need to keep your men on the landing. Your man told me you just needed coal. I suggest you load up and depart lickety-split."

"That's not particularly welcoming. What is amiss?"

"I ain't no welcomin' committee. I am the law, and for the good of public safety, I'm telling you, you all need to vamoose as soon as you can. All them freed slaves have been causing trouble for the God-fearing white folk. There's been a rash of thievin', bushwackin', and general lawlessness. They especially like to tussle with folks just off the boats and trains."

"Well, they are free now. I suppose that means they can go where they please. Now that they are free to buy and sell things, it will be good for business."

"That may be fine for you Yankees up Nawth, but not here. The Negroes have forgotten their place. They should be in the fields tending to the tobacco and cotton, not roaming about in town."

"Very well, Constable. We will endeavor to comply with your directives."

"Uh, just do as I say, and there won't be no trouble."

The newspapers have told this story all too many times. The blacks are now free by law. President Johnson even says recognizing the abolition of slavery is required of the rebel states to rejoin the Union. Tennessee already ratified the Thirteenth Amendment to the US Constitution back in April. But in the eyes of many, ending slavery did not mean equal economic opportunity, justice under the law, or freedom of movement. The end of slavery was just barely palatable to men like the deputy, and he felt blacks should know better than to leave the plantations. If that is enforced somehow, how would it differ than being a slave? This reconstruction of the Union could be a messy process indeed. No one seemed to have the answers. It is a shame Abraham Lincoln was not around anymore. Surely, he would be guiding the process wisely if he were alive. That Andrew Johnson fellow doesn't seem to be up to the task.

The coaling went well enough but took the rest of the daylight. All the boat officers chipped into the effort. Captain Bemis was the exception of course, and he used the time to drum up more business. A few small consignments and a handful of passengers were the result. I found the physical labor somewhat refreshing, but I did not want it ever to become a permanent vocation. The officers chipping in was not expected by the men, but it made a good show for most. The handful of Irishmen on board were not impressed and found our participation somehow patronizing. In thanks for a good job, I allowed two tankards of beer for supper. If anyone wanted more liquor, they had to drink their own. I made it known I expected all to be ready to depart Clarksville early in the morning.

The next obstacle that frequently caused trouble was Harpeth Shoals, which ran five miles downstream from the mouth of the Harpeth River near Ashland City. The shoals were bad enough in normal times, but with the low water, it was impossible to traverse the rocky bottom at all. In such times, steamers were sent from Nashville to that point to meet upbound boats and transfer cargo. It was a prime spot for ambushing during the war. Reb riders shot up many a boat there. They almost got my former boat here once or twice.

"Captain. Look there. There is a big muddy streak in the water drifting in the current. What do you make of that?"

"That, Mr. Swanson, appears to be mud and sand kicked up by a boat passing over a sandbar up ahead. I suspect that big steamer we saw yesterday made it by forcing its way over the shoals. Or at least trying to."

We found no boat stuck high and fast when we reached Harpeth Shoals. We did though find and use the route a boat recently made as it wiggled its way over.

The final obstacle to Nashville was a sandbar that habitually formed at Gower Island.

"Gentlemen, during the war, our gunboat was nearly stranded on a sandbar up ahead. We had to run a hawser to a large tree and winch our way across. The water is higher now, so we may get lucky."

We rounded the bend to find the steamer *Albatross* firmly aground on the bar. She was the mystery boat ahead of us all the way up the Cumberland. She had almost got across, but when the bow dipped, her paddle wheels rose up out of the water, leaving her helpless. She had the spars and rig to begin to grasshopper herself over but had not begun to do so. Her draft was at least five feet while ours was but three.

"Pilot, find a good spot to make a breach then heave to upon crossing over. We will then present an offer of assistance."

Mr. Swanson edged the boat to the bar gently and called for full power when the bow touched. Meanwhile, Mr. Voight had called for all hands and passengers aft to raise the bow a bit. The paddle wheels churned furiously, and the boat rose up onto the sand. When it reached the point of equilibrium, Mr. Voight summoned all human folk forward to shift the weigh in that direction. The boat heaved and shook but made it across.

"Good show, Mr. Swanson. That, Mr. Olsson, is how it is done. Bully! I see a skiff was launched from the *Albatross*. Let us try to remain here against the current."

"Aye, Captain."

The skiff came alongside, and I was impressed with the rowers' ability to overcome the current and the wash from our paddle wheels. Captain Lonergan Jinks introduced himself and his first mate, Sam Baseleon, an old salt from the coast that came west before the war. The bearded Captain Jinks was wearing the traditional steamboat captain frock coat but had four gold stripes on the cuffs in the navy tradition. He smelled of liquor but did not seem inebriated. I would probably be drinking too if my boat were in such an embarrassing predicament. "Salty Sam" wore a simple high-necked sweater and wool cap from the sea but sported a magnificent mustache.

"Good Captain, would you be willing and able to help us out of this predicament? We have perishables on board that must make it to Nashville soonest."

My reply was interrupted from a voice from behind. It was Mr. Bemis. No doubt our chief clerk had profit in mind and not any Christian charity. There was that old gleam in his eyes that I had missed for some time.

"If it is technically feasible, we will only charge the going rate. Five hundred dollars in gold or greenbacks. No bank checks or local currency. If funds are short, we might agree to cargo of equal value, especially whiskey or other fine liquors."

"Agreed. You drive a hard bargain, Captain, but I have had to pay more in the past."

I had not yet said a word. When finally given the chance, I said, "Have your men run a hawser cable, and we will give it a try. Use a green flag when in readiness. If unsuccessful, we will not hold you to the fare."

"That is more than fair, and thank you, Captain. We are an independent boat and don't have the capital to throw around."

"May I suggest then you wait for higher water in the future."

The task took over three hours, and with the use of both boats' capstans and a stand of stout hickory trees to latch onto with ropes, the helpless *Albatross* was dragged across the bar with much straining, groaning, and scraping of the hull. Thank heavens the bits on ours were not wrenched out in the process. I did not want to think of the damage to the hull of the *Albatross*. Mr. Bemis collected his loot in a combination of gold and paper. Naturally, it belonged to the company, but I authorized a dollar bonus to the men to be paid at the return to St. Louis. Bemis and I each received a bottle of whiskey to keep our mouths shut about the incident. Such news was bad for business. The label on the bottle said, "Clarke Distillery of Peoria, Illinois." That was upriver of my home of years gone by.

We left the *Albatross* behind to fend for herself and steamed on. Anna had reappeared in the pilothouse wearing a more festive dress, but without hoops. No doubt some mysterious device underneath poofed it out some.

This last stretch of the river snakes around a bit. We caught sight of the state capital building when we rounded Hardin's Bend. Anna was quite impressed. The architects of the cities out West were more interested in function than form. The state capital may be the most unusual building she has yet seen.

"It looks like a Greek or Roman temple I have seen illustrations of."

"That's why some folks call Nashville the *Athens of the South*, Miss Anna."

Swanson pushed the boat ashore at the landing with a gentle bump, and the crew went straight to work in securing her against the current. There were over a dozen boats here, but we apparently were the first to arrive from St. Louis this season. Nashville was platted mostly as a shipping depot for raw materials and not for ease of movement within the city. Here on the waterfront, the merchants stored wholesale grain, cotton, and tobacco in substantial brick warehouses in between Market and Front Streets that extended a whole block from the river into the city. The warehouses also handled bulk quantities of dry goods, hardware, and groceries for shipment down the Cumberland River. General freight was also brought up Market Street and sold from the storefronts along the town square. Conveniently, the boat was but a short distance away from the end of Broad Street, which winds up into the center of town.

The Union army had occupied Nashville in early 1862 without a battle and heavily fortified the city. There were no serious battles here until General Hood's invasion of Tennessee almost eight months ago. The Confederates were bloodily repulsed, and the city was spared. Most of the cotton plantations also escaped damage during the war and were in full production. Freed slaves still occupied the old contraband camps around the edge of town, and the number of Negroes within were growing as they looked for life beyond the fields.

The North needed cotton for its textile mills during the war. To ensure the flow of cotton, the federal government issued permits to allow plantations to operate with former slaves contracted for the labor. Of course, the system was rife with corruption. I was amazed that Bemis was unable to fully tap into it during the war. He said that cotton could be confiscated or purchased for as little as twelve cents a pound. It was then transported to New York for four cents a pound and then sold for up to $1.89 a pound. Much to his consternation, almost everyone got rich except him.

As for the former slaves, the desire for cotton outweighed what should have been simple Christian consideration. Instead of true freedom, the blacks are being denied economic and physical mobility by federal government policy, by the racial animosity of the whites, and by the enduring need for cotton labor in the South. The end of the war did not change this at all. Cotton exports were needed more than ever to pay off the war and to fund economic development, particularly railroads.

Nashville was still the principle deport for the Department of the Cumberland and a point of convergence of four operational railroads. The Nashville and Chattanooga, Tennessee and Alabama, and the North-Western railroads were running but still under Union army management. The Louisville and Nashville Railroad was under civilian management but was primarily hauling coal from the hills north of here. I couldn't complain too much about that. There was an advert at the landing for the Little Miami, Columbus, and Xenia Railroad that had three daily express trains to points east. One had to take a train into Ohio first to catch one. I momentarily thought how exciting it would be to take a train to Boston or New York. This boat certainly would never see those ports.

Bemis was already meeting with shippers and organizing the offloading of cargo. He moved about painfully on those confounded crutches. It may take him a day or two to organize a profitable cargo run to return to St. Louis. If that was the case, my plan was to let the crew ashore for at least a short time. I learned from captains before me to let the men blow off some steam on occasion. I would have Captain Bemis pay the men off with a few dollars to find some amusement. The trick is not to pay the men too much that they would get into trouble.

"Hello, Miss Anna. I need to drop a message off at the telegraph office. If you wish to accompany me, we may take a stroll through the city afterward. You can get off the boat for a while, and perhaps we can find a nice place to dine."

"That would be lovely, and I have a few errands myself."

For our sojourn, I wore a kid glove over my scalded hand and strapped on the Paterson revolver under the open frock coat. It would be less conspicuous there. The little Colt Root revolver in the suspender holster was usually enough for my sense of security, but Nashville was still a rough place. Perhaps more so than St. Louis. The provost guards could not be everywhere, and my steamboat uniform was too easily confused with the federal authorities. Walking alone with a lady made me a wonderful target for street thugs.

The layout of the streets of Nashville is a bit of mess, with irregular subdivisions and different lengths and widths. The riverfront was not exactly teeming with activity, and it was easy to avoid the groups of roustabouts and businessmen. We made it to Market Street unmolested by the various beggars and toughs who would like to part us from our currency.

Our first stop was for Anna's benefit. She quickly spotted the sign for Stephens and Janney and Company, a druggist and dispenser of apothecaries.

"Excuse me, my good captain. I need to make a few purchases."

"Do you need funds? My purse is at your disposal."

"Oh my, no. I have enough, thank you."

A woman's medical ailments and remedies were her own business and far too delicate a matter for a man to inquire about. She was in a good mood this morning, and I did not want to say or do anything to spoil that. I opened the door for her but remained outside to wait. The scene on the square across the street was not one for a woman's eyes anyway.

The public square was a place of business where vendors big and small come to sell their wares. The Negroes were allocated a small section on the corner. I could not tell the cause of the trouble, but four white men overturned a black man's produce table and beat him senseless. Satisfied with their efforts, the white ruffians melted back into the crowd. The other Negro proprietors helped the battered man up and restored the upturned table. Whites were venting the loss of the war and their current frustrations on the black race. It occurred to me the Negroes were treated better when they were slaves and considered property to be taken care of, or at least respected as belonging to someone else and be left alone. Many blacks did not have the social skills to defend themselves. They took the abuse or struck back physically. There seemed no other reaction in between.

Many men on the streets wore Confederate uniforms or bits and pieces of one. There was a law prohibiting the practice, but these men did not appear to have the means to replace them. They had a sullen defeated look about them as they ambled about trying to find a future. I had never seen a Confederate so close before. They were easy for me to despise. They were responsible for the death of my old crewmates and the damage to my boat. They were responsible for my scalded hand, Bemis's lost leg, and Anna's damaged state of mind. In a larger sense, they caused the war in their attempt to preserve the vile institution of slavery which resulted in so many ruined lives and the devastation of business and commerce. Their lack of contrition made their efforts to keep the Negro race down even more appalling to me.

My attention was broken by a young boy hawking newspaper from a pushcart. I bought the latest editions of the *Nashville Daily Union*, *Republican Banner*, and *Nashville Daily Press*. The latter had a headline announcing its planned merger with the *Nashville True Union*. I noticed an advert for the Western Insurance and Transportation Company in two papers. It claimed to be a "fast freight" company, and it featured an image of a train and a steamboat. I made a note to look more into this firm.

"Oh, there you are, my captain."

"Did you find everything you need, Miss Ann?"

"Oh, absolutely. I feel much better already."

We also made a stop at Singleton's Emporium on the corner of Church and Cherry streets. There Ann bought a story novel called *Jane Eyre* by Charlotte Brontë. It was written by some English woman years ago, but perhaps it would entertain her while I was busy on the boat. There were no books that piqued my interest. With the war, the pickings were slim. I wondered what the proprietor would do with the stacks of *Rifle and Light Infantry Tactics* by William Hardee. There wasn't exactly much demand for them anymore.

I usually do not purchase books. The last one was some years ago titled *The Midshipman's Revenge* written by John Townsend

Trowbridge. Instead of spending good money on a book, my usual practice is visiting the library in St. Louis. It has plenty to choose from, but the trouble is, the library doesn't care to lend books for weeks on end. Lending one to a riverman often meant never seeing it again. Any serious reading is thus done off season. While on the boat, there is the Bible and the newspapers we pick up at port. I would hate to admit publicly that the newspapers get more of my attention.

We walked for another hour or so and lunched at the restaurant I was familiar with. It is in the Germantown district, populated from immigrants from the old country. Here are large brick homes and worker cottages intermixed without class divisions. The menu items of the day were *Rinderroulade* and *Spätzle*. The beef roll was a bit overdone, but the egg noodles were just fine. Anna ate almost ravenously but kept her manners. She even had a beer, being parched from our strolling. Women did not usually drink beer in public, but she said we were in a strange town, and anyone who noticed or said anything wouldn't matter. She also spoke in German, much to the delight of the proprietor. I understood every word but kept my abilities secret. The first advice I received upon signing onto a steamboat was to hide my heritage. The "Dutch," or Deutsch immigrants, were reviled in many circles, and economic opportunities were often restricted.

We found Mr. Bemis speaking with a Union officer upon our return to the boat. Anna excused herself to deposit her purchases and "freshen up."

"Captain, may I introduce Captain James Rusling, the chief assistant quartermaster of the Department of the Cumberland. He reports directly to General Donelson. He has a proposal we might be interested in."

"Good day, Captain. I am charged with the removal of the heavy ordnance of the city's defenses and with its transport to Jefferson Barracks in St. Louis for storage. Most boats that land here belong to regular packet lines, and they don't want to disrupt their normal business. Others are owned by former Secesh and don't want anything to do with the Union army. Mr. Bemis here says you are a tramper and have the flexibility we need."

"What is the cargo, Captain Rusling?"

"More than one boat can carry, I'm afraid. I would like to load all the 32-pounder and 24-pounder siege guns I can and assorted field artillery until capacity is reached. Just the barrels, not the carriages."

"Seems straightforward. What do you say, Mr. Bemis?"

"At thirty cents a hundredweight, it might be a good trip. Those 32-pounder siege guns each weigh over seven thousand pounds. Once they are on board, we can't carry anything else except maybe the mail. No chance to pick up any other business along the way. But we would not have to have to stop except for fuel, and we would be in St. Louis early to make repairs to all the damage that is likely to occur."

"I like your calculations, but I'm worried about the deck. The boat will hold about seven hundred tons in these waters, but it must be evenly distributed. The main deck may not be able to hold such weight congregated in such a manner. It is not reinforced to hold cannon like our old gunboat. If one falls through the deck, it will pass right through the bottom of the boat. That much weight will push the keel down another foot, and we might have trouble getting over the bars."

"We can brace where we need to, sir. Such lumber is cheap. Besides, we're not going to fire the guns."

"All right, Bemis. Captain Rusling, you have a deal. We will make it happen somehow. Will you telegraph Jefferson Barracks to be prepared for our arrival?

"Indeed, I shall. Thank you, gentlemen. I was really in a bind. I will give the orders and set the wheels in motion. Most of the guns are already here and stored in that warehouse over there. We'll start bringing the rest down to the water."

After the army captain's departure, Bemis and I smiled at each other. Over the years, we developed the scheme to make the job seem exceptionally difficult to get a higher rate of shipping. It wasn't dishonest per se; it was business. If it were regular freight, we couldn't charge a quarter of that from here. No one could afford to pay it. As there were no fixed rates on the river, we simply charged what we guessed the shipper could pay. The axiom "supply and demand" was the rule on the rivers. Sometimes we won; sometimes we got the short end of things. You wouldn't complain if you did. That was the nature of the business. That the government was about to ship these guns at almost the cost of producing them was its problem, not ours.

We looked to the river to see our new friend on the *Albatross* was just reaching Nashville. Captain Jinks and his crew must have had more trouble, or perhaps they had to make repairs. He just missed out on a great deal. That's how it was in the business. Maybe he will get the contract for the gun carriages we were not asked to carry.

Mr. Voight approached from town kissing a good handful of money. He was quite proud of his achievement, wherever it happened.

"Me and the boys paid a visit to the Senate Billiard Rooms just opposite of the Commerce Hotel. They have fourteen fine Brunswick tables and a first-class saloon attached. Those soldier boys didn't know what hit them."

"Congratulations, but I would put all that back in your pocket and then in the strongbox for safekeeping. Captain Bemis here has a shipment lined up that will be brought here any time. Ask Mr. Swanson to move the boat over to the wharf boat over there for loading. It will be a very heavy load. Get the men ready."

"Aye, Captain. We'll get right on it. What is the cargo?"

"I don't want to ruin the surprise for you," I said with a smile.

I remained ashore as the boat was moved to a wharf boat, an old hull of a decommissioned steamer tied to the bank. From there, we could load our boat while it was fully in the water and maintain an even trim. Chance of blowing up the boilers when we tried to depart were reduced. I had never seen the boat in motion from this perspective. The water curling away at her bow was sheer poetry, but she appeared sluggish and slow to respond. I noticed then that Olsson was pulling the cords. I thought him too green yet for such responsibility, but Swanson was there beside him to avert catastrophe.

The guns were loaded with great effort, and the boat sagged and groaned under the weight. Mr. Voight already anticipated the need to adjust the hog chains in the hold, and he and a gaggle of men disappeared down below with the tools in hand. Captain Bemis was grinning ear to ear. His calculations must have shown a great profit in the making. With the boat loaded to capacity (and probably beyond), we cast off under a good head of steam.

Downstream, I later found Bemis on the boiler deck looking toward shore. We were rounding Bell's Bend, located about nine miles west of Nashville and past Davidson Brach Creek. But if I didn't know better, he was now upset.

"Hello, Captain."

"Something ailing you, Bemis?"

"Actually, yes. Back in December, the Rebs set up a four-gun battery on that knoll called Kelly's Point. They shot up and captured two transports. They then blocked the river from resupplying Nashville while that Hood fellow marched his Reb army upon the city. Our old friend Lieutenant Commander Fitch led a small squadron to break the Reb blockade. We recaptured the two transports, but our gunboat was shot up badly. I was in the pilothouse when a ball punched right on through and shattered my leg. I almost bled out until the men cauterized the wound with a firebox poker. We lost some good men, including Petty Officer Leighton. The boat ended up being condemned and decommissioned. Standing here now, I feel the men are calling out to me."

I always found the notion of dead spirits macabre and unsettling but saw the need to be understanding. I had been in his shoes before, and they still fit on occasion.

"I'm so sorry, Bemis. I never knew the particulars of the action. What do you think they are saying to you? Are they beckoning?"

"Might be a call for us not to forget or a beckoning. I can't tell."

"If it helps, tell them we will never forget."

Return Downstream

ownstream runs are naturally faster, but the dangers are more keenly felt. The velocity of the current creates less time to react to bars and obstructions. A boat must overcome the current, use the rudder to slow or stop. Fortunately, we were still enjoying the efforts of the Union army to keep the river open to steamboat traffic. Unfortunately, with the war over, the sight of a snag boat or dredge was increasingly rare. We didn't see one of them the whole way here. The river is queen and wants to return to her wild state and will soon cause additional difficulties for the boats. We refueled again in Clarksville and made it to Paducah before supply ran low.

With Paducah astern, I went to my cabin for some things in my trunk and to check again on Anna. She had been in good mood since Nashville and began to read to pass the time when my duties kept us apart. She was well into her novel *Jane Eyre*. I was a bit alarmed to find one of my trunks open and the contents obviously gone through. The other was still locked only because I had no need for it as it contained winter items. My Savage navy revolver was out of its holster, and my old pilot's frock coat was placed on the bed.

"What is the meaning of this, Ann? Why have you gone through my trunk?"

Her eyes were heavily medicated by those forsaken powders or maybe even alcohol too. The room smelled of whiskey and cigar smoke, but that was usual. I fought my anger down to the level of irritation.

"O captain! My captain! The ship has weathered every rack. The prize we sought is won. What? Oh, that? I was just bored is all. I tried on your old coat thinking I might want to be a captain someday."

Her voice was playful, almost seductive, but I was not having any of it.

"Not likely to happen. Pigs will use cutlery before that occurrence. You're no Anne Bonny."

"And you're no Calico Jack. There's no pirate heart in you. That is why I remain here alone and unmolested. And why are all these holes in your coat? Do you have moths on your little boat?"

"Not hardly. Those holes were produced by hostile musket balls. I have been meaning to have them repaired."

"I find that hard to believe. Most of these holes would have produced a wound. Where were you hit?"

"Not a scratch. The experience shook me for a while. I don't think of it often anymore."

"I may have misjudged you. I had always thought you were always safe in your iron boat while cruising the rivers and burning towns."

"We didn't distress any towns that didn't need a good burning. Now put everything back as you found it. I will return later."

"Aye, aye, Captain, sir! I will also swab the poop deck while I'm at it. Ah, ha-ha-ha!"

If a crewman had used those words and tone with me, he would be swimming in the river by now. I tried to feel an understanding of her pain and anguish, but the scene that just befell me left me with revulsion.

After supper and our nightly officer meeting, Bemis loitered to have a private discussion. Naturally, we kept our voices down.

"Captain, I want to know what your intentions with Anna are."

"They are honorable, Bemis, but I rediscovered I already have a boat to run. On this trip, I found there will never be time or opportunity for a spousal relationship, ashore or on the water. Certainly not with Anna. It is clear she does not care for life aboard a steamer. I'm not sure she cares much for me either. Sometimes she does, sometimes she doesn't."

"Careful about marrying your boat. It could strike a snag, burn to the waterline, or the boilers simply blow up."

"You can say the same for a woman, Bemis. At least a boat has a crew to help run her. Now look here. Ann—or Anna as she wants to be called now—and I grew up together. I was just a bit tickled at the possibility of getting together. But it has been almost ten years since I have seen her. I have changed and daresay she has too."

"Oh, in what way?"

"Her swings of temperament for one. It's like she has a bee in her bonnet, but I don't know what the subject is. Reminds me of our old Captain Favereau on the gunboat. The only times he was on an even keel was after a good chug of laudanum. She is using opium powders and perhaps other medicines, and that worries me. I suspect her experience in those hospitals in Quincy during the war has profoundly affected her. I don't know where we went wrong. I just know the feeling is gone, and I'm not getting it back."

"Hospitals would foozle anyone. I was there. Do I have your permission to pursue her interest?"

"Why would you do so? She is broken, perhaps beyond repair."

"So am I. Do I have your blessing or not?"

"You never needed it, Bemis, and best to you both. Give me an opportunity to inform her that I will continue my life's direction on the boat. She can remain in my cabin until we reach St. Louis. That will protect her virtue and reputation."

"Fair enough, but try to choose your words carefully. Give it some thought first. Let us shake hands on the matter as a gesture of good faith."

"Agreed. You are my friend and colleague, and I wish it to remain so. I rely on you greatly. I need to relieve Mr. Swanson for a spell and will see her afterward. From there, it is just a short run to St. Louis."

The boat entered the Mississippi at Cairo, and the waters were higher than they were when we steamed south. The current was slack though, indicating the surge from the rains was over. It was dark enough that I could not spot our old gunboat as we passed the levee back in Mound City. I went below to my old cabin to see Ann and discuss things between us. My hope was the medicines had worn off a bit, and she was more her old self. I was not looking forward to it but anticipated the relief it would bring. Running a boat and keeping Ann entertained was one job too many. Trying to do both meant performing well at one or the other or being bad at both.

I found Ann reading her story/novel, and she was well past halfway through. She had discarded her outerwear but was properly covered with a robe. It was amazing how often women changed their look and attire during the course of a day. I heard footfalls coming up from the boiler deck and closed the door for more privacy.

"Ann, when we reach St. Louis, I believe it is best that we part ways. I will provide fare to any point you desire and enough funds for incidentals. Captain Bemis is your good acquaintance, and he would surely care about your welfare as well."

I had inadvertently caused an explosion more powerful than any boiler mishap.

"What is this about? Is this retribution for me rejecting you years ago? I'm not good enough and you are passing me off to your bespectacled crippled minion as an outcast? You are not the only huckleberry on the bush! Verbrenne in der Hölle, mein guter Kapitän!"

Her transformation from damsel to demon was instantaneous. From my vantage point, she seemed to grow a foot in height while her eyes glowed and her hair ignited into an inferno. From a pocket in her robe, she produced a pistol, pointed it at my head, and fired.

The report of the weapon in the cabin sounded like a cannon, and I felt the bullet crease along the band of my cap. Fortunately, I had ducked as if dodging a thrown rock but, in the process, slipped and fell to the floor with a loud thud. The wind was knocked out of me, and I could not form the words to call for help. A panic began to rise in me.

With a shout of "Verdammt!" Anna dropped her derringer and produced my Savage navy revolver from under a pillow. Her fumbling with the complicated mechanism gave the seconds needed for Mr. Voight to burst through the door and to grab hold of the firearm. Unfortunately, he was unable to subdue her further. This was my opportunity to do some good, and from my prostrate position on the floor, I was able to kick Ann's legs out from under her. The three of us became a tangled mess on the floor with Ann finally capitulating in sobs and tears.

The first mate and I got to our feet and then hoisted the struggling woman up and rather roughly sat her in one of the chairs around the table. Defeated, Anna then took on a torpor state and no longer struggled. The vapors of liquor released during her struggle were strong. She just simply sat staring downward, shaking like a leaf.

"Mr. Voight, send for Captain Bemis."

"Yes, sir, but Captain Bemis is already here."

Indeed, he was. He silently stood in the door in shock.

There was also no need to summon further assistance as the discharge of the weapon was heard throughout the boat. Two crewmen armed with a coal shovel and an ax arrived within minutes.

"Captain, are you unharmed? Is anyone hurt?"

"Not physically, gentlemen. Do we have a physician on board?"

"No one claimed to be one while coming aboard, Captain. We're ready to put ashore at any landing to find one. Just give the word."

"No, Mr. Voight, we'll proceed to St. Louis, and I will go up and tell Mr. Swanson not to dawdle. In the meantime, have your men place Miss Anna and her belongings in the cabin I am currently residing and return my carpetbag here. Captain Bemis, escort Miss Anna to her new cabin. Mr. Voight, offer one of the women passengers five dollars to watch over her and tend to her needs for the duration of the trip. Have her check for additional weapons. No doubt the passengers and crew are curious. Tell them we had an accidental discharge of a weapon. That will be all for now."

With a unanimous "Aye, Captain," my orders were put in motion.

I retrieved her derringer from the floor and examined it. It was a typical parlor pistol of .41 caliber made in Philadelphia. Thankfully, she only had one shot. I also recovered my Savage navy revolver from the floor. Only the unique finger lever mechanism used to cock it kept her from finishing me off. She must have retrieved it from the trunk and loaded it. Was she planning this for some time, or did she feel in danger on board? I doubt I would ever know. I was grateful I had left my Paterson revolver in my carpetbag in the other cabin. It is a more conventional design and easier to use.

Examining my cap, there was now a lead smudge down the edge of band with some of the fabric missing. I could feel a headache coming on as the excitement of the event was over. Being grazed by a projectile was not helpful.

I sat in a chair at the table to make sense of it all. Within minutes, there was a voice at the door. It was Bemis.

"A word, Captain."

I dropped my cap on the table. It was the unspoken gesture that our conversation was a private one, man to man. He took a seat and did the same. He silently took note of the damage to the side of the cap.

"I can't say that went well, Bemis. I am at a loss to understand what happened. I don't know where we went wrong. I just know the feeling is gone, and I won't be getting it back."

"You never were one for tact with the ladies. That was like plowing through a logjam."

"You're right, of course, but we have always used direct discourse between us in the past. Being a woman, she couldn't help making a fool of herself."

"Captain, she is in a bedeviled state. Do you intend to turn her over to the law?"

"That had not occurred to me, Bemis. No, I think not, but I want to get some distance between me and her. You surely understand that. What I desire most is for her to find medical help. My first thought is to get her back to her family in Beardstown. That is in Illinois."

"That is on the Illinois River, isn't it?"

"It is indeed. About halfway between St. Louis and Peoria. I can't justify going there without a consignment or two to pay for the trip. Mr. Geldstein would have my pelt and my boat if I took a joy ride of that magnitude. The Illinois Packet Company runs three boats a week up the river, and we can ticket her passage on one of theirs. Do you have any other thoughts on the matter?"

"She professed no love for me in her little tirade, so I currently feel no strong obligation to take her under my wing. I have never seen that side of her. That was absolutely demonic, and she even spoke in tongues."

"She was telling me to burn in hell in German."

"What a language. It sounded like the devil himself. Captain, if we hand her over to a doctor, he would undoubtedly diagnose her with female hysteria and commit her to an institution. That is a family decision, so I agree we get her to her kin. They can then determine her treatment. I fear though that if we simply place her on a steamer, she will not complete the journey as planned. She would end up as a bohemian somewhere."

"It can't be helped unless we get the law involved. Bemis, we can't shackle her and take her against her will. We could be charged with kidnapping. We will have to determine what to do with her by tomorrow evening though when we arrive in St. Louis. Hopefully, she will agree to whatever we cook up."

"She is still responding to my directions but hasn't spoke to me yet. Let me try to persuade her. Where did she get that revolver?"

"Our old friend Captain Owens gave that to me upon his departure from the gunboat last year. You and the shore party had captured it from that Reb cavalry regiment we drove off from their camp on the Mississippi. Ann had been digging through my trunk in fits of boredom and found it. It was unloaded until she got hold of it."

We had already passed the port of Cairo, the last good opportunity to put Anna ashore. There in Cairo, a line of the Illinois Central Railroad ran north, but I had no idea if the rails went anywhere near Beardstown. The Rockford, Rock Island, and St. Louis Railroad has been looking at extending their lines to Beardstown for almost ten years, but nothing has come of it yet. Turning about and landing the boat without that knowledge would slow us considerably with the additional risk of wasting our time completely. We would stick to the original plan. The moon and stars favored steaming on through the night, and Mr. Swanson was sympathetic to our cause. We divided the time remaining into shifts and pushed on. The army would be gratified to have its guns, and the company would be pleased we arrived earlier than planned. Our few passengers would like it as well. After a bout of gunplay, most passengers want off a boat as soon as possible.

We finally made port in St. Louis to disembark the passengers and immediately pushed off again. We steamed a few miles downstream and landed at Carondelet, a small city just south of St. Louis. It was home to James Eads's Marine Ways, a boatyard that had the equipment and manpower to safely remove the big guns from the boat. The army will then move them to the storage armory at Jefferson Barracks at its leisure. Bemis disembarked after receiving the appropriate signatures and the balance of payment. He will deposit the government check and docket the bills of lading at the earliest opportunity.

I saw neither Bemis or Ann at the boat works' landing but was told they procured a carriage and proceeded to St. Louis. That was fine by me. I did see our Mr. Voight doing his job, offloading the guns and the army officer ashore directing their movement to the warehouses. We then steamed again up to our landing in St. Louis once that task was completed. In the pilothouse, neither Mr. Swanson nor Olsson brought up the subject of Ann. I figured they heard our conversation directly below. I suppose the whole boat did. The landing was uneventful, but I felt that all eyes were on us and the boat, as if somehow word of the incident had already spread. I hope it was just my imagination.

I went to the main deck to oversee the securing of the boat and the shutting down of the boilers and machinery.

"Mr. Vought, depending upon the successful efforts of Captain Bemis to organize the next run, my hope is to depart the day after tomorrow. Once the boat is offloaded, give the men twelve hours of slack time and have them return ready to haul cargo. I am going ashore to the company office."

"Aye, Captain. We'll take care of it."

The Company Office

The Negro doorman was at his station at the company office. The years were catching up to him, and he struggled with the heavy door.

"Welcomes back, Captain. We heards your boat's toot but didn't expect you so soon. Mr. Geldstein has a visitor at this time, but you can waits in the parlor."

Once summoned, I found Mr. Geldstein concluding a meeting with Joseph La Barge, the famous captain of the *Emilie*. His exploits are legend on the Missouri River. He is a distinguished-looking man, nearly six feet, and I would say about 180 pounds. Captain Sulloway matched his height but his bulk added at least thirty pounds more. A similar contrast was La barge's mild and agreeable sociable tones compared to Sulloway's bluff and bluster. They were discussing the possibility of chartering one of our boats to go up that stream. I arrived too late to overhear any details, but it is too late in the year to make a run to Fort Benton unless we wanted to winter in the Montana Territory. The first good opportunity for a run would be next spring sometime. I pity the poor captain who draws the short straw if a deal goes through.

"Ah, my good captain. You're back earlier than expected. How was the cruise with your Miss Ann?"

"We had a good run up, but there is increasing trouble with the roustabouts on the rivers. They are asking for higher wages. It is unbelievable how badly the Negroes are being treated. Worse now than when they were slaves. We came back with a boatload of heavy guns for Jefferson Barracks. Bemis is working up the numbers, but you can probably have enough to buy another boat."

"Always business first with you. Tell me about Ann. I would like to take some credit of getting you two reunited if things went well."

"It went from fine to calamity. The experience certainly shattered my illusions of love. I'm working on getting her home to pick up the pieces. It's my fault, I suppose. Juggling duties and spending time with her was an impossible task."

"That is a shame. They say rulers make bad lovers."

"Are you suggesting that I sell my share of the kingdom and go home?"

"Not at all. From what I've seen over the years, your place and best destiny is on a steamboat. Your telegraph from Nashville mentioned the Western Insurance and Transportation Company. What can you tell me about it?"

Thomas and I discussed at length about the state of the rivers, the boat officers, and the Western Insurance and Transportation Company. At present, all freight consignments are transferred from the cars of one railroad to those of another at cities where two lines meet. It's often the same practice with the steamboat companies. That complicates the shipping of freight over long distances and increases handling costs. The Western Insurance and Transportation Company finagled the authority of the State of Pennsylvania to make contracts with rail and boat companies to carry freight to any point on a single bill of lading. With this organization, shippers only pay one bill of lading with the assurance the company would see to the intricate handling of freight by various means to its final destination.

"If we could become part of that organization, we could tap into their trade."

"For once, you are thinking too small, Captain. This is what we should become, not just be a part of. Think of how little overhead and how much profit could be made. We wouldn't need to own all the boats or trains, just coordinate with them. Well done. This is the kind of solution I have wanted to discover for years. Thank you and get back to your boat. And let us keep this between ourselves, shall we?"

"Of course, Mr. Geldstein. Lips are sealed."

I departed his office needing a drink. Probably a cigar too. The nearest to be found were down the corridor in the company parlor. Waiting outside the office door was a man seated with a dour expression waiting his turn to see Thomas. He held a large box on his lap with what appeared to have airholes. Whatever it contained did not make a sound. This time, I wasted no time with my departure.

I found Captain Bemis in the lounge with the same idea as I. He said we cleared over $60,000 dollars on that run to Nashville. It wasn't a company record, but it was up there. At any other time, we would be quite festive. Not today.

"Bemis, where is Anna, and how is she doing?"

"I left her under the care of a lady friend. Anna may not approve of the seedy locale, but she is safe and watched over. I will retrieve her when it is time. You were unavailable to give permission, but I asked Mr. Voight to prepare a cabin from one of the storerooms on the boiler deck. I didn't think you would mind, considering the circumstances. She seems willing to go to Beardstown and shouldn't make any difficulties."

"What are your thoughts on getting her there?"

"Captain, here is the manifest for the voyage. We have a respectable load planned and can expect more cargo along the way. Since the company boat *Meramec* is having problems with one of the engines, I suggested we take the run so she would have no need to rush with repairs. We're simply filling in for her scheduled packet run. The clerk on the *Meramec* had it all set up before the breakdown. This would be all routine if it were not for Anna."

That response did not answer my question. Or maybe it did.

"This run takes us up the Illinois River, Bemis."

"Indeed, it does, Captain. There is even a planned stop in Beardstown. We will deliver assorted sundries and pick up a load of grain for Peoria. Word is that it at least sixty tons worth, maybe more."

"Well, I'll be. When can we depart?"

"The day after tomorrow if all goes well. The roustabouts on the dock want a higher wage, but I held firm and threatened to hire the Negroes. There's trouble brewing on the waterfront. Men of labor increasingly want higher wages and even demand an eight-hour day. The radicals are demanding a work-free Saturday. Nothing will ever get done if they achieve their goals. It wouldn't surprise me if things get out of hand someday soon. Mr. Voight will oversee the bills of lading if I am detained. Miss Anna has agreed to the plan and will remain where she is in the meantime."

"All right, fine. We just need to be loaded before the Sabbath. All work in the ports now shuts down then, but we can still steam. God help us. I just hope our hides do not end up here on the company parlor wall with all the other trophies. I am uncertain how our friend and boss Mr. Geldstein would take this."

"Can't imagine he would have an issue. It is a legitimate run with profit in the making."

"Not exactly."

A cough from behind us startled us both. It was if two schoolboys were caught in the middle of a prank.

"Captain Sulloway. Very good to see you."

"Indeed. Would you gentlemen care to join me in a drink and cigar. I'm buying."

With a run up the Illinois in the offing, I bought parcels of various sundries and delicacies for the family. I would place them in a box, register it as freight, and pay the fare for its transport. That way, our stop in Beardstown was further justified. I would also not be making a shipment on the company's dime. In addition to a clever saying, the freightage for the parcel coincidentally was exactly one seated Liberty dime.

Ann was out of my care, and this freed my time considerably. I slept on the boat studying the Topographic Engineer maps for the Illinois River and reading the pilot reports. It all seemed straightforward. The Illinois is a quirky little river but was slow and mild compared to the others of my acquaintance. The Illinois Packet Company found it profitable to run around sixteen boats on the river and employed several barges. There were rumors though its owners were considering selling out. If true, this was because trade on the Illinois River changed radically after the opening of the Illinois and Michigan Canal. Chicago was now a river port and the three hundred thousand bushels of corn and over two hundred thousand bushels of buckwheat previously shipped downstream to St. Louis now went north to Chicago.

With the completion of the canal, the Illinois River now connects Chicago to St. Louis and all the way to New Orleans. The Great Lakes and canals out east connect Chicago with New York and the Atlantic coast. This accident of geography spurred the growth of railroads, which reach out its tentacles to cities. The boats cannot go and are tapping into the river towns too. St. Louis has lost its competitive edge and will remain in second place unless a railroad bridge or two was built here over the Mississippi.

On the morning of our departure, I made my way to the pilothouse in the hope the coffee was strong and ready. I surely was not. Thank heaven the coffee was both. Mr. Swanson and the cub pilot were at their places.

"Good morning, Captain. Mr. Voight reports all freight and passengers are aboard. Mr. Weatherby reports he has enough steam for departure and will add more fire to the boilers once clear of the landing, and the cargo is shifted for an even keel. Give the word, sir."

"Mr. Swanson, I will be chief pilot on this run."

"I don't understand, Captain. Is there something amiss?"

"Yes, but certainly not with you. We are going up the Illinois, possibly all the way to Lasalle."

"I'm not certified for the Illinois. I don't recall that you are either."

"Exactly. That is why I need to be at the wheel. If disaster befalls us, it is on my shoulders, not yours."

"Are you sure this is wise, Captain?"

"No, I am not. But the *Meramec* is having engine difficulties of some sort. We are taking her place on her packet line, and Captain Bemis has set up a profitable run. Take the boat upriver, and I will assume the wheel once we reach the mouth of the Illinois at Grafton. I want you and Mr. Olsson here in the pilothouse from there on out. I want all of our eyes and experience on hand."

"I don't feel good about this, Captain."

"For what it is worth, I was raised on the Illinois and plied its waters for two years."

"Yes, but that was years ago, and you were a deckhand. Your boat was the *Garden City*, and it burned and sank."

"No one needs to know that, and for the record, I didn't start the fire. Here is a set of charts for you and Mr. Olsson. Think of it as an adventure."

"May fortune favor the bold, Captain. We are surely being bold."

The ready whistle from below confirmed steam was up, and Mr. Weatherby was standing by for orders. I watched as Olsson did the dance of the bells and whistles to get the boat out into the river while Mr. Swanson stood by to assure success. The young man seemed to know what to do, but he was hesitant and nervous during the process. His rapid signaling to the men at the engines no doubt was causing them fits as they attempted to comply. The cub pilot was having difficulty in anticipating the needed signals and was not allowing enough time for the men to respond. Our whistle greeting of "Hip, hip, hooray!" sounded like "Hoo, hoo, hoooo." Pathetic. I had had enough of watching this and was about to intervene. Swanson might have sensed my anxiety or not, but finally he took over the wheel. St. Louis is a busy port and is not the best place to learn backing into the stream until much later in instruction.

It was but a short steam of fourteen miles up to Grafton. I had time for two tankards of coffee before taking the wheel.

Up the Illinois

The town of Grafton is platted along the river at the foot of a stretch of an impressive limestone bluff. There is only room for three blocks before reaching the base of the steep bluffs, but two hollows lead to the backroads to the small farming communities beyond. The Methodist Church built on the hill between Cedar and Vine streets is the prominent landmark. Over ten years ago, the St. Louis and Keokuk Packet Company began shipping coal brought down the Illinois River in barges and delivered Mason's Landing. They sell to other boats but at a premium. The Slaten, Brock and Company here is in the business of cutting cord wood for shipment to St. Louis. It owns about fifty boats that are floated down river with the cordwood, and they are towed upstream by various steamers under contract. It is steady business, but the drifting barges are a hazard to navigation. Grafton is also famous for its ice industry, and the limestone quarried here is used extensively in the buildings in St. Louis.

At the landing were four steamers including the *Hudson*. She operated from La Crosse, Wisconsin, and must be here for the limestone. The folks up there already have enough ice. The mailboat *Adelia* used to be a common sight here, but she was taken in service during the war and seemingly has not yet returned.

From Grafton, the slow-moving Illinois River twists and turns 275 miles through its namesake state. This river differs from the other big rivers primarily in its slow fall, which averages only three inches per mile. This makes a slow current of only two to two and a half miles per hour. Because of its sluggishness, sandbars are quite common as well as fallen trees, creating logjam piles. Accidents on the river are still common, but they are caused more by negligence and complacency than nature. In the hierarchy of river pilots, those that plied the Illinois would never be the legends as those on the Mississippi, Ohio, and certainly not the wild Missouri. It may not be fair, but it was true.

Between St. Louis and Peoria, there is a whole lot of nothing from and economic standpoint. The land is dotted by small farming communities but no towns of importance. There is still a wilderness feel to it. The lower river here is still alive with game, and the fishing for bass, sauger, catfish, and the occasional walleye is good. Ducks, geese, and various waterfowl blackened the sloughs and lakes along the way. The navigation markers were easy enough to see in the daylight, and although often crude in construction, they were generally accurate. They had the good fortune of never being molested by Confederate guerillas during the war.

"Another sandbar ahead, Captain."

"We should have brought a herd of camels. It has been like crossing the deserts of Arabia."

Perhaps my observations were unfair. There is indeed a successful commercial fishing industry between Meredosia and Havana. Most of the fish caught were catfish, carp, and smallmouth buffalo. Fish markets in each town along the way processed and shipped tons of it. The buffalo is a rough fish. Some people enjoy it, but I always thought it best fed to hogs and such. Fishermen use a variety of handmade and manufactured nets and traps in their small boats. The most prominent type seemed to be the modified canoe called a duckboat. I tried to stay clear of the little boats as we passed by. It was the polite thing to do, and I certainly didn't want to foul the paddle wheels with an irate fishman's net. Our stern wash could not be helped, and it upset a boat or two on our ascent up the river. I couldn't hear the curses from my vantage point, but the pumping of fists clearly told me the wet men in the river were not happy.

The lands along the lower river here are generally flat and tilled for grain, but Beardstown doesn't become visible to the eyes until rounding a bend at the mouth of the La Moine River. The smoke rising from behind a stand of trees is the first tell-tale sign of inhabitance. There were no other boats at the landing, and I decided to push into the soft clay bank at the foot of State Street.

The first settlers to Beardstown were drawn by the richness of the soil and the salubrity of the climate that promised good farming. I had not been back since the start of the war, but it looked virtually the same as almost five years ago. Brick warehouses lined the waterfront, and clapboard structures were neatly organized for three blocks from the river. There still couldn't be more than two thousand people living here, but it was the largest town in the river between St. Louis and Peoria. Only two occurrences of note ever occurred here. One was the Duff Armstrong murder trial in '58. I wasn't there to see it, but back then lawyer Abraham Lincoln himself made a clever defense and spared the fellow from the gallows. The other was when Lincoln came then back a few months later and gave his famous "House Divided" speech.

Mr. Voight directed his men to secure the boat with hawsers and a gang of men ashore ran a long plank to the forecastle to handle freight and passengers. The one stage plank we carried aboard was far too short to bridge the chasm between the boat and the high bank. Maybe someday someone will conjure a better way to handle freight from the irregular banks along the rivers.

Ann appeared on forecastle with her arm under Captain Bemis's. It was unclear who was supporting who. She was wearing a rather whimsical and festive dress with hoops and a wide-brimmed hat with a velvet ribbon. A crewman waited impatiently under the burden of her trunk. I wanted this goodbye over with as quickly as possible.

"I am dreadfully sorry and ashamed for discharging my pistol in your direction. Although it is difficult to deny the act, I do not remember doing it at all. I do wish you well in the life you have chosen."

"Think of it no more, Ann. I hardly recall the incident."

I was lying and highly suspect she was too.

"Captain Bemis, please see Miss Ann off the boat. Her family home is but a few blocks from here. Someone should be there."

"I will see to Miss Ann, Captain. It will not take long. In the meantime, Mr. Voight is taking tally of the freight aboard and is preparing for its offloading as we speak."

There were no further words or gestures. For a brief period, Ann was in my life. My Christian teachings told me I should feel concern for her welfare. I wasn't feeling very charitable presently. Perhaps later. In fact, I felt nothing at all. If anything, I felt remorse for feeling no remorse.

Not wanting to watch her walk away, I turned around on my heel and nearly ran into my first mate.

"Yes, Mr. Voight? What is on your mind?"

"Chief Engineer Weatherby informs me the boilers, stacks, and mud drum all need a good scouring. He will need at least a full day."

"Will this delay adversely affect our consignments? Do we have perishables on board?"

These things I should know. It was embarrassing that I did not. With Ann gone, I can get back to the business of running my boat.

"According to Captain Bemis, there will be no detrimental effect on the cargo. However, it is a golden opportunity to visit your family. Pardon the liberty in saying so, Captain."

"I pray this opportunity is not the product of mischief on your part. I can well visit my family at the time of my choosing during the off-season."

"Not at all, Captain. I admit we officers discussed the matter, but there was no need for conspiracy. The feeder pump sucked in gobs of sand and muck while getting over all of those bars."

"Hmm. Very well, Mr. Voight, I am going to get some things from my cabin then depart the boat. See to the transfer of cargo. Mention to Captain Bemis not to take on cargo bound north of Peoria unless it is of great profit. I have a hankering to get off this river as soon as practical."

"Aye, Captain. Have a good visit with the family. We will be here when you return."

Packing up a carpet bag with sundries for Mother took but a few minutes. My original intent was to simply drop my purchased goods here for delivery, but the parcels fit easily into the bag. I left my Paterson revolver in the trunk as well as my flask of whiskey. No need to antagonize Mother, but I did retain the little Colt Root revolver in the suspender holster.

A distinguished gentleman stood on the dry ground next to the warehouse casting his gaze over the proceedings on the landing. I instantly recognized him as Mayor Arenz. He has been alternating between being an alderman or mayor here in Beardstown for over twenty years. I made my way over to him with greetings.

"Well, hello, young man. I thought it might be you. Your folks have mentioned the name of your boat at every chance. It's high time you brought her up the river to show her off."

"Good to see you, Mr. Arenz. Congratulations on your election to mayor. Or should I say reelection?"

"It was not technically a reelection as there was a year break since I last held the esteemed position. Mr. Haverkluft kept the seat warm for me. Are you here long?"

"Not at all. Just to drop off a shipment and load up whatever business my clerk can drum up. If I can catch a ride or rent a horse, I will have just enough time to visit the family."

"Your old friend James Black is a teamster in town and would surely oblige. His stable is two blocks west."

"Thank you, sir. I will see him straight away."

"Just a warning to you, son, but that circuit reverend Peter Cartwright fellow held a revival here a while back. He follows the teachings of John Wesley to a tittle. Near everyone who attended swallowed it up hook, line, and sinker, including our own minister. Many folks now shun worldly habits such as card playing, horse racing, and of course, the drinking of spirits of any kind. The Methodists here in town were already high-church types but now are nearly turning into Quakers."

"I didn't figure on doing any of that during my stay. If the boat is ready, I will depart sometime tomorrow."

"No one in town will give you any fuss, but I'm thinking of your mother. Those are some fancy duds you're wearing there. Looks like you have two watches too. Most of us can maybe afford one, if even that. Those under the spell of Reverend Cartwright won't approve."

"One is for local time and one is kept on St. Louis time. It is useful when telegraphing back to the company."

"Well, that's yet another thing. These revisionists don't care much for modern mechanical devices either. They say fancy clothes, the telegraph, and steam machinery separates us from God."

"Can't say that is true. I spend much time on my boat praying the boilers don't blow us up to kingdom come. Thy will be done and all that."

"Well, I can imagine so. Seems every week we hear of a calamity striking a boat. Well, welcome home, *Captain*. You have done us proud, and the townspeople will be happy to see you. Give my regards to your folks. Aufwiedersehen und Gute Reise."

I winced a bit and replied, "Good day to you, sir, and thank you."

Mayor John Arenz came to this country from Cologne, which was technically part of the Kingdom of Prussia. He spoke with but a slight accent, and he did not have the rigidness of the typical Prussian. He still likes to throw a German word or phrase to people of German descent thinking it would get him a vote or two. In most parts of the country, the German folk are still despised as filthy foreigners, and I have endeavored to keep my heritage concealed with uncertain success. Fortunately for us, the influx of the Irish gives new target to the anti-immigrant forces. If what he said was true about the Methodists in town, I might switch over and join the Lutherans. Father was one before he married Mother.

The good mayor did not mention Ann. Maybe he didn't see her.

I rounded the corner and saw the steeple of my old church. It was built in 1851 by the German immigrants on the corner of Fifth and State Streets. Pastor Ritter had recently left, and I could not remember the name of his replacement. After what Mayor Arenz said, I really didn't want to meet him anyway. A short distance further, I met my old friend James Black at his livery. We had not corresponded to each other at all over the years, but we took up where we left off. Men were like that. Together we saddled a mare. It would be returned sometime tomorrow.

"I saw Ann with one of your men from the boat. I hailed her, but she paid no mind. Looked sickly too. What's the matter with her?

"I brought her over from Quincy. She had been working in one of those big military hospitals. She must have seen some pretty awful sights. She even lost James Simpson to disease at Camp Butler."

"James Simpson did not die in any army camp. He tried to rob a grocer in Peoria and was shot dead. Did you make a play for her affections? You used to be sweet on her, but she never seemed to reciprocate."

"I suppose I did, but my efforts were in vain. I don't understand my problem with women. I mean, I like them just dandy, but they aren't particularly driven in my general direction."

"Well, with that puss, your only chance to get a girl is to trap one. Where do you meet them, at church or something?"

"I never get to go when the season is underway. When the 'lone-somes' get real bad, there is an improper house I frequent. I seldom go upstairs with one of the girls. Too much risk of catching something the doctors have no clue how to get rid of. Instead I remain in the parlor smoking, drinking, and chatting with the girls. They always like hearing about the boat and other stories."

"Did it ever occur to you that it is their job to be good listeners?"

"Until this moment, the thought never occurred to me."

"Well, now you have something to think about. They probably let you form some bad talking habits. Maybe you should grow a beard. It might hide some of your shortcomings. If women don't find you handsome, they should at least find you handy or wealthy. Go on and git. Bella here won't give you trouble. She's a good horse. There's a full feed bag under your carpetbag strapped to the saddle. Regards to the family."

The family home and farm are but five miles north of town and sit on the bluff overlooking the river. It was there I fell in love with the steamboats as they passed by. After me, my mother could have no more children, so there was only my brother and I to help on the farm. I left upon reaching eighteen years of age. My brother was two years older and left home when he joined the army back in '61. He was seldom much help anyway as he is one of the laziest critters I ever met. Letters from the folks seldom mention him anymore. I have no idea if he was still about here or not.

Family Ties

Beardstown proudly constructed a plank road over sandy ridges and marshes toward Bluff Springs ten years ago to allow farmers to carry heavier wagonloads over the sandy soil. To use it, a toll was collected over at the Zinn home on Fifteenth Street. The road was built mostly of cottonwood, which made for a very rough ride. Cottonwood is an awful tree and not fit for mush else. The road was made worse by the edges curling in the hot sun. Funding to extend the road to the town of Virginia was denied as state and county funds were diverted to entice the railroads. It was aggravating for us on the boats to see the government doing backflips for the railroads while we seldom, if ever, obtained such assistance.

I avoided the plank road and rode due north along the river. The family home soon came into view. The trees were bigger, and our faithful mostly Airedale dog was gone now. The lineage of Rufus was highly suspect, but he was a good and faithful dog. From out front here, not much else had changed. Father was smoking his pipe on the porch. His face lit up when he spotted me. It wasn't often a man with a steamboat uniform on horseback rode in from town. He stood up stiffly and waved, then turned and called, "Mother! Our riverman has returned." Mother and Father called themselves, well, *mother* and *father*. That tradition was similar to that on the boat. Everyone was called by their title if they had one.

I rode up and tied the horse before mother emerged from the house. That short ride from town had an inordinate effect on my backside. It had been years since I rode a horse. I got in a good handshake with Father before Mother burst through the door and overwhelmed me with motherly affection.

My sudden appearance embarrassed mother, for she had not prepared anything special for supper. In the pot she had sausage, potatoes, and cabbage. Although weary of eating of all three for weeks, it at least smelled better than what we had been eating on the boat. There was also Johnny cakes made from yellow corn on the table, which I'd never seen before. The yellow-dent variety was quickly replacing the traditional Indian corn across the country. It had a better yield, and people took to the uniform color. The dinner was made complete with a batch of yesterday's gingerbread cookies. It took some convincing to get mother to finally relax and sit with us to simply pass the time. They both looked well and appeared healthy, but they had aged considerably. They were both approaching sixty years, and few people lived beyond that. For that matter, few people seemed to make it to sixty. As we write regularly, there wasn't much new to talk about. It was just good to be together again.

I eventually brought up the subject of Ann and told them about as little as I did friend James Black. I did not bring up her old sweetheart James Simpson. They, in turn, told me of my brother's return from the war when his enlistment was up in the fall of last year. He had seen enough war and did not reenlist. My father was disappointed the army did not teach him the value of good work and some good morals. The Union army was not the Hessian Grenadiers, and from what I saw, Christian values were often in short supply in the army. Last heard, my brother was working on some barge on the upper lake north of Peoria or further up in Chillicothe. The only barges I knew of up there were the bawdy boats that pushed out into the river to avoid various vice laws. I thought it best not to mention that.

"Son, I want to thank you again for that J. H. Manny reaper you purchased for us. It goes through the grain fields like greased lightning. I was able to hang up the scythe for good. I can't do as much as I used to but have hired brothers Charles and Casper Bockmeier to help out. You may not remember them. They are about ten years younger than you. They are saving to buy their own place. I don't see why they don't just move out west. With the Homestead Act, you only must stay on the place five years and its yours. If you're planning on staying anyway, its 160 acres of free land."

The various sundries I had bought for Mother in St. Louis are difficult to procure out here. The parcels contained a candy called Turkish delights, mustard, curried powder, a box of sugar plums, tomato ketchup, and four pounds of white sugar. The most special was a large box of Bissinger's chocolates all the way from Cincinnati. The Bissinger claim was, the family has been making confections for European royalty for almost two hundred years. She seemed delighted but said the candies and white sugar were far too extravagant.

"Son, thank you, but we should all strive for a simple life. Too much of what is going on in the world is separating us from God."

"How would that be, Mother?"

"People separated from toil and want no longer seek salvation. It is easier for a camel to pass through an eye of needle than a rich man to get to heaven. It troubles me to see your finery and your purchase of these luxuries. I fear you may be drifting toward sin and darkness."

"Don't fear, Mother. This is simply my uniform, and the delicacies are for the special occasion. Why, you should see the doorman at the company office. He is but a Negro but sports a burgundy waistcoat with black velvet lapels and cuffs, yet he is a most pious man. Riches themselves don't keep us from heaven. It is how we use them. Reverend Manier in Cairo spoke often on the subject."

I hoped that would end the conversation on the subject. No such luck. She was about to say something else, but Father mercifully stepped in.

"Mutter, das ist genug zu diesem Thema. Lass uns über etwas anderes reden."

Yes, that was enough on that subject, and we should talk about something else. Thank you, Father, the one sitting here and the one in heaven. I chuckled to myself. While we were children, my parents spoke in German as if it were some secret-code cipher. To this day, they must think my brother and I don't understand, but we do.

We conversed well into the evening until we were all exhausted. When the time came, I retired to the room my brother and I shared when the family was complete. Only one bed remained. The ropes needed tightening, but I found myself too lazy for the chore. This must have been my brother's bed as it contained his curse. Sleep came easy. Perhaps it was the best sleep I had had in years. It was either for being at home or not having any coffee since morning. Either way was fine by me.

I woke to Mother calling us men to breakfast. The sun was just breaking over the horizon. I often cursed our luck in not having a hill or stand of trees to the east to delay its rise. My father and I were served boiled eggs, smoked ham, black bread, Emmental cheese, and cherry preserves. The meal brought back many memories. I regretted the apples were not yet ready for harvest.

"Can you not stay another day? You can ask your boss."

"Mother, our son here is the captain of his own boat. He *is* the boss. He has to set a good example."

"'Tis true, Mother. The men have been working in my absence, and I must go back soon. I can't let them think I am a slacker."

"I know, but you can't blame a mother for trying."

The goodbyes were difficult. We each silently knew it could be our last. They were getting old in life, and my profession was not a safe one. On the other hand, men and families who moved out west were usually never seen again. My father never saw his family after he left the old country, and the exchange of letters stopped years ago. We were actually very lucky. I still, though, had the blues, from my head down to my shoes.

I returned the mare to the livery, and James wouldn't take a dime.

"Take me for a ride on that big boat of yours sometime."

"Deal. Take care, my friend. You seem to have a thriving business here."

I found all was well on the boat. The engineer's men had scoured the boilers and flushed the mud drums of collected sediment. Bemis was back aboard and appeared in good cheer. It seemed almost as if he had one of his schemes in mind. If the circumstances were normal, I would say it was just like old times.

"Mornin', Captain. We have an interesting load to pick up in Peoria, and we can then make a triumphant return to St. Louis."

"Good morning, Captain Bemis. What, pray tell, is so interesting in Peoria?"

"Whiskey. All that we can carry. It may rival or surpass hauling those guns to Jefferson Barracks. We will be fully loaded, and the distance back to St. Louis is a fraction of that from Nashville. The savings from the coal expenditure alone is enormous."

"Well done. Let us proceed to Peoria and glory."

The boat slid out into the water with grace and proceeded upstream. But after less than three miles, we were quickly thwarted by a massive logjam along the breadth of a sandbar. The branches of the trees intertwined while the trunks had embedded themselves into the wet sand.

"Captain, it will take a few barrels of gunpowder to clear that or a snag boat. We are short on both."

"Indeed, Mr. Swanson. I have an idea we can try."

I rang the bells to reverse the port paddle wheel, turned the great wheel counterclockwise, and the boat spun about.

"Where are you going, Captain? You surely don't mean to ram the obstruction, so you?"

"Stop thinking of me as foolish, Swanson. We'll try Hager Slough."

"Hager Slough? It's not even on the chart. Are you sure about this?"

"No, I am not, but we will give it a try. Hager Slough was dredged some years back to get boats up the one hundred miles of the Sangamon River to Springfield. Abe Lincoln himself split rails for the project. The channel looked deeper than ever when we passed it. I surmise the logjam is backing up the water in the main channel and diverting it to the slough."

"Did any boat ever make it up to Springfield?"

"Just one. The *Talisman*. As she returned in a ruinous condition, only one other boat, the *Utility*, tried again. She bottomed out and became landlocked at Petersburg. Total loss."

"That must be decades ago. This endeavor does not seem wise, Captain."

"Have a little faith, Mr. Swanson. Pray a whole lot too. Besides, we're not going up the Sangamon, and the slough is my old fishing spot. It has not failed me yet."

The boat came about again as ordered and headed back upstream. No doubt Mr. Weatherby down below was perplexed as Mr. Swanson up here. Mr. Voight even came up to the pilothouse to find out what was going on.

"There's the slough, gentlemen. Steady as she goes."

Hager Slough was indeed full of water, higher than I had ever seen. But I kept the speed of the boat down to the pace of a walking man. No telling what trees and snags were lurking beneath the surface. The channel was just wide enough for the boat to fit, and the only way out if we were stopped was to reverse. No doubt we would crush the rudder and damage the paddle wheels if that came to be. Tree branches scraped and snapped along both sides of the boat, which alarmed the handful of passengers below. It did my nerves no good either.

To make the situation even more ominous, thunder boomed and rolled from the northwest. A heavy storm was moving in.

To break the tension, I asked Mr. Olsson to fill my tankard with coffee. I had to ask him twice as his attention was so fixed on the water. I even treadled the boat's signal "Hip, hip hooray!" as we passed by my parents' home. I glanced to see them waving back, but only for a second. My focus was on the river where it should be.

The two hours it took to regain the river seemed like a whole day. But we made it through, and all breathed a sigh of relief. Looking aft, the logjam at the sandbar had indeed created a substantial dam across the main channel. The water had nowhere else to go but down Hager Slough.

"That was the damnedest thing I ever saw, Captain. My hat is off to you, and I will buy you a drink at the first opportunity. You see that, Mr. Olsson? Our captain is not only bulletproof but a lord of the rivers!"

So a camel passing through the eye of the needle has a better chance to heaven than a rich man? Do riches separate men from God? Maybe so for some people, but for me, that was bunkum and balderdash. I just got the boat through Hager Slough praying all the way. I even got over fifty men and women to join in. Beat that, Reverend Peter Cartwright! If he had seen what transpired here, he would most certainly include the tale at his next revival.

Once in the main channel, I gave the wheel to Mr. Swanson with the promise to return shortly. I suddenly heard the call of nature and wanted to clean up. It was raining buckets by the time of my return to the pilothouse. Visibility was poor, but not bad enough to force a landing and wait it out.

The Illinois River is home to both the Illinois Packet Company and the Naples Packet Company, famous for their five-day runs between St. Louis and Lasalle. Each company controls ten to sixteen boats and own dozens of barges. They are both feeling the effects of the railroads just like all other boat companies. Rumors are there will be a dramatic change in both companies soon. There is talk of merging, disbanding outright, or just selling off excess tonnage. None of the boats we have seen so far flew either company banner on their jack staffs. Maybe they stopped the practice, or they are just far upriver taking advantage of the high waters. I probably wouldn't recognize any of their boats now anyway. Every company boat I knew when I was aboard the *Garden City* is long gone. Now all boats on this river are strangers to me.

Peoria was our destination, and it was but seventy-five miles or so up the river. It is a whiskey town on the river and not particularly known for a genteel tradition. The fair and growing city of fifteen thousand people had nine distilleries and at least six breweries up and running. For that, it is often called the *whiskey capital of the world*. That is a distinctive moniker when major cities in the country had at just one or two distilleries. Peoria was producing three times more than what was consumed locally, and that was a great amount in itself. Whiskey sold for $2.25 per gallon, including the hefty $1.10 per gallon tax slapped on by the city, state, and federal governments. It was still cheap enough and a high-enough quality that thirsty citizens across the prairies clamored for it.

The *Peoria City* passed us by with a full head of steam heading downstream. I wonder how she will fare at the sandbar we skirted around just north of Beardstown. I thought to put ashore at Havana for its high-quality coal, but we had enough to reach our destination.

Peoria is a typical river city, known as a wide-open town for men willing to look sideways at the law in the pursuit of making a dollar. The blocks just beyond the waterfront are jammed full of billiard halls, faro dens, fancy houses, saloons, and dance halls. It was just the type of place my brother would light upon, like a moth to a flame. It would break my mother's heart if it were true. With its rough reputation, I didn't care much for Peoria, but the wooded bluffs beyond the town to the north were perhaps the most beautiful sight in the world. This was especially true in the autumn. Someday I would like to take a drive in a carriage up there.

There were a dozen steamboats tied to the landing on Water Street. The sternwheeler *Schuyler* is a war veteran as well as the *City of Alton*. No dockmaster was seen, so I chose a spot in between the *Metamora* and the *David Tatum* of the Howard Boat Company as it offered the most space. The *Metamora* is a stern-wheeler of less than two hundred tons with only three boilers to power her two engines. She couldn't hold much and was no doubt only used in the local trade.

We made the landing without incident, although I wish it were a bit gentler. The boat came to a stop with a bump, which was startling but not damaging. The lord of the rivers indeed. This boat had a way of reminding pilots they were fallible. A sign on the landing read "Beware of Pickpockets and Loose Women." Both were in abundance here. Meanwhile, the rain was coming down more steadily. It was the kind that would hang over our heads for a long while. With my recent wanderings in mind, I remained on the boat. I would focus on my job once again.

The shipment of whiskey came in barrels from the Cole's Distillery. Almiran S. Cole built a 1,600-bushel distillery a few years back, but he was making bark juice here even before Peoria was founded. His facility was the most modern in town and created vast quantities cheaply. We took aboard all the boat could carry, filling the hold and the main deck. Some went up to the boiler deck. I thanked the builders again that this boat was designed as a freighter. Unlike most other boats, the boiler deck on this vessel was constructed stout enough to hold some cargo. The men rolled up all the barrels the vessel would carry before becoming too unstable. The cargo was far more profitable than any cabin passengers we would have carried there otherwise.

While waiting for the loading of the cargo, I read an edition of the *Peoria Evening Mail*. The one item that caught my interest was the announcement of the opening of the Union Stock Yard and Transit Company in Chicago. "The Yards," as they call it, was built on an old marshland. The railroads are bringing in cattle, hogs, and sheep for slaughter and then shipping the meat into the city. Plans are afoot to quickly make the facility a centralized processing area with the goal to ship meat across the northern states and beyond. This is a business beyond the reach of steamboats. We can move live-stock for sure, but not as many or at the speed of trains. Tarnation.

The boat pulled off the landing as announced, but there were four men missing. They were all deckhands, and I was not about to wait for them. It was their responsibility to be on time. My guess is they are in confinement somewhere in the city. In fact, most of the occupants in the river city jails were steamboatmen. Crewmen with money in their pocket often get into the red eye and trouble. The local law officers gleefully arrest rivermen with gusto with little provocation. Adding misery to such a fate, the company rule in such situations is that the men forfeit all wages coming to them. The rule is meant to dissuade bad conduct while ashore, but it has only moderate success.

Our voyage downstream toward St. Louis was uneventful, and I once again treadled the boat's call "Hip, hip, hooray!" as we passed by my parents' farm. No one was visible this time, probably because of the rain. In our absence, the logjam had been cleared by nature, and we were on our way. Woe be to any boat that was downstream when that occurred. I returned the wheel to Mr. Swanson once we passed by Grafton and reentered the mighty Mississippi.

Home Port

St. Louis was a welcome sight, and I looked forward to the next run. The autumn dry spell was just around the corner. Two men in black frock coats and topper hats waited ominously for our arrival. One wore a pair of those funny Frenchy pince-nez eyeglasses. The thin black cord hung down from one lens against his cheek and disappeared under his collar. That would be an irritant for me and was hopefully the only reason for the sour look on his face. This did not look good. I made my way below to the forecastle to head them off from any mischief they had in mind.

"Greetings, Captain. We are from the Missouri Steamboat Inspection Office. We understand you went up the Illinois. That isn't one of your usual routes, is it?"

"As you may already know, this boat is a tramper. We don't usually have a fixed route or schedule. We go where the company needs us. In this case, we were filling in for the *Meramec*, which had some sort of mechanical problem."

"We would like to see your chief pilot's certificate of certification for the Illinois River."

"I was the chief pilot on this run. Mr. Swanson up there only relieved me for short spells in slack water when the call of nature occurred. I was not expecting you, and my documents are in my cabin. I will return in a moment."

Well, this was it. I had no intention of deceit but planned to use the few minutes to gather my wits. My hope was that my experience on more difficult rivers would overcome the need for a specific certificate for the languid Illinois. Not long ago, a gold coin would suffice with inspectors, but these are new times. Bureaucracy was everywhere and getting stronger. I was prepared for a fine of some sort. What punishment the company would dole out was only in my imagination, and it wasn't a pleasant outcome. I would soon find out, though.

"Ahem. There is no need for that. I happen to have copies from the company office."

It was Captain Sulloway. He had somehow moved his bulk surreptitiously through the crowd at the landing and appeared as suddenly as a specter. His tone was grim. He must have overheard Bemis and me in the company parlor discussing taking Ann to Beardstown. If I didn't know his disdain for inspectors, I could easily suspect he contacted these gentlemen and was lying in wait.

The chief inspector opened the leather folder and leafed through its contents.

"Your boat master's certificate, certificates for the Upper Mississippi, Lower Mississippi, the Ohio, up to Louisville, the Cumberland, and Tennessee Rivers. There is a memorandum showing you proceeded up the Yazoo and the Red during the war, and another says you steamed the Missouri up to Leavenworth City some years ago. You sure get around, Captain. Oh, here it is, the Illinois. Why would you have this folder here and now Captain Sulloway? This is quite unusual."

"Yes, the good captain here was certified for the Illinois only recently, but in his haste, he departed before we could give him his copy. I came down here in person to bite off a piece of his buttocks. Our meeting here is purely coincidental."

"Very well. All appears in order. Be sure to have your certificates in hand, Captain. It will make both of our jobs easier. The same goes for all pilots. Good day, gentlemen."

I stood silently before my master, waiting for him to speak. The man was legendary for his volume and volcanic profanity. I knew well from firsthand experience as a cub pilot and braced myself to receive both. Instead, I was surprised to find neither in his words.

"Damn foolish thing you did. Anybody can pilot a boat on that excuse of a river, but you must have a certificate. The old days are over. We must now follow the regulations. I covered for you here but will not do so again. Besides, it was my foolish idea for you to take Miss Ann on the boat. I'm partly, only partly, to blame."

"I'm very sorry, sir, but we did have a profitable run. Very profitable."

"This isn't about profit, son. Remember old man Geldstein's philosophy? His son Thomas shares it to this day. We must uphold the company's reputation and image. Never do anything to diminish either ever again. No woman, or man for that matter, is worth that. Understand?"

"Aye, Captain!"

"Fine. Let us put this all behind us. Let's have a drink once you have everything settled here. I want to hear of your run. Oh, and you might want to get a replacement for your cap while in port. What the devil happened to it?"

"I brushed up against a hot pipe. Besides, these caps cost good money."

"Frugal is one thing, but you are the richest poor man I have ever met."

"Waste not, want not."

As I collected myself, I observed the deckhands and roustabouts unloaded the barrels of whiskey. It was amusing how they treated each with loving care. Barrels of vinegar were right smartly abused in comparison. Bemis had his stack of waybills signed by the receivers and departed for the company office. There the freight auditor would balance his books and sign off on the final bill of lading. The men would soon amble over there with their stubs too for pay off for the run. Most of them would be back for the next voyage, but there was always turnover. Some men went on to find their fortunes elsewhere, and others took their place.

I returned aboard and spent a few minutes to sort through my trunks and take inventory. Ann had placed everything back, but all was still in disarray. I was not happy to find that my two bottles of whiskey were empty and at least ten cigars gone. My reserve money purse containing nearly one hundred dollars was missing. No wonder she had money to spend on medicines.

That woman was trouble, all right. I had dodged two bullets with her.

BOOK 2

Down the Mississippi

Despite the profitable run, the usual elation of a good run was missing. Ann and the inspectors certainly did not contribute to any festive mood. The visit to my folks was a good one, but their aging in the past few years was a shock and a reminder that our times on earth was limited. I left the boat under the able Mr. Voight to continue to unload and made my way to the office to report to Mr. Geldstein.

Thomas had another visitor, so I spent the time waiting in the company parlor. Other boats were still on their runs, and I was the only captain among the few patrons. It was too early in the day for liquor and opted for coffee instead. I could not imagine functioning though the day without it.

An hour passed before another soul entered the room. I had hoped it would be a clerk summoning me to Thomas's office. Instead, it was my own Mr. Swanson and his young cub pilot in tow. He tacked his pilot report to the wall and gave a friendly wave to me across the way without words. From his standpoint, it was a profitable run on a new river. All was well.

Another hour passed before a young man summoned me to Mr. Geldstein's office. Thomas was in no better mood than me. He was now the owner of a steamboat company and Lord knows what other enterprises. His troubles came from many a direction.

"You haven't shaved. Are you growing a beard?"

"I'm thinking about it. Several people have recommended it, including you. Apparently, I am not aging gracefully."

I told Thomas of the run and the details of Ann and the episode with the inspectors at the landing. He would find out about Ann's gunplay eventually, and his signature was on the certificate. It was best he heard it all from me directly.

"I feel so foolish, Thomas."

"Don't kick yourself to death. It is all over. I want you to delay departure for a few days. There is a meeting of the board on Wednesday that I want you to attend. You haven't attended one in some time, being on the river and such. Primarily I want you to witness the proceedings and take note of each member's reaction and demeanor."

"It sounds ominous."

"It is. Nine o'clock sharp. Be there."

With the boat idle in port, the crew was left to their own devices while they waited for the announcement of the next run. The married men spent the time with their families while the single men typically amused themselves in the various billiard halls and taprooms near the levee. The engineer crew was kept busy for at least a few days scrubbing out the boilers and tinkering with the machinery. I had my usual haunts, but they were usually more genteel. The raucousness of the waterfront never appealed to me.

The most productive use during such idle times was preparing for the next run. This meant having laundry done, replacing worn items, and stocking up on various sundries to offset the monotony of the food on the boat. I did not return Ann's derringer pistol to her possession. It was too dangerous to do so. So I procured some .41 caliber balls and added it to my growing arsenal.

Wednesday could not come soon enough. I wanted this confabulation over with. Although it could prove interesting to watch the inner workings of the company, there were reports of the autumn dry spell effecting the rivers. We could easily miss out on a productive run if we did not depart soon. I had not seen Captain Bemis, but he should be collecting up consignments for transit.

My arrival at the company office occurred at the appointed time, fifteen minutes early, in fact. Directed to the parlor by the doorman, I found a gaggle of gentlemen deep in discussions and smoking cigars. They were dressed as men of means by all means. They reminded me instantly of the fat cat politicians comically portrayed in *Harper's Weekly*. My company uniform and lean frame stood out in stark contrast. I noticed Captain Sulloway across the room and gravitated to him. Two other boat captains present had done the same. The one I knew well enough was Doyle, captain of the *Piankeshaw*.

"Good morning, Captain Sulloway. This is quite a gathering. What will transpire here?"

"Morning, boys. In a few minutes, we will be called to enter the meeting room. I will point to where you three should sit. Mind your manners and watch and listen. If someone asks you a question, stand and say what you know and no hemming and hawing. This meeting might get scabrous, but Mr. Geldstein knows what he is doing. For God's sake, do not contradict him here. If you feel differently, we can talk it out later."

A Negro steward lightly rang a bell and announced the meeting would commence as soon as everyone was seated. Those who were already drinking took their glasses in with them.

The meeting room adjoined the parlor. It was a dark and foreboding with heavy wood paneling. Small, long windows ran the length of one wall high up along the edge of the ceiling. They produced just enough light but prevented viewing anything outside or inside from the street. Above the fireplace hung a portrait of Sylvanus Geldstein, the founder of the company and Thomas's late father. It was obviously done years ago. Until now I could never picture what he looked like as a younger man. I reckoned he was born old. A large walnut table dominated the center of the room with handsome padded chairs surrounding it. Someone had left upon it a copy of Tiffany's Blue Book, which claimed to be a study in virtuosity. Twenty chairs were pressed against the walls for those deemed not worthy of taking a seat at the high altar.

We three boat captains sat against the wall.

As soon as the last fanny found the cushion, Thomas entered the room, and the stewards closed the doors behind him. With the gloomy setting, all that was missing was the sound of a heavy bar locking us in the room. Thomas wore his usual black frock coat but wore a bright-red paisley-print vest for the occasion. Interestingly, he parted his hair in the opposite direction to fully expose is scalding injures from years ago. Frankly, he looked like the devil himself.

After brief welcoming remarks, he read the steamboat company's profits and losses and announced the dividends the holders of bonds and stocks could expect. I had never heard such high numbers used in a sentence before and found them astronomical. My surprise turned into revulsion as there was a general murmur of discontent among the assembled bigwigs.

"Gentlemen, if you are in a state of dissatisfaction, then I need warn you that we are in a deceptive 'Indian summer' of the steamboat business if we do not adapt to the changing times. Our southern packet lines had subsisted chiefly on the hauling of army supplies and returning with discharged soldiers and heavy armaments. With each haul, there are fewer soldiers to feed and fewer supplies to ship. The cotton crop is projected to be low this year as well. We can expect a virtual collapse of the cotton trade this year. There are too many boats for too little cargo. Our northern boats are confronted daily with competition from the railroads. With their government land grants and investment, the railroads are laying track daily to reach every town and village. I believe they are extending too fast and will find there is not enough business yet to make a profit, but it may be a few years for them to figure that out. In the meantime, we have to remain competitive and focus on our strengths."

"Mr. Geldstein, just what do you mean by that?"

"Railroads are known for being fast and can carry freight and passengers to virtually any point east of the Mississippi. They have built bridges at Quincy and Dubuque and are planning more across the Mississippi. Railroads will soon go all the way to the Pacific coast. People use the trains for speedy travel and pay a very high fare for doing so, but until major improvements are made, they cannot carry the tonnage we can. So we carry heavy freight far cheaper but at a lower speed. That is the nature of things, and the laws of physics cannot change it. If we do not adapt to the changing times, we will go asunder."

The murmuring of discontent showed Thomas had not convinced them.

"Gentlemen, I submit an example. New Orleans requires 360,000 tons of coal annually. The average coal car on a railroad carries fifteen tons. It requires 24,000 cars to transport 360,000 tons. Trains can pull but twenty-two cars of coal at a time. This means 1,091 trains, which the railroads do not yet have. Just eighteen steamboats with twenty barges can do the same job at fraction of the cost. The same math applies to all other bulk commodities. The railroad can't compete with us in these markets. That is our future. We must prepare for it by building the proper boats and barges to meet this demand. The days of the two- or three-deck packets are on the wane. Towboats and barges is the future.

A man at the table who seemed thoughtful and calm responded, "The railroads will still undercut us. With all of their federal financial backing and land grants, they will maintain an edge."

"Allow me to explain further."

Thomas then narrated a company reorganization close to what I described to him of the Western Insurance and Transportation Company when I returned from Nashville. He proposed this company make contracts with rail and boat companies to carry general freight to any point on a single bill of lading. With this organization, shippers only pay once with the assurance the company would see to the intricate handling of freight by various means to its final destination.

A bilious man four seats from me wearing a shiny gold vest that begged for notice rose to his feet. "With this arrangement, you would not even need to own boats! We would be a paper company with no equity! Outrageous!"

"Not at all, and resume your seat, Mr. Foley. We still need the fleet. We would just be harnessing other boats and the railroads to move freight more efficiently. It is the beginning of a new era. I realize that you can claim 8 percent of the dividends. That is a nice piece, but not enough to set policy. This meeting is only to inform, not to discuss."

"Geldstein, I don't see how it is possible. Such arrangements have never lasted more than a year. Remember the Union Express line? And as you say, the freight business is contracting. This is not the time for expansion. Everyone else is consolidating. I hear the Naples Line has even cut rates and wages."

"Yes, they have. The Keokuk Packet Line has also cut wages 20 percent. In response, our boat clerks and shipping agents will have to negotiate the best rates they can. If we are forced to cut wages, we will do so. But we will keep them just higher than the rest to attract and retain the best men on the rivers. We are on course into some lean times ahead, gentlemen. Dividends may not be to what you are accustomed."

The last sentence was the spark that ignited the calamitous uproar with everyone at the table voicing his displeasure. Thomas sat easily in his chair, no doubt expecting this reaction. He waited patiently for a few moments and glanced at Captain Sulloway. The unspoken signal was given. The old boatman lifted his great bulk from the chair and spoke in the volume usually reserved for an errant deckhand.

"Silence! Now get hold of yourselves, gentlemen. Mr. Geldstein and his family founded this company as one of the first on the rivers and have kept it afloat through the Great Fire and the epidemic of '49 and then the Great Panic of '57. A dozen steamboat companies have come and gone since then. While other boat companies shut down during the war, this one grew. We are in a new world now. Great changes are underway. If we don't change with them, the company will go asunder. Now take your seats and let Mr. Geldstein finish."

Momentarily subdued, the rhumba of vipers slowly coiled up again upon their padded chairs. They still eyed for an opportunity to strike. Thomas continued.

"Thank you, Captain Sulloway. I suspect some of you may not wish to risk your investments on the future I have spelled out. I am prepared to recall your bonds and interests in the company at face value. The few public bonds are not affected. Those who have holdings in the boats will be offered a buyout or release from the company if you buy out the company's share. Those stipulations are found in the company bylaws each of you signed. This is still a family company, and I am the owner. I will be available next Monday if you want to speak with me further. I pledge to make no major changes until the first of next month. At that time, I will require your support or the termination of our dealings. That is all for today. Good day, gentlemen."

Somehow the stewards outside knew the exact moment to open the doors. Those men with drinks downed them with one gulp and slammed their glasses on the table. The men with the most objections stormed out first, with more than one muttering threats to life and limb of Thomas. Others left dejectedly. A few went thoughtfully. Only three shook hands with Thomas and left with friendly words. My two fellow captains stood about awkwardly for a few minutes and left. I knew Captain Doyle was in a hurry as the *Piankeshaw* was scheduled to depart today. I could not tell his feelings on the matter. I sat numbly wondering what to do and what to make of what I just witnessed.

"Well, my good captain, perhaps you now realize why I stayed on the boat so long and came back only after Father's passing. Such men only think of money and profit. Having to contend with them is misery. I wonder sometimes if they have souls or are merely characters God places on earth to torture or amuse us. I understand the theory of the transmutation of species but highly doubt mankind will ever be entirely a noble one."

"I fear you are in danger, Thomas. Some of those men were claiming there would be hell to pay. That big fellow with the high open forehead and pockmarked features wearing the gold vest particularly."

"Oh, our good friend Mr. Foley. He is lower than a snake full of buckshot but holds a large portfolio of company bonds and is a majority owner of the *Kaw Nation*. Yes, I suppose there is a possibility of hazard until this is all settled. You don't need to concern yourself about that, though. You have a boat to run. If you would excuse us, Captain Sulloway and I have much to discuss."

The *Kaw Nation* was the boat I served on as a new relief pilot. It was an unhappy vessel with a milk and water captain and a tyrannical first mate. I don't know how things ran on the boat now, but it couldn't be much worse than it was then.

I walked down the hall to the contracting office to see about any opportunities. I was glad to see Bemis was already there. He was noticeably thinner than a few days ago. He looked gaunt and his eyes sunken.

"Good afternoon, Captain. Looks like we have an opportunity to make a run north to St. Paul or one south to New Orleans."

"What are the cargoes?"

"Whiskey, grain, and sundries outbound either direction. We can pick up some old cotton in Memphis. We don't have anything specific coming back up from New Orleans, but at this time of year, we will find something, colonial goods at least. A return from St. Paul is a log raft."

"Swanson has experience with log rafts, but the water is getting low up there. Let's go with the New Orleans run. I will speak with the clerk down the hall about posting our departure and assemble the crew."

One of the open secrets of our company was the prodigious use of the telegraph. Most other boat lines simply relied on the rhythms of their packet lines and blind luck. As a tramper looking for the low hanging fruit, we were able to schedule and arrange shipments here from St. Louis. No doubt this is how that Western Insurance and Transportation Company operated so efficiently. Too bad the board members had no appreciation of this modern technological wonder.

I continued down the corridor to inform Thomas of our plans. To my surprise, I found two large Negro stewards guarding the closed door to his office. They each carried a large revolver in a cross-draw holster and cradled a Henry repeating rifle. They said nothing but were obviously ready for anything. Thomas's personal clerk broke the silence. He looked over his spectacles as a teacher would an erring student.

"Can I help you, Captain?"

"I wanted to tell Mr. Geldstein of our upcoming run to New Orleans."

"Tell me the particulars, and I will inform him."

Two days later, the boat pulled from the levee. I had not the chance to speak with Thomas or Captain Sulloway. The company office had become a fortress, and those who entered surrendered their arms for the duration of the visit. The boat's departure was fine, I suppose, but it was sluggish to respond under Mr. Olsson's ringing of the bells. I was soon alarmed at the sight of a steamer approaching close from astern. My intervention was at hand when Swanson took the wheel and averted catastrophe. The young cub was bright enough, but he was being thrust too soon into handling the boat in a crowed port. I made a note to speak with my pilot about the matter in private. No harm was done, and I did not want to destroy Olsson's confidence.

The water was high and the current strong. Boat traffic had thinned out south of St. Louis, so there were no jams along the way. By and by, St. Mary and Kaskaskia came into view. At Rozier's Landing at mile marker 114, it was clear the Mississippi was increasingly overwhelming the Kaskaskia River. It would not surprise me that it would one day shear off the town of Kaskaskia from the state of Illinois. The irony was the town was the first capital of the state before moving to Vandalia and later to Springfield. The pitiful two-story capitol building has been ravaged by the frequent flooding and is now a private residence.

Swanson gave his student another point of instruction.

"The channel divides at Liberty Island up ahead, Mr. Olsson. We can take either one in this water, but the main channel is to west. Either way, the small Sheep Island just beyond is difficult to spot in the fog. One must be cautious."

Some miles further, I was in an uncharacteristically playful mood and decided to have fun with the cub pilot. Swanson replied to my wink with a mischievous grin.

"Look on up ahead there, Mr. Olsson. That ridge on the east bank is called the Devil's Backbone. That large stone at the end by the river is called the Devil's Bake Oven. It is a fine landmark to take note of."

"Yes, Captain. I see it on the charts, and we have passed this point on our last run. I'm quite familiar with it."

"Ah, but did you know those two outcroppings of rocks make excellent hiding places for Indians and river pirates to hide and wait for their victims to come along? In fact, river pirates became so bad one year that federal cavalry were dispatched to clear the area of them."

"Sir, their ain't no Indians or pirates here anywhere abouts."

"True. That was back in the early days. Now the site is more famous for the iron furnaces and the town of Grand Towers. Too bad about that young lass, though."

"What about the young lass, Captain?"

"Well, you see, the owner of the ironworks had a daughter he kept in that fine house up there. She took a fancy to one of the workers, but her father would have none of it. He paid the boy a handsome sum to forget his daughter and move on. She died brokenhearted, and her spirit walks the grounds looking for her lover."

"Or a suitable substitute," Swanson said in manufactured earnestness.

"A promising young steamboat pilot would suit her fine, don't you think, Mr. Swanson?"

"Indeed, I do, Captain. Fortunately, Mr. Olsson here is just learning the ropes. She wouldn't be interested."

The stalwart lad took the good-natured ribbing well. "It is fortunate you gentlemen are too old to attract her affections."

"Hm, well, yes. Uh, watch your helm, young man. You're drifting out of the channel."

We put in at Cape Girardeau for the night. It happens to be the biggest port on the Mississippi River between St. Louis and Memphis, and there is a good supply of coal here. It emerged from the war mostly unmolested. There was a brief skirmish nearby back in '63, but it was fought a short distance from the town and produced few casualties in comparison to the big battles.

Specifically, we put ashore at Green's Ferry, also known as the Waller's Ferry or even Smith's Ferry on some charts. On visits prior to the war, we used to pick up sacks of flour from the Bollinger Mill. The mill was burned during the hostilities for supplying flour to the Confederates. The rest of Cape Girardeau hasn't changed much in recent years except for four small forts guarding the town from Reb raiders. Fort D sat overlooking the landing, but there was no flag flying from the staff. Hawsers were run out and the boat tied to the bollards to keep us from drifting downstream.

The latest edition of the *Cape Girardeau Weekly Argus* was mostly full of gibberish. A few items caught my eye. "A young lady of color" with a fortune of over $500,000 advertises in *Galignani's Messenger* that she desires to form a matrimonial alliance. Maybe that was the kind of woman to pursue. It seems the rebel general Wade Hampton has written a letter discouraging the idea of emigration of southerners to foreign countries and recommending all who can do so to take the oath of allegiance. Well, at least there was something amusing in the miscellaneous story section. Two men had paid a small fee to hunt on a man's land without success.

> "Well, farmer, you told us your place was a good place for hunting. Now we have trampled it for three hours and found no game."
>
> "Justly so," the farmer replied. "I calculate, as a general thing, the less game there is, the more hunting you have."

It sounds like something my father would say.

My chief clerk interrupted my reading.

"Captain, I am going ashore for the evening. There is a small consignment set for loading in the morning."

"Of course, Bemis. Forgive my curiosity, but is there anything amiss?"

"Not at all. I am spending a short time with my folks. They still live here."

"You have never spoke of your background. I assumed you were from St. Louis."

"It is a good thing to be aboveboard, but generally a bad thing to be overboard. I was born and raised here. Schooled at the Cape Girardeau Academy and attended the Bethel Baptist Church under duress. I will return by ten o'clock. It will take that long for the coaling and uploading of freight."

"Baptist? You are the most unlikely Baptist I ever met."

"Yes, that's true, Captain. I more closely follow the teachings of Adam Smith. Permission to disembark."

"The economist? I suppose that is no surprise. Enjoy your stay and regards to your family."

The morning's events went as Bemis predicted. The uploading of coal and the small amount of freight took the crew until ten o'clock. The warning signal for departure sounded through the whistle a half hour earlier. I was just about to worry when Captain Bemis came into view. It was difficult to watch him hobble painfully on those forsaken crutches. The man I took to be his father helped him along. They embraced, parted, and Bemis made his way aboard.

"Looks like we are ready to depart, Mr. Swanson. Take the wheel and head downstream to glory."

My not-too-subtle command made it clear I wanted him and not the cub pilot at the wheel.

"Careful as we head downstream, Mr. Swanson. The ferryboat is still active at Green's Ferry. Mr. Olsson, you might be interested to know this is where the Cherokees were brought across the river during their Trail of Tears back in the late '30s."

"It's a shame what happened to those people. Uprooted and shoved to the western desert like that."

"That's what happens in the clash of civilizations."

"What do you mean, Mr. Swanson?"

"Whoever has the longest spears, the sharpest arrows, or the most guns decide who stays and who goes. The Indians have been pushing themselves around for hundreds of years. We came ashore at Plymouth Rock and were just better at it. I'm not saying it's right or not cruel, but that's the way it is. This nation is going to push all the way to the coast and take in everything in between. Any resistance the Indians off ere will be only an inconvenience."

"Let's change the subject, gentlemen. I am sorry to have brought it up."

"Aye, Captain."

Swanson steered the boat down the bend below Cape Girardeau. Some rivermen call it Steersman's Bend, but that's not on the charts. They gave it the name for it being one of the few places where there is plenty of water present in any season. This makes it a place where there is no fear that even a new cub pilot can navigate without supervision.

With the river running so well, we took a calculated risk and made Memphis in the late evening. There was risk indeed as roughly thirty miles north of the city, the river made a series of sharp bends as it flowed around Plum and Craighead points. We pilots considered this stretch of the river one of the more dangerous sections as inside these bends were usually a maze of snags and sandbars. The town of Plum Point on the Arkansas side was a successful waypoint on the Mississippi before the war and sold timber to the steamboats. It was too dark to tell if any was for sale now. The coffee in the pilot house kept us fully alert. My internal system was so used to the stuff there was no concern with falling asleep at the appointed time. My two colleagues kept up with my intake, and I suspected they would be awake for days.

Calamities and Mischief Afloat

We passed by the landing, came about, and approached from downstream. It was strange the company boat *Piankeshaw* was here. She left St. Louis two days ahead of us and should be on her way by now. As a big New Orleans boat, she was designed to haul large bales of cotton. She was loaded to the hurricane with remnants of last year's crop and looked like an iceberg. But there was no smoke from her stacks, and her boilers were stone cold. Swanson landed our boat alongside. Captain Doyle and two pilots were topside smoking cigars and drinking coffee. I had just seen him at the board meeting in St. Louis the other day.

"Ahoy! What are you still doing here? I figured you would be on your way by now."

"We have a broken poppet valve on the starboard engine. It happened sometime during the dogwatch. Looks like it was done with a hammer. No one has fessed up to the deed, but it could have been anyone. When I find out who committed the felony, there will be a keelhauling. All we can do is wait for the blacksmith to pound out another."

"Damnation. There has been unrest on the docks for weeks. Hopefully, it hasn't spread to the crews. That will spell big trouble for us."

"Keep a watch on any Irishmen you have on board. Those Dutchmen are bad enough, but the bogtrotters are even more a fractious bunch. I will hire a Negro crew if something like this happens again. They work hard and are loyal if you feed them well."

We soon discovered Memphis was indeed undergoing substantial turmoil. The old planter elites outside the city were attempting to restore their prewar social and economic status. Most of them had retained control of their land, but with slavery gone, they now had to bargain for the labor of their former slaves. That drove up costs that did not exist before and dug into the profits. To make matters worse for them, many freemen flocked to the city to escape life on the plantations. The white citizens were resentful of their presence anyway but became alarmed at the growing number of Negroes on the streets with no means to support themselves. The Irish immigrants were in direct competition for low-wage jobs and wanted the Negroes out of the city for good.

Tennessee also enacted laws and policies designed to keep the former slaves at work in the fields. The city leaders urged occupying Union troops to force blacks to work. The sympathetic commander Brigadier General Nathan Dudley ordered his men to take vagrant blacks into custody and force them to accept labor contracts on plantations. No doubt he had his fingers in the cotton trade. The colored units making up the bulk of the garrison counteract these efforts whenever possible. They tell the tell freed people that the threats to return them to the plantations are false and to ignore them. The Freedman's Bureau office here is Memphis is unfortunately no help and unsympathetic to their cause.

I learned the free blacks on the plantation were usually promised ten dollars a month for ten-hour days. A man forfeited a half-day wages if he missed two hours or work. That was a typical arrangement for most unskilled labor in the northern states except the blacks were being paid just over half of the average wage. In addition, the freemen were not allowed to leave the plantation without a pass. Those were seldom given. The newspapers say it was estimated that at least two-thirds of freemen are routinely defrauded of their wages.

I am more than a bit disgusted by the efforts of the bureaucracies to support the planters and former slave owners. We had just fought a bloody four-year war to defeat them. Under the newly established city government, the police, lawyers, judges, and jailers are in concert against the blacks with the implicit approval of the Union army leadership. Why were we so eager to reestablish the economic and political power of the old planter class? The greed for cotton must be the root cause.

We found few journeymen willing to work at any price. There was an ongoing strike for higher wages and less hours. I wondered how the *Piankeshaw* got her cotton loaded. Fortunately for us, the labor movement was not entirely organized. I would have preferred a Negro gang for transferring cargo just to spite the secesh whites, but the blacks were forcibly run off the other day. Relations between the races was deteriorating to the point of collapse. This all could blow up in our faces someday soon.

"Captain, I found a gang of Irish roustabouts willing to do cargo work. No Negroes in sight. Their price is 20 percent over the usual rate. Can't vouch for their speed or care of the freight."

"Offer our crew a five-dollar bonus to do the job, Captain Bemis. If you have enough takers, then do that. If not, go ahead and hire the insolent Irish. I would rather overpay and overwork our own men than pay those *verdammte Heiden*. Our boys shouldn't mind too much if it doesn't become a habit."

"Careful, Captain. You're sounding Germanic again. Next thing you know, you will call upon us to march against the Grand Duchy of Oldenburg."

My visits to Memphis during the war were not happy times. The gunboat languished in boredom during a coal shortage, and I had shot a man when he and his partner attempted a robbery of my person. I had no business in town, so I remained aboard. Some passengers departed, and a few came aboard. We should be able to shove off in the morning.

The new steamboat *Dictator* was moored down the line. She is on her long-awaited trial run, on her way from Pittsburg to New Orleans. What made her so special was that she was outfitted with experimental compound condensing Hartupee engines that promise great fuel efficiency. All the engineers at the landing were quite interested in taking a gander at the machinery, but her owner, Captain Donaldson, allowed admittance to the boat for a dollar. Our Mr. Weatherby thought it was worth the look. He reports the new engines are complicated and are significantly heavier than ours. He couldn't tell if the expense of maintenance and repair would be offset by the fuel savings. He remains happy with our current engines.

Steamboats terribly burn up tons of fuel, but coal is cheap and usually abundant. In normal times, the Bigley Brother's Coal company here in Memphis sells quality fuel at a reasonable price. The boat engines are simple in design, and maintenance costs are low. Although these new condensing engines may be the next step in maritime propulsion, I suspect they will be slow to be adopted. The status quo was just fine to move heavy cargo along the rivers.

Night fell upon the waterfront, but it took some hours for the quiet to reign. There was some sort of hootenanny up the way on Beale Street. The Negro quarter there was in a festive mood. Musicians of all types and levels of talent on the boats took up tunes as well. I was not surprised the martial songs of the war were omitted from the repertoire. Instead, the men played old romantic favorites like "Kathleen Mavourneen" and "The Girl I Left Behind Me." It did not take long for a musician of another boat to call upon combing the efforts to one song at a time. The tune took a few stanzas to become recognizable as each musician changed key and tempo and joined in as a united orchestra. The song was "Lorena."

> It matters little now, Lorena,
> The past is in the eternal past;
> Our heads will soon lie low, Lorena,
> Life's tide is ebbing out so fast.
> There is a Future! O thank God!
> Of life this is so small a part!
> Tis dust to dust beneath the sod;
> But there, up there, 'tis heart to heart.

The lovelorn song brought a tear to many an eye that night under the southern stars of Memphis. It had little meaning for me. Ann was gone. In fact, she was never there at all. Just a fantasy. But there was a future. I just not know what it held in store for the country, the company, the Negroes across the way, or for me.

We were prepared to depart around midday. We had a respectable load of last year's cotton, but the load only went as high as the edge of the boiler deck. Steam was up to pressure in adequate strength to get us off the bank and into the current.

"Captain. I request your assistance."

"And what could you need assistance with, Mr. Swanson?"

"Mr. Olsson here is having trouble getting the rhythm of the departure. Would you take him below and have him watch the engineers at their task? I believe it would be beneficial for him."

"I have held my tongue in suggesting that very thing. I would be delighted. Come along, Olsson."

Just as we arrived, the engineer sounded his ready whistle. Mr. Swanson, high above at the wheel, pulled the cords, signaling for both engines to reverse. We stood by the starboard engine but made sure we were out of the way of the men operating it.

"Now watch these men as they work, Olsson. Remember how long it takes for them to adjust the machinery and for the boat to respond."

The connecting rod from the engine piston ran to the rockshaft connecting to the paddle wheel. The reverse gear weighed over fifty pounds and required a strong set of arms to move. Two men were at the task this morning to ensure success. With the ring of the bells, they lifted the connecting rod off its hook at the bottom while a third man threw over a lever and raised the connecting rod about three feet. With the two men guiding the massive rock shaft, the connecting rod was dropped on to its upper hook. The throttle was opened, and the great wheels turned under power. The men made it look easier than it was. That came from practice.

The boat backed for some minutes, and the bells hanging on the walls rang the signal to move forward. The engineers closed the throttles, bringing the wheels to a halt. The men then reversed the process and hung the connecting rod on the lower hook on the rockshaft. The throttles were opened, and the paddle wheels churned the boat forward.

"Now you have seen what the men here must do when departing a landing. I think it is obvious to you that the two engines run independently, and you can send different signals to either one. But keep in mind that it is very easy to overwhelm these men when using the paddle wheels to maneuver in a stretch of a crooked river and while dodging about reefs and bars. The bells will tend to come faster than these men could ever answer them. You will learn to know how the process is going here from the sounds you hear and the bumps you feel in the pilothouse. Do you have a better understanding now, Mr. Olsson?"

"Aye, Captain, I believe I do. Thank you."

"Fine. When you have the chance, ask Mr. Swanson to provide you with a copy of *The Abortion of the Young Steam Engineer's Guide*. A man named Oliver Evans wrote it ages ago, but it is a good read for a new pilot. It will help you understand the mysteries of all this modern machinery. Someday you may not have as good an engineer as our Mr. Weatherby. Let me show you the boilers."

The four boilers are located forward of the machinery. The boatyard that built the vessel placed them at the center of equilibrium to balance the boat. They take up a vast amount of prime cargo space, but that cannot be helped. Each are made from overlapping iron plates and are thirty-five feet in length and thirty-six inches in diameter. The fireboxes are at the aft ends. Heat generated there passed through the center of the boilers through iron tubes and up and out of the stacks forward.

"The boilers here are the source of power for the engines. As you can see, we have four of them. Boilers are the greatest source of calamity on the rivers. They are temperamental, but if handled with respect and attention, they will serve you well. Oh, watch that man there."

The young engineer was tending the gauge cocks that protrude at the end of each boiler, which are used to determine the amount of water within. There are three on each boiler. He slowly turned the lever of the lowest one, and a small jet of water shot from it. Satisfied, he slowly closed it.

"Water came out of that, and that's a good thing. The water level is at least a third of the way up. If that were steam, we would be in big trouble. By the way, if anyone offers you boiler coffee, that's is where the water came from. It won't hurt you none, but it might give you the trots until you get used to it."

The engineer proceeded to crack open the middle cock.

"Here he expects to find either water, or steam, or a combination of both. I can see from here it is just water, and that's fine. If any steam came out, it would be time to add water. If it were a combination of steam and water, Mr. Weatherby or his designated assistant would be called to decide to take any action.

The engineer opened the top gauge cock, and a hiss of steam shot forth.

"See? That was pure steam, and there should never be water that high in the boiler. In such cases, the water is being sent to the engines, and they can't run on it. The casing could crack and ruin it. That can be prevented by opening the drain valve over there and letting some water out of the boiler."

"How do they add water to the boiler?"

"Good question. Come over this way. I will show you 'the doctor.'"

"The 'doctor,' or the water feed pump here, is a two-piston water pump that produces a volume of high-pressure water for the boilers. The doctor is a connected to the small steam engine there called the 'donkey.' This one is connected to the main boilers but can be operated by hand. The pump draws water from beneath the boat and forces it through those pipes into the boiler whenever an engineer opens the feed water valves."

"What are those glass tubes on the end of the boilers?"

"Another excellent question. Each of those is called a glass water column. When the engineer opens the top and bottom gauge cocks, simultaneously the tubes are filled with water and steam. The top surface of the water in the tube is the same level as the water in the boiler. It's very precise, and there is no guessing."

"Why not just use that method instead of opening all twelve of those gauge cocks one at a time?"

"Because we can't run with those valves open. The boat also runs in dirty water all the time. You can imagine the trouble caused when the boat runs into low water, and the pump sucks up mud and shoots it into the boilers. A mud-filled boiler doesn't heat well, makes the gauges inaccurate or useless, and damages the engines. On this boat, the engineers use both the old method and the glass water columns and clean the system regularly. We haven't blown up yet. All right. Get on up to the pilothouse. I will join you and Mr. Swanson directly."

I turned to find Mr. Weatherby and Mr. Voight watching the discussion with approving smiles. The engineer spoke with gratitude.

"Thank you for setting that boy on the right path, Captain. He has been ringing those bells like a call for supper on the farm. It causes more confusion than a mouse at a burlesque show."

The departure from Memphis was almost uneventful. The upbound *Mary T.* cut across our bow to regain her rightful place in the channel and caused a few nerves to fray. A notice in the newspaper expected her in Memphis for a visit, but she was bound for Mound City for sale. During the war, she was made into a gunboat but looked nothing like the boats the Union navy used. She was in fact the former Confederate gunboat *J. A. Cotton*. She was captured by the Union forces at Alexandria, Louisiana, back in June."

I lit the first cigar of the day and relaxed in my chair in the pilothouse. I dozed a bit as the miles glided by.

"All right, Mr. Olsson. You have undoubtedly reviewed the charts for today's cruise. What river feature and island are coming up?"

"Bolivar Bend and Island Number 74, Mr. Swanson."

"What significant event happened here?"

"For that I would have to defer to your wisdom, sir. These are new waters for me."

"Last March, the *James Watson* ran aground on that island. How might that happen to a two-year-old boat with a seasoned captain by the name of John Watson?"

"A loss of steering or some mechanical problem?"

"Those could be the reason, but the catastrophe was caused by running at night in a thunderstorm. To add to the misfortune, the boat caught fire. Thirty-five souls were lost, including twenty soldiers from the Thirty-Third Illinois Infantry. They had just received their discharge and were heading home. Three women and two children were lost too. Tragic incidents serve to remind all of us pilots that the river is still queen. We also tell you these stories to help you memorize the features on the river."

The nearby town of Bolivar, Mississippi, had its share of other misfortunes in the war. Besides the typical burning and looting, the levee protecting the town was cut by a Union gunboat. This caused significant flooding to the town and surrounding area. Neblett's Landing was left high and dry by the changing course of the river, and Bolivar is no longer useful as a port. Island Number 76 was used for a time as a woodyard for the Union navy employing freed slaves for labor but is now abandoned. Passing boats had since carted off all the wood.

"Gentlemen, if you would excuse me. It's time to make my rounds."

All was fine on the boiler deck, and there was no sign of mischief with the cargo. The whole deck could use a good scrubbing, though. On the forecastle, Mr. Voight reported all was well. The leadsmen were using their poles here to gauge the depth of the water and called "Mark Twain!" up to the pilothouse. Music to my ears and plenty of water underneath the boat. I made my way aft to confer with Mr. Weatherby about the machinery and the coal supply.

The engineer and I just exchanged greetings when an odd hissing interrupted our conversation. It was a sound that had no place on a steamboat. We both turned around and beheld what many boatmen saw last before their life was extinguished.

A hot jet of steam and water spewed from a growing fissure in the red-hot iron plate of boiler number 2. Some men were screaming as the hot vapor made contact with their skin; others were just overcome with fear. Within seconds, the boiler will erupt, killing us all. It would also detonate the two boilers astride it and possibly the fourth. The few fragments left of us mere mortals would feed the fish long before our scraps were scooped from the waters. The kindling wood made from the boat would stoke fires in the homes along the banks for years.

Mr. Weatherby yelled first, but my voice was louder.

"You there! Vent the steam! You there! Douse the fires!"

I shoved the engineer in the direction of the main relief valve to ensure the task was completed. I moved toward the fireboxes to spur the men there to get water on the fires. It felt as if all the clocks stopped, and I was wearing lead shoes. One man looked confused, as if he didn't understand the words.

"I say to you again, Dampf ablassen und Feuer löschen!"

The hypnotic spell was broken, and the men went to their urgent tasks, even the *schwachkopf* German. An astounding WHOOSH came from the paddle-wheel boxes, where the relief pipes disgorged the contents of the boilers. Seeing the men were doing their jobs, I made my way to the engineer-ready whistle and made five peals: the signal for emergency. There was still enough steam left to do so. I then rang the signal bell at the voice tube and flipped open the brass cover.

"Ahoy! Swanson! Are you there?"

"Aye, Captain! What has happened?"

"We lost the boilers, and you will soon be out of power. Point the bow upstream while you can!"

The first mate appeared from behind. His timing was perfect.

"Mr. Voight, we have lost power. Have the men heave the anchor over the bow and run out about one hundred feet of hawser rope. We'll use it to keep the bow pointed into the current."

With an "Aye, Captain!" he ran forward, collecting up a gang from the stupefied deck crew. I turned my attention back to the boilers. The engineer was applying the final touches to shutting them down.

"You men, there! Open the throttles wide open! That will let out the rest of the steam in the system."

"Mr. Weatherby, is the danger past?"

"Captain, if we didn't blow up a moment ago, I say we should see the sunset. Sweet Jesus, we were lucky. God be praised."

"I am going to the pilothouse. Take a good look at your machinery here and tell me what our options are. Find out how this happened."

"Aye, Captain!"

Although we were spared fire and brimstone, we were still in big trouble. About to go topside, I could see Swanson did not have enough power to bring us about and the boat was drifting sideways downstream. We could stove in our bow or stern if we hit the bank or collide against a bar, or even snag amidships.

Thankfully, I heard the *spaloosh* of the anchor hitting the water while I traversed the boiler deck. Mr. Voight yelled to his men to play out the line. That was somewhat reassuring. When I finally reached the pilothouse, Olsson's eyes were as large as teacups. He was turning the great wheel left and right with no effect.

"Captain! What in tarnation has happened?"

"A boiler mishap, Swanson."

"Oh, what a relief. I thought we were all going to die." His sarcasm gravy was ladled on thick.

By now the anchor was deployed and functioning as intended. As it dug into the mud, the bow swung gently into the current. Our progress downstream wasn't halted, but at least slowed to an old man's walking pace. The river downstream looked clear of obstructions and oncoming boats.

Swanson thought of something I had not.

"Mr. Olsson, take the red flag and place yourself on the stern. Wave away all boats that come from downstream. Those coming from upstream should see us at a distance, and the channel is broad enough to give us wide berth."

"Aye, Mr. Swanson."

"Captain, I fear there is damage to the paddle wheels. All that steam blew out the box sides. It was a majestic sight from here indeed."

Steam-relief pipes on most boats run up and through the hurricane deck to vent excess steam into the atmosphere. During the war, it was prudent to run the piping into the paddle-wheel boxes to reduce noise. Those pipes on the boat were not reconfigured at the cessation of hostilities as there seemed no need for the costly refit.

"Mr. Swanson, you have the deck. Unless Mr. Weatherby can produce a miracle, we are stuck here. Come darkness call for the torch baskets and lanterns to mark our position. I am going below to confer with our esteemed engineer. I will keep you appraised."

"Captain, how should I respond to a passing boat offering aid?"

"For now, thank them and send them along. Come morning, we may need a tow if our problems are not resolved."

"Aye, Captain."

Although relieved we were still alive and afloat, the quandary was how to get the boat to port in one piece. Boilers and machinery were fickle mistresses who did not care for being ignored or trifled with. I walked down the causeway to the main deck, and it came to mind for me to regain composure and to act as though it was just another day on the river. It would reassure the men.

Bemis was waiting for me at the hurricane deck landing within the Texas cabin. He was in his shirtsleeves but wearing his cap. His shoulders hung heavily in his crutches.

"I suppose I should feel lucky to be alive. Steam came up through the floorboards when the pipes cut loose."

"Are you inured, Bemis?"

"No, as I had the peace of mind to fall onto the bed and throw a blanket over me. Fortunately, the vapors were not strong and dissipated quickly. I would offer to assist, but I suppose you have the situation under control. You always shine under such circumstances as these."

"Thank you, Captain Bemis. We're still sifting the wheat from the chaff. I may need you in a bit though."

There wasn't much, if anything, Bemis could do to assist, and it wasn't for him being crippled. He was neither a pilot nor a mechanic. The first mate had his men doing all they could, and the engineer presumably was capable, although I was beginning to have my doubts. I proceeded to the main deck.

"What is the situation here, Mr. Voight?"

"Captain, the anchor is out and appears to have caught on a rock or snag. We're being held fast for the moment. You! Leadsman! What is the depth?"

"Quarter less twain, sir! Muddy bottom."

"Thank you, Mr. Voight, and to all to you men here as well. You kept cool and got us out of great peril. I am going aft to speak with the engineer. Carry on."

By the time I returned to the boilers, the engineering crew on the main deck had collected their wits but worked sheepishly at their tasks. The aft end of the boilers was where the gauge cocks and pressure glass water column gauges were located. There too is where I found the engineer and a pair of his men conversing.

"All right, engineer, let's have it. How did this happen, and can we get underway?"

"Fireman Bailey was minding the gauge cocks and the Bourdon gauge. Water ran low in number two, probably because the intake line clogged with silt. We are waiting for everything to cool before we can open up the boilers and see inside. We must have passed over a bar or something as we had just purged the mud drums an hour or so ago."

"The channel has been deep and clear for miles. Where is Bailey? I don't know him."

"He leapt into the water the water the first chance he got. He either feared an explosion or us lynching him. Either way, he is gone. Last anyone ever saw of him, he was being carried away in the current downstream."

"I'm not in a Christian mood at moment to assign men to launch the skiff to look for him. Perhaps we will come across him if we are able to get underway. Who was injured and how badly? Show me the damage."

"Three men have burned skin, but nothing life threatening. Thank God no one breathed in the vapors. That was a miracle. Come over here to see the damage, Captain."

Three of the boilers sat innocently in their cradles, but their sister was obviously the culprit. The long cylinder was bulged at the top. An area about the size of a supper plate rose a good three inches and still glowed red hot.

"There she is, Captain. The boilers are usually run interconnected, with incoming water from the river going to each simultaneously. The boat has a great deal more piping than others I have served. I believe we can valve off number two, but I must reroute some pipes. That means one boiler for the port wheel. We can operate that way or connect the center axle and propel the boat with one engine turning both wheels. I recommend the first option as the latter puts a huge strain on the entire system."

"Can we repair number two?"

"We can take a sledge and pound that cyst down flat, but this charcoal iron can be brittle. Heating it up under steam weakens it over time. These boilers are but a year, maybe two, years old. That is probably why we are alive at all. If we are blessed, it should reshape nicely. We can light the boiler dry to get the metal hot and more pliable."

"That gets it into shape, but the fissure is still there. The metal is weak there too. We can't trust it under steam."

"That is correct, Captain. We need to rivet a section of boiler plate over it and band it for good measure. We need at least six feet of plate and to shape it precisely. It needs to cover the split there and enough beyond it to rivet into sound metal."

"You do not need to tell me we have no plate or the tools to do the job here."

"Then I won't say it, Captain. Memphis or Vicksburg are the nearest yards capable of the job. Oh, as you probably know we blew out the outboard sides of the paddle-wheel boxes. The damage is mostly cosmetic, although we will splash about while underway. A few wheel planks are missing, but we have spares for those. Besides the boiler, the rest of the machinery looks fine so far. We will be at it well into tomorrow. We will need to build up steam slowly so we can check for leaks though. I can't make any promises."

I bottled up my anger and frustration. There was plenty of time for that later. Right now I needed the men to focus on their jobs and not sulk under chastisement.

"Engineer, gather your men. I want to speak with them briefly."

With a whistle through Weatherby's fingers, the men sheepishly gathered and formed a semicircle. Yelling at them would not shake them out of their sullenness. I decided a confident but truthful tone was needed here.

"It is my hope you men fully understand the dangerous nature of this modern machinery and the constant attention it demands. You must never let your guard down. You must tend to your duties as keep constant vigilance. We are alive only because of the providence of God. Be certain to give him your thanks. Now we are in a tight spot. The current is strong, and we have a long way to go. Our anchor is keeping us in place for the moment, but we could lose it at any time. Our bulk is too heavy for it to last long. Get to work and ready this boat to get underway. We are not out of this yet. Mr. Weatherby, take over. Get with the first mate for additional men as needed."

"Aye, aye, Captain!"

I turned to leave and saw the deckhands and passengers had watched my performance. Some seemed reassured while others had a desperate look in their eyes. Mr. Voight beckoned me.

"Captain, that was a nice speech, and you are right in that we may not have much time. With the current as strong as it is and our great weight with cargo, the bits and davits are straining. The strain could pull them off the deck or rip the bow off completely at any moment. We laid some additional ropes to ease the stress, but I cannot promise success."

"Thank you, Mr. Voight. We must add that to our list of prayers. Tell the men they have done a good job. If the boat breaks apart, get everyone off the main deck. The engineers aft are busy in their toils and will need to get the word."

"Aye, Captain."

Worked progressed through the rest of the day and into the night. I told the engineer to leave number two boiler as it was and focus on cleaning out the system of silt and other repairs. The men rotated in shifts to allow some rest. Passing boats hailed us and asked our condition, but their offers to assist were politely turned down. Our predicament was now mostly one of embarrassment. Storm clouds passed to the north, promising higher waters and stronger currents in the hours to come. We needed to get underway soon.

My sleep was fitful, and I dreamed of a similar circumstance during the war. Our boat was disabled by cannon fire, but the good work of engineer Thomas Geldstein saved the day. I did not have that confidence in Mr. Weatherby. A chief engineer was supposed to know every inch of pipe and could discern the condition of a boiler as a hen her eggs.

Awakening on my own told me there was no news from below. Thank the heavens we had not lost our anchor during the hours of darkness. While I washed up for the day, hammering commenced on the paddle boxes. Deckhands were affixing planks of various sizes to cover the holes blasted out by the steam. There was not enough wood, and the endeavor probably did little good except maybe reinforce the exposed frames. It did keep the men occupied though.

Mr. Weatherby came up to the pilothouse.

"A word, Captain?"

We went onto the hurricane deck. It was a wide-open space, but the bustle of activity down below should keep our words private.

"Say, what's on your mind besides your hat, engineer?"

"Sir, it's the doctor. Someone tried to sabotage it. Deliberately."

The feeder pump, called the doctor, fed river water into the boilers. It is the simple mechanism that I showed Mr. Olsson the other day that is steam-driven or operated manually. These contraptions are mostly foolproof unless clogged by mud and sand."

"How can you tell? Was it filled with sediment?"

"No, it was clean, as was the rest of the machinery. Someone removed the pin attaching the piston rod. There are also fresh wrench marks on the bolts of the housing. Whoever it was used a tool too large and nearly stripped them smooth."

"Who would do such a thing? Do you have any idea who it was?"

"I would wager it was Bailey, Captain, the man who leapt overboard at the first sign of danger. He was at the gauge cocks and let number 2 go dry. In fact, all the boilers were low on water even after the scoundrel told me he had just filled them. Number 2 just happened to give way first. Bailey must have disabled the feeder pump so we couldn't add water if we wanted to. He gave no warning to his crewmates, who were all about to be blown to atoms."

"How long have you known him?"

"Nobody knew him. This was his first run with us. Bailey had come over from the *Kaw Nation*."

"I know the part owner of that boat. A man named Foley. Sports a shiny gold vest. He was very upset at the board meeting a few days back."

"And you think he is connected to this somehow?"

"I don't know what to think. I do know that I want to get to a telegraph office soonest to let the company know of our condition. When can we be underway?"

"I'll do my best to have her ready first thing in the morning, Captain. God be willing."

We passed another day on the river as the men toiled on the machinery below. Naturally, I visited often to check on the progress. The boiler access plates were removed, and the smaller men were inside brushing and scrubbing them clean. Bore brushes were run through the pipes. The men found no other damage or obstructions. The chief engineer felt confident we could give it a try in the morning. That was good, for Mr. Voight detected some leaking in the hull at the bow. Caulking and oakum were doing their job for now, but that was an indicator our time was limited.

I called the officers together that evening and gathered at the table on the hurricane deck cabin. They all looked haggard. Even Bemis. I set the hour to light the fires for seven o'clock. Men will be fed by then, and we would have the whole day to make what distance we could. The men were to douse fires and vent steam if there was even a hint of trouble. If all goes well, we will head to the yards at Vicksburg for more substantial repairs and then to New Orleans to deliver this cargo.

I very much wanted to jettison the cargo and make all speed to St. Louis. If what I suspected were true, it was vital Mr. Geldstein and Captain Sulloway were warned. I could well be too late already. But the fastest way to get word back was to get to a telegraph, and from here, that was Vicksburg.

"All right, gentlemen, this is the plan. At first light, Mr. Weatherby will light fires and build enough pressure to check the system. If all is well, he will send three peals on the ready whistle to signal success and his intent to build enough steam to get underway. Once underway, Mr. Swanson will attempt to overcome the current and retrieve the anchor. He will then swing about and proceed downstream using just enough speed to navigate. Mr. Voight will haul in as much slack to the hawser and pull out the anchor when the bow reaches a point overhead. Cut the hawser and slip anchor if it is found wedged tightly in a snag. Be quick about it and use and ax if need be. Post leadsmen at bow and stern to judge the depth of water until turned about, then remain active at the bow until relieved."

Morning came, and the plan was put in motion. It all worked to the surprise and relief to all. Well, at least the cook had faith. He had made jelly cakes for all on board. He made them with three layers of thin cake with strawberry preserves in between. Fancy bakeries in St. Louis dusted them with powderized sugar, but we were no fancy bakery. In the festive spirit, I allowed two beers for the midday meal. Even the passengers were welcome to partake. That was good for business. We had an image to maintain.

With confidence in the boilers building, we stopped along the way for farmer piles and at various landings to take on additional cargo for Vicksburg and New Orleans. Word of our mishap had spread down the river quickly. Most shippers went ahead and consigned their goods to us, but some decided to wait for another boat. The missing planks of the paddle-wheel boxes obliterated the name of the boat, and that was probably a good thing. I thought to lower the company banner but decided against it. We should be proud to have escaped destruction, I supposed.

The Bayou Country Beckons

Vicksburg is Mississippi's largest town and is situated on a high bluff overlooking an S-bend in the Mississippi River. During the war, the Confederates heavily fortified the city and blocked the river to Union control for months. My old gunboat was here to witness the climatic running of the batteries during Grant's campaign to take the city. I felt a rather severe case of anxiety rounding Milliken's Bend and catching site of the courthouse high on the bluff. Memories of the war filled my mind for several moments. I hoped my colleagues in the pilothouse did not notice anything peculiar in my behavior. Vicksburg still serves as an important port and social center for the nearby cotton planters and is expected to regain its position as a prosperous commercial center. With the outrageous wharf fees here, they could build a Roman colosseum in no time.

I made my way to the telegraph office as soon as the bow touched the bank. It was all I could do to keep from running. Image was important, and steamboat captains simply did not run. The telegraph was still controlled by the army and its traffic had priority, even if it was as routine as a requisition for more hardtack. My hope was it was a slow day. Not surprisingly, the office was in a nondescript building just a block away from the waterfront with a short flagpole out front.

I nearly bumped into an orderly upon my rapid entry. It was a good thing the lad was fleet of foot and avoided my trajectory. My uniform was similar enough to the navy version to vouch for my loyalty, and the gold stripes on my cuffs indicated officer status.

Although the war was over and discipline declining, he was polite enough to usher me to the telegrapher's room. Maybe he was just bored enough to be helpful.

The telegraph was operated by a grimy man in his thirties. He wore a brown sack coat of the working class and a type of short topper hat I had not seen before. The telegraph device sat quiet at his desk, as useful as a paperweight.

"Good day. I need to send two telegrams, one to St. Louis and one to New Orleans."

"Not sure I can help you. Army traffic has priority."

I did not wish to haggle with the man, and I may get outright rejection if I somehow found an officer. I was anxious to get these sent, and he knew it.

"I addition to the usual fee, perhaps this could obtain a higher priority. Upon completion, there will be another."

The five-dollar gold piece worked its magical charm. It was disturbing how such a metal with no practical use was valued so highly. Yet men and kingdoms rose and fell because of it.

"Do you have the messages written out already?"

"Indeed, they are. The one there for St. Louis was the most urgent and is addressed to Mr. Geldstein. The second is intended for New Orleans to inform the shipping clerk of our delay and estimated arrival."

The man in brown read the first note aloud, "Urgent. Boiler mishap. No losses. Sabotage. Bailey from KN. Escaped. Beware gold vest. Will proceed to N.O. after repair."

I felt a huge sense of relief with the sending and confirmation of receipt of the fist message. I have done all that I could. The company messenger will find the note in the box at the telegraph office in St. Louis. Thomas should be alerted within the next hour or two, depending on how many times the telegraph had to be retransmitted over this great distance. I did not mind at all giving the lazy scoundrel the second coin, after both messages were sent, of course.

My return to the boat found four men from the machine shop ashore examining the boiler and discussing a method of repair. The yard had no means to roll iron plate of that thickness but suggested cutting a chunk of metal from another boiler of the same diameter. There were several steamboat wrecks nearby that should be fruitful.

Captain Bemis was on hand to discuss payment for the materials and labor. He hobbled over to me while Mr. Weatherby, and the yard boilermakers discussed the technical details.

"Captain, you seem to be in great haste to reach New Orleans. None of the goods we are carrying are perishable. We don't need to cut corners and endanger the boat. Aren't there better repair facilities in New Orleans?"

"It's not so simple as that, my friend."

I then told him all of what I knew and suspected. He was alarmed by the direction the company was heading as boat clerks could lose much of their autonomy.

"I find it of no surprise how the board reacted to the news. I might have sided with them if they hadn't just tried to kill me. But that such men would resort to sabotaging boats is alarming. Breaking a poppet valve is an irritant. Exploding a boiler is wanton murder. Stifled in those efforts, they may attempt even more direct measures. Geldstein and his allies could be in danger. Our parboiled owner has no kin to pass on the company as far as I know. Many of those board members have no scruples. Men have been killed for far less."

"That is why I feel compelled to return to St. Louis soonest. It is a desire I cannot shake loose even if there would be no benefit in reaching there."

All the passengers departed the boat upon landing and sought a safer means to New Orleans. There were six other boats here heading in a southerly direction including the *Independence, Annie E.,* and the *Nebraska.*

The *Piankeshaw* passed by landing. At least she was under steam again. Her officers mistook our waving as simply a friendly gesture and steamed along with her load of cotton. By the time we retrieved the red flag, she was downstream and out of sight. Only the smoke from her stacks rising above the trees showed her position.

Most of the crew was idle as the boiler repair was discussed. Mr. Voight put those with any carpentry skills to work on a proper repair to the paddle-wheel boxes and allowed those not employed to go ashore to stretch their legs. Swanson and Olsson went ashore too. They were all to return quickly at the ringing of the bell. In the meantime, they would probably go to an improper house, cockfight, or simply drink his time away. Most crewmen spend their money as soon as it hits their palm and then simply work for more. Those men were lionized by the port women. There was a strong Bethel Society chapter here in Vicksburg, and their results were admittedly disappointing. The men were reluctant to exchange their songs of vice for the songs of grace.

I decided to strap on my Paterson revolver and go ashore as well with a specific errand in mind. I quickly found Tillman's Saddlery and went inside. The proprietor was a bit perplexed at my request.

"You want a new holster for this old Paterson? Tarnation. I thought all these were shipped to Texas to fight the Comanches thirty years ago."

The holster that came with the revolver upon purchase had a large flap that produced a deal of fumbling and delay in drawing it. In these trying times, such a delay could be deadly. A gold coin insured the quick completion of the task.

While I waited for the holster, I went a few doors down and purchased two cigars and a copy of the *Vicksburg Weekly Herald*. Apparently, the familiar *Daily Citizen* was now defunct. Most of the locals believed I was part of the Union occupation and shunned me. Two ladies even crossed the street to avoid me. Curiously, there were no Negroes to be seen. No doubt the contraband camps outside of town were still occupied.

I quickly discovered the *Vicksburg Weekly Herald* was highly partisan to the Democrat cause. The lead editorial harshly denounced the proposed federal measures of Reconstruction. It chastised the United States Congress in "legislating solely in the interest of the Negro and to the injury of the white man of the South." I worried for the Negro race and wondered how this country could come together again.

I successfully retrieved my new holster after finishing my second cigar. It is a nice russet color, and the revolver withdrew from it easily. I strapped it on under my open frock coat and returned to the boat. I felt like a Mexican *pistolero* from a dime novel.

During my outing, it occurred to me the prominent home known as the Castle was missing. That was a shame, for it was stoutly built and even had a moat. In its place now was an abandoned earthen fort. The Washington Hotel though seemed to have escaped serious damage. I have read accounts of the civilians digging caves into the hillsides to avoid Union shelling during the siege. I did not have time to explore for them. My place was on the boat, and I have been gone too long.

I found the engineer and boilermakers eagerly awaiting my return.

"Captain! I believe we have an acceptable solution. There is a boiler of almost the exact dimensions a short distance from here. It is from a recent wreck and still in good shape. While these men retrieve it, I will get number 2 here disconnected and ready for removal. We can make the switch in the morning. We can steam the next morning if all goes well. We can perform a hydrostatic check on the whole system once we get to New Orleans. They don't have the equipment to do that here."

I was not surprised at the two-thousand-dollar price. I wasn't pleased either. The men needed to use a sizable boat to retrieve the boiler. The job also required all hands and the ingenuity of the engineer and boilermakers to orchestrate it all. Retrieving a complete boiler made me more at ease than a patch job on the old one. Six months ago, the *Sultana* exploded from a faulty boiler repair described exactly as the engineer's first option of making a patch. The *Sultana* was a big cotton boat severely overloaded with nearly two thousand souls. Most of them were Union soldiers just released from prison camps. When the boilers exploded, over half perished.

"Make it so. Coordinate your efforts with Mr. Voight and draw all the manpower you need from him. I will tell Captain Bemis to arrange payment."

"Got to hand it to you, Captain. Most boiler incidents are simply deadly explosions. You turned this into a five-day odyssey we might live to see through."

"It's not over with yet."

Lifting the damaged boiler out of its cradle was a dangerous and arduous task to be sure. Under the careful supervision of Mr.

Weatherby, the men disconnected various pipes and employed a series of block and tackles. The boiler was then moved forward to the waiting trundles on the deck. The stricken boiler was rolled to the bow and disgorged onto the landing. It was only good for scrap now. Maybe it would be cut up for use in making pots or something.

It took the remaining daylight to finish the job, and the men were released for rest. The new day would come too soon, but the delivery of the new boiler was promised early in the morning. There was no music, card playing, or general horseplay this night.

The morning brought a steam barge alongside with the replacement boiler. There was surface corrosion, but it looked in far better shape than the old number 2. The process of yesterday was repeated, and by nightfall, all the piping and connections were finished. The men even opened it up and gave it a good cleaning. There was no way to tell if it would hold together until we built up steam, and we would do that in the morning. After supper, I told the assembled officers:

"All right. Unless you get the word from me, we will operate the boilers absolutely no more than three-quarter pressure and run the engines at a constant speed as much as possible. Mr. Swanson will use only the rudder for steering, and let's hope we don't need any fancy maneuvering. For the most part, the Mississippi only gets wider and deeper from here. Light the boilers at seven o'clock, just after first light."

"Captain, what about the other boats at the landing? Should we tell them?

"It's probably the right thing to do. See to it, Mr. Voight. It wouldn't surprise me that some boats hightail it out of here."

Morning came, and I had two tankards of coffee before Mr. Weatherby was ready to light the fires. That was not a poor reflection on the engineer but a tribute to my consumption of coffee.

"Captain, I thought to enlist a blessing from the priest at St. Paul's Catholic Church, but Captain Bemis would not authorize the expenditure."

"Of course not. Priests bring bad luck to steamboats. It's true for some reason. Apply the match, good sir."

The downward current of the mighty Mississippi this time of year brought the boats up to the amazing speed of twenty miles per hour. It was potentially a dangerous situation as there was far less time to react to hazards and collisions with snags, bars, or other boats would likely result on the total loss of the boat. My hope was the velocity would reduce itself, or it would be a long slog upriver back to St. Louis.

We were entering the bayou country proper. Here the swamps and bayous teem with life where you can get a glimpse of alligators, armadillos, bobcats, swamp deer, beavers, and many other critters. None of them like to be around humans, and some let them know by trying to do them harm. The mosquitoes are especially irritating, but I never heard of anyone dying from them.

Just downstream of mile marker 155 is a tight bend in the river the Rebs fortified during the war to keep Union warships from ascending the river. Port Hudson was the name of fort, and it surrendered after a long siege just after the fall of Vicksburg to Grant.

Three bends beyond Profit Island lay Baton Rouge. The state house remained the dominant landmark, and it came into view well before the city. It did not hold the regular splendor of any capitol building I had ever seen and looked more like a penitentiary. Union troops occupied the building during the war, but it had caught fire on occasion and was now was a burned-out hulk abandoned and forlorn. The landing was busy though. Captain Compere's *Annie Wagley* was here, a fine side-wheeler used as a gunboat and now restored to her former glory. The *Hope* was here too, but she was a new boat for me.

We put ashore at Donaldsonville—or Port Barrow, if you will—for the night. The moon was reaching its fullness, but the overcast skies rendered it useless for navigation. Union forces had built Fort Butler here along the river, but like most of the small forts, it was now abandoned. The town was a haven for escaped slaves, and they easily composed the majority of the people here now. Although there are some fine homes in town, most of the buildings were simple clapboard affairs. There was no reason to go ashore, although a few of the passengers did so out of curiosity. Two passengers did not heed our departure bell and whistle and were left behind.

Come morning, Mr. Weatherby built up steam, and the boat proceeded on her way. We fell in with a small procession of steamers that got the jump on us this morning. Just ahead of us was the *New Era*. I saw her during the expedition up the Red River being used as a transport. She now flew under the flag of the newly formed Red River Packet Company. I don't envy her captain. The Red River is a temperamental wench, looking for every opportunity to snare a boat.

It was at Bell's Point that I finally began to relax a bit and believe we would actually make New Orleans in one piece. There was just thirty-five miles to go. No doubt Mr. Voight would get the crew fed shortly, so they would be ready to work once we landed.

New Orleans slowly came into view in the distance. The black smoke rising from the boats is the first clue on clear days like this. I had been here at least five times over the years. For the boat, it meant the end of the line. There were indeed another 160 miles or more to the Gulf of Mexico, but there was no appreciable trade below the city. A riverboat on the open water would fare very poorly on the swells and high winds.

New Orleans was occupied early in the war and did not suffer from battle. It had been under the ham-fisted occupation of General Benjamin Butler though. To me, New Orleans seemed stagnant. The suburbs of Faubourg St. Mary, Marigny, and Tremé showed signs of neglect. Their rows of single-story plastered and tile roofed Creole cottages looked run down. The last time I walked through the city, even the Pontalba buildings that form two sides of Jackson Square needed a good cleaning and some repair. That had not changed over the years. The block-long, four-story buildings still retained their original purpose though and the ground floors still held shops and restaurants. The upper floors are rented out as apartments. Some of the wealthy-quarter residents relocated to Esplanade Avenue and North Rampart Street, both of which are probably the most pleasant and attractive residential streets in the city. From here, though, it appeared the city had its usual bustle of activity.

Mr. Swanson found an empty space at the levee, although he had to vie for position with the *Carrie Poole*. As a stern-wheeler, she was not as nimble as we and Swanson was able to cut her off smartly.

We were fortunate to be near the warehouses and the rail tracks to Lake Pontchartrain.

The site for New Orleans was originally selected for its relatively high elevation amid the surrounding low-lying swampland. About five miles to the east lay Lake Pontchartrain, which provided a safe harbor for ocean shipping. Newcomers were often surprised to learn that the big ships from foreign lands seldom came up the river. Instead, the levee along the old French Quarter was usually the realm of the steamboats.

The Pontchartrain Railroad was chartered back in 1830 and has been carrying people and goods ever since. The railway is vital in transferring cargo and passengers between ocean-going ships docked at the lake and the riverboats here. For years, passenger fare has been fifteen cents for a one-way trip and twenty-five cents for a round trip. Someday I might find the time to see the big ships on the lake. They must be a sight. The shipping agents receiving our cargo would no doubt be pleased by the convenience at our berthing site. I met both Mr. Bemis and Mr. Voight on the forecastle.

"Gentlemen, let's get the cargo unloaded and see to arranging a hydrostatic test of the boilers."

"Captain, we will not be allowed to test the boilers here. We will need to push off and proceed across the river to Algiers over yonder."

"Damnation. All right. No sense in me crying about it. It is what it is."

"Captain, I suggest you give the men some time ashore. I will keep just enough men here to operate the boilers and machinery."

"That's probably a good idea. I will stay aboard as pilot. It will give Mr. Swanson and his cub a break."

The men got to work in earnest upon learning of their pending time ashore. The token engineer crew was disappointed, but they were promised some hours in the city when the time came to load the upbound cargo. Swanson wasn't as eager as the men to go ashore.

Swanson was no fool as he has been here before. The closest avenue to the waterfront was Gallatin Street, and it was one of the most dangerous thoroughfares in the world. Local lore claims that if you could make it past Gallatin, you could make it anywhere. Gangs such as the Live Oak Boys were so slick and so quick that their victims never knew their throats had been slashed until they were already dead on the street. Of course, there were also pickpockets and thugs galore. Scammers and swindlers were copious in their number too.

Some of the most ruthless in town were the women. Prostitutes in New Orleans were known to kill their inebriated patrons and to dispose their bodies in the swamps. Folks are often surprised to find that white women comprise the vast majority of the whores, and nearly all these were Irish immigrants. The great potato famine was to blame for that. The Irish poured into New Orleans, and the women did not have the skills or education to do much else for a living.

"Captain, this unloading of cargo and then pulling off the levee to have the boilers tested seems like a waste of time and fuel. Can't those mechanics test the system here? The boilers got us here without mishap. Is this really necessary?"

"Afraid so, Mr. Swanson. It's too dangerous to perform the test with so many other boats in proximity. Without the test, no shipping agent would consign his freight on this boat. His insurance underwriters would not fund him. The only freight we might get is a boatload of dirty immigrants. We're here, and we'll get it done. Besides, I would like to know if we can trust the boilers at full steam. We will need the power to get back to St. Louis."

We had landed between the steamers *Mittie Stevens* and the *Henry von Phul.* The latter was a fine boat that was used by the Union army as a transport, hospital, and quartermaster boat throughout the war. I was only acquainted with her captain, James Allen, but knew the pilot well. Sam Bowen is as good as they come, and he gave a friendly wave from atop the hurricane deck.

"Haven't seen you in a coon's age! You still packing that old Paterson revolver? How about we get some of the old pards together to meet up later for a drink?"

"I have no need to carry the revolver as often with all the Rebs disarmed. Good to see you, and that the *von Phul* there made it through the war none too worse for wear. We'll be pushing off here in a bit and heading over to Algiers to have a boiler looked at. Have a drink on me."

"I assume your boiler trouble is minor. If it were serious, you wouldn't be here at all, would you?"

"We had a close call. I just want to make sure everything is in order with a hydrostatic test."

"Can't be too careful. Take care of yourself. Keep a close eye on Bemis. He can filch an orphanage so slick that they thank him for the service."

All reputable boilermakers performed a hydrostatic testing of their products to establish the safe maximum pressures allowed. The steamboat inspection offices of each state were becoming more persnickety about periodic testing after the spate of boiler explosions in recent years. My issue with this was the added bureaucracy and the fact that almost all boiler mishaps were due to negligence, not mechanical failure. It seemed only another opportunity for the states to stick their hands into our pockets. Lord, help us if the federal government someday gets involved. It would mean even more regulations and more fees. The man Bemis admired so much, Adam Smith, once said, "There is no art which one government sooner learns of another than that of draining money from the pockets of the people." That was true enough to earn a space in the Bible.

The crew and the journeymen from ashore emptied the boat quickly. Captain Bemis then paid the men five dollars each for time served on the boat. It was enough for some amusement, but hopefully not enough to get into serious trouble. Paying them off in full probably meant some would not return to the boat, and I needed a full crew to return home. Bemis remained ashore to drum up some business while our small crew got the boat underway. Without cargo, she rode high and nimble. I was able to use just the rudder to maneuver her to the landing on the other bank.

The town of Algiers is located directly across the river from New Orleans, and it had none of the splendor of the Crescent City. It was an industry town with workshops, machinists, and the eastern terminus of the New Orleans, Opelousas, and Great Western Railroad. Three ferry lines ran almost continuously between New Orleans and Algiers. I was pleasantly surprised when one of them, the *Southerner,* gave us wide berth while I turned the boat back upstream to make a landing.

Two vessels at the landing caught my interest. A barge with the name *Regina* roughly painted on the side was being fitted with steam propulsion. This did not look like a successful endeavor as there will be little room for cargo upon completion of the task. The other was the *Iberville*. I had seen her on the expedition up the Yazoo back in '63. Since then, she had extensive fire damage and was awaiting either reconstruction or scrapping. I landed the boat next to the *J. M. Sharp*. Although she looked like an older boat, I could not recall ever seeing her. New paint on her paddle-wheel boxes proudly proclaimed she was under the flag of the Bayou Sara Mail Company, with A. J. Dye as her master. I always thought painting the captain's name on the boat was a bit pretentious, but c'est la vie.

Early in the war, Confederate officials destroyed what property they could in Algiers that might benefit the invading Union troops. Fortunately for us, the repair shops with the capability to build mechanical parts for steamships were back in operation. Unfortunately, by the time we arrived, it was too late in the day to conduct the test. The technicians had gone home and would not return until the morning.

I procured copies of the *Daily Picayune* and the *Louisiana Staats-Zeitung* from hawkers at the landing. Both were rather thin in news today, but the *Picayune* reports that two days ago, President Johnson declared the War of Rebellion officially over. Confederate privateers like the CSS *Shenandoah* were still prowling the seas, but they were being pursued by the Union navy. They were expected to surrender once they finally figured out the South was defeated, probably in some foreign port. The *Zeitung* was in German but had some adverts in English. Both papers at least served as entertainment for the evening as morning could not come soon enough.

The hydrostatic test consists of filling the boiler with water and pressurizing the water to at least one and half times the maximum operating pressure for thirty minutes. Every part is subject to more than the maximum stress of normal operations. Any weak link should fail during the test. If all is satisfactory, the pressure is released gradually, and the engineers visually inspect for any signs leakages or wetting of the surfaces. To be certified, the test is witnessed by inspection agents, who then approve and sign off on the test.

I watched with interest as my engineers and the shop technicians prepared the machinery and administered the test. Most of us on board had never seen the procedures for this, and even Mr. Weatherby had only participated in these a few times. The boilers were fired, and all eyes were on the Bourdon gauge as the needle climbed past 150 pounds, our normal operating pressure. The boilers were originally rated for 180 pounds, and my nerves were very much on edge when the needle surpassed that and continued its climb. Several men were absentmindedly backing away, as if the distance of a few feet would make any difference in a mishap at this point.

The chief technician finally gave the word to begin venting steam and let the fires burn out. He turned to the assembled men on the deck and gave a wide grin. He must have found our worried looks quite humorous.

"Captain, we still need to look over a few things, but I believe you will be pleased to learn the boilers passed the test. Those lunkheads up in Vicksburg did a good job for once. I will prepare the certificate, and you can be on your way in a few hours."

We used the time to obtain coal from the yard. There was an abundance of it as the Union navy had stockpiled it for the river fleet and the blockading squadron on this stretch of the gulf. With the certificate finally in hand, I ordered the chief engineer to fire up the boilers for the short run across the river. The document was fancy enough for framing. Considering how much the yard charged, they should have thrown in a gilded frame on the deal.

The dockmaster ashore directed me to berth alongside the *Nebraska*, an older boat that had been put to use as a transport during the war. I remember seeing her on occasion above Vicksburg in the weeks Grant was preparing to move against the city. My goodness, that was over two years ago already. Captain Bemis was watching our approach and hobbled on his crutches across the levee and up the stageplank.

"We didn't expect to see you back so soon, Captain. I have arranged a few consignments, but they won't be ready for loading until the day after tomorrow. The shipping agent company Goldenbow and Lesparre is trying to fill the boat, bless their hearts. In the meantime, I will try to scrounge up some more. I assume all went well over there in Algiers. Otherwise, you wouldn't be here."

"Well enough, I suppose. I didn't see anything the technicians did that we couldn't have done ourselves. They did give us a certificate, though."

The boat signal "Hip, hip, hooray" had announced our arrival, and the crewmen left ashore returned in small groups throughout the evening and night. They were in various states of drunkenness and no doubt penniless. A few men were still missing at breakfast, but they should be along. Storm clouds to the southwest meant rain was on the way. That would be welcome upstream, but here it would turn the landing into mud, making the handling of freight treacherous.

The evening on the boat was a quite one. The promised rain passed to the south. Aside from the dogwatch guarding the boat on the forecastle, everyone aboard was sleeping off the labors of the day or the liquor. I pulled a chair onto the hurricane deck to enjoy a cigar. For a while, I faced the city and marveled at the revelry that continued well into the night, wondering when and how the people ever slept. I then spun the chair around and gazed over the serene river and tried to spot a star or two through the clouds.

Morning came, and with the return of my able first mate, Mr. Voight, I decided to stretch my legs and perhaps replenish my various sundries. I strapped on the old Paterson revolver under my open frock coat. The little Root revolver was in its usual place in the suspender holster. Those of the engineer crew wanting to go ashore did so with the warning to return no later than seven o'clock in the morning. I wanted to get underway as soon as the freight was loaded.

New Orleans is a city of full of degenerates to one degree or another. It is a drunk, merrymaking, corruption-embracing kind of port. Here, the basic concept of morals slowly dissolves in a brightly colored solution of sugar and grain alcohol. People of all races and creeds live here with tolerance and sometimes acceptance, depending on the value of their skills, labor, or wealth. There is also every class of deplorable known to the calendar of crime. New Orleans is indeed a grand medley of humanity living in a seedy dark underworld that will swallow up a naïve man or unescorted woman, never to be seen again. Alive or dead.

Before the war, the people of New Orleans held an annual carnival in the spring they call Mardi Gras. The Catholic Church's discouragement of intimacy and meat during Lent encourages the flock to raise hell a week before Ash Wednesday. Get all the sin out of their system, so to speak. My parents spoke of the carnival as being called *Fasching* in the Germanic states and Austria. It was much the same for the Catholic mackerels there. I couldn't see how the intentional debauchery was pleasing to God, even with the pious fasting and prayer during Lent. Such was New Orleans. Word is the people here are planning to restart this Mardi Gras tradition this next spring.

My first challenge ashore was to cross Gallatin Street. Ramshackle buildings filled with low groggeries line the street and were the dens of the worst of both sexes. Prostitutes, some missing limbs or teeth, lured sailors off the street like the sirens of Homer's *Iliad*. Both of my revolvers were recently cleaned and had fresh powder and ball for this outing.

Crossing Gallatin without incident, I found an interesting sight on the next block. A gaudily dressed man on the corner turned the hand crank to his barrel organ to play the tune "Johnny Roach" while his mongrel dog looked at passersby with sad eyes. The man looked foreign, perhaps from eastern Europe. The name Vincenzo Gianoni was painted on the pull cart bearing his barrel organ. Maybe he was one of those gypsy people. The upturned hat by the dog beckoned whatever generosity ebbed from the people of New Orleans. Only a heart made of stone could resist the pining of the poor animal. I dropped two bits into the straw skimmer and patted the dog's head. My hope was it would go to feeding the rangy dog. No doubt it was a forlorn hope. The operator of the musical contraption needed his animal to look sad and thin for his scheme to work.

During the outing, I hoped to finally get a glimpse of Marie Catherine Laveau, the famous practitioner of voodoo and a renowned mystical healer. Miss Marie apparently mixed Roman Catholic saints with African spirits to form her occult religion. While not conjuring her black magic, she worked as a hairdresser in prominent white households of the city. She is said to walk about the streets as if she owned them. I had no wish to engage with her in conversation but thought of her as another of the sights of the city to behold. So far, she proved to be as elusive as the quadroon balls, which are talked about but never actually seen.

My main purpose ashore was to send a telegraph to St. Louis to inform Mr. Geldstein of our condition and expected return. I found the office of the American Telegraph Company on the corner of St. Charles and Gravier. Mr. E. W. Barnes was the manager and he kindly reduced my rambling note to a concise message ready for one of his operators to transmit across the wire. I wondered if Mr. Foley with the gold vest was still invested with the company or was otherwise engaged is some nefarious mischief.

A short distance away on Rampart Street, I bought two boxes of cigars from Jose Acebel, a man who claimed to be from Cuba. I normally avoid the Havana tobaccos and cigars as they are too mild. No taste to them. He had a nice supply of Carolina tobacco cigars at a fair price.

"The weather seems fine this trip, Mr. Acebel. I have seen it so hot here that the only cool place to be found was by the fire."

"Ah, señor, I have seen it so hot that dogs melted and trickled down between the bricks in the pavement."

There was tension here in the city. I noticed right away but took me some time to find the cause. My assumption was people were at ill ease because of the ongoing occupation by Union troops. That certainly didn't help matters, but there was more to it. With the war over, there were still soldiers walking about, but not nearly as many as before. More in number than soldiers were the newly freed slaves of the South. Quite a few, in fact. Just like in Memphis, none of them seemed to be employed in any productive endeavor, and they clearly intimidated the citizens of New Orleans. Once again, my blue steamboat uniform provided a shield to any thought of anyone pestering me. Maybe too a glimpse of my revolver did the trick.

There was a time I didn't think much one way or the other about slavery. Once employed on a steamboat, I soon saw the economic shortsightedness of the institution. People were held in bondage who could otherwise be engaged in trade, and it took the owners much effort to keep them in place including overseers, slave patrols, laws, and politics. It finally occurred to me during the war that there was also a basic immorality at play here. The slaves were not soulless livestock but people. Fellow Christians for the most part. They too should be able to decide their own destiny. It took a couple of the war years to make an abolitionist out of me, but that's where I now stand.

Unfortunately, President Johnson seems all too quick about letting the Old South rejoin the Union without first addressing the Negroes' problems. Allowing the ex-Confederates back into power beforehand will forfeit all leverage and ensure the black race remains in bondage, even if the lawbooks say they are free. It makes me wonder why we fought the war at all and think the next election could not come soon enough. That was nearly three years into the future.

I had absentmindedly wandered off to the west several blocks on St. Charles Avenue and stumbled onto Lafayette Square. The city hall is located here, and it is another example of Greek architecture found across the South. It is no accident the Southerners admired Greek and Roman building styles. Those ancient civilizations were based on slavery as well. The irony is that both the Greek and Roman empires exist now only in the history books. So too the Confederacy.

It was past time to return to the boat, but along the way I stopped to buy a bottle of winter strained oil to lubricate my firearms. I also paid a quick visit to Dutrey's for a pint of Guinness extra stout to lubricate me. Situated at the corner of Decatur and Madison Streets, this coffee shop did very well, serving German food to the hungry crowds who worked at the Creole Market. Stouts were usually too heavy for my taste, but there was no way I was going to drink the water here. We had arrived toward the end of the yellow-jack season, but I did not want to take the risk of drinking tainted water as the fever made for a gruesome death. After catching it, people came down with a high fever, and their skin turned a sickly yellow. In addition, the victims felt a host of nasty symptoms such as nausea, convulsions, and delirium. Then came the blood. Eventually, the poor wretches start to bleed through their eyes, nose, and ears. The entire process of dying took only a few days. In the epidemic years, the yellow jack could kill off 10 percent of the city's population. The worse season to date was back in '53, when over eight thousand people of New Orleans gave up the ghost. So no local water for me. I would stick to the stout or something stronger.

While I enjoyed the beverage, a Negro outside the widow was engaged at separating people from their money with a game of three-card monte. The man sat with a blanket spread before him and placed three cards facedown. The dealer showed the target card (in this instance, the queen of hearts). He then rapidly rearranged the cards to confuse the player about which card is which. The player then selected one of the three cards, attempting to locate the queen. If a player finds the card, he wins an amount equal to the amount the dealer bet. The player loses his money if the target card is not picked. Naturally, the odds are in the dealer's favor from the start, and he is certain to win anyway with various sleights of hand and other tricks. The whole game preys on the greedy and stupid. The poor sap had lost two dollars to the Negro before I finished the stout and was on my way again.

I found the boat where I left her. Men were unloading a large freight wagon and carrying the boxes, crates, and barrels aboard. "Goldenbow and Lesparre, Shipping Agents" was painted on the side panels. The freight was already weighed at the scales up the way. Lord only knows if they were accurate and if they favored the shipper or the boat. Mr. Voight and Captain Bemis were supervising the whole affair.

"Hello, Captain. Did you get everything you needed?"

"Indeed, Mr. Voight. I sent a telegraph message to St. Louis and purchased some cigars. How did you fare ashore?"

"Lost five dollars to a faro dealer with six fingers on each hand. It was my fault. I shouldn't have plied the liquor beforehand like I did."

"What is the cargo situation, Mr. Bemis? When can we depart?"

"A few more wagonloads between now and dark. A consignment for, hmm, let's see, Grieff A. D. and Company should be particularly profitable. Barrels of French wines, cheeses, and fancy liquors des-tined for St. Louis. You won't like it, but we will have a boatload of filthy Russian immigrants bound for St. Louis too. They have a mind to settle in southern Illinois of all places. Their ship arrived from Europe today, and they are coming by train from Lake Pontchartrain. They should arrive as a herd at first light. No Chinamen, though, or livestock. Thank Christ."

"Don't be blasphemous, Bemis."

"I am not, my good captain. I thank him in all earnestness."

Everyone looks up and down on people, but mostly down. The style of clothes worn and how you carry yourself betrays your status in society. That said, the color of skin is the first thing considered. Aside from that, upon introduction, people ask of your profession and where you are from. I don't like to admit to the fact I am guilty of it as well. I never met a Chinaman and have no prejudice yet, but for some reason, I never cared much for Hoosiers. I can't explain it, but it's true. For myself, my Germanic ancestry has done no favors, as if I or anyone else are able to choose our parents or location of birth. It's a foolish way to judge a man. His deeds should be the measure. I resolved to work on that.

The steamer *St. Patrick* landed to our starboard side during the late afternoon. She was a familiar sight on the Tennessee River during the war. I thought she was on the Memphis-Louisville trade route, but here she was now. Captain Archer is her master, and we exchanged friendly waves.

The men were awfully quiet on the boat after supper. Most must be sleeping off their time ashore or the work Mr. Voight assigned them. One young man down below was playing a twangy tune on his Jew's harp. I knew who it was from up here on the hurricane deck. One of his front teeth was cracked in half from the device when he played it under the influence of cheap whiskey.

The Russians Are Coming

There was a fog on the river in the morning, but it promised to lift shortly as the sun rose. A steady wind from the south brought a hint of salty sea mixed with the smells of death and decay of the bayous. The crews of the boats along the levee roused and the general clank of machinery, cursing and shouting of the mates. The rush of boiler fires sounded the beginning of a new day. A pleasant feature of the morning was the cornucopia of odors produced by the cooking of breakfasts on the boats. Some particularly smelled quite delicious. Most crews found disappointment that the delicious-smelling meal was not to be found on their plates. I made my way to the wheelhouse and met Swanson and Olsson just as they were unlocking the door. The cub pilot automatically went right to the stove to get the first pot of coffee to boil. Good man.

"Will we be departing shortly, Captain?"

"All the cargo is aboard, but Captain Bemis has accepted a boatload of immigrants. We will shove off as soon as they are aboard."

"Oh Lord."

As if on cue, a long line of humanity emerged on the levee. The fog gave the people an unearthly appearance, as if they emerged from the vapor itself. There were men and women of all ages, and at least a third were children. They were all dressed in browns and blacks without a hint of color. They surely must be serfs off the estates. Some looked frightened; others were beaming. A typical sight for immigrants. Bemis had said there were about three hundred, but the unending line looked far larger than that. At the head of the procession was Victor Gerodias, whom I knew as the deputy sheriff for the parish. Just before the war, he had fought a duel at the halfway house. The choice of weapons was shotguns loaded with ball at the distance of forty paces. The deputy's adversary plunked his projectile in the fleshy part of his leg. He was extremely lucky it was not amputated. The limp was a constant reminder of that day. I had made his acquaintance on occasion when he returned drunken crewmen to the boat. I imagine he was there to make sure every Russian got aboard. New Orleans had enough problems already.

We could hear the footfalls on the gang stage as our guests came aboard with their trunks and sacks. The ready whistle down below soon pealed for my presence.

"Oh my. This is going to be a long trip. A boatload of these people will be the end of me. At least there isn't any livestock to foul the boat. Excuse me, gentlemen."

I made my way to the forecastle where I found Bemis and an exotic woman deep in conversation. She looked about thirty-five years old but may be much younger. A Russian peasant's life was a hard one. She wore a dark-brown sarafan dress as all the other women and a patterned scarf about her head. Upon noticing me, Bemis snapped to attention and rendered a rather snappy naval salute.

"Good morning, Captain! We will have these people on board and settled within the half hour."

This behavior was odd to say the least, but I played along with it for the moment. In normal times, I would take such exaggerated respect as an insult. Bemis was up to something, though. I returned his salute. A throng of immigrants stood about us in wonder and silence.

"Captain, this is Irina Oblonsky. She speaks wonderful English and is the guide for these people."

"How do you do, Ms. Oblonsky? I understand you want transit to St. Louis."

"Pleased to make your acquaintance, Captain. We are bound for Anna, Illinois. Our patron, Ivan Turchaninov, will be waiting for us at Hamburg Landing. You would know him as John Turchin. He was a great general in your army during the war."

I vaguely remembered some news account of a General Turchin, but it wasn't a good one. Something about a court martial.

"Very well. The voyage will take about six days, depending on the current and weather. Mr. Bemis here will tell you the rules of the boat. It is most important that you do not get in the way of the crew or break into the cargo."

"We will follow your rules, and we are not thieves. Do not worry about your cargo."

I departed with some pleasantries and made my way toward the pilothouse. As I did so, the immigrant men removed their caps, and the throng parted to make a clear path. I was as impressed as Moses must have been with the parting of the Red Sea.

"A word, Captain?"

It was my chief engineer and first mate. They had a worried look about them.

"Morning, gentlemen. Are we almost ready to depart?"

"Captain, we have two men absent. O'Fallon and Murphy. Both are firemen. We hired them just before leaving St. Louis."

"We can't afford to wait for them. Perhaps these immigrants know how to shovel coal."

"That is true, but their leaving was odd. They had already spent time ashore and jumped the boat sometime during the night. One did not even bother to take his seabag, and neither were paid off."

"That is odd. Tell the men check the coal supply. Break up any chunks larger than a potato before tossing them into the fireboxes. Look over the machinery too."

"I'm not following you, Captain. What will that accomplish?"

"If those men left an incendiary, we would find it in the bunkers before we blow ourselves to kingdom come. Calamity would come too if they molested the valves, gauges, or whatnot. Find out what you can about those scoundrels from their mates."

"Why on earth would they do such a thing?"

"Don't forget about the boiler and the tampering with the doctor. I fear there may be a larger conspiracy afoot."

I left my two officers with their eyes wide and their mouths agape.

I felt much better once I reached the pilot house. The mass of humanity made me uncomfortable to say the least. They were packed in every open space and along the rails. A few women were obviously pregnant. I soon felt the boat develop a list to port as I poured a tankard of coffee. Before I could make mention of it, there was a woman's voice down below yelling in a strange foreign language. The boat assumed an even keel as the immigrants shifted into position along both sides of the boat this time. The engineer's ready whistle soon pealed that all was in readiness, and Mr. Swanson backed the boat into the river and proceeded upstream.

"Captain, with this current, we should make no further than Natchez by dark."

"Steady as she goes. I will tell Mr. Voight to make plans to take on coal there. There are slim pickings between Natchez and Vicksburg nowadays."

I made my way around the boat to check on things. The immigrants must be exhausted from their ordeal as they were huddled in masses and trying to sleep. Unlike most passengers who moved the cargo about to create shelter, these people have so far left everything in place. Fortunately, the weather was fine but humid. Autumn was beginning, and the temperatures would drop as we steamed north. If these people were from the steppes, they may hardly notice. I found the engineer at the boilers.

"How are things here, Mr. Weatherby?"

"The machinery is in good shape and no hint of trouble from boiler number 2. The firemen are scrutinizing every lump of coal that goes in the firebox. No issues from all these immigrants, not even the children. They are giving everything a wide berth. They are more obedient than slaves."

"Back in Russia, there isn't much difference between serfs and slaves. It must be in their nature. Any word about our two missing men?"

"Yeah, and it isn't good. Both are Irishmen that came from the *Kaw Nation* just before we shipped. What is going on here, Captain?"

"Wish I knew for sure, Weatherby. First the boiler, and now two men mysteriously jump ship. It appears men from the *Kaw Nation* mean us harm."

"Why on earth would they be hostile? We seldom cross paths with that boat. It has a regular run up to St. Paul. For heaven's sake, we both work for the same outfit."

"Thomas Geldstein is thinking of making some changes to the company, but none of them would affect the men. The changes would be good ones and keep us on the river for decades to come. I don't fully understand any hostility either. Have your trusted men keep a vigilant watch on the boilers, machinery, and the coal bunkers day and night. From now on I do not trust anyone from the *Kaw Nation* or Irishmen. I want to get back to St. Louis soonest."

"Aye, Captain. As do I. On a happier note, whatever the cook is fixing up in the kitchen smells better than what he has boiled up so far."

"Indeed. He must have gone shopping while in New Orleans. I have grown tired of his cabbage, potatoes, and sausage. I wonder what these immigrants brought to eat."

I looked out from the main deck and noticed we were already passing Donaldsonville. The star-shaped Fort Butler looked deserted. Few white folks live there anymore as they were either run off during the war or otherwise supplanted by the influx of freedmen. The coal pile made for the Union boats was almost depleted and probably wet.

I enjoyed a smoke in solitude on the hurricane deck. My chair was placed on the stern instead of the bow so the men in the pilot-house would not be watching the back of my head the whole time. I was greatly worried for the boat as one man with malicious intent could create great harm. It occurred to me that a single match could destroy the boat, and perhaps it would be a good idea to collect up all the matches from the men and restrict smoking to the hurricane deck here. All the stores of kerosene needed to come under lock and key too. It is a very disquieting feeling for a captain when he cannot trust his own crew.

During my second cigar, we were overtaken by the steamer *Tarascon*. She is a fine boat, probably about 230 feet and powered by oversized paddle wheels. She has just returned to the river trade. The *Tarascon* had previously supported the Union fleet at Mobile and was present at the famous battle there. Her captain pealed her whistle as a challenge to race, and Swanson did not reply. He would have caught hell from me if he did. My guess was she was returning to her regular trade out of Evansville, Indiana.

A return to the boiler deck found the immigrants back on their feet and engaged in sweeping the boat stem to stern. All work stopped when I appeared, and the people spread apart to make a clear way for me. I felt like the czar himself. If they kept this up, the boat would be cleaner than the day she was launched. I found the same exercise on the main deck with Mr. Voight and his deckhands watching in awe and a bit of embarrassment.

"They're putting us all to shame, but I'm not complaining, Captain. This keeps them busy, even the children. They aren't running around playing games and getting in our way."

The supper bell rang none too soon, and I went to the main deck to get a plate of whatever produced that wonderful smell all afternoon. It was a great surprise to find immigrant women dishing out a thick soup and large hunks of course black bread. Captain Bemis sat on a crate next to Ms. Oblonsky watching my reaction with one of those mischievous grins on his face. Once my presence was noticed, the Russians went silent, and I was almost forcibly ushered to the front of the line.

"Blagoslovi tebya, kapitan. Prikhodi i yesh'!"

I had no earthly idea what was just said. In my ear, they sounded as the inhabitants of Venus. It was spoken in a friendly, almost reverent tone, so I nodded and said, "Thank you."

The portly woman they called *Babushka* ladled a heaping portion into a bowl, gave it to me, and said, "Solyanka!" I didn't know if that meant "here you go" or if it was the contents of the bowl. I fumbled with the spoon and nearly dropped everything. The assembled throng gasped but broke out in cheers when I recovered myself without loss of soup or dignity. I gave greetings to Ms. Oblonsky but sat next to Bemis. The soup contained sausage, ham, as well as cabbage, carrots, onions, and potatoes. There were even some chopped pickled cucumbers. My guess was, this meal was made with a combination of our food and that of our guests.

"Bemis, what the devil is going on here? First all the cleaning and now the food."

"These people were a bit short of cash, so they are working off the balance. I suspect you will be further pleased along the way."

"That is quite an assumption that I am pleased at all right now."

"Eat your food, and I'm sure you will come around."

The river approach to Natchez from the south is an easy one, even in the quickly fading light. Swanson edged the boat in for a gentle bump. We were in search of coal, and there was no other need to go ashore. Our immigrant passengers were more than happy to remain aboard. They had been weeks at sea, no doubt in the awful conditions of steerage. Here they found contentment in the open and airy steamboat on a calm river. The steamboat *John Kilgour* was already here and loading bags of sugar. We saw her last in New Orleans, so it meant she was heading north, probably to St. Louis.

Natchez is a sugar and cotton port that suffered little damage during the war. At one time, General Grant made his headquarters in the Rosalie mansion, and it was said the town just wasn't worth the effort to burn it. The plantations of the area were brought under Union control and continued to produce their crops under contract. So things were pretty much the same here as before the war. The sign for D. Moses and Sons "Cheap Cash Store" still hung near the waterfront, and St. Mary's Cathedral was still not finished. No doubt the continuous line of two-story stores and mercantile shops still operated along the length of Main Street.

The coal yard was still open, but the proprietor did not see how we could finish the job that evening. He had promised the *John Kilgour* first dibs in the morning, and our departure would be delayed considerably waiting on it. I was naturally flustered, but Bemis simply waved his cap back at the boat.

All the Russian menfolk disembarked and formed a human chain from the boat to the coal pile. While a group filled the scuttles, the men of the chain passed each to the next man and onto the boat. A handful of the men ran back to the coal pile with the empty scuttles to have the process repeated. The boat was coaled in a fraction of the time of using the normal roustabouts. I was starting to like these immigrants.

My good feelings here at the moment were dashed. Mr. Weatherby beckoned to me. His face was grim indeed.

"Captain, my men found three of these in the coal bunkers just before we landed. Your fears were correct."

In his hand was what appeared at first glance a lump of coal about the size of a small melon. He handed it to me, and it felt much lighter than what coal should be.

"It is a thin sheet metal casing containing gunpowder. Probably two pounds' worth. It was dipped in beeswax and pitch and rolled in coal dust while the mixture was hot to conceal its true purpose. Just one of these in the firebox would have set off the boilers. I have sworn the men to secrecy, but no doubt the crew is aware. Something like this can't be kept secret for long."

"Damnation. I am at a loss to conceive a man so vile as to do this. Thank God in heaven your men found them. I trust your men searched the remaining supply in the bunkers?"

"I didn't even have to ask. When the first one was found, the boys digging though and around examining every nugget."

"If Mr. Swanson is up to it, we will push on to Vicksburg and maybe all the way to Memphis without stopping. Light the boilers by four o'clock in the morning. We will take on all the coal we can carry so we won't have to stop."

"Aye, Captain."

I soon told Messrs. Voight, Swanson, and Bemis of my plans. The first mate was aware of the infernal devices found in the bunkers, but Swanson Bemis had been blissfully ignorant. That reminded me of many times the goings-on of the boat that went unnoticed by me secluded in the pilothouse. I asked Bemis to rouse the telegraph operator and send a message ahead to Vicksburg to prepare a coal flat for us to take in tow. We would empty it while under way. This was an extravagance I had never partaken, but we needed to get home quickly.

"Captain, we have ten Sharps rifles stored aboard. Should I issue them to the men?"

"I suppose not, Mr. Voight. We might just be arming an enemy of ours. Gentlemen, let us turn in for the night. The next few days will be long ones."

For Swanson and me, it was certainly time to turn in. No doubt the Russian men would find sleep easily too.

I returned to my cabin and was surprised to find my bed made and room swept. The Russians had been here too. A quick check of my trunks showed all my possessions and money were still there. The boat was deathly quiet as I quickly drifted off to sleep.

I took first watch at the wheel in the morning and backed the boat out into the current. The *John Kilgour* was still dark and silent with only its fire watch awake. It would be hours before she loaded coal and followed us. I wonder if we left her enough to get very far. The horizon to the east was warming up, but the sun had yet to peek over the horizon. Wisps of fog hung to the water, but the sight of each bank was clear. I really didn't get my sea legs, though, until approaching Fairchild Island some fifteen miles upstream. There was just so much on my mind. Like all river islands, Fairchild grows and diminishes with the water level. Today at high water, it is small, willow topped, with scrubby bottoms with privets and vines. That was a good sign. It meant plenty of water between the keel and the river bottom.

Around six o'clock, there was a knock on the pilothouse door. A Russian woman sheepishly entered with a bowl of steaming contents and said "Kasha!" I still did not know if that meant some sort of greeting or the contents of the bowl. I replied, "Thank you" and bade her goodbye. I wondered if she saw the Paterson revolver strapped on beneath the open frock coat.

The bowl contained some type of cereal or porridge that looked and tasted like buckwheat groats. In such dishes, the grain is first roasted, then soaked, and then slowly simmered it until soft. The meal had a strong nutty flavor and firm texture with a slightly gummy consistency. I probably wouldn't have eaten it if was smooth and creamy. I want food to chew by golly. The meal was oddly satisfying and a nice change from leftover cabbage, potatoes, and sausage. It washed down well with the strong coffee in the pot.

I wasn't sure of the immigrants' religion, but they were strange enough in their appearance and eating habits that my guess was they were Hebrew of some sort. More than one woman, though, wore a cross necklace, but they had an additional short crossbar above and below the usual one. If there was a holy man among them, I couldn't tell.

"Ninety-five miles to Vicksburg. We have eight feet of water in these parts. It's another four hundred miles to Memphis."

Alone in the pilothouse, I was talking to myself already.

The boat was running well, and I heard hardly a peep from below. Normally, a boatload of passengers is raucous and distracting. Oftentimes the people had to be told to stay quiet so the men could hear the bells. That must be it. These Russians were told to remain quiet and were dutifully following orders.

Progress up the river seemed painfully slow. The *Cleona* overtook us with ease and disappeared around a bend. The *Cleona* is a small packet, maybe 120 feet, engaged in trade between New Orleans and Washington over in St. Landry Parish. I didn't feel so bad after noticing she was riding high, meaning she had little cargo aboard. At Coffee Point, the river begins to double back on itself for miles in tight turns, and I was wishing someone would just cut a channel across and straighten the river out. My anxiousness to get to St. Louis was overwhelming. There were nearly four hundred souls on this boat that were counting on me to get them there safely. Was I willing to take risks to get us there soonest?

Yes, yes, I was. I wasn't proud of the fact, but there it was.

I flipped open the brass lid to the voice tube and pulled the bell cord. Down on the main deck, the engineer on duty answered with an "Ahoy!"

"This is the captain. Bring up the boiler pressure to 180 pounds, but no more. Maintain that until further notice."

"Uh, aye, Captain!"

The firemen would apply more coal to the furnaces, but it would take several minutes for the effect to be felt. In these conditions, the thirty additional pounds of pressure should get us an additional three, maybe four miles per hour. The thought reminded me of serving with naval officers in the war. They all spoke of speed in "knots." All the maps and charts out here are in miles, and that required some adjustment on their part.

Swanson and his cub pilot came up to the pilothouse at quarter to noon, fifteen minutes early. They brought me a large chunk of black bread split down the middle with a slice of beef and sliced pickled cucumbers between the halves. I wondered if the Russians ate this way normally or were taking lessons from our cook. I was running my internal boilers mostly on coffee and did not care for a tankard of beer presently.

"Good day, Captain. Is all well here?"

Swanson must have known we are operating above the maximum boiler pressure I usually allow. I suppose the news got around the boat quickly. His tone of voice was a mixture of inquisitiveness and concern. I replied as a pilot about to be relieved.

"We are near Mile 345, approaching Big Black Island and Point Pleasant. The river is deep and smooth. Vicksburg is thirty-seven miles ahead. Mr. Olsson, take the wheel."

"I have the wheel, Captain!"

It was the first time I had asked the young man to handle the boat, and he did so with relish. It occurred to me that this could be an exceptional moment for him. Perhaps he would remember it as the first time I displayed confidence in him. I wouldn't want him to know that I thought the river was fairly tame in these parts and the boat would need only its rudder to make the turns. Any cub pilot could do it.

"Mr. Swanson, I will be in my cabin but will return by the time we get to Vicksburg. If Bemis was successful with his telegraph message, there will be a coal barge waiting for us. We will take it in tow and replenish when our reserves on board are expended or when darkness puts us ashore for the night."

"Aye, Captain. I assume you want to maintain best speed to St. Louis."

"Indeed. Carry on, gentlemen. You have the watch."

I used the few hours getting to Vicksburg with a quick walk through the boat and a retirement to my cabin to lie down for a bit. There was too much coffee in my system to get any real rest. Too soon, the peal from the whistle summoned me to the pilothouse. We must be approaching Vicksburg.

My arrival in the pilothouse found the barge operation underway. Swanson pulled our boat alongside the towboat, pulling the coal barge and slowed to match its speed. The hawsers were transferred to our boat and secured. Our boat then pulled ahead while the tug drifted astern free and clear. I didn't get to see it, but Bemis no doubt had tossed the packet of money to the towboat to pay for the coal and the delivery service. Both crews made the endeavor look easy. But pulling a loaded barge slowed our ascent of the river. I tried to do the math in my head to ascertain if this was worth the expense and saved any time all. I tried to convince myself that it did.

"Excellent work, gentlemen. I will return shortly. Get a feel for the boat and estimate how far we can go upriver before a halt is required."

"Captain, the full moon for this month of September was back on the fifth. It has been on the wane and will reach the last quarter tomorrow. Not many stars out tonight. I know you want to push on, but my recommendation is to put ashore at Crow's Landing at Lake Providence, Louisiana. It will also give Mr. Weatherby a chance to tinker with his machinery down there."

"Damnation. That means we will make Memphis in the evening the day after next. Depending on the coal situation we may be delayed there ten hours or more."

"Sir, we won't make St. Louis at all if we lose the boat."

"Thank you for speaking the obvious, Mr. Swanson. All right. Proceed to Crow's Landing, but we will push on if the conditions allow it."

"Aye, Captain."

Working in shifts, we steamed on in the darkness with the torch baskets illuminating the shores. Swanson and I finally got the boat to Crow's Landing but could not safely go further. We put ashore in near total darkness, and I silently thanked the Lord for delivering us here in one piece. No lights were seen from the town or nearby plantations. The men at the boilers were exhausted and slept about their machinery. Mr. Voight organized his men and brought the coal barge alongside. With the help of the Russians, it took but a few hours to fill the bunkers. There was enough left to get us to Memphis.

With the engines shut down, the Russians chatted endlessly, catching up on what they would normally have said throughout the day. Four men and woman produced their stringed instruments and began to play a lively tune that provoked a round of dancing. The boat decks trembled with the stomping of hundreds of feet. I sat next to Captain Bemis and Ms. Oblonsky, who explained what was transpiring.

The primary musical instruments called *balalaika* resembled the common mandolin but were a triangular shape and only had three strings. In a supporting role was what they called a *gudok*. It is a three-stringed pear-shaped instrument held vertically and played with a bow. The strumming, plucking, and drawing were all done with a rapidity that until now had been unseen by my eyes.

The dance, I learned, was called a *gopak*, a folkdance originating from the infamous Cossacks. The men knelt, jumped, kicked, and pranced about like a whirlwind. The women twirled and fluttered about. If there was a rhyme or reason to the acrobatics, my uncultured sensitivities did not catch it. Their physical exertions were immense and was certainly beyond the abilities of the ballroom patrons of St. Louis. How the engineers remained asleep through all this was a testament to their exertions of the day. I told Mr. Voight to light lamps fore and aft to alert our presence to any boats on the river. They were safer than the open torch baskets burning oily rags.

Bemis and Ms. Oblonsky excused themselves to find refreshment while I spoke briefly with Mr. Voight about the business of the boat. All was well, so I soon retired to my own cabin. Fortunately, the music stopped after but a few dances. The river became calm again. There was thunder to the west, though, meaning rain sometime in the morning.

Some months ago, I bought a newfangled mechanical alarm clock in St. Louis. Although quite expensive, it served me well after a night like this. The sonorous ringing of the twin bells usually brought me out of any sound slumber. The impulse, though, was to throw the annoying mechanism across the room. Remembering the cost of the device always kept me from doing so. I strapped on the gun belt, donned my frock coat and cap, and exited my cabin. With luck, there would be some coffee in the kitchen already boiled up.

In the causeway, I was more than surprised to find Ms. Oblonsky exiting Captain Bemis's cabin, although she was probably more surprised to see me. With a sheepish smile, she passed by me and went below. I gave her a few moments then went down the causeway in search of coffee.

There was a steady drizzle falling already and the air felt like a heavy rain was soon to follow. I met Mr. Voight in the kitchen with the same idea as I. I told him to allow the immigrants on the main deck to move the cargo to make shelter but that he should supervise the enterprise. To our satisfaction, there was a cauldron of coffee ready for the crew. We each took two apples from the bushel on the counter. They were still a bit green, being so early in the season. I then filled my tankard and headed topside. I wonder if the Russians even knew what coffee was. Russia would never be a great country unless they developed a coffee tradition and brewed a good beer. There was no need to check with the engineer as I could tell the boilers were already lit.

The ready whistle pealed just as I lit the pilothouse stove and placed a pot of coffee atop of it. My fellow pilots would be up shortly. I backed the boat off the landing without fanfare but pealed the boat's "Hip, hip, hooray" after ordering the engines ahead. The Russians had taken to cheering when they heard the signal. I found that amusing. Within the hour, a Russian woman brought up a bowl of *kasha*. It was perfect for the foul weather outside. I was sorry she had to get wet in its delivery, but these were hardy folk.

Another full day was spent chugging up the river. The current was still strong and progress agonizingly slow. We always strived to make good time as it was good for business. I also understood the pilot's yearning to get to port on a regular packet line. But as a tramper, I had seldom been under pressure to reach a destination at a specific time. This yearning to get to St. Louis was self-inflicted, but that made my anxiety worse, not less. By nine o'clock in the morning, the rain came down heavily but did not hinder my vision to the point of requiring putting ashore.

The boat had peacefully passed Shipwith's Landing, Pilcher's Point, and Ashton, and was coming in sight of Grand Lake when Swanson and Olsson entered the pilothouse. I hadn't noticed until now that Swanson was wearing his Remington revolver in much the same manner as I wore my Paterson. I could not tell if young Mr. Olsson was armed. My assumption was Swanson was on my side, come what may. My assumption too was that Olsson would follow Swanson's lead.

"Good morning, gentlemen. We have another good nine hours of light left. If the rain doesn't stop us, we should make Victoria or maybe even Laconia."

"How are you holding up, Captain? You haven't had much rest."

"I would like one of you to spell me for a while. I'm going to take a nap on the bench there."

I drifted in and out of sleep as the boat passed by the familiar landmarks of Egg's Point, Bachelor's Bend, Greenville, and Island Number 82. The young cub pilot was coming along on in learning the river but had trouble remembering the details. This was his first time on the Lower Mississippi, so it was understandable. Swanson, though, was using a far gentler approach than Captain Sulloway used on me. My old master put the fear of God into me should I make a mistake.

I awoke after about four hours of fitful sleep and did not feel refreshed. A good tankard of coffee would finish the job. Maybe a cigar or two would help. The rain had slackened off to a drizzle.

"Captain, we are coming up on Concordia. I think we can just make Victoria before darkness shuts us down."

"Very well, Mr. Swanson. Any word from Mr. Voight and Mr. Weatherby?"

"They both stopped by, but report all is well. Captain Bemis looked through the glass at one point but did not enter."

I chuckled to myself at the sight of Bemis peering inside. No doubt he thought to discuss his night with Ms. Oblonsky. I didn't condone fornication on my boat but was glad to discover he was apparently still able. I caught myself imagining how he performed the act with but one leg but quickly put that out of mind. Well, I tried to.

We landed at Victoria without whistles but rang the bell three times to announce our arrival. There was no need to wake the town. The coal barge was brought alongside and its remaining contents transferred to the boat's bunkers. It would be just enough to reach Memphis, which was just seven hours upstream. The Russians had another bout of dancing and frolicking as they knew they were near the end of their long journey. For the evening meal, their womenfolk prepared stuffed cabbage rolls they called *golubtsi*. My mother made better, and she called them *kohlrouladen*. I did marvel at how they made so many rolls for so many people. My mother toiled for just four people.

Morning came with the promise of good weather. The engineer lit the boilers and had steam up by six o'clock in the morning as expected. Swanson and Olsson came up to the pilothouse within the hour of departing upstream bringing a bowl of *kasha*, and chunk of black bread, and two pickled cucumbers for me. Swanson took the wheel while I ate. I procured a jar of peach preserves from my possibles bag to aid in the eating of the course bread. There was a flash of envy in the cub pilot's eyes.

"Have some preserves, Mr. Olsson. Once the jar is open, it needs to be eaten before it goes bad."

"Thank you, Captain!"

The boat passed Laconia, Friar's Point, and the familiar port of Helena. It had been an important supply point for the Union forces in the war but was not a friendly place for the soldiers stationed there. They had aptly called it "Hell in Arkansas" due to the boredom, disease, and hostile Confederate activity. There was even a battle fought there, but the Confederates under Generals Holmes and Sterling Price were soundly defeated. Memphis was now just seventy miles upstream.

I was quite overjoyed at seeing Memphis come into view. Although we were still 440 miles from home, there was ample coal, mechanics, dry goods, and a telegraph here. My plan was to get enough coal to finish the journey, or at least get us to Cairo, just 252 miles upstream. I would also get a telegraph off to Thomas Geldstein. Mr. Weatherby could use the rest of the day and the evening to clean his boilers and lubricate his machinery.

Captain Bemis and Mr. Voight were successful in procuring coal. Once again, the immigrant men greatly assisted in loading the boat and barge. From the boat, we witnessed several fights between gangs of white men and the Negroes. The Negroes never had a chance as the white men used rocks and sticks as weapons while the black men had only their fists. Armed men, presumably the law in these parts, quickly appeared and finished the job. Those Negroes that could not escape were rounded up, beaten some more, and carted off to jail. I was ashamed that the Russians witnessed this. As an oppressed people, they stood in cold silence and horror at the spectacle.

Supper was a dish called *pirozhki*, which turned out to be small stuffed pies filled with meat and potatoes. I was told these things could be filled with any ingredients imaginable, but the Russian women aboard used what was on hand. Again I marveled at how these delicate pastries were made in vast quantities for so many people.

Swanson and Olsson had the early morning watch, and the boat pulled from the landing with ease. We steamed to the coal yard where the barge was waiting, and it was quickly secured and brought under tow. The steamer *Bart Able* briefly got in the way and nearly caused a collision. Her pilot, Pink Varble, cursed at us roundly but pulled his boat into the channel and out of our way. "Pinky" is a good pilot, one of the best in the business, but he is a short man and carried almost three hundred pounds. His diatribe was rendered comical by his appearance, and we all got a good laugh. That made him even madder. The Russians too chortled and guffawed at the sight.

A few hours later, the boat approached Craighead Point, about thirty miles upriver from Memphis. Here the river turns east against the foot of the First Chickasaw Bluff. Atop the bluff, the Confederates built Fort Pillow and stocked it with some forty heavy guns. The fort was captured by the Union early in the war, though without a battle. In the spring of '64, that devil Nathan Bedford Forrest attacked it and ended up massacring the garrison. Most of the black soldiers there were simply murdered. It was absolutely disgraceful.

We reached Columbus in the early evening when I ordered the boat to land. Being here, there was no need to land at the busy port of Cairo just upstream, and it was too dark to push on to Hamburg Landing. Columbus was heavily fortified by the Confederates early in the war to block the Union navy from descending the Mississippi

River. The battle at Belmont was fought just across the river by General Grant himself. The Rebs abandoned Fort DeRussey without a shot when they lost Fort Henry on the Tennessee River and Fort Donelson on the Cumberland. Those losses left the position here flanked, and the Rebs had no chance to hold it. The Union garrison was now gone, but the abandoned fort still frowned down upon the river.

Once the boat was tied up, I told Ms. Oblonsky to announce to her Russians we would reach Hamburg Landing by tomorrow night. The outbreak of whooping and stomping was immense. The music began, and the men passed around a clear liquor they called *vodka*. I did not understand their words, but their numerous toasts were followed by either "Za Dorovie!" "Davay!" and "Poekhali!" After each toast, the men downed their glasses. The women too, for that matter. The liquor had no taste and went down the throat like fire. I can hold my liquor, but the effect of this kerosene went right to my head. After two respectable glasses of the perilous fluid it, I had to decline any more. I still had a boat to run. Mr. Voight produced a bottle of whiskey that was sampled but resulted in a sour expression from the Russians. They appreciated the gesture, but the St. Louis bark juice was as foreign to them as the *vodka* was to us. The music and revelry went on into the wee hours. Only with the help of that vodka was I able to get to sleep.

I felt the excitement of the Russians the next morning as I awoke. There was a general clamoring about on the decks below as they moved the cargo back into place and swept and cleaned the boat yet again. Breakfast was bought up to the pilothouse and consisted of a heaping plate of *pirozhki* for each of us. This time, it was filled with fruit preserves. The Russian women must have been up the whole night cooking these up.

We passed by the down bound *Ingomar* a few miles upstream of Columbus. She had gotten an early start or had steamed on through the night. She was a moderate-sized boat and received her engines from the retired *Aurilla Wood*. It is a common practice to reuse engines and place them in new boats as they took far longer to wear out than the wood hulls. The *Ingomar* is a familiar sight in St. Louis and ably mastered by Captain P. E. Burke. Our signal received a friendly reply.

Three miles above Cairo, we took note of the wreck of the steamer *Blackhawk*. My old gunboat served alongside her when she was flagship of the fleet that ascended the White River and attacked Fort Hindman. We saw her again during the Red River campaign. Back in April, the *Blackhawk* accidentally burned and sank here. They say her hull and machinery are still, intact and there were plans to raise her. It's too bad. She was a fine boat.

The land around Hamburg Landing is generally flat and prone to flooding, but the rolling hills to the east promised good land for farming. The town of Anna lay ten miles in that direction and was the destination of the Russia immigrants sponsored by John Turchin. I remembered him now from the newspapers as a sort of a cad and fortune-seeking bounder. Hopefully, his plans were in earnest with these people. There were four large freight wagons at the landing waiting on the throng to take them to their promised land. There certainly was not enough room for all of them, so presumably the wagons were for their belongings. I doubted these hardy people would think much about walking the ten miles to Anna. It wasn't even raining.

Swanson pealed the whistle and rang the main bell with aplomb, and when our "Hip, hip, hooray!" reverberated over the fields, the Russians erupted in cheers.

The immigrants had shed their earth-colored garb for their festive native dress. The women in particular now wore bright fabric resplendent in a cascade of colors. The men too looked quite dashing in their finery. Bemis was on the forecastle receiving the thanks, kisses, and hugs from the adoring Russians. The longest goodbye was reserved for Ms. Oblonsky. There was no delay in their departure, and no one could blame them. The immigrants had spent weeks or even months in the travels from their old country to their new country. I wondered if my father's voyage so long ago was so jubilant.

BOOK 3

Hostile Intentions

"Captain, we need to push off now if we are to reach Ste. Genevieve this evening. We don't want to tangle with those sandbars in the dark."

"Very well, Mr. Swanson. Back us out and take us upriver."

We spent the night at Ste. Genevieve alongside the steamer *Illinois*. She was on her way up the Ohio and Tennessee Rivers. We had but sixty-nine miles to go. With a good start, we would be home in the afternoon. I was tempted to go ashore with some of the other officers, but instead contented myself with a bottle of good St. Louis bourbon and a cigar. It was too windy and cool to sit comfortably on the hurricane deck, so I retired to my cabin. The sounds of revelry from the town came through the closed widows. Quite a raucous crowd for a town of just twelve hundred souls. The boat, on the other hand, was quiet. So very quiet after our throng of immigrants departed.

There was a light knock at the door. I called for the intruder of my solitude to enter, and Bemis hobbled in. I don't think he noticed my hand had been on the handle of the Paterson. Beckoned inside by me he made his way to the bed at sat on its edge. It was easier for him to sit there and no doubt more comfortable than these hard table chairs. My cap was already off, and I did not put back on. He dropped his on the bed once his crutches were laid out across the mattress.

"Barring any calamity, it looks like we will be in St. Louis tomorrow, Captain."

"That is true, but despite my efforts, we didn't set any speed records. It was hardly a respectable run even with all the preparations and expense."

"Can you imagine what those keelboat men had to contend with before the steam engine? That same trip would have taken months. We are surely in a modern age."

"I'm not so sure I like this new era, Bemis. It appears to me we have lost a certain measure of our innocence. Honor between men seems lacking. Raw greed and the quest for power seems to rule the day. Look at how despicably we are treating the Negroes now. Worse than when they were slaves."

"It is the story of mankind since his ousting from the Garden. You just might be more aware of it now in your position as captain. You used to be quite detached from the world up in that birdcage of a pilothouse."

"How do you cope with this world, Bemis? You have been wheeling and dealing with these people all your life. You certainly like your profits, but to your credit, you don't seem to crave power."

"Oh, I like to make a hefty sum, all right. But I see the whole enterprise of life as a game. The money is nice, but I really enjoy sticking it to the men who think they own the place. Especially when they don't own a piece of it at all."

"Like how? You mean Thomas Geldstein?"

"No, Thomas owns his company fair and square. I will let you in on little secret. I can't be prosecuted now anyway. Remember that time in Galena we were accused of aiding an escaped slave?"

"Indeed. The constable almost brought up Captain Sulloway up on charges."

"Sulloway had nothing to do with it, although he had his suspicions. That night, I let lose twenty slaves onto the good people of Galena."

"The devil you say!"

"At one hundred dollars a head, it was quite worthwhile. Fun too. Can you imagine the look of an owner's face when he discovers his stock has up and gone? Hilarious!"

"How long had you been running slaves?"

"Just about eight years before the war ended the vile institution. I have almost five hundred Negroes to my credit. I wish the war went on for just a little bit longer so I could have the rounded number. Just joshing, of course."

"No wonder you were so popular with the contrabands on the gunboat."

"Yep. I got some out every time we put into port while on patrol. Some were kinfolk to the Negro crewmen. I had to take extra care with Captain Owens, though. He was always poking about like all naval officers do. No need to worry about you, though. You were always quite serene up in the pilothouse. Though I didn't think you would have made a fuss even if you did find out."

"Bemis, you are a good man. You just want people to think you are a scoundrel. Let me pour you a drink. Have a cigar too."

We never got around to speaking of Ms. Oblonsky. It was probably for the best.

The voyage up the Mississippi to St. Louis was routine. There were boats ahead of us and behind, and a good dozen or more passed by from upstream. The waypoints Penitentiary Point, Calico Island, and Bridgewater Island slowly passed astern in succession. I had told Mr. Weatherby to return to our normal 150 pounds of pressure and was regretting it. With the twenty-two tons of humanity and baggage unloaded at Hamburg Landing, the boat was steaming faster, but the empty barge still held her back some. But my anxiety was rising with each passing mile. I was just about to give in and order more steam when Widow's Beard Island came into view. With but twenty miles to St. Louis, the whole exercise was rendered moot. There was no need to burn the extra coal.

On the final approach to the landing, Swanson instructed the cub to make a sharp turn to port. Perturbed, I was drawing in a breath to speak harshly when I caught sight of the towboat *Dan Hine* overtaking us from the starboard. She was out of Savanna pushing a brace of barges filled with coal. She should have cut in behind us, at least that was the polite thing to do. Good manners were often lacking on the rivers.

"Captain, the dockmaster is waving his green flag at us. He's directing us to land four spaces below our usual haunts."

This was unusual but was only an irritant. I spotted the probable cause. The *Kaw Nation* was here. We would come to at a spot some distance from her. I also spotted the friendly steamer *City of Alton*. She was present with us during Grant's campaign against Vicksburg. My goodness that was over two years ago. She now ran between St. Louis and Memphis under the command of John Brunner.

"Very well, Mr. Swanson. Once secured, I will tell Mr. Voight to have the men detach the barge we are towing and secure it. You have the boat."

The landing was uneventful, and somehow our arrival was expected by the customs agents. They had a nice new customs house on the corner of Third and Olive streets. Too bad they did not remain there. With our load of foreign goods picked up in New Orleans, they were checking if the duties were collected. They would probably add a few fees more to line their pockets. Fortunately, that was between them and the receivers.

On my way to the company office, I swore I felt an uneasiness and tension in the air. Looking about, I saw no signs of trouble and dismissed it. I had been running on coffee and Necco wafers today, and it was probably nothing. My anxiety was probably more to carrying the three explosive devices we found in the bunkers in an old flour sack.

The first sign that something was truly amiss was the old doorman was gone. He was an escaped slave whom the Geldsteins offered sanctuary and employment. The Geldstein family claimed for years it bought him fair and square, and when no one claimed him after a decade or more, they announced his freedom. The man on duty now was a large young Negro armed with a large cane. It was decorative and went well with the burgundy waist oat and black topper hat. But in his hands, it could be a deadly weapon.

"Welcome home, Captain. Mr. Geldstein is expecting you. Please wait in the parlor, sir."

This man was speaking the white man's English. I liked the sound of it more than the butchered English of the slaves. It showed the world that he was a free man.

"Thank you. Where is my old friend that is usually at the door?"

"Some white trash beat him badly for no reason. He just killed him and ran off."

This was sad news indeed, and it troubled me so. I remembered our first meeting. He had told me to go right instead of left. I was a good-natured jab at the white man that I still chuckle about on occasion, but not today. I was ashamed to admit that I did not even know his name.

Once inside the foyer, I turned right and into the company parlor. A clerk was posting a pilot report next to the large map of the Tennessee River and a steward was bringing a bottle to the only patron here at this early hour. In one hand, smoke rose from a massive cigar; in the other was the last swig of brown liquor. The drink was downed in a gulp, and the man poured a new one from the bottle. The steward must have grown weary of serving the him and finally gave in by just leaving the bottle. His large frame, dark-blue officer coat, and respectable beard of white could only belong to Captain Sulloway. He did nothing small, only large. From food to drink, from boats and voyages—it was large. His choice of weapons was large too, and his big Colt dragoon pistol lay on the table pointing toward the door. The only thing that would slow him down before shooting was deciding whether or not to finish the drink first.

I am glad for his eyesight being sharp still. He picked up his new drink and waved to me with his cigar hand. Ashes dropped him onto the table, but he was more concerned about getting any into his drink and moved the glass.

"Ahoy, young man! I see your toting that old Paterson of yours. You really need to consider getting a new Colt or Remington. They at least hold six shots as opposed to the five in that old thing."

"I've had this revolver for four years and never had a real chance to fire it besides long-range plinking. Never hit a thing but came close. Can't see spending good money on something I so seldom use. Besides, you've carrying that big-horse pistol for more than twenty years."

"You're the poorest rich man I ever met. And this Colt dragoon has been handy more than a few times over the years. Pull up a chair and join me."

Captain Sulloway refreshed his glass of whiskey and poured two fingers worth for me. He then offered a cigar, but I had my own. He had grown fond of those large but tasteless Havanas. His taste for liquor has not changed nor the copious amounts he drank of it.

"You know, young man, I'm getting too old for this. The threat of gunplay does get the juices flowing, though and there are times I feel again as a young man in Mexico ready to take on Santa Anna's entire army. But those moments are fleeting. This is just an ugly business. It's difficult to tell who's on what side. Most of the company men just want a job when it is all over. They don't care who runs the place. I'm thinking though that when this is over, I will settle down. Get a house and marry a good woman. Yes, I'm going to find some widow half my age and marry her. The war made a surplus of them, so the pickings should be good."

"Get married? Why you surprise me, sir. I never thought you to get lovestruck again."

"Love? At my age, you settle for mutual tolerance. If she would tolerate me, I suspect love just might pay a visit. How could I not love a woman who would put up with me? Hell. Maybe I could find one that likes a snort on occasion and maybe a cigar on Sundays."

"Would you stay in St. Louis? I would like to pay a call on you occasionally."

"Not likely. St. Louis is getting too big. I want to build a house overlooking a river somewhere. I would spend the days watching the boats go by, drink good whiskey, smoke cigars, and think of good times past."

"You will hear our signal every time we pass by. Depending on which river you choose, you will hear it often and for many years."

A Negro steward entered and announced Mr. Geldstein would see me now. I followed him down the corridor. Two Negro stewards armed with Henry rifles guarded Thomas's door. To the side, his personal clerk sifted through piles of paper in frustration.

"Knock three times and go on in, Captain. Don't wait for a reply."

I did as was told, and the office door was closed behind me. The room smelled stale. An open window or two would refresh it, but they remained closed with curtains drawn. There were stacks of papers and folders on the desk. Normally, Thomas's deck was neat or even clear of papers. The room was darkened, and that did help conceal the enormity of the old burns on his face. His disfigurements were hideous from certain angles, I'm sorry to say, but there was a good man underneath.

"How are things here, Thomas? I've been quite worried for your safety."

"Your telegraphs were quite helpful to us in avoiding any major difficulties. Thank you. Our new charter is expected from Governor Fletcher any day now, and we can begin to reorganize into a full-fledged transportation company."

"What about the bondholders, especially that Mr. Foley fellow with the gold vest?"

"Foley is friends with the governor and contributed to his campaign too. But our proposal has the potential to bring in much money from out of state. As a true politician, Governor Fletcher will follow the money trail to us."

"I take it Foley isn't going away quietly."

"We have thwarted his feeble legal moves, but he has yet to either acquiesce to the plan or surrender his holdings with a buy-out. He should have contributed more to the winning political campaigns. Don't you go taking any advice from him in choosing a horse at the track. He has been reduced to subterfuge, which I believe is behind the nefarious activities lately. You may not have heard, but your colleague Captain Doyle of the *Piankeshaw* was assaulted while ashore in New Orleans. No motive or suspect. I was glad you were not accosted. My guess is that beard you are growing threw them off."

"The devil you say! First his poppet valve was intentionally damaged, and then he was attacked. Meanwhile we found three of these in our coal supply.

I placed the bread bag containing the incendiary devices on the desk. Thomas pulled each out and examined them carefully.

"Pretty crude facsimiles of coal but close enough. A fireman in haste would never notice. Fortunately, no other boats had any such incidents, but they are closely watching for anything."

"Thomas carefully returned the explosive devices into the bag and deposited it into the bottom draw of his desk." He paused for a moment before continuing."

"Your missing man was found a few days back."

"I'm missing three. One leapt from the boat during the boiler incident. Two others were left behind in New Orleans."

"Must be the first fellow. He was found along the riverbank just north of Port Anderson, Mississippi."

"Drowned?"

"No. He was shot in the forehead."

"I guess that shut him up for good. There's no way to pin that on Foley?"

"Not likely. He's been spending his time aboard the *Kaw Nation*. He has the protection of his crew there. The ones in the know will vouch for him. The others will follow their officers. I have asked the chief of police to investigate this, but I don't have much confidence in him. Foley pays him under the table too."

Shouts and gunshots down the corridor interrupted our conversation. The loud *ba-booms* must surely be coming from Captain Sulloway's dragoon pistol.

"Captain, throw the bar across the door!"

I quickly rose from the padded chair and did as told. The men guarding outside clearly had joined in the fusillade. They had gotten off five or six shots from their Henry rifles before their bodies fell back against the door. They were clearly severely wounded as the sounds of their cries and moans seeped under the door. Within moments, a heavy thud sounded that shook the door and frame. Someone was slamming a heavy object against the door attempting to gain entry.

"Follow me, Captain." Thomas's voice was just above a whisper.

I turned and saw that he had opened a bookcase behind his desk exposing a corridor that led into darkness. He was motioning me to enter. I did so as quickly and quietly as I could. In my haste, I slammed my thigh against his desk. I suppressed the pain, cursed my foolishness, and hoped the aggressors outside did not hear. I passed by my parboiled employer and entered the darkened space. Thomas followed me in and pushed me further to gain room for him to enter and shut the bookcase. With that done, he placed an iron bar across the hooks and secured the entryway from this side. With a match, he lit a candle lantern and withdrew a respectable revolver. In the light, it looked like a Remington.

"Follow me and stay quiet."

The corridor led a good twenty feet and opened into an opulent lounge, complete with a liquor bar along one wall, padded chairs, and a fireplace. The light from the candle lantern showed that we had entered through another bookcase. There were no other doors in the room, but there were other bookcases. We could still hear the pounding against the office door and the occasional gunshot somewhere in the distance.

"Hold the lantern and remain here."

With that done, Thomas edged to a wall and slowly slid open a slat. He peered through and smiled at whatever was on the other side of the wall.

"Would you like to get some good use from that Paterson? Come over here and shoot those men in the head. Do it quickly."

It was the oddest thing ever asked of me. Without too much thought, I withdrew my revolver and walked over to the slit. Thomas took the lantern from me. Was this some test of loyalty?

"Go on. Be quick. They are almost through the office door."

I peered through the slit and saw two men with a marble planter stand using it as a battering ram. They were maybe ten feet away. The two negro guards looked dead at their feet. I pushed the long barrel of the Paterson through the slit and took aim at the furthest man. The one closer had his back turned to me and would not see where the shot came from.

The Paterson fired and produced little recoil. The projectile found its mark on the cheekbone, and the man slumped, dropping his half of the planter stand. Perplexed, his associate frantically looked about to see where the round was fired. He let go of the planter and spun around, fanning the hammer of his revolver to empty it quickly. His astonishment of looking down the barrel of the Paterson was ended with the pull of the trigger. This round landed higher, right in the forehead.

Thomas pulled me back, looked out briefly, and shut the visor.

"All right. We'll stay put for a while and see what develops."

We waited a good five minutes, but it felt like hours. Thomas was about to pour us a drink when we heard the voice of Captain Sulloway call for us.

"Let us return to my office. Take the lantern."

We retraced our steps and closed the bookcase. I was directed to unbar the door and did so. Outside we found Captain Sulloway and a handful of men. The big man had thrust a captured pistol under his waistbelt and retrieved a Henry rifle from one of the dead stewards. His big Colt was holstered and presumably empty. It still smoked from the discharge of powder.

"Are you two unharmed?"

"Indeed, Captain Sulloway. What were our losses?"

"The guard outside, these two here, and two others in the corridor. Your clerk there got under his desk and is shaken but otherwise unharmed. The bodies of eight scoundrels are littered about. I can't account for how many were outside and skedaddled. They all look and smell like Irish boaters. Most of their effort was aimed at the strong room where we keep the cash. Fortunately, the clerks there all got inside and closed the iron door. Only these two came in this direction. How were they shot? They were already down when we got here."

"Thanks go to our good captain here with his trusty Paterson revolver. The weapon was good enough against the Comanches at Bandera Pass, and it was good enough for these rogues. Did any make it upstairs?"

"No, sir, as far as we can tell. Uh, young man, are you sure you are unharmed? Take a gander at your cap."

"Oh, that damage was done some time ago…"

I took off my cap and examined it. It had a new set of holes punched clean through. One of those errant rounds must have come through the slit I was firing from. How it did not empty my skull is a holy miracle. I then looked at the wall we fired from behind. The hidden slit was underneath the clock and the lines blended with the patterns in the paneling. There were two nearby bullet marks but no holes. The wall must have an iron plate backing. That was fine by me as either of those bullets would have struck me down.

Mr. Geldstein had more to say. "Captain Sulloway. Have the men reload their firearms and take a guarding position. The devils may be back. Send a messenger to the police station. Tell them what has happened and that I demand police protection. My hope is that the gunfire has summoned them already, but we can't count on that."

"Mr. Geldstein, I am going to check on my boat."

"Go forth, but be careful, Captain. You only have three shots remaining in that Paterson."

"Actually, only two. I carry it on an empty chamber."

Captain Sulloway chortled. "That's a bad habit, son. Always have a fully loaded revolver when you go into the lions' den."

A crowd had gathered outside the office building with gawkers peering in the doors and windows. Two Negro stewards stood in the entryway barring admittance. Each held a Henry rifle. I squeezed between them and walked briskly to the waterfront. Police officers were just arriving as I made my way around the corner. Commercial activity at this end of the waterfront was halted, with roustabouts, boatmen, and shipping agents milling about and wondering what had happened. I avoided the clumps of spectators and made my way up to the forecastle. My fist mate, Mr. Voight, was here with two men armed with Sharps rifles.

"Captain, we heard of the attack on the company office. Are you uninjured?"

"Besides being in an unsociable mood, I am fine. What is the situation here?"

"Two guards are posted here on the forecastle, and there is also one to port and another to starboard up on the boiler deck. No one has approached the boat."

"Keep guards posted until we depart. That may be tomorrow or the next day. Mr. Geldstein knows much of the crew had pinched out on us due to the boiler mishap. He will send men over. I will be in my cabin for a while if needed. Are you armed?"

"Not really, Captain. I possess a small Allen pepperbox. It is in my cabin and not even loaded."

"Come up to my cabin. I have one for you to use."

We went to the cabin on the hurricane deck, and I retrieved the Savage revolver from a trunk. It was still loaded from the incident with Ann.

"Have you ever used one of these before?"

"I am familiar with revolvers, Captain, but this one is unusual."

"You can't pull the hammer back with your thumb. Use the ringed lever under the trigger with your middle finger and then pull the trigger like any other. It's awkward, but it works. Here is the flap holster, but I would recommend just sticking it through a waistbelt."

"Yes, sir. Thank you for the loan."

"Mr. Voight, I believe that scoundrel Foley from the *Kaw Nation* is behind all this. He is upset with the company reorganization and the lowering of dividends. Mr. Geldstein didn't want to cut the men's pay to pay the fat cats. You can tell the men if shooting starts, they are defending their jobs and wages."

"Yes, Captain. I will tell them. Just who is this Foley fellow?"

"From what I understand, he is a major bondholder of the company and some others as well. He also owns an improper house or two. He does no real work and lives off the dividends—you know, profits, from his investments. They support his sybaritic lifestyle. Foley is upset with the planned reorganization, but I suspect there is more to it. As far as I know, Thomas Geldstein has no children or kin to pass the business to. If he dies, the company might be broken up and distributed to the bondholders. Men like Foley could make a great deal of money. In the meantime, he is doing as much damage as he can."

"Why don't we take Foley off the *Kaw Nation* now?"

"I suppose Mr. Geldstein doesn't want a gunfight here on the waterfront. The police aren't being too helpful, and the blame for all this could fall back on our laps if we rush his boat."

"You know, Captain, if they push off into the river, jurisdiction becomes a very cloudy issue."

"It does indeed. Once I'm finished here, I will return to the company office, but I plan to be back and spend the night on the boat. Carry on, Mr. Voight."

Once I cleaned and reloaded the Paterson, all five cylinders this time, the hammer was lowered between two cylinders, and hopefully that would be safe enough. I also put fresh caps on my little Root revolver. I thought to retrieve Ann's derringer from my possibles bag in the pilothouse but could not conceive needing it. Once I locked both trunks, I departed the boat.

The crowds were dispersing, and life was returning to normal on the levee. The occasional gunshot was common on the riverfront, but a protracted battle was not. I found a police detective in the company lounge interviewing the employees about what they saw. I gave my statement but did not mention Mr. Geldstein's secret lair. The detective did not ask how I shot two men without opening the door or shooting through it. I was relieved, but if he was this lax in his questioning, he was incompetent by nature or on purpose. Mr. Geldstein was holed up in his office with Captain Sulloway, and the rattled clerk told me to come by in the morning.

We men on the boat scrounged up some food from the kitchen and, of course, the beer. It was nearly a sleepless night. The bed ropes needed tightening, but I was not going to do that now. In times like this, I wished I had hired a cabin boy. Usually, they were an extravagant waste of good money. I took the precaution to sleep in the other bed in case of an intruder. Pillows under the covers of my usual bed were meant to imitate my form and confuse an attacker. The pillows and sheets of the new bed still smelled of Ann. I wonder how she was faring.

I was surprised to awake at sunrise without the boat on fire, shot up, or sinking. I strapped on the gun belt and donned my frock coat and cap. The cap felt odd, and I then remembered the rough handling it had received yesterday. The riverfront was beginning to stir with the new day, but nothing seemed out of the ordinary. I then made my way to the company office, and the stewards let me pass with my weapons. The clerk announced my presence and allowed me to enter the office of Thomas Geldstein.

"Good morning, Captain. Is all well with the boat?"

"Yes, sir. The guards I posted reported no irregularities."

"Very good. Well, at least we have that good news. On the other hand, there are more troubling developments. We have been informed Captain Bemis is in City Hospital. He was attacked with a knife while at a Chinese teahouse somewhere over on North Tenth Street last night. He is in bad shape but expected to recover barring any complications."

"A Chinese tea shop? I didn't even know there was one in St. Louis. What was he doing there? I know he doesn't care for tea, and he can get coffee anywhere. Who did the deed?"

"There's but one Chinaman in St. Louis, and he goes by the name of Alla Lee. He runs a small opium den in the back of his shop. I've been to Lee's once before. They serve the beverages in bowls if you can believe that. The quirky custom was too much for me. Anyway, I imagine Bemis went there for pain relief from those oriental water pipes. An Irish ruffian did the actual deed. Mr. Lee pointed him out to the police, and he was arrested. All signs point to him just being a typical thug, but he isn't talking much. He is expecting someone to bail him out."

"Why the devil was Bemis attacked? The man is a cripple. Was it for his money?"

"Could be, but the Irishman simply entered the establishment without a word and went right for him. The Chinaman drove him off with some great curved sword from the Orient. I have sent a man to the hospital to learn what Bemis has to say and another to watch over him. I know you are friends, but I need to you to focus on your boat. There is enough water for one more run before the winter season is upon us."

"You want us to leave? Seems like you can use all the men you can get."

"There's more to it than a routine freight run. The *Kaw Nation* is preparing to depart. She is expected to head to St. Paul on her last scheduled run of the season. The police are not much help here and will be useless once Foley is out of their jurisdiction. I want you to follow the *Kaw Nation* and apprehend Foley if you can. Kill him if he resists. Speed is of utmost importance. I hope you can apprehend him within the next eight hours. Once he is under our control back here, you can go on your merry way and ship as much freight as you can afterward."

"My God, Thomas, are you serious?"

"Deadly. Will you do it, or will you not?"

"After what he has done, I will do so with all earnestness, but we need to coal. For that and other expenses along the way, I will need a new chief clerk. Bemis had not named a mud clerk assistant or recommended one yet."

"I have a man ready for you. His work in the past has attained a fine prominence in the profession. He goes by the name of Bosun Joe. He won that moniker from his service in the navy before the war."

"*Bosun Joe?* You want me to give the job of chief clerk to a man that goes by 'Bosun Joe'? What is his real name?"

"His given name is Jeff Davis."

"Never heard of him by either name. Any relation to Jefferson Davis?"

"None that he would admit to now. He fought in the Missouri Brigade during the war but was formerly a shipping clerk with the company."

"Uh, the Missouri Brigade? Who was his commander?"

"I don't recollect, but he has sworn his oath of allegiance. It is duly recorded in the records office. He has it on his person if you wish to examine it."

"Oath of allegiance? He was in Confederate service? Oh, that's just dandy shines. An ex-Reb as a chief clerk and sporting a cockamamie nickname to boot."

"Give him a chance, Captain. He won't disappoint. He has been quite useful since his return. Very recently, in fact."

"He needs to be good. I have relied upon Bemis greatly in the past. We can't afford to lose money on account of an incompetent or disloyal chief clerk. In any case, I will need him to report to the accounting office to go over the books and sign for the accounts. He will need a company frock coat and cap too."

"Already being done."

"I take it this was a done deal from the start. I have no say in this matter?"

"Not this time, Captain. See if you can get away from St. Louis today or at first light. The water won't be rising any until the floods next February if the almanac is accurate. All it will do in the meantime is drop."

"I understand the situation, I think. Getting a crew may be a problem, though. After than boiler mishap, some of the boys are giving up the river for good."

"I will send some men over to fill any gaps. They may already be on the way. Reliable ones too. Examine your coal supply as well. I don't want your firemen to toss in any infernal devices and blow your boilers."

"Aye, aye, Mr. Geldstein. I will go to the boat and make all preparations."

"Oh, a word of advice. In the event of gunplay, remember that Foley is a southpaw. He shoots with his left hand."

I returned to the boat quickly and found my boat officers waiting for me. I saw provisions being loaded and would not ask about them for now.

"What's this all about, Captain? We received a summons from the company to report to the boat without delay. I'm fine with that, but it upset the wife, being so highly unusual."

I wanted to tell them then and there what was afoot, but there was no time for that now. The question was ignored.

"Gentlemen, when you think we have enough men to operate the boat, we will build up steam and depart. Mr. Weatherby, how much coal do we have aboard?"

"Not much. After building up pressure, we can go for three hours, maybe four."

"Very well. We will make for Alton and take on coal there. We will thus avoid the congestion at the yards here in St. Louis. Once coaled, we will head north toward St. Paul. I will want an officers meeting at noon. I want then to address the men at one o'clock. As you can see, many of them are new, and I want to discuss our trip."

"Captain, aren't we taking on cargo here first? We're leaving with an empty hull. And as you know, departing on a Friday is considered bad luck."

"Those are our orders, Mr. Voight, and luck is made when preparations meet opportunity. There is just enough water left in the season to reach St. Paul. All profits will be made along the way and back. Get all preparations done without delay. We push off as soon as possible. That will be all. Let's get to work."

With the events of yesterday, the officers set about their duties with alacrity and without further questions. Surely, they could tell I was in no mood for any delay or hesitation. Swanson silently tugged the cub pilot's sleeve and went topside.

In Pursuit of the Kaw Nation

T he excitement of yesterday and the lack of good sleep was catching up with me. I went to the pilothouse to lie on the bench. The engineer-ready whistle pealed from down below, and Olsson backed the boat out onto the river. His technique was much improved.

The town of Alton, Illinois, contained the souls of some six thousand people and was located near the confluence of the Mississippi, Illinois, and the Missouri Rivers. In its early days, it had the potential to be an even greater city than St. Louis but was undercut by my home port and the town of Grafton. The bank here rises steeply from the river, and the landing is perfect for shipping the area's grains and produce. There is one large grain silo here with more planned for the future. The despised railroad is here too. The Chicago and Mississippi Railroad runs to Springfield, Bloomington, and Joliet, linking up with the Chicago and Rock Island Railroad to Chicago. Anyone getting on a train here can be in New York in three days or less. The coal yard here supplies both trains and boats as do more and more river towns nowadays. I wished the Russian immigrants were here to help with the coal and get us on our way soonest.

Swanson landed the boat smartly, and Mr. Voight's men secured it quickly. Ready with his billfold on the forecastle was Bosun Joe. It was important for a captain to work in concert with his chief clerk, but his background was not inspiring. That he was thrust upon me caused resentment, and the filling of Bemis's shoes (or shoe, in this case) did not seem possible. This was our first meeting.

He was a pudgy man of below-medium height dressed in brown workman's clothes that looked new. They must have been recent replacements for a butternut uniform, but the red corduroy trousers were smudged by coal dust already. A gentleman would have brushed them before reporting for work. A battered tin coffee dipper hung from a hook on a waistbelt. Probably a relic of the war. The dark-blue company frock coat and cap looked quite out of character, being too formal for this man. Like applying lip rouge to a pig. Upon seeing me, he took off his new cap and held it in two hands as if he were a slave speaking with his master. His head was as smooth as a billiard ball and highlighted a face of elfin intensity. I was surprised to see a scalp of such magnificent barrenness as he could not have been thirty years old.

"Ah, you noticed. Well, the men of my family skin out early. Pleased to meet you, *Skipper*. I'm afraid we will be severely taken advantage by the coal yard here. We could have acquired coal across the river in St. Louis at a far better price. The journeymen act as though they are still asleep."

This Bosun Joe's tone was that of a rather jovial fellow. In normal times, I would find it refreshing, but these were not normal times.

"Glad to make your acquaintance and welcome aboard, but never again call me *skipper*. Never could abide that term, even when in endearment."

"Uh, aye, Captain."

I called out to the roustabouts. "All you men there! There will be a two-dollar bonus to each of you if this boat is loaded within the hour! A bottle of whiskey to the man who totes the most!"

That had the desired effect. There was no more lollygagging, and the Illinoisans almost put the Russian immigrants of our previous voyage to shame. Almost.

The whirling dervish of activity soon filled the bunkers with good bituminous and then the main deck, for which we paid an exorbitant price. The men loaded all the bagged fuel on the main deck, but once underway, I told Mr. Voight to have the men stack some on the forecastle and some forward on the boiler and hurricane decks. The object was to make parapets from which the men could take up covered positions. The bow ran low upon completion of the that task, so other bags were shifted aft to obtain a level keel.

The officers assembled in the pilothouse at noon. I wanted Swanson to hear too and could not legally trust the cub pilot in these waters alone at the wheel. Also, with Negroes now aboard, the cabin with the great table reverted to their use. I noticed Swanson's gun belt hanging on a hook over the chart table. Toting around three pounds of gun iron does get tiresome.

I told the officers of our mission to overtake the *Kaw Nation* and bring the villain Foley to justice one way or the other.

"Captain, I don't feel easy with all these armed Negroes on board. There must be twenty of them, and at least ten have them Henry repeating rifles."

"Are they following your orders?"

"I suppose so, but with no cargo aboard, that hasn't been put to the test. We haven't had Negroes on board all season, and well, it takes some getting used to."

"Get used to it, Mr. Voight. The rest of you too. Issue out the ten Sharps rifles we have on board to any man not working the machinery. Instruct the men in their use."

"Do you expect gunplay, Captain?"

"Let us hope our armed party is enough to persuade Foley to come to and be taken into custody. Remember that this man attempted to explode our boilers. One of his men disabled the *Piankeshaw*, and most likely he sent others to attack Captains Doyle and Bemis. Foley's men stormed the company office and killed some good men. Damn near got me too. If he resists, we will take him by force, but take him we will. Is that understood?"

With all the dots connected, I could see their hesitation melt away. All but Mr. Olsson. He was squeamish about killing to the point I wondered how he stomached eating meat. But for the officers, this was no longer some great mystery. It was the pursuit of justice, maybe even a little retribution.

"Mr. Weatherby, we will make best speed. Put the pressure to 180, and if she holds, increase gradually to two hundred. Back off at the first sign of trouble."

"Uh, aye, Captain. Two hundred pounds it will be if the feeder pump keeps up. We've never gone that high while underway."

The assembled men looked about each other with worried looks. I was worried too, but the hydrostatic test in New Orleans proved the boat could take it, at least in theory. The first sign of trouble was usually an explosion though.

"I wish I knew how much coal the *Kaw Nation* was carrying. That would be helpful in calculating if we could catch her before the rapids at Rock Island."

"She has only enough to make it to Hannibal, Captain. The firemen will reach the bottom of their bunkers in eight hours or less."

"How, pray tell, do you know that, Bosun Joe?"

"I was aboard her yesterday."

"What? Explain yourself."

"I went over to collect my things. It was planned that I would be their new mud clerk. I had just reported yesterday. I was hired by Mr. Geldstein himself. When your man Bemis was incapacitated, he sent for me. I am grateful for the opportunity, Captain."

"What can you tell me of that boat? Who is in command? Who are her pilots?"

"Last heard, Mr. Foley himself would captain, although it is clear he is no riverman. I was introduced to the some of the officers, but I'm embarrassed to say I don't recall their names. They were in quite a hurry to depart and had only part of their cargo aboard. The chief clerk was mighty upset about that as the shippers would not be pleased at all. Sorry I can't be more helpful, but I was only aboard for a few hours."

Later the crew was assembled between the boilers and engines so I could speak to all at once without the engineer crew leaving their posts. I repeated what I had told the officers and promised a five-dollar bonus for every man on this run. My speech was not worthy of Daniel Webster, but it had the desired effect.

As we traveled upriver, farmers at the landings along the way hailed us by waving kerchiefs. They called to us to pick up their sack piles. We used the voice trumpet to say we were unable to upbound but would stop on the way down. We would be going the opposite direction, but at least their grain would reach market somewhere. I felt awful about it and added that to the list of grievances against "Gold Vest" Foley. He would have stopped at all these points already if he was doing his job.

I remained in the pilothouse and scrutinized every steamboat along the river with the spyglass. I also examined every river, branch, stream, and slough a boat could go up and hide. We had pulled that trick to escape old Nathan Bedford Forrest ourselves when he attacked the Union depot at Johnsonville. No one was going to pull that stunt on me.

Two boats were a few miles up, but they were too far away to identify. Either one could be our quarry. I recalled the reading a book years ago about the exploits of Admiral Horatio Nelson. In the sailing days, warships would go for hours or days trying to outsail their opponents before firing their cannon. I thought too about my time in the war on the gunboat, and a queasiness nearly overtook me. I saw too much death and destruction, and it was all coming back too fast. My boiled left hand was throbbing. I absentmindedly rubbed it. With little so sensing remaining, it felt like my right hand was handling a piece of cold meat.

"Are you all right, Captain?"

"Yes, but I don't think our cook's fare is sitting well with me. I will be fine in a moment."

A few hours later, I could ascertain the identity of the nearest boat. My heart lifted and stomach sank, realizing it was the *Kaw Nation*. She was steaming serenely as if she had not a care in the world. I rang the arranged signal from the main bell, and I could hear the men below spring into action. For another moment, I was back somewhere on the Tennessee River.

"Gentlemen, up ahead is the *Kaw Nation*. Let's go get her."

"Captain, if they start shooting, we are going to be mighty exposed up here. This glass and these boards won't stop a bullet. They will be concentrating their fire here first to disable the boat. Maybe we should get some coal sacks stacked up against the pilothouse here."

"If they shoot get low under the glass. You will be fine, Mr. Swanson."

"How so, Captain?"

"This boat was built for war service. There is half-inch iron plate built into the walls of this here pilothouse."

"Well, I'll be. Pull up some chairs next to the wheel, Mr. Olsson. We can duck in comfort."

It was clear we were gaining on our quarry and should be soon within shooting distance of the long-range Sharps rifles. The Henrys fired fast but not far with their puny .44 caliber rimfire rounds. The men were not to fire though until I pealed the whistle three times. To give the *Kaw Nation* the chance to come to, I gave a long blast from the main whistle. It was about to get dark, and I wanted this over before having to come ashore for the night. Foley could then escape into a town or into the darkness beyond a landing. The men in the pilothouse up yonder spun about in surprise at our whistle and pulled the bell ropes. We could not hear the signal from here, but my hopes of a quick and peaceful conclusion to our chase were dashed.

"Captain, heavy black smoke is coming from her stacks. She's putting on steam. They must have dumped a whole barrel of resin on their fires."

"We are already running at our absolute top speed. If she pulls away, we may be in trouble."

The *Kaw Nation* quickly matched our speed and began to pull away slowly. Relief came upon us when discovering she was not so fleet as to lose us. At this rate, she would remain in view for some time. If Bosun Joe was correct, she would be soon scraping the bottom of her coal bunkers any time now.

"Steady as she goes, Mr. Swanson."

I had just lit a cigar to pass the time when a mighty explosion tore through the *Kaw Nation*. She had blown her boilers. Two of the massive cylinders tore up through her upper decks carrying away her pilothouse and spraying a forest of lumber upon the water. Her remaining boiler fires communicated with the woodwork, igniting what was left of her. Men—living, injured, and dead—bobbed in the water. Their cries, moans, and screams were carried across the water.

"Swanson! Signal our engineer to slow. Take up a position to bring aboard those men. Swing wide to avoid that burning hulk. I'm going to the forecastle."

"Aye, Captain!"

I passed through the boiler deck and saw the men at the rails standing in dumb silence. There was no cheering. Just a state of bewilderment and shock. We had all witnessed firsthand the nightmare of all rivermen.

"You men here! Go below and be ready to rescue the survivors. Place your weapons here in a pile, and you there, guard them."

The Negro with the Henry rifle nervously nodded.

I found Mr. Voight on the forecastle getting the men ready with ropes at the rails to assist. He had already sent men aft to launch the skiff into the water. I only had to tell him to collect up the arms and get them secured. Two remained at arms lest a crewman from the *Kaw Nation* got any ideas.

The men worked frantically to fish out as many men from the river as possible. There appeared to be no women, children, or other passengers, thank God. The fire roaring from the burning hulk lit the scene and helped in the endeavor. The current was strong enough though that our men first had to concentrate snatching up those showing signs of life first. Those unable to move or call out drifted downstream.

The mangled men of the *Kaw Nation* were laid out on the main deck and made as comfortable as possible. Of the fifteen we fished out, only a handful would probably survive. Some were vomiting blood, and some were suffering sudden and uncontrollable bloody diarrhea. These men had severe trauma to their innards. Others were coughing up blood, a sure sign of damage to the lungs.

Meanwhile, the *Kaw Nation* snagged against the shore. There she would burn to her waterline.

There was no sign of that Foley scoundrel. If he was in the pilothouse, he was launched into eternity and as good as dead. If he was in the river, he was already swept downstream, and his chances were only slightly better, unless a fabled *Klabautermann* saved him. I felt a measure of remorse. Before the war, I had served on the *Kaw Nation* for two years as a relief pilot. It was not a happy time, but it was not the boat's fault. She was stout and dependable. Her demise was not deserved. If any of those men on the boat were innocent of crimes their misfortune was not deserved either.

My new chief clerk caught my attention.

He had taken off his frock coat during the exertions of the rescue. His shirtsleeves were heavily soiled past his elbows.

"How did you get so much coal dust on you?"

"Oh, yesterday I was helping the boys on the *Kaw Nation* move some coal about, Captain."

"That's unusual for a clerk, isn't it?"

"Oh, we clerks are called on special missions on occasion. We're quite handy at all sorts of things."

Once we gathered what survivors we could, I ordered the boat to proceed to Hannibal at best speed. We would have set a company record for this trip had we not stopped to pluck up the men. From the survivors, we learned that Foley was apparently on board, but we did not find his body in the fading light. We didn't see too many bodies at all. Maybe half of the men on board were accounted for. While underway again, the crew removed the parapets and brought the coal bags to their usual place on the main deck. Mr. Voight collected all the arms and locked them away. I left my Paterson in my cabin as well as the Savage revolver, which Mr. Voight returned.

Hannibal was now close ahead. A long blast from the whistle aroused the town and alerted those ashore something was amiss. James Morris is still the harbormaster here and is a good chap. He directed the boat to the foot of Hill Street with his green lantern when he heard the signal we had injured aboard. Hill Street is the quickest avenue to the hospital. He had even summoned the vehicles of Smart Brother's Omnibus Line to carry the men there. With the injured men gone, a strange quiet fell over the boat. It was well past midnight when the boat settled in for the night. We set up a fire watch, but otherwise, the men went to sleep with their own thoughts. I did as well, and I had much on my mind.

In the morning, I left the boat to send a telegraph back to St. Louis. I had not even noticed we had landed between the *Belle of La*

Crosse and the *Alex McGregor*. Idle crewmen on those boats queerly stood and stared at our boat. I left without another glance and found the office of the Western Union Telegraph Company right where I remembered it. I entered and wrote this message to the operator. He had come in early, expecting a busy day.

> Came upon KN. Destroyed by boiler mishap. Fifteen men recovered and in hospital. All officers missing. Will await reply and instructions.

I was watching the operator at his task when a man burst into the office. My immediate reaction was to draw my Paterson. I quickly remembered I had left it on the boat. If the dapper man was an assailant, he had the drop on me. My hand went for the little Root revolver, but I foolishly froze. Fortunately, he was not hostile but only excited and out of breath. He introduced himself as a reporter from the *Hannibal Daily Messenger*.

"Captain, would you care to make a statement about the calamity last night?"

"No, not really. It was quite a tragedy. We are all still shocked by it."

"It is rumored that your two boats were racing. Is there any truth to that?"

"No one has said any such thing. You just now made that up. No sane man does it at all and certainly not at night. Moreover, I am well known for not participating in such foolishness. I was only making the best possible speed to reach this port to deliver the injured men."

"Can I have your name for the record?"

I told him my name and asked that all credit for the lives saved go to my men.

"My, that's a Dutchy name by God."

"You cut me to the quick, good sir. It's American. I was born and bred in the heart of the western wilderness. Beardstown, Illinois, to be precise. I expect you to be just as precise in your reporting."

The reporter left not learning much else. Upon the man's exit, the telegraph operator told me the *Hannibal Daily Messenger* was probably going to close any day now. Most people here read the *Daily Quincy Whig and Republican*. With reporters like that, it did not surprise me in the least.

My plan was to give the men time ashore here in Hannibal while I waited for the reply to my wire. My guess was we would be told by St. Louis to finish the *Kaw Nation's* run up to St. Paul. She had left a day early, and we both hightailed it up to this point. This left us a well ahead of her schedule, and we had the time for loafing a little bit. Shippers upstream would not be ready yet, and there was no sense to press on today. Still I wanted to see the reply to my note to the company before departing. Telegraphs are quick, but a messenger would have to take the note to the company office, a reply formed, and brought back to the telegraph office. That could take some hours.

I had been to Hannibal on several occasions, but this was the first time since the beginning of the war. The *T. R. Semel* was still the ferry here, but Captain Davis may have moved on by now. The town looked about the same, nestled on a small plain surrounded on three sides by hills. There were about ten thousand people residing here, mostly of Union persuasion. The Hannibal–St. Joseph Railroad had its eastern terminus here and the trains and boats shared the coal yard. If someone famous ever came from here, I hadn't heard of him yet.

As a river town, Hannibal had its share of saloons and fancy houses, which outnumbered the churches by two to one. Captain Sulloway had once taken me to the Arcade Saloon and Restaurant on the corner of Third and Broadway under the post office. It was too early to partake of any refreshment, and my proper place was on the boat anyway.

I found Bosun Joe at the landing speaking to two men who were introduced as commission merchants. Neither Messrs. Bellard or Stilwell were dressed as men of means, and I was not too impressed. They had heard of the disaster last night and rushed right down. Fortunately for them, they received a telegraph that their cargo due from St. Louis was only left behind and not lost. They were sorry for the loss of the boat but relieved their property was not floating downstream. Fortunately for us, they did have a shipment bound upriver, and my chief clerk was negotiating the terms. A good portion of it was one hundred barrels of beer from the Hannibal City Brewery. A man by the name of Schambucher had come from the old country and set up his brewery on Bay Mill Road just above the ferry landing. I remember it being a good lager.

I ordered the payment of the five-dollar bonus to the men. No doubt most of the men would enjoy themselves immensely while in Hannibal and return with empty pockets. It's in a boatman's blood.

"How many do you think we will lose, Mr. Voight?"

"Three to five as always, Captain. All the Negroes will be back, though."

"Huh. Look there, Mr. Voight. A lawman comes approaching. I wonder what he wants."

We quickly learned the man was James Munson, the chief of police for the city and township of Hannibal. He was in a traditional police uniform but carried no weapon that we could see. He got right to the point as lawmen usually do.

"Good morning, gentlemen. I have come from the hospital. More than one of the men claim their boat was victim to an explosive charge in the coal bunkers."

Mr. Voight and I were certainly surprised by that news and could not help but take that as an accusation.

"I take it, Mr. Munson, that you are warning us to examine our coal supplies for other such devices to prevent such an occurrence on my boat."

"That would be a wise precaution, but those injured men think you all had something to do with it."

"We were a good one hundred yards astern of the *Kaw Nation* when her boilers blew. None of my men could throw even a potato that far with such precision. How could we have done such a deed, and why? That boat belongs to the same company as ours. We had friends on that boat. May I suggest the injured men are in painful delirium or under heavy mediation? Their accusations make no sense."

"No, they do not, but I had to follow through anyway. Boiler explosions happen all the time. You all have a safe journey."

"By the way, Mr. Munson. We fished out everyone we could in the darkness, but others may have been swept downstream. Have you received word of any other survivors?"

"No, not yet. In such cases, passing boats will fish out the bodies as they come across them or report their location for us to retrieve. Newspapers along the river make a big fuss about survivors that show up, though. That will go on for days or weeks until nature takes its course. I suppose you are familiar with all that, Captain."

"Unfortunately, we are, good sir. Good day to you as well."

The Hannibal police chief turned and walked back into town. As with all lawmen, he left us not knowing whether he had shelved the matter or not.

"What the hell was all that about, Captain? Those scoundrels on the *Kaw Nation* pushed their boilers beyond their limits. It was clear to all of us."

"Uh, that is what happened, Mr. Voight. If you have not done so already, let the men ashore by watch. They will tell our side of the tale all about town."

"You don't mind them telling of us trying to run down Foley?"

"That will come out anyway, and no doubt the tale is already being told in St. Louis. I would rather have the truth be told than some dastardly lie we somehow blew up their boilers by an explosive device. People will see clearly that Foley blew himself up, avoiding justice."

"I hope you are correct, Captain."

"As do I."

A boy soon arrived with a telegraph from St. Louis. The handwriting was remarkably bad for a Western Union operator. He must be busy and hurried today.

> Your note received. Sad news. Pay off injured men. Retrieve bell and strongbox if possible. Proceed St. Paul. Geldstein.

The note included a list of the scheduled stops along the way. That would go to my new chief clerk. I showed the note to my first mate.

"I understand about the strongbox, but what's that about the bell?"

"Mr. Geldstein has all the old bells on display in the company parlor, Mr. Voight."

"Huh. Well to each his own, but the force of that explosion probably sent both into the next county."

"I reckon so, but when we depart, we will examine the wreck. We can then report we tried at least. Fortunately, it is but a few miles from here. We won't get too far off the schedule."

Bosun Joe proved successful in securing the freight consigned to the late *Kaw Nation* and a little more. His methods were not the cold and ruthless of Captain Bemis, but they got the job done it seems. His jovial manner was disarming, and the shipping agents signed the contracts with a smile. My worry was ol' Joe there was offering discount rates. I can't think of any other reason the agents would be smiling so.

"Hello, Captain. So far, we have that beer bound to Quincy, lumber from the Hannibal Lumber Company to La Grange, and a shipment of assorted dry goods from the Cohn Brothers to Keokuk. The Eagle Mills is preparing barrels and bags of flour for the town of Fort Madison."

"Those are all short hauls. I was hoping my new chief clerk could land some bigger fish."

"They are short hauls indeed. That is the nature of the packet trade in these parts. All the processed goods go north and south but the heavy commodities like coal, lumber, and iron ore all move south. It will be that way all the way to St. Paul and back to St. Louis. I took the liberty of sending telegraphs to the regular stops the *Kaw Nation* routinely made to let them know we are coming in her stead."

"Good thinking. I see you have cleaned up a bit. No more coal dust."

"Oh, that. Well, as it says in the Bible, cleanliness is next to godliness."

"That's not from the Bible, but it is sage advice. I credit my mother for the origin of the saying. Carry on, Bosun Joe."

Steamboat clerks in this company received fifty dollars a month plus 2 percent on obtaining freight. That was a mite less than on other boats. It was still a respectable sum on good runs and the arrangement insured the clerks worked aggressively. Although he has just started, Bosun Joe appeared to have the makings of a good agent. Maybe I was wrong about him at least about that.

It was nightfall before all the goods were loaded onto the boat. That was quite fortunate as Hannibal shuts down for the Sabbath. Most of the men were sober enough to earn their pay for the day. The others were too drunk to care. Just as Mr. Voight predicted, three deckhands and one oiler were in the city hoosegow on charges of drunk or lewd behavior.

We cast off at first light to survey the wreck of the *Kaw Nation*. We found her just about where we left her, just north of Saverton, Missouri on the Illinois side. Scavengers, mostly teenage boys, were already poking about the burned-out hull but did not appear to have collected anything of value. They, of course, skedaddled when we passed by, spun about, and anchored pointing upstream. Those few that lingered were put to flight with a peal from the whistle and the lowering of the skiff.

I remained in the pilothouse and scanned the scene with Swanson's field glasses. They were suited to the task better than my spyglass. The steep bank lined with trees prevented much vision beyond. Wood planks and even a chair hug from the branches.

Swanson said to no one in particular, "What a filthy job those men have, having to poke around like that."

"Could be worse, sir."

"How so, Mr. Olsson?"

"It could be raining."

There was a moment of jubilation when the company flag was recovered from the broken jack staff. Only bits of the fine elm wheel were found. Those pieces were probably larger than any we would find of the pilot who stood behind it. We heard a whoop, and a crewman emerged from the trees along the bank carrying the bell. There was no sign of the strongbox. It was the consensus that it was somewhere down in the nearly submerged hull or somewhere in the river. The current was too strong and the waters too cold and deep to ask a man to dive and fish around for it. Fortunately for the crew, there were no other bodies found. After a few hours, I recalled the men on the search. A light rain began to fall just as the skiff was hoisted aboard. The boat moved serenely upstream.

The seventeen miles up to Quincy went by quickly. The last time I was here was to pick up Ann from her work in the hospital. There were no journeymen at the landing, being Sunday and all. The deckhands rolled the beer onto the landing and made a neat assemblage of the one hundred barrels. Our clerk affixed a label identifying the new owner. The sleepy Sunday watchman had the responsibility to prevent theft. That was the risk involved with closing the landings on the Sabbath.

We repeated this unloading of freight after steaming up the twelve miles to La Grange. The lumber would patiently wait for its new owner. At least there was less risk of pilferage. Well, maybe.

The boat steamed the additional thirty miles to Keokuk, and Swanson made a nice landing. It is here where the Des Moines River meets the Mississippi. On our approach, we could feel the spill of the Des Moines pushing us toward the east bank of the Mississippi, and the wind added its force. Three islands at the confluence contribute to the hazard. Mr. Swanson did a fine job at the wheel. Our young cub pilot was amazed the boat was for a time pointing in a northwesterly direction but was steaming due north. That is the power of nature, and a steamboat can't fight it. It must adapt to it. It was early evening, and we would wait for the roustabouts to arrive in the morning to unload the goodly supply of dry goods. The rain was coming down a bit heavier, and the freight would have some protection in the boat.

Keokuk is a handsome city with almost ten thousand souls and is most proud of her former mayor, Samuel Ryan Curtis. He had become a general in the war and was most noted for his victory at Pea Ridge in '62 and defeating Sterling Price's invasion of Missouri last year about this time. My guess was he returned here recently for a visit as there was patriotic bunting hanging all about town. Maybe it was all still up for welcoming returning soldiers.

Most of the men stayed on the boat on account of the rain, but mostly because they were out of money and nursing the effects of alcohol from the nights before. That was too bad as Keokuk sported over ten fine saloons, but being a Sunday, they were closed anyway. Pastor Kirchkoff of the German Creek Evangelical Lutheran Church here in town dropped by to ply his trade. Many of the men gathered round on the boiler deck to listen while a handful slinked away to other parts of the boat. The good pastor read from Ephesians the verse proclaiming that by grace are we saved through faith and not by our worldly good deeds. It is the gift of God and not of works, lest any man should boast. I suppose it was something all we sinners needed to hear, especially the miscreants working the main deck. Looking about the men, I could see many of them appreciated this over-the-usual fire and brimstone other clergymen feel inclined to use when speaking to rivermen.

In our haste to depart St. Louis, I had not replenished my sundries. The rain was coming down harder, and I was too lazy to break out the mackintosh raincoat and walk into town. It was near seven o'clock anyway, and most shops were closed for Sunday. I was thus reduced to drinking the coffee served to the crew. It was strong at least. I needed something to do while we awaited the end of the Sabbath.

There were two local newspapers in Keokuk, and the hawkers plied their papers at the landing. Competition was fierce as the lads nearly came to blows. I bought the latest editions of *The Gate City* and *The Constitution* and retired to the pilothouse to read them over a cigar and tankard of coffee. There was news that the Cheyenne and Arapahos signed a peace treaty at the Little Arkansas River out west in the Colorado Territory. It is hoped that in a few weeks, the United States and all the major plains Indian tribes will sign it too. The government wants a general peace and unmolested traffic on the Santa Fe Trail. It also wants the Indians to remain south of the Arkansas and excluded them north to the Platte. There was no map in the newspaper so I could not tell what all that meant.

Conversely, the Indians demanded unrestricted hunting grounds and reparation for Chivington's massacre of Black Kettle's band at a place called Sand Creek. I did not know of the massacre or how bad it was. It might have been during the war and drowned out by the big battles closer to home. To show their good faith, the Indians released several white captives, among them a woman and four children from Texas. Another bit of news was that Connecticut held a vote to legalize black suffrage in the state. Two-thirds of the people voted against it. So much for black political equality. The women may get to vote before the Negroes, and Lord help us if that ever happens.

Swanson had gone ashore attempting to purchase personal provisions at Harris and Brown's Mercantile, leaving his cub pilot aboard. Mr. Olsson probably didn't have the money to spend anyway. In addition to paying for his instruction, the Boatman's Association wanted its cut. I remember well having to count each penny in my early years. He was here in the pilothouse sweeping up and generally just passing the time. There were moments when I thought he was about to ask me something, but he went back to sweeping. I smiled to myself that I must intimidate him as Captain Sulloway did to me when I was a young cub. He still does in a way.

Morning came with dark overcast clouds, the kind that would linger overhead all day. Autumn was certainly in the air, which chilled the joints, making them stiff. By eight o'clock, the men were loading the freight destined for the upstream stops. Andrew Brown and Thomas Heaight were the steamboat agents in town and were bargaining with Bosun Joe on the landing. Our direct competition here was the Keokuk Packet Company, and they had the hometown advantage. None of their boats were here today and presumably steaming under load already.

The roustabouts under the employ of commission merchant Andrew Brown trundled up the various goods produced here. There were barrels of beer from Baehr and Leisy Brothers, salted beef from Billings and Davis, and nails and hardware from the Brownell Brothers. There were also enough barrels of sorghum that would supply a modest town for the coming winter. Some lucky farmer upstream would receive his plow and thresher made by the Hawk Eye Plow Factory. The boat could hold far more than she was carrying, but I reminded myself this was a lead packet run.

We pushed off by eleven o'clock, which was the regularly scheduled departure. Between here and Nauvoo were the dreaded Des

Moines Rapids. To prepare for them, Swanson went below to answer a call of nature, leaving me and the cub pilot alone in the pilothouse. The young man had finally summoned the courage to ask me his question.

"Captain, may I ask you something?"

"Of course, Mr. Olsson. I find great pleasure in passing on any knowledge or wisdom of the rivers."

"Word is going around that you killed some men during the assault on the company office."

I was taken aback as my assumption was that he wanted to ask about the boat or navigation.

"That is a delicate subject. If you want to know if that is true, then yes, it is. I won't lie to you."

"How may did you get?"

"You ask as though I was hunting squirrels. Two is the precise number and don't let anyone tell you it was more. I don't wish to discuss this further. I don't enjoy the practice of killing and do so only out of necessity."

"I ask because the Bible says, 'Thou shall not kill.'"

"A naval chaplain in Mound City gave a sermon on that very subject. The original Hebrew translates to 'You shall not murder.' The commandment not to kill is regarding unlawful killing. Anyway, I don't believe the Good Lord intended we walk about unable to defend ourselves. In this cruel world, there wouldn't be many Christians left. Let me ask you something. Did you serve in the war?"

"No, Captain. I bought my way out."

That answer came out too quick and even smug. He should best keep that news under wraps. If the crew found out, there could be trouble. Men who bought their way out were held in low regard. He certainly dropped a few notches with me. I wonder if Swanson knew.

During the war, a man could pay three hundred dollars to avoid service, which was at least a year's pay for most laborers. Someone figured that it was better to let men buy their way out than force them unwillingly and receive poor service. Olsson seemed to have qualms about killing anyway, so it was probably best he didn't serve. Unfortunately, for the average man with little money, only the well-to-do could afford the three hundred dollars. No wonder many called it a rich man's war and a poor man's fight.

"I'm sorry I asked. Well, let us drop this matter. It has no place in the pilothouse. What is the next mile marker and the coming obstacle upriver?"

"Uh, I don't know, sir."

"That proves my point. Take the wheel for a spell. I will remain until Mr. Swanson's return."

"Aye, Captain."

With Swanson back at the wheel, the rapids and shallows were passed easily. For once they seem well marked, and the water was at its optimum height with a slack downstream velocity. No boats vied for position, and those coming from above stayed on their side of the narrow channel. God be praised. I mean that truly.

This far north, the river bottoms and banks are much rockier, and the river less prone to a change the course of the channel. Yet there were still sandbars, reefs, and such. The wing dikes are a hazard too if you wander out of the channel. With the timber industry in full swing, there seemed far more errant trees in the water called deadheads. Plying upstream was quite dangerous as the trunks sank to the bottom, and the tops remained just below the surface. Such trees formed a spear ready to pierce the hull that were often invisible to sight. They are still a menace going downstream, but often a boat could ride over them. A good pilot would not put it to the test though. For a while, we followed the steamer *Die Vernon*, who would blaze a trail for our boat. Better for them to hit such a snag than us in my book.

Steady as She Goes to St. Paul

The boat continued up the Mississippi, stopping at various land-ings large and small to load and unload cargo. Of interest to me was Muscatine, Iowa, which held the largest black community of the state. It consists largely now of former fugitive slaves and free blacks who had traveled up the Mississippi from the South. It was good to see the town was growing quite well and appeared prosper-ous. We landed briefly, but there was no letting the boilers settle as time was short. As a result, a full head of steam was maintained in the period between landing and pushing off again. These were the moments I feared most as the boilers could easily overheat and explode. Most boiler accidents occurred at these times.

We passed through the rapids above Davenport and Rock Island, and memories of my last visit flashed across my vision, causing a cold sweat. Back then, we had almost been run down by a massive log raft that had broken free of her towboat. We got through that scare with only a battered paddle wheel. That was almost five years ago, but I can still see it clear as if it were yesterday. After that, we used a local pilot when we got between Rock Island and La Crosse. The five-dol-lar fee was worth it, considering the loss of the entire boat and cargo if we strayed out of the ill-marked channel and run up on the rocks. We ran far into the night and beyond what I would normally con-sider safe, but I wanted to make Dunleith to stay on schedule. We could have put into Dubuque across the river, but Dunleith was a small town with less chance for the men to get into trouble ashore. If we continue to lose three to five men at each overnight stop, we wouldn't have anyone left to man the boat by the time we got to St. Paul.

The next morning, the discharge and loading of cargo in Dubuque were problematic as the journeymen there demanded higher than normal wages. The matter was made worse as the clerk on the *Andy Johnson* gave into the demands. Bosun Joe tried to hold the line but ended up paying more than we usually would. Even so, there was not enough of the roustabouts to do the job quickly. The deck crew was called in to assist, and the whites balked at working alongside the Negroes.

Once past Galena, we were on a stretch of the river I had not seen for some years. I swallowed my pride and consulted the charts often. It was a good lesson for young Mr. Olsson. Don't let arrogance jeopardize the boat. I caught Swanson taking a sideways glance at the charts on occasion.

Unfortunately, the men were getting restive. The frequent stops and lack of journeymen at the landings were overworking the deck crew. The engineers had even less rest as they had to clean and service their machinery when it was not in operation. The five-dollar bonus to the men was already paid out and gone. The ready whistle on the main deck pealed the captain's summons after the breakfast meal. It was certainly not the best fare we had eaten, and it shouldn't have surprised me that was the spark that ignited the fuse.

"Steady as she goes, Mr. Swanson. I do believe our next stop is a delivery at Cassville in about twenty miles. Feel free to give Mr. Olsson a chance at the wheel."

"Aye, Captain. We'll hold down the fort."

As I closed the door, I overheard Swanson telling his cub, "See? He trusts you. It just takes a while."

I wouldn't go that far. It is an easy piece of river, and Swanson will be there watching his every move.

I descended to the main deck and found Mr. Voight facing a semicircle of white deckmen. The Negroes were gathered to the side. The engineers aft were looking on as well but couldn't leave their positions. My hope was Mr. Weatherby or someone else was watching the gauges.

"What's all this about, Mr. Voight?"

"Some of the men are upset and want to speak with you. This here is the ringleader and self-appointed spokesman."

My anger rose, but I tried to keep it under my hat, or at least what was left of it. I had never seen such in all my days. My mind raced to determine what actions on my part might have caused this. Captain Sulloway certainly would not have tolerated such a challenge.

The ringleader was a strongly made man with a sallow and much freckled complexion and large prominent teeth. He was as dirty as everyone else, but unlike many of his mates, he did not wear a Union bummer cap from the war. His eyes glowed in defiance, and I disliked him immediately, "What is your name, young man?"

"McKinney."

My first mate jumped right in, "That's captain or sir to you."

"Fine. McKinney, *Captain.*"

"Ah, that's Irish, is it not?"

"And what of if? Uh, *Captain?*"

I wanted to slap him into next week but suppressed the urge to do so. I would talk with this *dummer Trottel*, but I was really speaking to the men with my reply.

"My people came over as immigrants and have not been treated well over the years. I am trying to be tolerant and welcoming to yours. My recent experiences with the Irish and with you here now are making that difficult. What are your grievances?"

"You work us from dawn well into the darkness without respite for days on end. The food is not fit for man or beast. You won't let us play our music unless the boat is stopped. I have been cooped up on this scow for days and have to share it with darkies."

I could not imitate the bombastic Captain Sulloway and would not try. Instead, I adopted a cold, steely look and calm manner of speech. If these men really thought I was a killer of men, women, and children, this tactic might prove effective. Whatever I did, I needed to prevent an all-out mutiny.

"You signed on under your own free will for the wages and conditions of this boat. The work is hard, and the dangers are many.

I pay a fair wage and expect you to work a fair day's labor. If you were in my shoes, you would expect no less. We feed you better than most boats and let you go ashore whenever it is practical. The rules enforced are for the safe and efficient operation of this vessel. Now I am a Christian man and run this boat according to the New Testament. If this skullduggery continues, you will find me operating this boat in accordance with the Old Testament. If you cannot abide, tell me now, and I will drop you off at the nearest landing. That will be the end to my Christian charity."

"Is féidir leat uilig dul go hIfreann!"

I did not understand the words of the Irish, but the message was clear. "Mr. Voight, we will be passing by Potasi on the Illinois side in a few minutes. Take McKinney here to the stern and give him a proper send-off."

"Aye, aye, Captain! Thank you, sir!"

The first mate grabbed the miscreant by the shoulder, spun him around, then took him by the collar and seat of the pants. Off balance and on his tip toes, the impudent Irishman was rushed through the gang of watching crewman toward the stern.

"Wait! You mean to throw me overboard? "Cac naofa! A Thiarna déan trocaire!"

Mr. Voight replied with an almost evil pleasure, "Spare your wailing. Be thankful he's putting you off the stern. Off the side means being ground up in the paddle wheels. It's your lucky day!"

I did not feel the satisfaction I thought would come. I had never had to resort to putting a man ashore, and certainly not over the rail. If I had spoken like that in my deckhand days, that would have been the expected result. There would have been no explanation by the captain. In the navy, the man would have whipped him for such insolence. The Negroes onboard rejoiced in the man's fate, and they were smiling from ear to ear. As for the remaining whites, I would have to wait and see how they responded. My hope was that McKinney fellow was a lone malcontent. Perhaps hearing the splash and slosh of the odious man hitting the water would have helped me in my thoughts. I am now sorry for missing it.

I had some last words for the crew.

"Gentlemen, we will put ashore tonight at La Crosse to take on coal. The Milwaukee–St. Paul Railroad maintains a sizable pile there. We will be in St. Paul in two days. We will remain there a few days at least to arrange down bound cargo. You are all free men. If you feel you are being mistreated, abused, or cheated, you can remain ashore. Although unusual, while there, I will be willing to pay you off for the days you have worked. If you are not aboard when we steam, you will be left behind. As long as you are on board, I expect a fair day's work each and every day until we return to St. Louis."

A crewman in the back asked, "What is the downbound cargo, Captain?" He was using his deck mates as a shield between me and him.

"We expect a log raft. We have word it is being assembled now and will be ready by the time we want to depart. It is the last run of the season. That means we will go down the river lickety-split and stop only for coal when needed. Take over, Mr. Voight! I am going aft to speak with the cook. That breakfast did not agree with me."

The crew briefly cheered with that last remark.

My speaking of the cook was meant to remind the crew that I ate what they ate. I was no William Bligh dining on partridges while they are given gruel. I saw that many of them were heartened to hear they would get some loafing done in St. Paul and that the log raft promised a quick return to St. Louis. I could understand their anxiety as most of them were hurriedly recalled to the boat and had not expected to steam all the way upriver. I wondered what Captain Sulloway would have thought of my performance. I secretly wished he were here right now.

Returning to the pilothouse, I was asked what had happened. No doubt the ruckus was heard up here, but they could not make out the words. They certainly couldn't hear the splash the Irishman made when he hit the water. I filled them in, and Mr. Olsson stood with his mouth agape. I knew then he would never fill the pot with boiler coffee. I changed the subject.

"Look there, Mr. Olsson. Up ahead is the foot of Coon Slough, just short of Warner's Landing. Avoid taking that route at the risk of all other hazards. The *Lady Franklin* snagged there some years back, and her wreck is still on the bottom. The Galena Packet Company has never learned that lesson and lost a few more boats up that slough. La Crosse is about thirteen miles ahead, and we will stop there for the night."

Both of my colleagues visibly sighed in relief. They were both dog-tired. So was I.

The men had been quiet for the rest of the day, and we made La Crosse in good time. Barrow's Island was easily avoided during the approach, and once again it was well into the evening when we landed. There was nothing to do but tie up and wait for the five thousand souls of the city to awake in the morning. The city landing is at the foot of State Street. Two nice wharf boats are located just upstream but were occupied by steamers I could not identify in the dark. Substantial three-story brick warehouses run along Front Street, but no light emanated from the windows. Even the row of saloons on Front Street were now quiet. The railroad depot is off to north side of town along the Black River. We would move to the coal yard there in the morning. If any of the men wanted to, they could catch the midnight train to Milwaukee.

The "Willow Dock" here is the most unusual on any river I had plied. It was built by ingeniously weaving willow shrub branches together in bundles to form a dock 136 feet long and 160 feet wide. They say that over fifty thousand branches were used. The willows sprouted and grew, creating a permanent living dock. By its looks, it will last for the ages. Just beyond is the newly built Eagle Hotel and the older Elgin Hotel. La Crosse is also home to the Eagle Foundry and Coleman's Sawmill. There is a three-story brick brewery under the ownership of Gottlieb Heileman here as well, but it is struggling to make a profit. Apparently, it has little market outside of La Crosse. From the sign painted on the building, his claim was his beer was brewed in the "old style," whatever that meant. If it meant rye beers, his brewery would never achieve prominence.

Mr. Voight set the watch schedule and put the men to bed. There was no card or checkers playing, singing, or dancing. The men were tired. I called an officer meeting in my cabin to discuss matters, but I had no intention of it being a long one. We kept our voices low as the crew were just down the corridor.

"We had an unpleasant day. What are the men saying?"

The first mate was the first to pipe up, "The Negroes quite enjoyed seeing their antagonist put ashore. The whites will stay aboard until at least St. Paul and see if conditions improve."

Mr. Weatherby added, "I believe my engineers just need a rest of a day or two. It was a hard slog up the river with many a stop along the way."

Swanson rarely said much during these meetings, and his cub, Mr. Olsson, never did. He surprised me with, "I must admit, Captain, I could use a break from the pilothouse as well."

"Very well. Even if the log raft is ready upstream, we will stay in port for two days, unless we get word the river is falling. It's getting colder too, and we don't want to get trapped by ice. We will unload and prepare the boat to depart once we land. We will luxuriate once that is complete. If we lose the crew, at least the boat is ready for anyone we can hire."

"I don't think we will lose many at all, Captain. Winter is coming, and it gets downright cold and snowy up here. Most of the boys are from Missouri and parts south. They will freeze up here. As for the Negroes, they aren't all that welcome up here and have nowhere else to go. Everyone just wants to go home."

"I wish I shared your confidence, Mr. Voight, and please remind me never to hire an Irishman again."

We spent a few minutes talking about the boat and the river ahead, but even I saw all the officers just needed a reprieve. The men did too. Tired and cantankerous crews made mistakes that damage cargo or the boat. As much as I wanted to, I couldn't head home tomorrow. We had consignments aboard for St. Paul and several tons of logs to push downriver. I did decide not to make any further stops along the way to pick up cargo, but even so, we still had another 160 miles of steaming. If Swanson were up to it, we would push on all the way to St. Paul without stopping. It was time to call it a night.

Morning came too soon for everyone.

The steamers *Bill Henderson* and the *James Means* were the boats I saw last night docked at the wharf boats. They are both little stern-wheelers of about 140 feet that were handy on the upper-river tributaries such as the Chippewa and Wapsipinicon. They could get up those streams to deliver supplies to the logging towns and push down small log rafts for assembling into large ones for market. I have seen both on the Mississippi running between Davenport, Galena, and Dubuque. Their crews retuned our waves but weren't exactly acting friendly.

Mr. Swanson brought up the latest editions of the *Wood County Reporter*, the *Daily Wisconsin*, and the *Prairie de Chen Courier*. I would read them later.

We were in the realm of the North Western Packet Company, which was just organized two years ago. It had at least eight first-rate steamers on the upper Mississippi running between St. Louis and St. Paul and is known to be investing over $100,000 in building barges for hauling grain. If true, that is at least thirty or forty barges, and they were signaling they understood the future of steamboats on the rivers. Our fleet is larger but is spread across the rivers. Here, we are merely minor interlopers and not considered a threat. If Thomas Geldstein gets his way, we might someday buy them out. If we're not careful, they may do the same to us.

We coaled up enough to get to St. Paul and to get back here in case the cost of fuel was prohibitive upstream. With that chore done, we steamed on. Mr. Voight reported that we hadn't lost any men at La Crosse.

Our journey took us up a rather uninhabited stretch of the river. On the Upper Mississippi, there is scarcely room for a town or landing due to the rocky nature of the banks and bluffs. The towns of Fountain City, Alma, and Wabasha passed by with hardly a notice. At Point Douglas, we took note of the wreck of the *Fanny Harris*. She had been crushed in the ice three years ago. As the boat entered Lake Pepin, we knew our destination was just seventy miles or so upriver. The lake has a nice wide channel, and we gave Mr. Olsson a chance behind the great wheel. He quickly learned for himself that the wind was a force to reckon with and pointed the bow to the northwest to compensate.

St. Paul is nestled in a series of stone bluffs. Lambert's Landing was our destination. There were over a thousand steamboat landings here before the war, and the newspapers say those numbers will soon be exceeded. The city is the gateway to the frontier beyond. The mighty Sioux tribe occasionally had something to say about that, but they were defeated during a brisk little war a few years ago. Fort Snelling just upriver was the army's base of supply in these parts. There was no reason for us to steam there, and Beef Slough and St. Anthony Falls prohibited further navigation for this boat anyway.

The last obstacle before the landing is the Wabasha Bridge spanning Hennepin Avenue and the Flats. It was completed ten years ago or so and was the first bridge across the Mississippi anywhere along its length. Fortunately for the steamboat business, it is not a railroad bridge, at least not yet. I must admit it is a handsome wooden bridge, of what they call a suspension type. Cables stretched between the twin towers on each bank, which held up the roadway. I doubt though the timber construction will last long in this hostile climate. While it exists, the tolls people pay to cross it will bring the owners considerable profits.

"Captain, that bridge is too low for us to pass under. We will need to step the chimneys to pass underneath.

This is the reason bridges are the bane of steamboats, that along with their cursed pilings that often were driven in too close to the channel.

"Proceed on, Mr. Swanson. Mr. Voight will have his men on the hurricane deck momentarily."

In times such as these, the boilers are brought up to full pressure to give the best chance of power to clear the bridge. When the stacks are detached and folded back, the draft of the fires is severely reduced, and there is a substantial loss of steam generated. The idea is to take down the chimneys close to the bridge, then get them back up quickly as soon as possible. Most of the men on board have never performed the feat, let alone even seen it done. I went on deck to oversee the procedure but left Mr. Voight in charge. I hate to admit that I was quite the novice in the procedure myself.

The bolts were loosened, and the cables released under the stewardship of the first mate. Only a few times did he have to raise his voice and only once use an invective. Fortunately, there were no ladies present. I was pleased to report that there were no serious injuries, but I was embarrassed that Mr. Voight had to tell me to stand aside or get crushed by of the stacks.

We passed under the bridge without striking a piling or causing any other incident, and the stacks were erected and secured. The harbormaster directed the boat to what was probably the last open slip on the landing. We had passed the steamer *Minnesota* down bound on the lake, and she probably was the boat that made this opening for us. She is a good boat and has beautiful prairie murals painted on the paddle-wheel boxes. Four steamers were docked outboard of those at the landing for want of space. Two were our old acquaintances, the *Warsaw* and the *Hardy Johnson*. No one cared to dock in such a manner as cargo had to be moved across another fellow's boat to be brought ashore or loaded. Departure for the inboard boat could greatly disrupt the outboard's schedule, and theft and fights were common. We squeezed in between the *City Belle* and the *Northern Light*. The *Northern Light* was another attractive boat festooned with paintings of the aurora borealis on the paddle-wheel boxes. She also had a decorative orgy of a boiler deck saloon with oil paintings, fancy moldings, plush furniture, and thick carpeting. The expense of those furnishing was over half the cost of the boat. A foolish expenditure in my book. Such showboats sought passenger traffic and became steamboat legends in the public eye. No one wrote happy songs or stories about the workboats and freight packets.

I had been to St. Paul only twice, but I found it a delightful city. There was hustle and bustle of enterprise here, brought about by the opening of the frontier as well as the need to prepare for the harsh winters. Autumn was almost gone up here, and store owners needed to stock up on items to get them through the winter. Producers of goods wanted to ship their wares while they could, and farmers wanted to get their grain to market. Once secured to the bank, the roustabouts quickly began their work. Apparently, the labor unrest to the South had not reached here yet. It was just like old times.

There are over seventy saloons in the city, all ready and eager to separate the rivermen from their money. Adverts at the waterfront hawked the Lahr House on Union Block Corner. The restaurant and saloon claim to be "the place" and invites all to come and see the enormous and trained Tygomelia. There was also signage for the May Flower restaurant on Third Street. It serves meals at all hours and fresh oysters daily. The attached saloon serves kangaroo cocktails, equinoctial punches; and with the Christmas season approaching, the May Flower also served Tom and Jerry cocktails that would make Pierce Egan proud.

A rather tasteless sign advertised the Chicago and Northwestern Railroad. Its patent ventilated cars connected St Paul with Chicago. Dang railroads.

A ruckus brewed up on the landing while the men were still securing the boat. The noise was different enough from the cursing, yelling, and general racket of machinery that men stopped what they were doing and looked about for the source. From our vantage point up here, it was easy to spot. One man of immense stature and a foul mouth of equal dimensions was squared off against a spindly lad half his weight. Swedes were common in these parts, and some specimens were known to grow large. The two combatants were ringed by at least sixty men cheering them on. From here, we could not tell the cause of the coming clash or if it was truly hostile or a donnybrook challenge for the sake of puerile entertainment.

We were all soon told of the cause through the yelling and taunting. We heard all the way up on the hurricane deck that after days of name-calling and other acts of impolite behavior, the small man had had enough and suggested the matter be finally settled. An officer from their boat made his way through the circle and addressed each man. Each combatant then stripped to the waist and waited for the officer to give a signal to commence. The big man eagerly agreed and even accepted the condition of fighting under something called the Marquess of Queensbury Rules.

"It looks like they will be fighting according to the Queensbury Rules."

"What the devil are those, Mr. Swanson?"

"I'm surprised you don't know those, Captain. You have been plying the rivers for years and haven't seen a fight settled so?'"

"No, the fights I have seen are over within thirty seconds and usually involve a heavy tool or a knife."

"Actually, the rules are very new. Some Englishman made a list of them to cover boxing to make sure it is a clean fight. I would be surprised if either man down there actually knows them."

"I am surprised you know so much about boxing, Mr. Swanson. You must have the heart of the gambler."

"Only in matters of such competitions, Captain. Never fared well in games of chance, but I believe I am a good judge of horseflesh."

Gambling is in the riverman's blood, and the event unfolding below drew bets as thick as a swarm of Memphis mosquitoes. The stakeholders were busy with calling out odds and collecting money.

With the signal given, the small man made two quick swings to the Swede's potato trap. Both of those missed, and now off-balance, he was vulnerable. The big man did not hesitate and landed a blow that sent his target stumbling almost into the water. The Swede smiled as if he thought the contest all but won, but the little man made up his mind to be quicker in his attacks and landed a solid hit on the jaw. The blow caused the big man to hit the ground and to fill his mouth with a quart of sand. The pair then went to a lengthy period of sparring, neither able to land a telling blow.

One of the spectators suggested that both men were tired and should retire for drinks. He disappeared in a flash when asked if he was buying.

The fight resumed with vigor, and blows began to strike home. The Swede's nose took much abuse, and the smaller man's chest was black-and-blue. When the Swede finally got the upper hand, the smaller fellow broke off and ran to his boat to find allies. It was just as well as the police arrived in force. They quickly found and arrested the little man, but somehow the big Swede melted into the crowd and disappeared. It is strange to relate that the police never found him. I went back to my duties as the gambling men below argued how to disperse the winnings.

The landing soon returned to its usual chaotic mayhem of loading and unloading. Our upbound cargo was relieved from our care, but we were informed the log raft was not yet ready for transport. It would be another day or two. More time and money wasted, and there was no guarantee the discontented men would remain with the boat for long. I reminded myself of the promised reprieve for the men and tried to shrug off the delay. I would write home to the folks. That would pass some time, and they have not yet received a note from St. Paul. In their twilight years, it is best to write them often.

With the excitement over and the coffeepot empty, I could not remember my last professional haircut. Weeks of neglect had made my strands uneven and resistant to the hair grease that was usually able to keep them in place. It was time for a new coiffure and perhaps a trim on the beard. The Merchant's Hotel was just a block from the landing on East Third Street, and it would certainly have a skilled barber. A short walk later, I found the barber parlor with ease.

The name Maurice Jernigan was on the shingle, and I found him to be an amicable Negro. Haircuts were five cents, marked down from ten, and shaves were three cents. As I didn't need a complete shave, I was irritated he charged the full three cents. I suppose trimming the beard in addition to the unruly locks was more than a typical haircut, so it all balanced out. The splash of tonic swung the scales to my favor. I tipped the man five cents, for which he seemed genuinely grateful.

"Thank you, sir. Business has been slow of late."

"Why would that be? Are the folks around here growing their hair long for the coming winter?"

"No, sir, it is on account of me being part of the Sons of Freedom. We aim to get the vote for the black man."

"I wish you luck on that, Mr. Jernigan, I truly do."

I now knew how Captain Bemis felt about sticking it in the eye to the men who thought they owned the joint. I gave the man a five-dollar piece for his fledgling organization. I'm not sure I cared at all about the Negro vote. But making the lives of those so violently opposed to it miserable felt pretty good.

A quick stop to the Minnesota State Telegraph Office was in order. No messages were awaiting our arrival, but I sent an update to St. Louis.

We needed a heavy wooden butting block to protect the bow of the boat to push a log raft of any size. To save costs, we had never hired a full-time carpenter, relying on the ingenuity and strength of the crewmen we hired. To make the crib, the Daniel Shaw Lumber Company sent over a man to supervise the project. He was called "Chips" like every carpenter on the river boats. Within a few hours, the job was done. It greatly detracted from the elegant lines of the boat, and I looked forward to heaving it overboard at the first opportunity.

An idle night on the boat was not what I had in mind. I changed into my clean uniform that was reserved for fancy occasions. My intent was to catch a show or two at the opera house. With the new haircut, white gloves, and the splash of tonic, I was dressed to the nines.

The Ingersoll Hall is located on the corner of Wabasha and Third Streets, a comfortable walk from the landing. It advertised itself as "the easiest to sing in, in America, the best seated in the state, the best ventilated this side of Italy, and the best lighted in the world." The auditorium included the entire third floor of the building. Daniel Ingersoll had his dry-goods business on the ground floor, and the second-floor housed insurance and other offices.

This was the end of the theatric season and probably the last week of opportunity to see a show. The traveling troupes counted on multiple stops to make a profit, and winter was approaching. The opera house here in St. Paul has stoves for heating, but the venues in the small communities in the surrounding counties did not. Few patrons wanted to see a show while shivering, so it just didn't pay for the actors to remain so far north. Admission was seventy-five cents for the dress circle parquet, and that was fine enough. It was foolish to spend five dollars for a private seat in a box. I arrived with plenty of time to spare and enjoyed half a cigar in the lobby. There were at least six other steamboat officers here in uniform and any number of rivermen in the audience in "civilian" garb. Some of the officers evidently called St. Paul their home port, for they had their ladies in attendance.

I settled into my seat with a nice snifter of brandy. I had a craving for another cigar, but there were now ladies present. I perused the miniature playbill given to all at the entrance. Typical opera companies have a lengthy repertoire of plays and operas, and artists sang and danced when they were not acting. *Kitty O'Neal!* was the opening act this evening, and I remembered seeing it back in St. Louis just before the war. Mollie Williams was the featured comedienne and chanteuse tonight. The back of the playbill proudly exclaimed she was well received in Montgomery, Alabama, a few years back. I would be more impressed if the little Rebel had played well in the opera house back in Peoria. Next spring the opera house was looking forward to the plays *The Daughter of the Regiment*, *The French Spy*, *The Hunchback*, and *The Honey Moon*. Perhaps we will be up here again for one.

The play went well enough to get my mind off the boat and the troubles in St. Louis. For the first time ever, I was looking forward to seeing the end of a season.

The second play was the celebrated protean farce *A Day in Paris*. Mollie Williams played five parts with aplomb, especially the role of Emilie Grenville, the lass betrothed to Windham. The actress Cordelia O'Conner was not having a good night and missed several of her lines.

Thunder rumbled menacingly in the second act, and the unmistakable patter of rain struck the roof. There was a collective groan among the audience as few, if anyone, brought along suitable protection. An hour or so ago, there was not a cloud in the sky, and the stars shone brightly. The actors and the orchestral gems did not miss a beat—though, a tribute to their experience and intrepidity in their profession.

With the last fall of the curtain, the assemblage made their way to the exit with the worst expectations of getting soaked to the skin. If they were looking forward to the experience, they were not disappointed. To my astonishment, a woman latched on to my elbow and exclaimed, "Come along, or we will catch our deaths!" Before I could formulate a reply, I was pulled off-balance and down the street. She had drawn her opera cape about her head to protect her coiffure, and it restricted her vision as blinkers do a horse. My attempts to gain her attention remained unsuccessful, so my efforts went to keeping my balance and placing the unlit cigar into my coat pocket to preserve it for later. Three blocks later, we arrived at a magnificent two-story house. My assumption that my duties of seeing her safely home was complete was rendered asunder when she dragged me though the front gate, up the walk, and up to the front door. Only then was her attention diverted to me when she asked me for the key to the door.

After a good ten-second scream, she collapsed into a faint. It was a silly gesture as women never really fainted so, and men had to pretend they believed it. She was remarkably heavy for her size, and I would judge her as around forty years old, but maybe younger if the light were better.

"You, there! Unhand my wife!"

I turned to see the man entering the gate and approaching us. He was wearing a steamboat uniform and sported a beard just slightly longer than mine. With my arms full of his wife, there was no ability to reach for my Root revolver without dropping her first. That would, of course, infuriate the husband even further, and there was no convenient means of escape.

"Hold there, good man. I believe there is an issue of mistaken identity. Your wife shanghaied me at the door of the opera house in the rain and dragged me here. I certainly did not accost her. She just now fainted upon the discovery and your approach."

Fortunately for all, the husband saw the light and even found it humorous. I politely declined the offer to enter the home and join him in a brandy.

"Ah, I know how it is away from homeport. First business is to the boat. I am glad though it was you instead of one of the local men. Word would get around town here, and she would not leave the house for weeks in the shame of it. Good travels, Captain."

With handshakes done, I loitered only a moment to light a cigar. There was a break in the rain now, but I was surely soaked to the skin as I made my way back to the boat. With a little stretching of the truth, I could claim I met a respectable woman in St. Paul. Held her in my arms as well.

There was usually little trouble on the landings during a heavy rain. The crewmen spent the time under the shelter of the boat playing cards, checkers, and with the usual tomfoolery of the young men daring one another to do some foolish thing.

I woke refreshed and hoped to get word today that the log raft was ready for us. I found to my chagrin though that the rain played upon my shoes last evening and shrunk them a size, maybe two. I finally got my feet inside them and started my day. Mr. Weatherby's men had scoured the boilers and greased the machinery and only needed the order to light the fires. The men could go ashore by shift, and most hightailed it straight for the nearby Matteson Saloon and Billiard Room.

With not much else to do, I went into town as well but pledged to come back in far better shape than the men. As well as a box of cigars, I purchased two packets of Gayetty's Medicated paper. It claimed to be the greatest necessity of the age, guaranteed to be made of the purest materials. It never occurred to me to use the purest materials when the call of nature came. A poke sack full of horehound candy ended my shopping spree.

I bought a copy of the *St. Paul Pioneer*, the self-proclaimed cheapest newspaper in the West. At fifteen cents a week, it just might be. The front page heralded the feat of a farmer growing three beets weighing between fourteen and seventeen pounds. The man also claimed forty-eight bushels an acre this year. If true that was impressive, especially in these climes. In national news, the rebel Captain Henry Wirz was found guilty of conspiracy to kill large numbers of Union prisoners at Camp Sumter. He was also convicted of eleven of thirteen counts of acts of personal cruelty. It is expected he will be hung soon. We had all heard the rumors of Andersonville during the war, and they must have been true.

I arrived back at the boat in time to find a minister of some sort scolding one of the mates. He had made his way up onto the forecastle.

"Sir, do you know where you are going?"

"Why, preacher man, we are heading south to St. Louis once all is in readiness."

"No, with all that cursing and lewd behavior, you are going to hell, faster than your steamboat."

"Oh, then you know your destination, preacher man?"

"Of course, for I am going to heaven."

"No, you are going into the river!"

Matching the action to his word, the mate took hold of the preacher and tossed him over the side. With all the wailing and thrashing, the man may have drowned, but the mate nodded to the men, and they fished him out. Drenched and furious, the minister produced some cursing on his own, which earned him the laughter and derision of the boatmen. I was too late to intervene, but I spoke to the mate as the minister stumbled off in the direction of town.

"Tarnation, mister. Are you trying to bring the wrath of God down upon us?"

"Why, no, Captain. Actually, if feel as though I was the hand of God in this affair."

"Don't be blasphemous. What is that you are chewing? You look like you are chewing your cud."

"Spruce resin gum, Captain. It don't taste too good and becomes brittle the more it is chewed. It's said to be good for cleaning the teeth and gums."

"Uh, fine. You and the men get back to work. If you can't find any, I'm sure Mr. Voight has a list of chores."

"Aye, Captain!"

I shook my head in frustration. That boy may be strong as an ox and perhaps just about as smart. My chief clerk Bosun Joe caught my attention. I had not seen him since we landed.

"What have you been up to? How were the profits from the upbound run?"

"Good day, Captain. We had a good return for our efforts. I will have a precise number for you shortly."

"I would have thought you would have one by now. Where have you been?"

"I had heard there were some, uh, former colleagues of mine in town. I thought to look them up and perhaps offer them a means to return home."

"Confederates? In Minnesota?"

"Indeed. They were prisoners of war who volunteered to serve in the Union army on the western frontier. They joined up to get out of the hellholes that all you all called prison camps. You probably have heard them called Galvanized Yankees."

"Those Union camps were better than that Andersonville place. Did you find any?"

"No, Captain. The ones who passed through here were sent into the Dakota Territory. I did though follow a sign to see a fabled Tygomelia. It was not the creature of legend but only a young freakishly-mottled moose."

"Any word on the log raft?"

Bosun Joe was able to gather the details of the log raft consignment that would take us south and toward home. The load of timber comes from the Daniel Shaw Lumber Company headquartered in Eau Claire, Wisconsin. The firm has grown rapidly over the past seven years and owns thousands of acres of virgin timber in the Chippewa River Valley. This was probably the last raft of the season, and the owners are quite anxious for us to get underway. I was happy to oblige and was quite satisfied with the ninety cents per foot board measure. In normal times, boats could count on only seventy cents, maybe eighty. I could not ascertain if Bosun Joe was a good negotiator or if the lumber company were that desperate. It really didn't matter. If Bemis were here though, we would have undoubtedly told the lumbermen of all our woes and troubles to get the best terms. Bosun Joe claimed the log raft would be ready for us sometime tomorrow.

"Ah, Mr. Voight. You are just in time. Sound the signal to assemble the crew. We will depart at first light. We will proceed to the southern end of Lake Pepin and meet the log raft that should be assembled and ready."

The boat's "Hip, hip, hooray!" soon reverberated through the streets of St. Paul and echoed off the hills beyond. I wondered how many of the men would answer the call.

The Log Raft

I went to bed tired and dispirited, notwithstanding the pleasant events of the day. I poured myself a good slug of whiskey and poured it down the hatch. It was not my usual brand, and the strength caught me by surprise. I was glad no one saw me gag and cough. It was amazing how much and how often Captain Sulloway put away. He drank at all hours of the day and in very generous amounts. I could only imagine how he stayed on his feet, let alone expertly pilot a boat on any stretch of the river.

Morning couldn't come early enough. When it did come, I was even more anxious to get underway. I had kept the company appraised of our status but had not received a reply. That was not unusual, but the past several weeks had not been usual times. I went below for a tankard of coffee and found Mr. Weatherby had already lit the fires. My trusted first mate, Mr. Voight, reported that all but two men were accounted for, a fireman and a deckhand. That was less than expected. We couldn't tell though if they missed the boat for drunkenness, being in the hoosegow, or run off. They weren't paid off, so they probably weren't malcontent.

Using the current of the river, we slipped under the bridge much easier than the other day. We then cleared all the obstacles and reentered Lake Pepin. The lake is twenty-five miles long and averages about three miles wide. The ice here is from three to four feet thick in the winter. We did not want to be caught up here and meet the fate of the *Fanny Harris*. For the voyage home, we in the pilothouse were bracing ourselves for the likely low water and westerly winds this time of the year.

The log raft was assembled at Reads Landing, located at the southern end of the lake just opposite of the mouth of the Chippewa

River. It is the residence and headquarters of several raft pilots and logging companies. Reads Landing was originally named Waumadee and from here began the main trail for the Sioux and Lakota tribes of the Indians. The white man has displaced the natives, and as long as the white pine lasted on the Chippewa River and its tributaries, the logging industry would reign supreme here. There were at least twenty-five saloons at Reads Landing that run day and night every day of the week. Poker is the game here, they say. The residents do not go to church, for there is no church to go to. This was one place on the Mississippi I had a hard time imagining would ever be fully Christianized.

Timber rafts are typically 275 wide and 600 feet long, consisting of about 3,500 logs. They have a surface area of 4 acres to give some perspective. As the last one planned for the season, the raft assembled for us was at least this large, maybe more. The logs were held together with boom chains and hemp lines, but I couldn't see how they would hold up to the stress and strain of the river. The bow of the boat was made fast to the stern of the raft by the lumber company men who had performed the task countless times. I hoped that my men below were watching and learning.

To steer this mass, the boat would swing to port or starboard by a newly invented means of guy lines running from the stern of the raft to the steam capstan on the boat. When put in motion, the capstan played out a hawser on one side and reeled in the other. In this manner, the raft was steered primarily by pushing on its stern at an angle. For tight turns, the boat will use a technique of steering called flanking. This is done by throwing one or both engines into reverse as the raft enters a turn. This maneuver checked the forward movement of the raft and gave more time for the turn. In difficult places, like rapids, a second steamer called a "bowmate" may be attached to the bow. We would gauge the river and call upon one if needed. There always seemed to be at least one loitering around such hazards awaiting employment. They weren't cheap, and we would avoid using one if possible.

"Mr. Swanson, you have experience in towing and pushing rafts up here. I have none whatsoever, I'm afraid."

"It has been a few years, but yes, Captain. I would be happy to instruct you. My belief is that you will catch onto the particulars quite readily. Usually it takes but a gentle touch from back here. The oarsmen on the bow of the raft do some of the work."

"Oarsmen? Do I need to assign men out on the raft? I doubt any have such experience."

"Not at all, Captain. They come from the lumber company. They will reside in and rotate in shifts from the hut they erected out there on the raft. I am told they are quite adept and will need little guidance from us. I will go over the signaling procedures with you along the way."

"Mr. Olsson, I hope you appreciate the wealth of experience you are accumulating on this boat. You wouldn't get a fraction of it running a packet between St. Louis and Keokuk."

"I do indeed, but I would most appreciate living to tell the tale, Captain."

"Proceed downriver when all is in readiness, Mr. Swanson. I'm going to the forecastle to see the crib and capstan in action."

The raft was secured within an hour, and we were on our way. I could see by the men's faces there was a sense of relief that we were finally on our way home. We had all left St. Louis in haste and not necessarily in the direction we had planned. Some of the boys were on board solely to help run down the *Kaw Nation* and were not prepared for a long voyage. They have had their time ashore, some slack time on the landing, better food, and were now heading home. There was no room for complaint in my book.

"How are we doing here, Mr. Voight?"

"Just fine as far as I can tell, Captain. It is a strange sight to have such a mass of timber off our bow. The capstan is under stress but should bear up. It turns freely with the motion of the boat. Mr. Swanson says he will signal if we need to apply power to it. One ring on the bell for the warning, followed by one short peal on the whistle for starboard or two for port, then three to return to neutral."

"As good a system as any. I will be up there to relieve him on occasion."

"Have you ever pushed a log raft, Captain?"

"No, I have not. If you are about to ask me if I feel unease, no, I do not. At least not for the boat. Between here and La Crosse, the river channel is at least one quarter of a mile wide. With that forest of trees in front of us, we can barrel right through sandbars and most other hazards. God bless those who might get in our way though. With this current and the load of coal aboard, we should make excellent time to St. Louis. We will stop only when darkness or fog forces us to do so."

I returned to the pilothouse to find Swanson and Olsson at the wheel with a good turn in the distance. I was glad to see the lumbermen on the raft hoisted a red flag at the bow to mark it. The piece of cloth seemed very far away. A steamboat was already in the turn ascending the river and closing. The law governing the passing of two boats is that the ascending boat must blow one whistle, providing she wants to pass normally to the right. The descending boat must answer that whistle. Then if the descending boat wishes to pass to the left, she must blow two peals, and the ascending boat must answer and govern herself accordingly. The number one rule on the rivers was that descending boats have the right of way as they are far less maneuverable running with the current.

As we had a log raft, we took the outside of every turn to provide more room to make the maneuver. Swanson pealed the whistle twice and the other replied with one. The oncoming boat dutifully hugged the right bank to let us pass. No doubt she had been called upon to do this often in these waters.

Swanson ordered the reverse of both engines and applied full rudder to swing the boat to an angle from the raft. I took note that it sometimes required opposite rudder to get the boat into the position. This might not be so easy as Swanson made it out to be.

Our cub pilot was still thinking of the signals we used and asked who came up with them. I answered the question as Mr. Swanson had his hands full.

"Mr. Olsson, persons not acquainted with steamboats naturally think that Congress thought these up under the Steamboat Act of 1852. It's not true, though, at least directly. The president appoints a supervising inspector for each district, and they appoint local inspectors of licenses, boilers, and of hulls. They are all former rivermen. The supervising inspectors meet annually in Washington City and make laws governing the steam vessels navigating the inland waters of the United States. Now let us watch and learn the prestidigitations of Mr. Swanson."

I soon had my spell behind the wheel while Swanson was still fresh enough to provide instruction. The handling of the boat was sluggish and at times counterintuitive. The Upper Mississippi was straighter than the stream below St. Louis, so I had no trouble keeping the raft in the main channel. The issue of concern for me was the current. There is a drop of some eight hundred feet in elevation between St. Paul and St. Louis, which meant an average velocity of five miles an hour. Normally, to maintain rudder, a boat would have to steam at least three miles an hour above that. I was attempting to keep that speed, which was in error.

"Captain, no offense, but you need to back off. You are fighting the log raft. Make it work for you."

"What do you mean by that, Swanson? If I reduce speed, there would be no control."

"Think of the raft and boat combined as one vessel. The boat is now simply the rudder. The bow of the raft will by nature remain in the main channel. The boat will push it along surely but will tend to push it out of the channel and into the outside bank during a turn. Let the river push along the mass of logs. Use the boat to swing the stern of the raft free of the banks on the inside turn."

I did as he said at the next opportunity, and all went well. The men at the bow did not have to frantically ply their oars, and the turn was negotiated easily. At least now I knew how to turn to port.

"Well, hog gravy and chitlins! That is how it is done, Captain."

"Thank you. Let us be sure to give our young cub pilot a chance at this. Log rafts and barges are likely to be more common for us in the future."

We had in our possession the measurement of every span of each bridge across the river all the way to St. Louis. Before departing, we confirmed the raft would fit, but there was little margin for error. I was most concerned with the rapids at Rock Island and Keokuk.

Before the war, a boat lost its log raft, and it nearly caused the end of us while we were ascending. I certainly did not wish to cause such a calamity nor be a victim of one. Fortunately, this late in the season, it was a moderately low stage of water, and the river was slacker than it was a few weeks ago.

There are at least four rapids pilots living in Le Claire at the head of the Rock Island Rapids. Swanson reversed the engines two miles out and was able to bring the massive raft almost to a standstill at the landing. A pilot was waiting and rowed his skiff to the raft, secured it with the help of the lumbermen, and clambered aboard. After an examination of his license, I allowed him to take the wheel, and we continued downstream.

At such rapids, when boats pushed or towed a log raft, they must not let other boats pass them before they made it through the chute. If a boat got by them, they will be delayed until the river ahead was clear. Astern, the steamboat *Lucy Bertram* saw we were ready to make the decent, and by the thick smoke from her stacks, she wanted to cut in front of us. She was too far off though and had no chance.

It was a white-knuckle event for me as I watched the rapids pilot at work. Swanson was obviously feeling unease, and Olsson was mesmerized. The raft buckled and swayed with the current, and there was no doubt it struck rocks at least a dozen times. The great mass of the raft did not care a wit and continued onward. The lumbermen on the raft moved about like fleas on a dog's back checking and adjusting the chains and hawsers. I was quite relieved when we reached Davenport, where we let the freelance pilot ashore. It was ten dollars well spent.

Our experience was repeated at the Keokuk rapids. We went through sure enough, but I was just as nervous. With that behind us, I did find increased confidence in handling the great log raft. It helped that I was fortified by Swanson's presence in the pilothouse. Mr. Olsson had his chance behind the wheel and was surprising adept at it. It was not his fault the upbound steamer *Hannibal City* nearly collided with the raft. The pilot had failed to heed our signals.

During our voyage downstream, we landed to rest in Lansing, Dubuque, Rock Island, Burlington, and Hannibal. The log raft had no place at the landings, so it was lashed to the bank just downstream of each town. South of Hannibal, we came upon a snag boat working on the carcass of the *Kaw Nation*. The engines would surely be recovered as well as any cargo not ruined by the explosion, fire, or submersion in the water. I wondered if they would find the strongbox. Its contents would be worth more than anything they would otherwise salvage.

Once past the rapids, the river grew wider and deeper. We could relax just a bit. Swanson showed Olsson how to use a watch as a makeshift compass.

"Just hold the watch horizontal to the ground and point the hour hand at the sun. Approximately halfway between that point and the twelve o'clock mark will point to the south."

"Sound easy enough, but I have never seen a compass in use on this steamboat or the need to do so."

"Never pass on the opportunity to learn something, Mr. Olsson. Might come in handy someday. You never know."

We surely won no races taking almost half again as long to get to St. Louis as we would have without the raft. We were all at the end of our ropes when we unceremoniously landed the mound of timber at Bloody Island near east St. Louis. We pulled off as soon as Bosun Joe received payment and an agent's signature from the J. A. Holmes and Company. We arrived at our usual landing thirty minutes later, and the crew cheered with our signal "Hip, hip, hooray!" There was no cargo to unload, and once the boat was secured and cleaned, the men would be paid off and sent along their merry way.

Yet there was a hitch. At the landing, we were greeted by the harbormaster and two well-dressed gentlemen. I had seen them from the river and went below to the forecastle to greet them.

"Good day, Captain. There are reports of cholera in the city. We are here to warn you and to ask where you have come from."

"We are in from St. Paul. We put ashore for rest while pushing a log raft but did not enter any towns. No sign of the disease upriver. Where is the sickness here in town?"

"There are outbreaks among the residents along the River des Peres and Dutchtown. It always seems to begin there for some reason. I suspect the influx of dirty foreigners that were brought it in. We also have two men from the *Rob Roy* under observation."

"This is our home port, good sir, but I will inform the men."

"Very well, but I advise staying clear of the Dutchtown section and avoiding any Germanic folk. Irish too."

Between Seasons

A s usual lately, I made a beeline to the office once the boat was secured. Mr. Weatherby and his men would be busy for a day or two scrubbing out the boilers and preparing the machinery to remain in idleness through the winter season. Mr. Voight had already set the deck crew to work cleaning up the boat days ago as there was little else for them to do. They would be released soonest.

It felt as if it could snow any time. It was cold, but not enough to wear a greatcoat. I had strapped on the Paterson but felt awkward with it. With the cold weather at hand, I had buttoned my frock coat and wore the revolver outside in plain view. The russet leather contrasted sharply against the dark blue fabric and instantly caught the attention of every passerby.

From the outside it appeared the company office had returned to normal. There was a Negro doorman out front sporting a burgundy coat as before, but there was no sign of a weapon.

"Welcomes back, Captain. Mr. Geldstein has been expecting you. Youse are to waits in the parlor and should hang up your gun in there."

There was a respectable crowd of boat officers passing the time there, and the tobacco smoke rose thick from the tables. This is how it used to be. Some of the men were engaged in that came called poker. They were playing it with far more dignity and calm than the deckhands on the boat. Maybe it could be a gentleman's game. It appeared more sociable than faro.

As I entered and took off my cap, the room fell silent. I looked behind me to see what could have caused this, but there was no one else there. Some of my colleagues looked surprised at my entry while others had a cold, accusatory countenance. It was not a warm welcome. With nowhere else to go, I strode to the bar and took a seat. My hope was that my walk did not look like a slink of the guilty. I certainly felt no guilt for recent events. Well, I wasn't all that proud of tossing the Irishman into the river. Maybe they have heard of the event already. My guess was most, if not all, these gentlemen had done such a thing in the past themselves.

I handed my gun belt to the bartender, who hung it up on a hook. There were five others already on the wall. The grips looked like they were Colts, but I was no expert. I unbuttoned my frock coat but did not surrender my little Root. The Negro behind the bar apparently did not see it. I removed my cap and noticed the threads around the bullet holes were quite frayed now. Even I had to admit that it needed serious repair or replacement.

I wordlessly finished two fingers of good whiskey and was about to order another when a porter beckoned me to the office of Mr. Geldstein. A door was now installed in the corridor, blocking easy access to Thomas's office beyond. The heavy marble planters were gone and replaced by much lighter iron ones. The porter and the Negro behind the door exchanged words, and I was allowed through.

Mr. Geldstein's personal clerk was where he was supposed to be, and the wall behind him showed no signs of the gunfight of a few weeks ago. He rose and knocked twice on Thomas's door and opened it. With a gesture, he motioned me to walk through. It was another wordless conversation.

"Good to have you back, Captain. I trust your journey was a profitable one."

Thomas did not rise from his desk as usual, and his tone lacked the usual friendliness. His old burns were redder than usual, and I could not account why that might be. He used his hand to signal his desire for me to have a seat.

"How was your run, Captain?"

"My clerk is preparing the exact numbers, but it appears we made a respectable profit, considering."

"Considering what?"

"Considering we paid premium price for coal at Alton, burned through it to reach Hannibal without stopping to pick up sack piles or any other business along the way. We received excellent terms on the log raft which will compensate for that and then some. How goes the salvage work on the *Kaw Nation*? We observed it underway while proceeding here. We have the bell and her flag."

"The good news is, we have her strongbox and soon both her engines. There were no incriminating papers against Foley in them, but the cash was intact. The bad news is that Foley himself is still unaccounted for."

"If he was in the vicinity of the pilothouse, he is a good as dead."

"I don't share your confidence, Captain. What if he were in his usual aft cabin on the boiler deck?"

"He would probably have drowned or burned to death. We saw no one emerge from there. Has he been spotted here in St. Louis?"

"Nothing confirmed, but there are rumors. I have recalled all his bond holdings in the company. Various lenders are calling for the liquidation of his assets to pay off his debts. He is by all accounts financially ruined, at least here in St. Louis."

"That sounds as though he has no power to cause mischief for the company or you personally, Thomas."

"The desire for revenge is powerful, and if he is alive, he is still a danger. It is unfortunate you could not apprehend him. The loss of the *Kaw Nation* and her crew was a blow to the company. We had some good men aboard, and as an old boat, she carried no insurance."

"We were almost within hailing distance, but she poured on the steam and blew her boilers."

"Yes, that is the official story, Captain, and we will stick to it."

Mr. Geldstein sounded as if we shared a secret, but I was not sure what that was. When I thought of the darkest possibility, I did not want to know.

"Thomas, how is Captain Bemis? Has he recovered from the attack?"

"He recovered enough to take a steamer to Cape Girardeau. His family is there. I know not if he will return to the trade. His body cannot take much more and will require a great deal of time to heal fully."

My hope was that Bemis would be fit enough to return to the boat. It looks like I will be stuck with that Bosun Joe fellow for a while.

"Captain, your season is over. Ice is forming upriver and is due here within the next week or so. Direct Mr. Swanson to take the boat to the Eads' yards in Carondelet. She will get a complete overhaul on the machinery and her hull looked over. While the boat is being worked on, I want you to take the opportunity to rest up and prepare for the next season. Maybe you can take a proper holiday."

"Sounds like you want me to lie low and get out of town."

"That's the general idea."

I rose to leave but had one more question to ask. I was very much afraid of the answer.

"Uh, Thomas, whatever happened to those three incendiary devices disguised as lumps of coal?"

"I had them delivered over to the police as evidence."

"You entrusted a man to do this?"

"Indeed so. He is man I trust implicitly. I was not going to walk all the way to police headquarters myself. I have several companies to run, you know. Now go to your boat. You have matters to attend to."

With my revolver retrieved, it was time to get back to the boat quickly before Weatherby and his men had taken apart the boilers. My arrival was almost perfect as only the first cover to one of the ash boxes was removed. Swanson and Olsson were already gone. With a skeleton crew, we took the boat the few miles down to the yards in Carondelet.

James Eads had built the best construction and repair yards on the Mississippi. Cement rails topped by iron ran in rows and extended into the river. Below the water waited wheeled cribs. We pulled the boat up along the bank, and the yard crews secured the boat with hawsers. Once that was done, a huge steam engine was put in motion that winched the boat completely out of the water upon the waiting cribs. The boat was brought up all the way into a waiting shed where workers could ply their trades in all weather.

We unloaded all the company property of high value, to include the strongbox and papers, and the weapons. Two deckhands hauled my trunks, one of the privileges of being a captain. Wagons and carriages were waiting to take us back to the company office in St. Louis.

I procured a room at the Barnum Hotel and arranged for the delivery of my trunks. Until they came, I had the contents of my carpetbag and the possibles bag I retrieved from the pilothouse. Before I made captain, my usual practice was to arrange off-season lodging at a boarding house on Fifth Street between Chestnut and Pine Streets. I avoid it now as the residents would no doubt badger me for money or even take it by theft. Hotels were an extravagance in my book, but they offered better meals and certainly more privacy and security. The Barnum Hotel was well known and convenient but was now aging. That was to my advantage as its rates were more reasonable.

With not much to do for the rest of the day, I caught up with the latest editions of the papers. President Johnson has been in the news quite a bit as his relationship with the Republican leadership quickly crumbled. A faction called the Radical Republicans, led by Thaddeus Stevens and Charles Sumner, dominated the party and were calling for Johnson for a more stringent reconstruction of the Southern states. It seemed to me the president was very lax, hoping bygones could be bygones. With his policies, all I could see the war did was kill thousands of people and put the black race back onto the plantation and treated worse than before.

In the morning, I dressed and went through the contents of my bags and trunks. Now was the opportunity to take stock of my earthly belongings and repair and replace worn items. Socks and skivvies were always the first in need of replacement after a year on the rivers. Shirt linens as well. With a mental list in my mind, I took the omnibus to the company office to be paid off. I was not surprised to find Captain Sulloway in the parlor with a cigar and a drink in hand. It seems as if he appropriated the lounge as his office.

"Well, hello, young man. Have a seat and tell me of your last run."

I told him of our pursuit of the *Kaw Nation* and its destruction and then the details of our journey to St. Paul and our return here. He changed the subject, much to my surprise.

"How much money do you have now? With your captain's pay and dividends from company bonds, you must have a respectable nest egg. Lord knows you hardly spend a cent. You act as though you cannot afford a new hat."

I would normally play discussions of money cagey, but this was my mentor Captain Sulloway. He had never steered me wrong, even when drunk as a skunk.

"Uh, I am not too sure. I have an account at the Boatman's Savings Institution and a cashbox in their vault. My guess would be just over $20,000 and another ten in government bonds."

"Good heavens, son! You are what they call *nouveau riche*, a man of means in his own time. But most men in your position have more to show for it besides a bank ledger. Your handling of money is about as bad a stuffing your mattress with it or burying it behind the barn. You should at least invest your surplus funds and let the money grow. You surely know of the parable of the talents found in the book of Matthew, chapter 25, I think. You really don't know how to spend money, do you?"

"Well, there are some things that are worth the cost, such as good tobacco, liquor, and coffee. There's no need to scrimp on those necessities."

"Consider depositing more into the bank's account and get a gold certificate of deposit for six months. At least those draw 4 percent interest."

"Captain Sulloway, I remember well the Panic of 1857 when many banks failed. I see no safe place to invest. I also have a great fear of being hornswoggled."

"Well, don't purchase a Kansas turnip farm. Buy another share in your boat and receive more dividends. One or more of the other three shareholders would probably accept an offer. Buy more bonds in the company and never have to work again unless you want to. As Lord Melbourne once observed, on some matters, the clever fellows get it wrong and the damned fools get it right. You never can tell with life. Live it while you can. The Good Lord certainly has provided you with the means. Laissez les bons temps rouler!"

"It's treasonous, but investing in railroads seems to be a wise choice."

"Nonsense. When it comes to money, there is no concept of loyalty. Just avoid what they call paper railroads. They may look good on the map, but many of those will never get built, and the investors will lose out.'

"I shall consider what you said, sir. There's a great deal to think about."

"Don't take too long with that, son. Life is too short to worry about it so. Oh, and keep an eye on your government bonds. Word is that Secretary of the Treasury McCulloch is arguing that the Legal Tender Acts authorizing them in the first place were temporary war measures. He wants the government to retire them all and return to the gold standard. It appears the House of Representatives will soon endorse the secretary's argument. Even the greenbacks may go the way of all things."

"By the way, Captain Sulloway, what will you be doing during the off-season?"

"I will be plenty busy here, but I am considering finally looking for that piece of property on which to retire. I'm well into my sixties now, and the Good Lord promised us only threescore and ten if we lived, right? That means I'm probably on borrowed time."

"I figure we are all on borrowed time the way things have been transpiring around here lately."

"Oh, don't let all that that worry you none, my lad. You just do what is right, and it all works out. Get out and live a little. You are too tied to the boat. There is more to life than the rivers."

"None that interests me yet."

"Tell me, boy, just what do you want in life? What are your ambitions?"

"That's an interesting question. I was asking that myself on our way down from St. Paul. I have exceeded my boyhood dreams and reached the top of my profession. But it feels as though I will remain where I am for the rest of my life. The Good Lord has provided for me in abundance. I should be grateful and satisfied."

"But you are growing anxious for a different challenge, eh? That is the natural state of mankind. If contentment were found so easily, man would still be living in caves. I envy you that you are asking these questions in your youth. Too many men find they are too old to do anything about their plight in the world and die miserable."

"Do you have regrets then, Captain Sulloway?"

"I have the good fortune to say no to that. This era of time was the perfect one to exist in. I saw this country in its youth, and one thing or another has kept me quite busy over the years. I miss the rivers certainly, but running the operations of this steamboat company leaves me little time for such yearning. I thought the job would be a huckleberry over my persimmon, but I dare say things are running smoothly."

Like most everyone else, the war took four years of my life. There was no time or opportunity to give much thought about anything else than getting the boat through to its next destination. My brief and timid attempt to find a wife blew up like a faulty boiler. I had at least two months before the rivers cleared of ice and enough water returned to carry the boats. That was a great deal of time to mull over things.

I left his presence with a handshake. His massive hand could crush mine, but he deftly exerted just enough pressure to be sociable.

The rest of my day was spent pondering the advice of Captain Sulloway. He was a bigger man than I would ever be. He had fought in the war with Mexico, ran steamboats up all the wild western rivers, was a commander in the navy in this last war, and now helps run this great company. He overcame his losses in the great fire and cholera epidemic of '49 too. All he asks of life is full bottle of whiskey, a big cigar, and a position of usefulness.

One night I had a case of the lonesomes and decided on a sociable evening. St. Louis had many things going for it, and one of them was all the right ingredients for a vice district. A convenient locale, personal anonymity, low rents, cheap eats, and strangers coming and going at all hours. Some blocks away from the landing was a club for gentlemen that I frequented on occasion. Being on the river most of the year meant that steamboat men had little chance to properly meet ladies of quality. It was the curse of the profession. The front parlor was where the women waited and a man with means could spend the night conversing and dancing while in the company of the friendly high-strung girls. The bawdy rooms were upstairs. I was warmly received by the hostess, who remembered my patronage of the past. I couldn't exactly claim to be a regular as I frequented the establishment only in the off-season. Well, sometimes between runs, but not always.

The matron introduced me to a fine trio. I said my customary, "I'll buy you a drink, you sing me a song, take me as I come because I can't stay long." Judging by their forced but polite reaction, I might need to work on something new.

I sat with the three lovely creatures who all wanted to hear of my exploits. I was jolted into reality upon the realization that they were simply paid to be so attentive. My old friend James Black in Beardstown was right. No woman would be interested in the travails of navigating through a wooded slough. Well, that didn't stop me. I figured they could earn their pay this evening.

Another steamboat uniform caught my eye across the room, and I instantly recognized our cub pilot Mr. Olsson. He was enraptured by a young lass and seemed to be having a fine time. My assumption proved correct as she led him to the stairs. He did not see me as far as I know, and I would not want to disrupt his evening by approaching him. I would wager he had visited such establishments back home in Jacksonville, Illinois.

I was content with the cigar and neat cognac, along with the conversation with the "spellbound" ladies. I even bought them some fancy drinks. One desired a gin sling, of all things. I was offered a taste and quickly returned to my drink.

I left the establishment shortly before the scandalous hour of midnight. The matron did not mind that I did not venture upstairs as I paid handsomely for the company of the ladies in the parlor. It suddenly occurred to me, though, that none of them pressed their calling all evening. Could it have been my cologne? Maybe I should change brands.

The last weeks of 1865 were proceeding agonizingly slow. There have been nearly constant snow flurries but fortunately the streets of St. Louis have been kept mostly clear by the city's work crews. The almanac says this winter will be a cold one, which means ice will form in the river above St. Louis and will close it down until the spring melt.

Upper Mississippi boats came south for the winter seeking refuge from the snows and ice. Many laid up at St. Louis, Alton, and even in ports further downstream to escape the ravages of nature. The west bank of Arsenal Island was considered the safest winter harbors, but only a fraction of the boats could fit. Owners had to decide to cut their season short to ensure a spot, which meant a loss of revenue. Despite the short winter season, the St. Louis waterfront was sometimes gouged by tons of ice that choked the channel at that point.

The winter ice did indeed form shortly after our return to St. Louis, halting all steamboat traffic north of Cairo. At the waterfront, we could tell this ice came from the Upper Mississippi. Missouri River ice is light and porous, mixed with clay and sand, and it seldom comes in large fields. The ice before our eyes was formed in the deep cold water of the north and was clear and free from impurities. This stuff was as solid as iron and sharp enough to cut through a boat hull with ease. The great weight of this mass covering the river could smash a boat to matchsticks without slowing down. Until the sun arose and ruled the days, no boat could venture out into the stream.

The sun did make an appearance for a few days, and the warming temperatures caused many to doubt the veracity of the Farmer's Almanac. The ice groaned and cracked, and the ice that had covered much of the river north of St. Louis started to break and cleave. The chunks that broke apart, drifted downstream, and piled up to form a temporary dam upstream of St. Louis at Mosenthein Island. It was substantial enough to hold back the river for several miles. As the water behind the jam built up, it rose and broke apart more ice. That action built the pile up to even higher levels, at least ten feet above the surface. Downstream of the jam, the boats at the landing beyond were left stranded on the river bottom as the water drained away.

Several boat officers and owners assembled at the company office to be kept appraised of this perilous situation. I found myself there out of curiosity as last I heard, my boat was still up on the ways in Carondelet waiting its turn for refurbishment. Thomas Geldstein appeared in the lounge to deliver a grim warning. He was using a cane now.

"Gentlemen, if you have valuable property on board your boats, you best get it all off promptly within the hour. After that, it is expected the ice gorge will give way. Do not risk your lives or those of your men further than that appointed time."

Only a handful of men made for the doors with any rush. Most of us had the good sense to remove all valuables and papers from our boats at the end of a season. I took note it was December 16.

As if on que, one hour later, the fire bells rang furiously at the waterfront. We all rushed out to witness the calamity we all knew was coming. Hundreds of people were present to watch the proceedings. I was able to find a good vantage point at the foot of Chestnut Street with some other company men. Thomas was not present as far as I could tell, and he as probably watching from the office. The upper levels of the company building surely held a spectacular view.

Upstream, all could hear the ice breaking with thunderous claps and snaps. Once the water started moving again, sheets of ice passed under the *Sioux City* and *New Admiral,* lifting them up and smashing them against the *Empire City* and *Metropolitan,* carrying them all downriver. The *Highlander, Geneva,* and *Calypso* were wrenched from their moorings and joined the procession. Four wharf boats and at least seven barges were pulled from their resting places to join the dance. This was just the beginning of their travails as they were ground up in the sharp ice and deposited in smashed heaps on the west bank near the hamlet of Kosciusko. The recent arrivals of German Lutherans from the region of Saxony are building a school there and will have some lumber to add to their efforts. The water then rose at the levee, and fortunately, all present were fleet enough of foot to reach higher ground.

With the passing of the shock, the sounds of moaning, mourning, and cursing arose from the witnessing assemblage. Those seven steamers, the wharf boats, and barges represented an investment of at least a million dollars. Surely many owners lost heavily, maybe everything. The dozens of boats that escaped catastrophic loss were surely damaged, being tossed about and pressed against one another and the riverbank. It looked as though the *Grey Eagle* was sinking, and she was in the middle of the distraught fleet. Our company had landed its boats on the south end of the levee after the season and did not lose any steamers outright. There was no way to ascertain the extent of the damage until the danger was past, but there must be some to every boat on the river. The whole affair lasted three hours. It seemed like only a few minutes.

The next day showed the desolation of the waterfront with a depressingly jumbled mass of boats. The great river behind them coursed at full speed, apparently making up for lost time. Large chunks of ice dared anyone to venture out. To add insult to injury, it began to snow heavily, and the temperatures dropped lower than what they had been.

Three days later, the boat owners and captains gathered at the company. Captain Sulloway chaired the meeting with the aim to provide an assessment to known damages to our boats and the outlook for the next season. He did not look well, but his news was a bit reassuring.

"Eight of our twenty boats here received damage from that ice gorge. The most serious was the crushing of a paddle-wheel box on the *Otoe*. We can fix that at the landing. Damage to the other company boats such as the *Quapaw, Auxvasse,* and the *Meramec* was generally confined to the superstructures, which are cheap and easy to repair. We were fortunate in the extreme. The steamboats above Chestnut Street were crushed or pushed into the bank while those south of that point like ours were just jostled together. Our boats undergoing refit at Carondelet are fine."

There was a general mummer of approval.

"How did the other companies fare?" an owner I did not know had asked.

"Good question. The North Western Line lost the *Metropolitan,* but she was almost ten years old. In fact, five of the seven boats sunk were far older than average. The Missouri River boats and the Upper Mississippi companies suffered the brunt. Oh, I'm told the *Grey Eagle* sank this morning, but they expect to raise her and put her back in service. Our major competitors are still strong or will be after repairs."

More murmuring, but more of disappointment.

"Careful, gentlemen. Let us not rejoice in the misfortunes of others. The Good Lord may take note and dish some out for us to swallow. Give thanks for our blessings. This reminds me of '56 when such a disaster struck. We lost a score of vessels then. It can happen again. Now the winter season is not yet over and won't be until late March or April. Do the best to safeguard your vessels. The carpenters of the company will be very busy for several weeks. Employ others as you see fit. We will keep you informed of any further developments."

I had received a short letter from my patents in reply to mine written in St. Paul. Back in Beardstown, Ann had suddenly boarded a steamboat heading downstream a few weeks ago now heading to parts unknown. Naturally, her family was distraught and anxious and were asking me if I would look for her and make inquiries. I would, of course, but she could be anywhere by now. It would have been helpful if they included the name of the boat. It was good to hear, though, that she had been weaned off the opium but had taken up using St. John's Wort as a substitute. I was thankful I got my reply of assurance in the mail before the forming of the ice. The ferry boats were now stranded where they were until spring.

Christmas passed without much notice from me, but I had a grand time at a party celebrating New Year's. Boat captains from all companies met at the ballroom at the National Hotel. Captain Sulloway of course was the life of the party, engaged in swapping stories with the legendary Horace Bixby. I found an interesting chap named Grant Marsh to converse with. He had been up the Missouri River three times in the last two years and was chaffing at the bit for another run. His description of the many obstacles and hostile aborigines did not inspire me at all to steam up the virulent river.

One of the dinner courses included lobster, which I did not find appealing. The issue for me was not that it was shipped from rail at great expense from New York. The hitch was that it resembled a giant cricket and was unappetizing. Out here, lobster may be exotic but back East, the locals feed the horrid creatures to their cats. Although the liquor flowed freely, we men generally behaved ourselves as ladies were present. We all hoped and toasted that the year 1866 would be a good and prosperous one.

Two weeks later, the St. Louis newspapers proclaimed new warnings for an ice breakup expected any day. Those of us with boats on the river received the news with dread and resignation. Nature was in charge, and we had to bow to her whim. Boats had received general repairs since the calamity a few weeks ago, and a few were able to move to more secure ports. My boat escaped damage but was back among the flock of sheep at the landing.

The sun indeed shown forth in its winterly glory in the second week of January. The almanac was wrong again. The ice floe broke apart upstream from the landing, and huge chunks floated by ominously hugging the eastern bank. Many of us thought we might escape serious damage, but word was soon received an ice dam was forming downstream at Cahokia Bend. On Friday the twelfth, the restrained river rose ten feet within thirty minutes. The ice flowing downstream now felt free to spread and soon pressed against the boats at the landing. The *Memphis*, valued at $85,000, was crushed into an unrecognizable pile of scrap, as well as the *Prairie Rose*, *Julia*, and *Warsaw*. The *Memphis*, which had been test-boring for a piling for a proposed bridge by James Eads, had become frozen in the ice days ago. There was no chance to save her, her hulk grounded on Duncan Island. A gargantuan frozen block stove in the hull of the ferry *John Trendly* and dumped her carcass on the Illinois shore. Another scraped off the stern of the *Omaha*. All the other boats were jostled and battered about like toys in a child's washtub. I knew my fine boat was damaged but could not tell how badly. At least she was sill afloat.

Nightfall brought no relief for us as the Mississippi was not through with her torment. We were all powerless, and sleep did not come that night to any riverman. At first light, I made my way to the bank to see what could be left of my boat. It was difficult to spot her in the jumbled mass, but she was afloat a few hundred yards downstream from her mooring. Thanks be to God.

Not all could give such thanks. Seven more boats were listed as a total loss. These were the *Nebraska*, *City of Pekin*, *Hattie May*, *Diadem*,

Viola Belle, Reserve, and *Rosalie.* The two-day scourge also claimed five rock boats and two wharf boats, one of which was the old *Alton.* The *Nebraska* was loaded with furniture and equipment recovered from the *Memphis,* which was stricken yesterday. Of course, all the other boats received more damage above that from the day before. I should not have thought it strange that the stern-wheel boats inordinately received greater damage to the paddle wheels. Their sterns faced the ice and had no structures to protect them.

I overheard a man remark on the *Rosalie,* "She was asking for it, all right. She was launched on a Friday, always sailed on a Friday, and now she was sunk on a Friday."

As if to add credence to this superstition, a cold, steady rain began to fall, which lasted for two days. It was just as well. The Sabbath and the rain gave men time to collect their wits and let the river calm itself before venturing out into the mass of timber to assess the damage.

After four days of waiting, I found the needed for a stiff drink and retreated to the company lounge. There on the board were an initial assessment of all the company boats. For each boat, the list of damages nearly filled the entire page.

I found that the damage to my boat was significant, but her hull and machinery were intact. Not surprisingly. her rudder was smashed, and collisions caved in portions of hurricane deck and the outer edge of main deck. Five days of dedicated repair could get her back on the river. The company's *Otoe* was not sunk, but it was deemed she could not be economically returned to service. She was just over ten years old and well beyond the average age of a steamboat. I suspect she will be made a wharf boat.

"Ah, do you think this is lamentable? The damages back in '56 were worse."

I turned to find Captain Sulloway. I should have guessed he was behind me as the smoke from his harsh cigars and smell of his liquor was unmistakable.

"Come by sometime, and we will discuss in detail the spring season. Mr. Geldstein and I have something special in mind."

"What might that be, sir?"

"You have often lamented the taming of the rivers, with all the markers, dredging, and snag work. You will have a chance of going up the Missouri, all the way to Fort Benton. You might want to find the time to study up on the river and all the native peoples found along the way."

"You can't be serious. Assuming the boat will be ready, she wasn't built for it. She's no mountain boat. Too big. If she doesn't snag, she will be blown upon the bank by those prairie winds. Maybe those wild Indians will attack. The little red devils hate steamboats going through their happy hunting lands. What would be the cargo?"

"General household goods and provisions up, buffalo hides and gold on the way down. If you have space, you can move freight as the opportunity arises along the way. Let us wait until later to discuss the details. In the meantime, you get some rest and think about the necessary preparations. By the way, you look terrible. You need a hair of the dog. Let me buy you a drink. That will fix you up."

The weeks after the ice gorge was spent by the boat companies in getting their boats in shape. The boatyards were full of the most serious cases, so work was done at the landing. With so many boats lost, there was plenty of room for all. Work continued around the clock, with the night illuminated with basket torches and lanterns. Every owner desperately wanted his boat ready for the upcoming season.

I was reading accounts of the mighty Sioux Nation when interrupted by the clambering ringing of the alarm bells at the landing. There had been no word of another ice gorge. It slowly dawned on me there must be a fire. I did not even bother with an overcoat and scrambled out of the company lounge at the run.

Smoke and flame erupted from boats at the foot of Market Street. Fire-hose wagons were already in motion, and soon their pumps would be in operation—that is, if they could get a hose through the ice near shore and into the water. Boat nearby the conflagration were cut loose and pushed into the stream, but their steam was not up, and they were powerless. I gathered up what company men responded to me and made preparations to cut the boat loose from her mooring.

Fortunately, that was not necessary, but four St. Louis steamboats were lost. The *Luna* of the Atlantic and Mississippi Steam Ship Transportation Company and the *Peytona* were a total loss. The *Leviathan* under Captain George Pegram of the Eagle Packet Company was heavily damaged. There was just enough left of her to make her into a wharf boat. The *Dictator* was the most spectacular loss. She was the boat with the fancy new compound-condensing engines and new-style flue boilers. I wondered if she was the cause of all this misfortune. I'm sure many thought the same thing even in the absence of facts. Once again, our company escaped the wrath of nature and man.

"Uh, Captain, does this belong to you?"

A weathered workman held out my cap in his hand. I had not noticed it missing. The cap had not fared well with its short stay on the ground. It had been trampled into the mud and snow by many feet on the landing. The company wheel insignia was cracked in two. It was beyond salvaging, even by my low standards.

"Well, on top of everything, I need to purchase a new hat."

With nothing else to do, I took the omnibus to the Beltzhoover and Bobb Hat Company. It would be ready in a few days. In the meantime, I would walk about bareheaded, which felt unnatural and uncomfortable.

My studies continued. I already knew the Missouri is one cantankerous river as I had been up to Leavenworth City. But that was years ago. I had the river charts and planned to seek out the pilot reports. All rivers jumped out of their channels on occasion, and sandbars and snags appeared and disappeared at whim. But the Missouri was another matter altogether. The channels shift and move around in a manner that denotes a constant search for something long lost. They changed so much and so often the charts were nearly useless. They call it the "Big Muddy," say it is a mile wide and an inch deep, and that the water is too thick to drink and too thin to plow. The water is black as pitch at night with no chance to see snags even with a full moon. And six inches of water looked the same as six feet in such conditions. There would be no running at night. This could be a great adventure, but I was filled with dread. They say men are generally capable of more than they know, but they generally lack confidence, the drive, or the opportunity. I have been very lucky to date, but I could easily lose my boat.

The newspapers all reported of a shocking crime upriver. A bank in Liberty, Missouri, was robbed of its contents by a gang of former Confederate bushwhackers. They did it on a cold snowy day in broad daylight, the first robbery of its kind. They made off with $60,000 worth of cash and certificates, quite a sum. The thieves even had the foresight to demand the stamps required to cash the certificates. The robbery was bloodless until they shot and killed a young college student on the street. Unfortunately, the gang managed to get to their horses and across the water aboard a ferry boat before a posse could intercept them. This is a devastating loss for the people who kept their money in that bank. Life savings vanished in an instant. What is this country coming to?

The Mercantile Library Association contained over eighty thousand volumes, but there was a dearth of books about the Missouri River outside of fiction and novels. I found three reputable sources I thought might be helpful. There was *The Book of the Indians of North America* by Samuel G. Drake, but it was written way back in 1833 and covered mostly the eastern tribes. *The Life, History, and Travels of Kah-Ge-Ga-Gah-Bowh* was published in 1847, but that tribe was from the British Possessions north of the border. There was a copy of the senate report titled "Disbursements for the Benefit of the Indians in 1863," but it did not teach me anything at all beyond the millions of dollars appropriated for the Indian peoples. As the government moved the Indians onto reservations, it took on the responsibility for feeding and equipping them for farming. I could only guess the graft and corruption behind those numbers, and I could imagine a great deal.

I was able to make some generalizations of the Indian from what I read and had already heard. They are an exotic people, without much religion as we know it or government. Some writers, like James Adair, thought they were descendants of the ten lost tribes of Israel. That may be the best way to fit them into Christian history, but that didn't seem quite right. What was clear to me was, the Indians were far behind the white cultures in technological achievements. They had no concept of the workings of the steam engine and could not even smelt iron. All their knives, guns, and even cooking pots came from trading or stealing from the whites. If they were to advance toward modern civilization, they required substantial help from the government. Those Indians that did not wish to modernize risked annihilation in the clash of civilizations. Westward expansion of the United States was a foregone conclusion. The question was how the Indians would fit into it, if at all.

The upper reaches of the Missouri were the lands of the Sioux and Blackfeet. When they were not killing one another, they went after the settlers that strayed from the Emigrant Trails and infiltrated their lands. The army was out there to keep everyone separated but was undermanned and often outgunned. I was to take the boat right into the heart of this mess on a dangerous river. I could lose both my boat and my scalp.

BOOK 4

Up the Missouri

S pring was slow in coming this year, but March brought warmer weather, and a rise in the river was at hand. Then began a whirling dervish of activity at the riverfront. Workmen made final repairs to the boats, and roustabouts brought goods from the warehouses for loading onto the boats. Many rivermen were anxious to get back to work to draw pay as their onshore habits emptied their pockets weeks ago. Boat owners desired their vessels underway to make their profits. I think many of us too just wanted to escape the misfortunes St. Louis endured through the winter.

Those boats planning to head up the Missouri River had at least a few weeks longer to wait. The snow up in the northern mountains had not yet melted. The company advertised my boat's planned departure and called upon men to sign up as crew. Notes were left for me from the officers who sailed with me last season expressing their intent to return. The note that Bosun Joe character left seemed particularly eager. The thought crossed my mind that maybe he was on the run from the law.

I did not often see Thomas Geldstein while I visited the company office. Ever since the assault on the building last season, he mostly remained behind the heavy doors and guards. Naturally, I found Captain Sulloway in the parlor lounge. He was heavier than usual and slower in motion. Perhaps with the return of spring, he would get up and move more. That would do him some good.

"Oh, there you are, lad. Have a seat. Are you all set for your cruise up the Big Muddy?"

"Not yet. We still need to round out the crew, and the cargo isn't scheduled for loading until after the first of April."

"I am not speaking of the boat, silly. I am inquiring about you."

"About as ready as I will ever be."

"Don't be so glum. You act as though we are sending you over Niagara Falls. Such an attitude in infectious and will be noticed by the men. The Missouri is just a river. Like a woman, it has its moods. Because of its great length, you will simply encounter more of them."

"I never had to contend with the Indians before."

"That is correct, but you faced Confederates throughout the war, and those boys had cannon."

I nodded in assent but not in earnestness.

"The best thing to do is to just let the Injuns be. Anchor out in the middle of the river when you stop for the night and post guards to watch both banks. Don't let the men take potshots at them. That tends to rile them up."

"But I would think a good musket volley would make them scamper."

"Don't ever underestimate the red man. They are fiercely proud, and all their actions are guided by that. They are crafty and clever in defending their lifestyle and lands. Don't give them a reason to attack beyond your mere presence. Injuns prefer to strike first from ambush and will simply disappear if they feel they are outgunned. Many of them still use bows and arrows, but more each day carry firearms. They can't hit the broadside of a barn at any distance, but up close they are deadly and will show no mercy."

"Sounds like the Rebs during the war."

"There you go. That's the spirit."

The company posted notices for deckhands and mechanics for the upcoming voyage up the Missouri. At my request, the notice included "No Irish." I had my fill of them and more.

I met with the boat officers on the first of April to discuss the voyage and to identify any problems that we could address before departure. The boat was now repaired, and workmen were applying white paint. Once dry, a few skilled men would repaint her name on the paddle-wheel boxes. One of the laborers had remarked that all our boats had Indian names. It was a flash of the obvious to me. Old Mr. Geldstein thought the natives were a noble breed and paid homage to their spirit. I closed the meeting with a prediction we would steam away on the seventh of April.

Our cub pilot was sporting a black eye and some bruises. I did not mention it at the meeting and figured he had run afoul of a dance-hall girl or her boyfriend. I asked Swanson when the chance arose. No need to embarrass the boy.

Word got around he was a three-hundred-dollar man who avoided service in the war. Olsson was roughed up by some men in a saloon, but not badly. Maybe he won't act so smug about it anymore. I thought Jacksonville, Illinois, was full of patriots. General Benjamin Grierson hailed from there, as I recall.

"Tell me, Swanson, why did you take him on as a cub pilot. He is learning, but his pace is slow. He is just plain odd sometimes."

"Well, the money was the kicker. But he came highly recommended from a company boat."

"Which one was that?"

"You won't like to hear it, but it was the *Kaw Nation*. You know how he feels about killing and such. He was only a mud clerk, and I can't imagine how he could have been involved with any of Foley's shenanigans."

"You are probably right about that. He did his job with us without hindrance or complaint about our actions."

The riverfront became quiet when all the downbound boats departed. What was left were those waiting for good conditions to steam up the Mississippi or the Missouri. Any time, though, boats would begin arriving from other ports. My plan was to allow a few boats take the lead up the Missouri and follow in their wake. They presumably knew the river better than Swanson or I did. Most of the goods on board were on consignment with a merchant or agent already awaiting them. There was no need to race ahead to ensure a good price.

The preparations for the voyage came to fruition as planned on Saturday, April 7. The boat was fully loaded with cargo two days ago, and today 205 passengers shuffled aboard. I disliked carrying passengers as they were nothing but trouble, but Bosun Joe convinced me that the three hundred dollars fare charged to each passenger made it quite worth the potential irritation. They were all considered deck passengers, but we arranged to tarp off the stern quarter of the boiler deck. There, the womenfolk could find refuge from the foul language and habits of the men.

I made my way to the pilothouse and found Swanson and Olsson. Olsson's face looked much improved.

"Good morning, Captain! The coffee is ready. Oh, I see you purchased a new hat. Looks fine. We're just waiting on Mr. Weatherby to signal he has steam up. That will be any minute. First Mate Voight reports his deckmen are ready to cast off."

"Well, with this auspicious beginning, this should be a fine voyage. Shove off as soon as steam is up, Mr. Swanson."

A quick look up the landing showed a grand sight of at least two dozen boats getting up steam. The dockmaster was pacing with his green flag waiting for the first boat to signal she was in readiness to depart. There was no sign of any ferry craft coming from the Illinois side, so all in all, the river was free and clear to navigate.

A deep *harrumph* and shouts of men interrupted the proceedings. It was an unmistakable sound that filled every riverman with dread. Our young cub pilot, Mr. Olsson, spotted it first.

"A combustion, Captain! Looks to be the *Frank Bates* on fire up yonder!"

That it was. The flames spread remarkably fast and quickly alighted the *Nevada* and *Effie Dean* moored close by. Panicked passengers scrambled to collect their belongings and get ashore, but it quickly became a race to just save their lives. Horses and other livestock screamed in terror and pain. Someone had the thought to open the chicken coop on the hurricane deck on the *Nevada*, and the birds flew to freedom. Freedom is not the same as safety as most of them ended up in the river and swept downstream.

"Mr. Swanson, give the signals to depart immediately. We will operate with whatever steam Mr. Weatherby has cooked up so far. Take a position just downstream so we may render assistance if needed."

The boat was soon out into the water and in safety for the moment. I retrieved my spyglass and witnessed the latest disaster to hit St. Louis. In her haste to depart and escape the fires, the *Alex Majors* blew her boilers and set the *Fanny Ogden* alight. The boats afire remained on the bank as the inferno was too hot to allow the men to get near enough to cast them off. The towboat *Dan Hine* tried to assist but found the flames too dangerous as well. The remaining steamboats moored up and downstream of the conflagration made it safely into the river or were too distant already to be molested. I was glad to see our company boat *Tamarod* safely underway. Swanson had kept the boat in position out in the river for a good thirty minutes before I gave the order to proceed upstream and head for the Missouri. There was simply nothing to do but watch anyway. The loss of those boats was quite a shame, especially since they were all just recently repaired and were fully loaded with cargo. The loss of the *Effie Dean* was especially ruinous for Captain Joseph La Barge. Yesterday he balked at the high prices of insurance for cargo and boat and denied coverage. The famed riverman lost everything. I learned later that with his good name, he was able to secure enough loans to build a new boat, the *Octavia*. She would be ready in the autumn.

Boat losses since last summer have been horrific. St. Louis lost its fair share, but such disasters had happened in other ports too. The newspapers reported that fifty-four boats were lost in the Red River alone since last June. Insurance rates on cargo are already high, and the merchants will have to shoulder even higher prices in the future. More general freight will be lost to the railroads if steamboat safety cannot be reestablished quickly.

Mr. Olsson groaned and held a hand to his lower gut. Maybe he was overcome by the happenings on the St. Louis landing. Mr. Swanson asked the obvious question.

"What ails you, cub? You look a little peaked."

"Not sure. Sometimes it hurts to urinate. I need to be excused for a minute to answer the call."

I absentmindedly said, "Merry Christmas." He looked at me with astonishment. As far as I know, he did not see me at the bawdy house several weeks ago. He must wonder if I had detectives tracking his movements.

"Sometimes you're a hard man to like, Captain."

"Only a dod-limbed fool is rude when there is no need. My apologies, Mr. Olsson. Tend to your business. Mr. Swanson, I am going below to make my rounds. Steady on as she goes."

St. Louis has long been known as the gateway to the West with good reason. First the steamboats and increasingly the railroads emanating from here take goods and people deep into the continent. The fur trade started it all, but the America Fur Company fell on hard times and was sold off a few months ago. The Montana and Idaho Transportation Line was also formed a few weeks back, promising to become the largest company sending steamboats emanating from St. Louis and steaming up the Missouri. Our company was still not focused on any particular river. That has been good practice in the past as it has been able to shift boats to meet demand. On the other hand, such companies can dominate a single section of a river and squeeze us out.

I found my first mate on the forecastle instructing the new men in the use of the leader ropes and poles. These men will be quite important when we enter the Missouri. They will be used almost continuously to sound the bottom all the way to Fort Benton, over two thousand miles upstream.

"We have a very novice deck crew, Captain. Almost all are greenhorns to be sure. Over half are Negroes too. It's the best we could do. The more experienced men already shipped out with the boats heading down the Mississippi. Two of the Negroes are said to be fair at carpentry. They may prove to be useful in that profession when we venture beyond civilization."

"What do you make of the passengers, Mr. Voight?"

"Mostly settlers with some miners, gamblers, and general riff-raff thrown in. They are all armed to the teeth. The men have at least two revolvers, a rifle, and a shotgun. The St. Louis gunsmiths are all represented. I've seen every type and caliber from Hawken, Gemmer, and Dimick. A fair number of surplus muskets too. Lord knows what the women are packing."

"I'm glad to see no livestock at least. I won't collect up the firearms just yet. Pass the word, though, that I will do so at the first hint of trouble. The passengers should just pack them up until perhaps we get into Indian territory."

"Aye, Captain. I will see to getting the word out."

I had little doubt that the passengers would comply with Mr. Voight. In normal times, he is a kind man. Get him riled, though, and that 180 pounds of gristle he consists of turns into a formidable juggernaut.

"Speaking of firearms, we still have the ten Sharps rifles aboard, and the company again loaned us ten of those Henry rifles. Once we reach St. Joseph, we will need to instruct the crew on their use."

I meandered my way to the oilers and engines. The main deck was overcrowded with people and cargo. The settlers were keen-eyed and alert, but they all seemed dirtier than they should have been just starting out. With their dull-colored clothes, these people may well be from the Southern states and looking for a new home. The men and some of the women were engaged in the national pastime of chewing tobacco. They were already fouling the decks with their nasty habit. I wondered if they realized fully that they would probably never see their families and kin left behind. Pioneer settlers seldom did.

I knew the coal bunkers were filled, but there was an inordinate amount of coal bushels stacked about. I went aft to inquire about it with my chief engineer. I found Mr. Weatherby instructing the men on the steam gauges. Good man. He stopped at my approach.

"Mr. Weatherby, it appears we have a great deal of fuel on board in spaces we could have been used for cargo."

"Aye, Captain, 'tis true, but coal will be getting scarce the further we go up the Missouri. After we pass St. Joseph, we will be burning wood for a few thousand miles. Just like the old days."

"Very well. We will try to replenish what coal you burn along the way, but supplies may be limited indeed. We should reach St. Joseph in eight days. It appears you have several Negroes in your department. Do you foresee any problems?"

"They should work out fine. Most here will tend the fires, but some show an aptitude to be oilers. One, though, claims to be a talented blacksmith. Although I brought along a veritable cornucopia of bolts and various spare parts, he may come in handy."

"That's fine. Be sure they wear their company pin. I want it made clear to the passengers these men are part of the crew. I will put ashore anyone who thinks they can mistreat them."

"Aye, Captain. It will be a pleasure."

We spoke loudly enough for the gawking passengers to overhear. Word should get around the boat quickly enough.

I had not seen my chief clerk yet and decided to pay him a call. I had hoped to find a reason to replace Bosun Joe but could not conjure one big enough to bring up to Thomas Geldstein. There was a bond between those two I could not quite grasp. I found ol' Joe in his office, sitting like a dragon on his hoard. My old friend Captain Bemis always gave me the same impression. I wondered how the uniped was faring.

"How are the accounts looking, Bosun Joe? If all goes well, should this be a profitable voyage?"

"Oh my, yes, Captain. We have a full load of trade goods for the wanting people of the far-northern reaches. We even have a stamp mill for the mines. It is broken down and crated just forward of the boilers. We're being paid a whopping dollar and twenty-five per hundredweight. I know you don't like to carry troublesome passengers, but they have paid a premium price for the ride. When their food runs out, we will charge them for feeding."

"The Montana Territory is quite a distance from old Dixie. Will you be able to adjust?" I was attempting to be jovial. Bosun Joe was jovial in return.

"Oh, I am very much looking forward to reaching Fort Benton and its environs. Good Confederate territory."

"What? What are Rebs doing that far north?"

"Lots of them went upriver to avoid the war and start mining. Some say the left wing of Sterling Price's army skedaddled up there after his raid in '64. The men thought it best to avoid persecution for their war service under Yankee occupation."

"Well, maybe you will run into a few old acquaintances. No offense. At least you need not worry about an Indian wanting your scalp. There is not a hair on it."

"Oh, I don't know about that. It would make a nice pair of moccasins."

The boat steamed along under fair skies and light winds from the northwest. We made the mouth of the Missouri in good time only having to dodge a few chunks of ice. They floated low in the water, indicating their origin was from the Upper Mississippi. By all appearances, the Missouri was now ice-free. With the ongoing mountain-snow melt, there should be plenty of water.

I returned to the pilothouse and found our cub at the wheel. Swanson was reclining on the bench smoking a pipe. That was new for him. He had been smoking cigars. Young Mr. Olsson also had a pipe in his mouth. He was clenching it with his teeth, and it was not lit. There was just over half a pot of coffee on the stove, and half of that went into my tankard.

"How is the river, gentlemen?"

"Gracious. There are snags aplenty. I counted forty on that last bend. Every cottonwood tree they cut down makes another. We are keeping in the middle of the river and hoping for the best."

"Do your utmost. It would be a pity to be thwarted at this early stage."

During the day, we serenely passed Howard Bend, Creve Coeur Lake, and came up on Bon Homme Island. That was the name on the chart, but it was also known as Good Mans Island and Isle au Bon Homme. The burned-out hulk of the *New Lucy* served as a reminder of the dangers of fire. She was known as a fine floating palace but caught fire while laid up. Only her charred hull on the bank was left. Steaming up further, we came across the famous huge sandstone bluff called Tavern Rock. Lewis and Clark made note of it in their journals, and it was used by French and Spanish trappers and traders as a shelter. Tavern Rock rose to a height of three hundred feet and was a prominent landmark. The last time I was on this stretch of river, I had missed the spectacle. I was off shift and slept though the passing.

We passed the hamlet of St. Albans and then Augusta. This was wine country, and the vines lined the hills on both banks. Here they grew the famous Norton and Catawba wine grapes that people of the entire country clamored for. The Mount Pleasant Winery was making a fortune for Georg and Friedrich Muench. I knew this by reading the labels on the bottle.

We did not land but pushed ahead to put ashore at Washington for the night. These were strange waters for Swanson and me, and it made no sense to endanger the boat on this largely unmarked river. The boat's signal "Hip, hip, hooray!" reverberated for the first time on this river. Washington was populated with just under two thousand pro-Union antislavery German immigrant families, which had pushed out most of the original slave owners. The town was ransacked by General Sterling Price's Reb soldiers in '64 but was rebuilding. We found just enough coal to replenish what we burned during the day. Two boats that departed before us got the jump on the limited supply.

We had steamed over eighty-four miles on the river but were only fifty or so miles from St. Louis as the crow flies. Such was the nature of the winding circuitous river. Surprisingly, we all had a quiet evening once all the coal was loaded. Some fellow on the boiler deck had brought along one of those large Spanish guitars and played rather melancholy tunes until the folks drifted off to sleep.

The events, or more like the lack of notable events, continued as we steamed upriver. The crew was kept active feeding the furnaces, sounding the water depth, and keeping everything running smoothly. We had a new cook on board, and he was doing a fair job. At this time of year, there was no fresh produce, and our diet consisted of foods that were salted, smoked, dried, or pickled. At least he knew how to bake, and the various breads were actually quite good. True to Bosun Joe's prediction, the number of passengers who wanted to purchase food from us grew. At this rate, we would need to get groceries when we came ashore at nights. Navigation became easier when we fell in behind two steamboats heading upstream. They were the *Mollie Dozier* and the *Waverly* out of St. Louis. They were both side-wheelers about the same size as this boat, and where they could go, we should be able to as well. We would follow them closely as long as we could.

While making my rounds, there was time to speak with the men. The white men were quick to complain to the mates, so I reckoned I knew how they were doing. The Negroes were a silent lot. That could mean they were doing just fine or simply suffered in silence. I found a group of five at the stern taking a break.

"Gentlemen, how is the trip so far? Are you being treated well? How is the food?"

"We can't complain much, Captain. The bosses work us hard, but that still beats chopping tobacco."

"Do you feel you are treated more harshly than the white crewmen?"

"Well, they don't have to work the fireboxes or scrub out the boilers, but everything else is the same. Even the food. That surprised us."

"Tending the machinery is the job of Mr. Weatherby's crew, which you are part. The deck crew tends to the rest of the ship. I don't know what you signed on for with my chief clerk, but you will be getting paid the same wages as the white fellows. Keep that under your hats as I don't what any trouble from the rest of the crew."

"My gawd, sir, won't that get you in trouble with your boss and the other boats?"

"The company owner, Mr. Thomas Geldstein, insists upon it. I will tell you what I tell every man on this boat. We pay a fair wage but expect a fair day's labor. There will be good days and bad. I will treat you like the men you are until the day you cross me. Do we have an agreement?"

"Yes, Captain, sir. You sure do."

"Very well. Carry on."

Departed their company I could overhear their excitement. My euphoria was brought back down to reality when one man questioned my sincerity and thought my comments were a ruse. He called his accomplices "Uncle Toms" for being so trusting. I vowed to prove that man wrong even if it had to come from my own pocket. I didn't start slavery, but I helped end it. Now it was time to get the black race up on its feet. It was just not an economic issue for me anymore but a moral one. It was nearly time to relieve Mr. Swanson, so a return to the pilothouse was in order.

Following the steamboat *Mollie Dozier* came in handy at the sharp bends at St. John's Island. My inclination was to take the southern chute, but she went to the right instead. I soon saw why. The southern chute was spitting out trees like a meat grinder this morning. This boat was drawing about three feet and a half of water and the *Mollie Dozier* probably four. Wherever she went, we could too. My only complaint with this arrangement was that the *Mollie* had only three boilers and was not steaming as fast as I would like. I could overtake her, but her pilots knew the waters better.

We were still in wine country as we passed Herman, Missouri. Wooded bluff and rolling hills graced the south bank. Some folks call this the Missouri Rhineland on account of all the grapes grown here. The soil could support other crops, but the steep slopes of these hills were best used for viticulture.

Mr. Voight came up to the pilothouse to inform us that a family needed to depart the boat at the next landing. Their children had taken ill, and of course, we had no means of medical treatment. We briefly put ashore at Shipley's Landing just below the mouth of Loose Creek. I directed Bosun Joe to give them a partial refund, just charging for their travels here. That wasn't required by law or tradition, but it was the Christian thing to do. They had enough troubles.

We made an overnight stop at Jefferson City, the capital of the state. Here we were able to replenish our coal, but as the railroad came through here, the competition drove the prices up. After four days on the boat with weeks to go, most of the passengers took the opportunity to disembark to stretch their legs. Some noted deficiencies in their preparations and went into town to purchase various items. I noted with some satisfaction that I had prepared well for this season by stocking up on cigars, whiskey, various sundries, and even wine. I was thankful we had not resorted to burning wood yet.

Jefferson City should be an attractive town by now, nestled in the valley with wooded hills beyond. The war, though, brought a stagnation to its businesses; and the series of entrenchments ringing the city were an ugly scar on the land. They were built in haste to deter an attack by Sterling Price's army during his famous raid through Missouri. I could see why he did not attack the town. His army of cavalry would have not fared well against these fortifications.

The settlers and crew were warned that we would depart promptly at the appointed hour with or without them. All the crew was accounted for and I have no idea if all the passengers made it back. We seldom kept a list of them. Certainly not when we were carrying this many.

The sun was slow to rise. So too were the crewmen, even then Negroes. It was early April, but the mornings were still cold. There was a dampness in the air that seeped down into the joints. The mates stomped about and shouted for the men to rise without immediate effect. Passengers on the boiler deck cursed and shouted for quiet. The tossing of a man from his bunk did the trick. The men yawned, stretched, and moaned their way below to the main deck to start their day.

Some riverboat captains complained about the shallow Missouri River and the difficulty of finding parts deep enough to navigate. So far, I would not blame them. Even at high water such as this, finding the channel has been a challenge. Little has been done over the years to improve it as a useful waterway. Just some wing dams here and there. It has been nerve-wracking, and I could see why some captains would say that crews navigating the Missouri needed more whiskey than those on other rivers. Some captains were known to fill a bucket full of liquor every few hours and put it on the deck to help deckhands unwind. I was not so carefree with the liquor. For this voyage, I did allow crewmen to buy a snort for five cents no more than three times a workday and one more if we labored into the night. If he wanted any more than that, he had to bring his own. I was not running a saloon. What we did provide the men in abundance was the cauldron of coffee. The cook sold it by the cup to the settlers, but often that was the boiler-coffee variety.

The boat was ready to depart, but we waited for the *Mollie Dozier* to back out onto the river first. Her pilot, George Keith, was hesitant to do so as we were in position to be given the right of way. A friendly toot on the whistle and wave of a cap reassured him we would not collide. I could not blame the man as most times steamboats vied for position on the river. Our yielding the lead must have seemed unusual. Maybe, but his boat will find the snags and sandbars for us. I met Captain Frank Dozier at the New Year's party in St. Louis. He is quite proud of his new boat and named it for his wife.

We passed by the hamlet of Nebraska, which never recovered from the flood of '44. After that tragic event, most of the inhabitants moved their lives over to Providence. Providence is a busy port for the local trade with boats dropping off cargo to be carried to Columbia. Packet boats come by too, picking up Boone County's goods bound for St. Louis or the City of Kansas. The town its famous for its whiskey, said to be the best in these parts. Unfortunately, the railroad chose to bypass Providence, and its future is uncertain.

The Confederate hotbed of Booneville came into view. The town was settled in the early 1800s by the bothers of Daniel Boone himself and was active in the frontier trade. The railroad ran through town and hosted General Price's horde for several days during their raid through Missouri late in the war. Boonville is also a starting point for the Santa Fe Trail. It is here that we landed for coal and to depart some passengers with their goal of trekking down that trail into the desert. Good luck to them. We now had more than 230 miles under our belts.

"Gentlemen. The chart here annotates the wreck of the *Twilight* in these parts but says nothing of the cause."

"The charts seldom do, Mr. Olsson. If the wreck is along the river, the cause was probably a snag or a sandbar. If on a bend or near port, chances are, it was a boiler explosion. What is important is that it shows a location of potential danger. The wreck could pose a threat as well. Do you know of the *Twilight*, Captain?"

"If I recollect correctly, there was an account in the newspapers last fall that said she was snagged there opposite Fire Creek. I remember it because she was reported to have a large amount of good whiskey on board."

We came upon a prominent flint-bearing bluff on the river called Arrow Rock. It is a grand sight and was home to Dr. John

Sappington, the man who years ago developed quinine to treat malaria from cinchona bark of all things. It is far more effective than ingesting calomel. That stuff just makes things worse for any ailment. The town of Arrow Rock has been stagnant for years and suffered a brutal fire two years ago. As the railroad bypassed it by several miles, its future is uncertain. The steamboat trade has been keeping it alive. Arrow Rock's population is about a thousand and is dropping rapidly.

We encountered the dreaded bend at Lexington, Missouri. It was here the *Saluda* exploded her boilers back in '52 attempting to push through the narrow channel and stiff currents at full steam. Dozens of people were killed and injured. Captain Lebarge's brother was the pilot who was killed in the blast. I saw the good captain speaking with Captain Sulloway at the New Year's party in January. Quite a shame. We did not have the troubles in navigating the bend as did the *Saluda*.

The City of Kansas was the next urban center, and it was originally a fur-trading outpost. For years, the economic powerhouse in the area has been the city of Westport just two miles up the Kaw River. It was there that General Sterling Price's Confederate army was soundly defeated in the autumn of '64. We could see no signs of entrenchments or battle damage from the river. Westport has an excellent landing, but the Missouri Pacific Railroad decided to end its terminus in the City of Kansas, or Kansas City, if you will. No one seems to be agreeable on what to call the town. The charts say "City of Kansas." A few months ago, though, the Union Pacific connected here with its lines to the west. The town across the river is called Wyandotte, and I suspect it will never amount to much. All the trade was over here. We joined several boats at the landing, but we had no trade to conduct. We were interested only in acquiring coal. This was also our last opportunity to conduct any major repairs before heading upriver. Mr. Weatherby, though, was confident all was well with the machinery. He only procured more lubricants as a precaution, and we pushed on.

"Gentlemen, the chart says the *Arabia* wreck is nearby. What caused her demise?"

"I defer to you, Mr. Swanson. What can you tell Mr. Olsson of the *Arabia?*"

"Not much beyond that she hit a snag and sank quickly about ten years ago. There was no loss of life, but the hulk filled with mud so quickly the cargo was not recovered. She is not even considered a navigation hazard."

Just ahead, Leavenworth City, Kansas, came into view. We have come exactly five hundred miles from St. Louis according to these miserable charts. The city is just as dirty and dreary as I remembered it from six years ago. The yellow flea-bitten mutt was still here too, barking his greeting to arriving steamboats. The grand Planter Hotel was missing, though. As its lot was still vacant, my guess was that it suffered a catastrophic loss such as fire. The town was growing, though, by the looks of the new buildings expanding now at least ten blocks from the river. By my reckoning, Leavenworth must be grateful to the proximity of the fort sharing the name. Fort Leavenworth most certainly shielded the town from Confederate attack during the war.

The Great Western Stove Company and Foundry had expanded their business, occupying several blocks near the landing. The company originally made steam engines and steamboat parts, but the signage now proudly advertised its wood- and coal-burning stoves. With the state of the river traffic, there was far more demand for stoves than steamboat parts. At the landing waited a dozen wagons for the firm William Russell, Alexander Majors, and Waddell. It is said these experienced freighters hired 1,700 men as teamsters and owned 7,500 head of oxen and 500 wagons. If you wanted to ship freight down the Santa Fe Trail from here, this was the firm to hire.

The *Waverly* passed by, and I decided to leave the *Mollie Dozier* behind. We had need to only drop off some freight while she had more involved plans. We pulled off the landing in friendly pursuit of the *Waverly* and steamed north into strange waters for me.

The boat steamed north and, within three miles, passed the landing at Fort Leavenworth. The fort was built in 1827 and named for the War of 1812 veteran General Henry Leavenworth. Its main purpose was to separate the warring Indian tribes and to protect pioneers along the Santa Fe Trail. It never has come under direct attack by anyone but served as a training ground for new regiments during the war and as an arsenal and supply depot for all the forts scattered across the West. Just upstream, we easily avoided Kickapoo Island.

Seven miles further is the town of Weston, Missouri. In contrast to Leavenworth City, Weston, Missouri, is a fine town with brick buildings indicating a permanence not given by wood-frame construction. Steep wooded hills form a semicircle around the town adding to its beauty. It seemed strange to me so far north, but this here was tobacco and hemp country, and Weston was the chief port of export. The landing looked well-tended and quite handy at the food of the main street. I never set foot here but have partaken of the fine lager beer of the Weston Brewing Company and whiskey from the McCormick's Distillery. The war was not kind to Weston, though, and her population dropped from five thousand to just over one thousand.

The Missouri River is also cottonwood country, and in early spring they produce tiny red blooms that are pleasing to the eye. This is followed by masses of seeds with a cottony covering that blow across the land covering it with a layer of white that resembles a frost. The fluff gets into everything, even finding its way into clothing. I could not discern what practical good comes from a cottonwood tree.

We passed by Atchison, Kansas, Columbus Landing, Maysville, and Hart's Landing without a need to stop, although other boats had found a reason to. Indeed, the Lower Missouri was teeming with boats so far. This particular stretch of the river was quite pleasant, and Swanson gave Olsson an extended time at the wheel.

Beyond Civilization

The boat reached St. Joseph in the late afternoon, an hour earlier than I expected, a full 595 miles from St. Louis. The hated Hannibal and St. Joseph Railroad ends here and is the last point of civilization for us and for settlers heading west across the vast prairie. St. Joseph became nationally famous with the establishment of the Leavenworth and Pike's Peak Express Company. Most people called it the simpler "Pony Express." Riders rode at a gallop in relays all the way out to Sacramento, California, and back carrying mail at exorbitant prices. That ill-fated venture was never profitable as it took too much infrastructure to work. The business couldn't stay in the black while caring for horses, waystations, and paying dozens of men. The telegraph quickly surpassed and replaced it after only eighteen months in operation.

St. Joseph appeared to be an industrious city. Two lumberyards were visible from the landing, and I could smell a vinegar factory somewhere. The Occidental and the Pacific hotels each had signs at the riverfront, but there were surely more hotels with a city of this size and importance. There was also an advert for Dr. C. Adams, a noted occultist apparently. I thought it might be fun to inquire to our fortune on this run and then compare notes with him upon our return. I quickly thought better of it. No need to antagonize the Good Lord at this critical juncture.

I enjoyed a smoke of a cigar while the men tended to the boat and the roustabouts unloaded and loaded more cargo. The working men of St. Joseph reminded me of the good times at St. Louis just a few years ago who toiled hard for a good day's wage. The settlers and passengers broke out their musical instruments and played like they were going to town. As always, I forbade the practice while underway as the crewmen could not always hear the bell and whistle signals over the instruments and stomping. We weren't the navy, though. The people on board could whistle all they liked, and here they could sing if they wanted. The passengers now retrieved their weapons from their baggage. Upstream from here was mostly Indian territory. Except for a few small towns or outposts, it is a lawless land of gypsies, tramps, and thieves. Only the residual goodness found in man or a loaded gun kept the peace, and that wasn't much to bank on.

Across the way, Bosun Joe broke from a group of shipping agents and strode toward me. His face had an anxious expression, and his step was quick, almost breaking into a run. This was obviously the result of something of importance, so I made my way forward to the forecastle to meet him. He again took off his hat and held across his chest like a slave talking to his master. I believe he was just using these opportunities to show off his glabrous head. The shine from it nearly blinded me.

"Captain! Those men over yonder are forwarding agents for the Woolworth and Barton Company. They did business with that scoundrel Foley but a few days ago. He doesn't have his own boat but arranged a shipment of Indian trade goods and several barrels of whiskey on credit aboard the *Marcella*."

"That is too miraculous to be true. If so, he must have caught the railroad in Hannibal and came here. Tarnation. Where is he headed? We haven't yet come across the *Marcella*."

"Upriver is all they know for sure. One man thinks he may be headed up the Yellowstone. Another says Fort Benton."

"Any accomplices?

"None they know of, but in the past, Foley always had some men handy. Do you mean to overtake the *Marcella* like we did the *Kaw Nation*?"

"I saw the *Marcella* in St. Louis. She is a nimble little stern-wheeler at about seventy tons with a good head start. She can go up almost any tributary, and we cannot follow. The chase could end up resembling the pursuit of a will-o'-wisp in the bayou. We will have to settle for keeping an eye out for her and for any sign of Foley. We will push off when the handling of cargo is finished, and we have all the coal we can carry. We will be burning wood when that is depleted."

A man was sent to the Missouri and Western Telegraph Company office to wire back word that we made St. Joseph in fine shape, and we had an intimation of old "Gold Vest's" whereabouts. Runners were sent to the Empire Billiard Hall to alert the crewmen who had sauntered there for amusement. The allure of the place was understandable. If you believed their advert, it is the largest and most commodious billiard hall in the West. There are five new and beautiful tables made by Julius Balkes, a bar stocked with the finest liquors, wines, and cigars. I strode over to the tobacco store owned by Deichman and Fuelling to stock up for the long slog that was to come. My tobacco habit had increased to five a day. They say that General Grant smoked early two dozen a day. I don't see how he does it, but then again, he doesn't drink, according to him.

It was time for me to get ready to enter Indian territory. While in St. Louis, I procured some papered cartridges for the Paterson revolver. They were made for the Colt navy pistol, but the shopkeeper assured me they would work. The powder charge and bullet are in one piece, and all one must do is insert it into one of the five holes in the cylinder and clamp it down with the special loading tool the Paterson requires. Other revolvers would just use their loading levers. The standard percussion cap ignites the powder and sends the ball along its way. The thin paper is treated with some chemical and thoroughly combusts, allowing a reload without too much fuss. Unlike most revolvers, the Paterson requires a partial disassembly, and the new cartridges do not correct that deficiency. If these rounds work, it will mean no more reloading with an awkward powder flask.

I was not to be disappointed. The first lead ball I tried was a tight fit, testing the gun metal to the limit. The lead projectile seated and left a nice residual ring of metal, the telltale sign it was a good fit. I also found use for the new cartridges in the Savage navy revolver. I had never fired it before but have practiced with it somewhat while unloaded. The last time I had seen it in action was when Ann tried to blow my head off and fumbled the job. If I ever used it, I didn't want to follow her example. I left the Savage in a trunk in my cabin. The little Rood revolver in the suspender holster got a good cleaning and fresh powder and caps. The Paterson went to its holster as I ascended to the pilot house. The gun belt got hung next to Mr. Swanson's Remington revolver.

"Good morning, Captain. Coffee is on the stove."

"Good morning gentlemen. I see you are prepared to defend yourself, Mr. Swanson."

"Indeed, Captain. She is all cleaned up with fresh cartridges and caps. I don't want a misfire when the need arises."

"Mr. Olsson, are you armed?"

"No, Captain. I don't hold with personal firearms. A man could get hurt. I'm just an innocent bystander."

"They are the ones that usually get shot. If you change your mind, I have a one-shot derringer in my possibles bag hanging over there. Help yourself when the need arises."

"No thank, sir."

"Suit yourself."

With steam up, we pushed off the landing and followed in the wake of the sternwheeler *Cora*. She had half the tonnage of this boat and could navigate on a damp sponge. With her shallow draft, we couldn't blindly stick to her. She might at least show us the main channel.

We passed Brownville, Nebraska, a well-established town dating back to 1854. Passing through Weeping Water Bottoms, the town of Nebraska City then came into view. We nosed onto the bank to procure wood. It was all cottonwood, one of the poorest fuels a boat could use. It produced more smoke than heat and fouled the stacks with creosote. Cottonwood was not good for much of anything, and when it was put to good use, it was usually fences or cargo pallets. It was all that was available, though; and as feared, it would be our primary source of fuel for the duration of the voyage. I pondered the cost and benefit of buying the buildings and furniture of the town to burn instead. The cottonwood won the calculations but just barely.

The hamlet of Nebraska City had grown out of the remains of Fort Kearny, which the army abandoned back in '48. A sidenote on the charts named this place Table Creek, but I trusted the sign at the landing more than the charts printed way back in St. Louis. Here was also the *Deer Lodge*. She is a handy little stern-wheel boat at about 170 tons, less than half our size and length. What amazed me is that she was equipped with a portable sawmill. Nothing fancy, but enough to process her own wood or fuel. I so much wanted one now. The *Cora* stopped here too. She was slightly larger than the *Deer Lodge*, but I now remembered her as sunk by a snag last year up this river somewhere. She must have been repaired and put back into service.

Passing up the narrows through Florence Bend, we made it just to Omaha for the night as the rain was coming in intermittent showers, being pushed by a fitfully gusting wind. We made plans to refuel and steam the next morning. We were burning between thirty and sixty cords of wood a day, depending on the poor quality of the fuel. At an average of three dollars a cord, this was one expensive run. Not much rest would come for the crew. The stacks and boilers were in much need of cleaning. As expected, there was no appreciable amounts of coal to be had. What little there was to be found was meant for the local blacksmiths and the few homes that could afford it. My regret for not landing across the river at Council Bluffs was lifted when told there was no coal there either. I knew the Union Pacific railroad planned the transcontinental line to run through here, and President Lincoln himself proclaimed Council Bluffs to be the starting point. I smiled to think that the railroads would have to haul coal here at considerable trouble and expense. The railroad-construction boom attracted hundreds of Irish immigrants to Council Bluffs who congregated in "Irish Hollow." Maybe they were more suited to railway work than steamboats. In the last year and a half, the railroad has spent over $500,000 in surveying and construction and only has forty miles completed to Fremont. At this rate of construction, it would be years before the line is completed.

Our departure in the morning was delayed due the efforts of cleaning the boilers and stacks. I was disappointed in Mr. Weatherby and his men, but they did work all through the night. Few on board slept well with all their banging and cussing. The *Deer Lodge* and *Cora* both left without us, and there were no other boats in sight. It was time for Swanson and me to earn our pay as pilots. We had been on this Missouri River for several days and were becoming in tune with its moods, so to speak.

We came upon Desoto Bend and the site of the wreck of the famous steamboat *Bertrand,* one of several steamboats in the "Mountain Fleet" of the Montana and Idaho Transportation Line. The *Bertrand* was only a month old and on her maiden voyage when she caught a snag and sank. That was just a year ago, and she carried a full load of cargo for Virginia City. Curiously, she was not salvaged. We could not locate the wreck as the sands and mud of the river claimed her carcass. I had met her captain, James Yore, back in St. Louis during the party for the New Year.

The tilled fields and wooded hills had given way to the vast rolling prairies. There was unbroken wilderness, where nothing dwelt except wild animals and wilder men. Sights of deer were common as well as giant flocks of waterfowl and ducks. This was indeed unspoiled land where no civilized habitation greeted the eye. We had a few days of rain here and there, but they were not troublesome enough to require a halt. But at the end of each, the tallgrasses were taller and greener than before.

A knock on the door of the pilothouse broke the spell of the beauty around me. Unfortunately, it woke Swanson. He needed all the rest he could get.

"Yes, Mr. Voight?

"Mr. Weatherby reports we are running low on wood and suggests we stop at the nearest woodpile. We only have a few hours of it left."

"Damnation. It looks as though a daily search for wood will be our lives for weeks to come. Very well. Have the men ready with axes and saws. We may be required to cut our own."

"Captain, the chart here says there is a woodcutting outfit ten miles upstream just beyond Onawa Bend. Perhaps that is an opportune opportunity."

"Very well. We'll make for that, Mr. Voight."

We had passed a few such outfits since St. Joseph. They were generally located at a small landing with a log cabin or tent and displayed a small flag or rag tied to a pole to attract attention. We landed with a short peal to the whistle to announce our arrival. I went below to the forecastle with Bosun Joe. Perhaps we could negotiate a good price.

A man awaited us on shore. He was dressed in a red flannel shirt, and canvas trousers were stuffed into midcalf boots. He was the only man at the landing, but when the engines shut down, we could hear chopping and sawing a short distance away in the stand of cottonwood trees. A fine Dimick hunting rifle was propped up against a tree within easy reach. I kicked myself for forgetting my Paterson up in the pilothouse. I then noticed that Bosun Joe had strapped on a smoke wagon but could not tell the make or model.

We exchanged greetings with our newfound friend. If I had thought of him as odd at first, his name confirmed my suspicions.

"Chester County White? Is that your name or where you are from?"

"My name of course," he said with a sly grin.

"Just a moment. Isn't that a breed of pig? We had a drift of them when I was growing up."

"Yes, my folks had a strange sense of humor. You shouldn't hold my given name against me."

"I will not, but your flagrant use of the full contents is a little disturbing. I would think you might drop the middle name in all but the most formal circumstances, like silently signing your name and such."

I left the negotiations to Bosun Joe as I probably lost a measure or two of good will with the man. Dang foolish of me, and I knew better. This was the beginning of the season, and these woodcutters knew they had us over a barrel. The choice was to pay their price or chop our own. That could save money up front but use up valuable time. Time was money. Ol' Joe was able to procure two days' worth at three dollars a cord. That was outright robbery in my mind, but Bosun Joe told me it was reasonable in these climes and times.

Mr. White told us that the Sioux Indians were feeling restive and would surely take a shot or two at the boat as we steamed further into their lands. They did not take kindly to the harvesting of their cottonwood trees and occasionally tried to stop it. The work party here was ambushed a week or so back, but the Indian braves did not press home their attack. "They had us pinned down flatter than a brown tick on a white dog. They weren't too serious, or we wouldn't be here now. They're waiting on the boats laden with supplies." He added the neighboring Blackfeet tribe was fighting off and on with the Sioux and should be more friendly if we encountered them. That didn't mean they would welcome us with open arms, though. It meant they were probably receiving their fair share of government subsidies more or less on time. That we heard was a rarity. Government shipments were often delayed, and corruption was widespread. No wonder the Indians were in a constant state of irritation. We went along our way.

"Up there ahead, Captain. That is Blackbird Hill according the chart. We're making good time. Have you heard the legend about this place?"

"Afraid not, Mr. Swanson. Do tell."

"It seems about twenty years ago, a young woman thought her fiancé died at sea and married another man years later. The fiancé, in fact, was alive and found her and her husband living on the Blackbird Hill by chance. The woman asked for a divorce so as to marry her old love, and the husband killed her. He gathered her up and jumped off the cliff into the river. The young seaman wandered the prairie in grief until near dead. He was saved by a band of Indians and returned to civilization."

"Why did not the seaman prevent the murder?"

"He had waited by the river to await the result of the conversation. He was too late to intervene, Mr. Olsson. They say, though, that every October, her ghost is seen and heard upon the hill there."

"That is enough, Mr. Swanson. I do not wish to be a target of your joshing."

After days of steaming through the wilderness and obtaining wood from the forsaken camps, the town of Sioux City was a welcome sight. Only some three thousand hardy souls lived here, but it was a beacon of civilization and for us looked a large and promising as St. Louis. Of course, in actuality, it was just another wide-open frontier town filled with gamblers and hardcases. The town was on a basin bordered by three rivers that to me looked just fine for growing just about anything a farmer set his mind on to plant. Naturally, this and other towns were encroaching on Indian lands, and there was a constant threat of attack. I had read that four years ago, an Indian named Chief Little Crow had become angered by broken promises and delayed annuity payments. He became so riled that he led a revolt of the Sioux over in Minnesota. The Indians' wanton killing of men, women, and children as well as the destruction of property created panic throughout the region. In response, fearful settlers in Dakota Territory here abandoned their farms, stock, and crops to seek refuge in Sioux City. That is all over for now, but Sioux City still relies on the steamboats for goods, and we were heartily cheered upon our arrival. We had some cargo for offloading here, which suits me fine. The river ahead would become more shallow, and the loss of some weight would reduce our draft.

Over the next several days, we stopped at such places as Ponca, Elk Point, and St. Helena for wood and to tend to the machinery. The mud drum needed almost constant attention. Most of the time, it felt as if we were a ship in the middle of an ocean of land. The blue-green foliage of prairie grasses grew upright and strictly clumping, three to eight feet in height. Their flowers are tinted red to purple, and small groupings really make a statement. Off in the distance, we occasionally saw vast herds of buffalo that stretched far beyond view. We also saw small groups of men on horseback, which we presumed to be Indians on the hunt. Of the towns we encountered, Yankton was one of the few with promise, only as it was the capital of the new Dakota Territory. There were probably about three thousand people living here. At the tiny hamlet of Niobrara, we found a large log cabin that obviously doubled as a fort and a sawmill to cut the cottonwood trees. At least here, the prices were more reasonable for the awful cottonwood fuel in my mind.

It was twenty miles upstream of Yankton where for the first time, we saw an Indian party on horseback up close. Well, not exactly up close. We used the spyglass to get the best look at them. Each had a rifle of some sort and paint on their faces. What little I knew of them said they used paint in war and sometimes to bring them luck while hunting. They were just out of range for muskets, and if it were true that they were poor marksmen, they certainly couldn't hit us.

A shot rang out from below, and three or four more followed in quick succession. Passengers were being trigger-happy. I pulled the rope to the main whistle and gave a long peal. My hope was that it would startle the shooters down below and warn the Indians out yonder.

"Mr. Olsson. Take the wheel. Try not to hit anything. I am going below. Send for Mr. Swanson if I am gone for more than ten minutes."

Strapping on the Paterson, I departed the pilothouse and nearly tumbled down the causeway in my haste. Upon reaching the boiler deck I found a group of men were slapping themselves on the back and exchanging money. Others looked sheepish at me, as if children caught snitching cookies from a jar. Mr. Voight and a handful of crewmen showed up at just the right time.

"What in tarnation is the meaning of this? Shooting at Indians for sport? There will be none of that on this boat. Do I make myself clear?"

"No harm done, Captain. Did you see them scatter? Ha!"

"You are a damnable fool. Did you think for a moment they will not collect up what men they have and lay in wait for us to steam by? We may have to face odds that are not in our favor. If this happens again, I will collect up the firearms of all of you and put ashore the men who did it. No doubt the Indians would love to make your acquaintance."

"Didn't know you loved the Indians as much as your Negroes, Captain."

"You are a foolish clod. When you reach your destination, you can antagonize the Indians as much as you want and live and die accordingly. Until then, I have a responsibility to get this boat up to Fort Benton. We may have left civilization behind, but everyone on this boat will remain civilized by God! Now go back to whatever you people do, except for shooting at Indians or each other."

A young child broke the tension and ended the conversation. "My mother says if you haven't got something nice to say about someone, it's time to change the subject."

With the excitement over, the children went back to amusing themselves with games of red rover, tag, and hide-and-go-seek. They tried the game of crack the whip but quickly found there was no room. If they did not interfere with the crew or come up to the pilot-house, I did not care what they did. They would learn a life lesson if they touched a boiler or got their hand caught in the machinery.

With the Indians no doubt riled up, I made a point to land at the military outposts along the way for protection, even if that meant losing a few hours of good steaming time. We had had remarkable weather up to this point, and I was quite proud that we had navigated a strange river—all of it beyond St. Joseph without the assistance of following a steamer. We have had to grasshopper over several sand-bars, but nothing out of the ordinary. I did have to admit though the sheer length of the journey was bearing down on us all. The days were long, the nights short, and the monotony was tiresome. Our cook was doing the best he could with what was available, but our diet became a routine of soups, stews, and whatnot. Fortunately, his baking assistant was capable, and our plentiful sugar supply and canned fruit allowed serving various desserts on occasion. By now, too all the passengers were paying the boat to prepare their meals.

Not all was peaches and cream with the passengers. They left the crew alone, but not each other. Fights were common, usually about the encroachment of someone's claimed territory. Men won and lost their fortunes by way of gambling, and the losers did not always take it well. I always felt gambling was somewhat foolish, but I could see why the Baptists labeled the practice as sinful. Theft proved to be the most common and dangerous transgression. Snitching an item brought swift and immediate punishment, long before a boat officer could quell the situation. Beatings were common, and eventually one man was killed. We buried him on the bank and marked the spot with a wooden cross. No doubt the grave and its contents would be swept away with the next flood. That was assuming the coyotes wouldn't get to the body first. If there was good to be found in the affair, it was that thieving in general petered off.

Although only early afternoon, I ordered the boat to put ashore at Fort Randall. It was a time for a decent rest before a grand mistake was made at the boilers or the passenger engaged in gunplay. Fort Randall was one of the first permanent military outfits along the upper Missouri River and over two hundred river miles upstream from Sioux City. The army built it ten years ago to protect travelers along westward trails and to mitigate relations with Native Americans. Since the war, the most important mission of the fort was to mount expeditions attempting to control the many Indian tribes on the Great Plains, especially the warlike Sioux. The boat's signal "Hip, hip, hooray!" brought whoops and hollers from the lonely soldiers who expected a shipment. We were greeted by a soldier with the chevrons a quartermaster sergeant. The light-blue denoted infantry. He had been left in charge of the fort as the captain led a patrol somewhere to the east.

"I am disappointed you are not the supply boat we have been expecting. Four steamboats passed by without so much as a wave of the hand. We don't have enough food to feed you, but you are welcome to stay long as you like. Maybe you can tell us what is going on back in the States. We're all from Iowa, and any news would be welcome."

The passengers quickly put ashore on their own account. The boat's crew needed to get to the stacks and boilers right away, though. The machinery was simply easier to clean before the metal got too cold. Mr. Voight passed the word that the men could go ashore as soon as they finished with no restrictions. They all worked at a fever pitch.

We found that Fort Randall was a series of twenty-four one-story log buildings that could house six companies or about five hundred men. They were all arranged around a large central parade ground. There were the officer's quarters, barracks, the commissary, and a quartermaster building. Other structures included the guardhouse, hospital, morgue, warehouse, and a sutler's store. They all seemed of good construction, but the cottonwood logs were obviously splitting and warping and needed copious amounts of oakum to fill the gaps. The whole fort was on a flat plain with majestic hills in the background. There was no protective wall here, which I was told was not a typical feature of army posts in the West. They were apparently the product of the imagination found in dime novels.

I learned the location of the fort is at the confluence of the Niobrara and Missouri Rivers, which was handy as the post served as a supply base for Indian agencies and other forts in the area. The fort's mission is to prevent Indian attacks as well at the trespassing of Indian lands by white settlers. While not on campaign, the soldiers' duties at Fort Randall were the routine and often monotonous post-maintenance tasks. As ammunition was expensive and hard to come by on the frontier, the soldiers were not issued any for practice firing. The officers picnicked and hunted significantly more than they trained their men to fight.

"Mr. Swanson, I want you and Olsson to go ashore and have a good time. Get some rest too. We still have a long way to go."

"Aye, Captain. Be sure to do so yourself. You may not have noticed more gray hair coming in."

"That's all I need. By the way, where is our young cub?"

"He went up to the hospital as soon as he could. His, uh, condition hasn't improved much since leaving St. Louis. When he urinates, it feels as if he is passing hatpins. He was hoping to get a dose or two of calomel."

"I learned to walk the straight and narrow during the war, Swanson. Well, I stay on the path usually. I saw what happened to sailors that came down with such ailments. Why physicians would think mercury injections on the afflicted area helped is beyond me. It made things worse from what I saw."

"They should tattoo the navels of those afflicted, and good luck with these saw-bone regimental surgeons. All they know is how to amputate limbs."

"Let's hope it doesn't come to that."

We looked at each other for a moment and had a hearty laugh at the boy's expense. Poor lad.

Frontier forts are lonely places indeed, and our arrival was a cause of celebration. Passengers, crew, soldiers, and the few of their family members mingled freely. The black crewmen kept mostly to themselves but still had a fine time. The soldiers had recently killed a buffalo and cooked it up over a massive pit of cottonwood embers. Our cook contributed to the feast as well. Whatever stores were used was made up for with the buffalo meat and hospitality. After some calculations, I put a bottle of whiskey into the kitty. I had been drinking too much of it anyway. As they were making a punch of some sorts, I figured no one would get roaring drunk with it. It was a waste of good whiskey, though, diluting it like that.

The festivities went well, and there was but little trouble. The men swapped war stories, and even the former Rebs chimed in. Most of these Iowa boys at the fort saw action early in the war and were then sent out here. They were all looking forward to their discharge in five months. The only instance of vexation I witnessed dealt with an errant child. They had all been playing well, finally able to play crack the whip and other outdoor games.

One lad, about ten or so, had taken a dessert from a child half his height and about half his age. A solder was at hand and grabbed his wrist as quick as a viper. The boy did not yelp in surprise but was obviously in discomfort at being caught and finding his hand caught in a viselike grip. Yet not a word he spoke. I suspected he had been in this predicament before. Often, in fact.

"Now look here, boy. That is unacceptable. You must learn to mind your elders and protect those younger than you. In a few years, if you pull a stunt like this, you will be likely shot by those you bully."

The boy did not heed the words and the soldier, and the man peeled back a young finger at a time as if he were shucking an ear of corn. With the tart exposed, the hand was lowered to the waiting child.

Those of us witnessing the event were stunned in the head, wondering what to make of this. We now expected a parent to show up with either a lecture or a kick in the pants for the child.

"Say there! Unhand my boy!"

Apparently, it was the tike's father. He was taller than the soldier, but he had the build of an office clerk. The same type clothes too.

The soldier released his grip, and the crowd, told of what transpired, shouted their approval of the soldier.

The father was not satisfied and saw no reason to let the incident go. The soldier straightened and turned to face the man. His eyes were mere slits, and his teeth were clenched. The soldier seemed to grow in height and bulk, ready to take on a bear. He looked as though he could successfully do so. The father's hostility was doused with great rapidity.

"Uh, I mean to say that I should thank you for showing my son some virtue. I can't watch him all the time."

The father departed in great haste following the path of his son's egress. I suddenly felt badly for the boy, the cowardly father, and those of us who had to witness the whole affair."

The gaiety returned to the festive throng after a few awkward moments as if nothing had happened. I took a moment to peruse a copy of *The Union and Dakotaian* newspaper out of Yankton. Although it only printed a few days ago. there was nothing of interest on the two pages. Being this remote, there was little to print. A purdy young thing presented me a platter of buffalo steak with boiled potatoes. It came with a wink and a smile.

A corporal whispered in my ear, "Careful there, sir. She is a fine girl, but her mother is a gorgon."

I knew better than to seek release of sexual attention with this one, even though she was quite pleasing to the eye. To her, I was only the means of entertainment or escape from this frontier isolation. The meat was fine but just a tad overdone. I shouldn't have even noticed as I was hungry and certainly tired of the canned salted beef we had been subsisting on. Even the cook's renowned redeye gravy was not much help anymore. I was going through my supply of Beecham's pills to keep my gut pipes in motion.

We spent an enjoyable two full days at Fort Randall, and we pulled off the landing with some contrition. We still had at least two weeks to go if all went well to cover the last long miles to Fort Benton. It was unfathomable that Lewis and Clark poled their boats all the way here and on to the western coast. I gave the good sergeant a small bag of horehound candy and promised we would stop by on our way home to pick up the mail for delivery downstream.

I was pleased to learn the Negro blacksmith was put to work in his profession. Mr. Weatherby had need of a new poppet valve spring, and the man made one lickety-split. If a black man can make such an intricate part, he can do anything a white man could.

Indians and Scoundrels

s always, we stopped at various woodpiles and had yet to engage the crew in chopping wood. That was a blessing. Anchoring in the middle of the river so far had prevented any mischief from any hostile Indians. The boat went on to land at Fort Rice and at Fort Peck. At the former, we encountered the *Yellowstone* and the new owner of the fur trade in these parts, a Mr. C. P. Chouteau. I asked him about Foley on the chance they were doing business together. They were not presently, and by his reaction, I doubt Chouteau would ever do so again. The small garrisons were friendly but did not match the hospitality of Fort Randall. No one though could tell us of our nemesis Foley or his whereabouts. Even when the *Marcella* landed for fuel some days ago, he apparently was lying low.

Up ahead in the distance, we could not believe our eyes. Stretched across the horizon was a black smudge of which we could not fathom the cause. The smell was the first real clue of what we were witnessing. The winds blew in a dank, musky odor that only meant one thing: buffalo. There were thousands of them. The boat churned on and on until we could finally make out the individual animals. They were as massive as the books said, but not a sound was heard from them. A herd of cattle of this size would be heard for miles. Unfortunately for us they, had decided to cross the river here and were effectively blocking it.

"What do you think, Mr. Swanson? Is there any chance we could just push through them?"

"I advise against it, Captain. The bulls are two thousand pounds or more, and the cows are a menace too. If they don't bust up the hull, they will wreck the paddle wheels."

"Damnation. We are thwarted until they move on. Signal the deck crew to anchor here in the meantime. I don't want to get any closer as those fools down below will start taking potshots at them for sport."

We remained in place for two days before the river was clear enough to push through. In those days, the majesty of the buffalo gave way to feelings of irritation on my part. A violent thunderstorm was their motivation to move on and our salvation. The deck crew managed to snag four small animals that had drowned upriver, and efforts at fishing sauger and paddlefish were largely successful. Only one catfish was caught, but it was a respectable eighty-pounder. They found the trick was to let the lure settle deep into the eddy below a rock. The fresh meats were welcome additions to our monotonous diet.

The undulations in the courses of the river again looped back on themselves many times over, and the tight bends often required use of both rudder and engines to complete the turns. As we came out of a particularly tight turn, we encountered a line of mounted Indians astride the river. They certainly could not stop a steamboat, so it was a bluff of some sort. I had never seen an Indian up close except for the wooden statues promoting cigar sales. The visage of these Sioux was magnificent. Their physique was perfect for these lands, as if sculpted from red granite. The red riders wore breechcloths with leggings and buckskin shirts. Each was armed with a musket and wore face paint. Some of them sported rather colorful maquillage while others endeavored to make their countenances quite grim. I had to remind myself they could not physically prevent our passage. I could even tell the location of the channel as the water came all the way up to the bellies of the horses on each side of the gap.

"Hold the boat in position, Olsson. Send someone for Mr. Swanson. He should be asleep in his cabin. I'm going below."

"Guess you know what you're doing, Captain."

"I don't know what I could have said to give you that idea. Both engines ahead full, with whistles pealing and guns blazing if they take a shot at us. Don't wait for an order."

While on the way to the forecastle, I shouted to the passengers to ready weapons and fire only on my command or if fired upon. I threatened to leave anyone behind who violated that admonishment. I took the voice trumpet from one of the leadsmen upon my arrival at the prow. I had no idea what to say. Mr. Voight and Mr. Weatherby were standing to each side and were at a loss as well.

From behind, I received a friendly tap on the shoulder. I turned to find a man dressed in skins and a wide-brimmed hat. He leaned against a long Pennsylvania rifle and sported a holstered revolver and a wicked knife on his waistbelt. He hadn't shaved or cut his hair in months, maybe years.

"Captain, are you a man who can partake of some friendly advice?"

"I am a living example of a man who values sound advice. What is your name, and what do you have to offer?"

"My name is Trapper J. I have spent a few years up in these parts and can speak with those savages out there."

"Is that Jay as in j-a-y, or j-a-y with an *e*, or just the letter *J*?"

"The letter *J* if you if you please, but I answer to all three."

"Fine. What do you make of all this? Do these jaspers always appear at mealtime?"

"Well, while you have been staring down each other here, you might not have noticed Indians on each bank have swung around behind you. They want some form of payment to allow you to pass unmolested."

"That will not happen, I assure you."

My hand movements had caught the attention of the band leader, the one with the most feathers, and he boldly prodded his horse forward. He stopped but twenty yards away. It would be easy to pick him off with a pistol, but we would then have to deal with dozens of infuriated Indians. This was a brave man or extremely foolish. If I were a betting man, I would place my money on brave. He shouted at the boat in a mythical language and used his arms for emphasis.

"Well, I'll be. You can see that Injun is very curious about your left hand and is asking how you got it."

"An incident involving steam almost two years ago. Not a very remarkable story. Why do they use their hands so when speaking?"

"These men are hunters and warriors, Captain. They could recite the collected works of Ellen Sturgis Hooper in sign if they wanted. It's useful when sneaking up on prey or a foe. Comes in real handy, in fact."

"Go ahead and speak with him, but I will not pay him any tribute."

Trapper J spent a few minutes conversing, far longer to say what I had told him. The Indians had a look of shock and fright when told whatever tale Trapper J cooked up. The leader of the band spoke to his men in that singsong language of theirs. After some murmuring, the warriors rode away at a trot.

Once they were out of earshot, Trapper J slapped his thigh and laughed until tears flowed from those weathered eyes.

"What the devil was that all about? Out with it, man."

"Well, first they respect your actions with the buffalo herd. They figure you might just appreciate nature. Most boats that pass through here love to shoot up the herds and leave the carcasses to rot. Such a waste of food and hide. On the other hand, I took some liberties with your story, Captain. I told those wagon burners you took the hand of *Wakíŋyaŋ*, the thunderbird himself, and lived to tell the tale. They have never seen such an injury before and swallowed the yarn whole. They think you must have powerful medicine indeed. You now even have an Injun name."

"What might that be?"

"*Napa Lute*. It means 'red hand.' That is a very spiffy name for a first meeting. I think they will leave the boat alone until they had a chance to talk it out among themselves. I suggest you start off slow then hightail it out of here. They may be superstitious, but they are not stupid."

"Uh, don't we smoke a peace pipe or something?"

"This would not be the time or place, Captain. They still want you gone or dead."

"We will be gone shortly. Trapper J, you have blessed me with a most enjoyable day. Thank you. I have a bottle of whiskey for you. I will bring it by shortly."

"At your service, Captain. A pleasure."

The excitement died away, and a sense of normalcy returned to the boat, whatever that was. Days and weeks went by endlessly and in a haze. There were moments, I believed, my watches had stopped only to realize time was simply moving as slow as winter molasses. It was times like these I had wished to have kept a journal. Some captains kept a deck log, but I found that a useless chore and never did. Captain Sulloway abstained from the practice as far as I know, so it must not be all that important. I was though taking copious notes about the river in the event of a return someday that helped pass some of the time.

We came upon two more herds of buffalo, but they were off in the distance. We made landings for wood at the hamlet of Harmon and several unnamed woodpiles along the way. One was owned by a fellow named James Bellows, and he probably owned the best landing along the river. It is a fine site for a real town someday.

Just two miles above this landing, we encountered a fleet of small boats drifting from upstream. None were under steam power, and the larger ones were of wood construction. These could not have been made by the natives. They were even equipped with a mast and sail, but the winds were not favorable presently. They were all using poles and the current for propulsion. Swanson knew of these vessels.

"Those big ones are called mackinaws, Captain. They can reach a length of fifty feet or more. Those small ones are called bullboats and are of Indian design. They have a light wooden frame with a buffalo skin stretched around it to make a hull. Those men must be anxious to get downriver with their gold and fur. That or they unwilling or unable to pay for steamboat passage."

"I have seen the mackinaws before, but not the bullboats. I have read about them but never thought to see one up close."

It took some doing to avoid the vessels drifting with the current. We did our best but would not jeopardize the boat by running close to shore and hitting a snag. There was a copious amount of swearing and cursing as the men on the river frantically paddled their way clear of our advancing prow.

The Missouri River had taken a tact to the west and should remain on this general heading until our destination. I was fine by that as it meant we had but five hundred miles to go. As the winds were generally from the west, we might not have to struggle so much against them. They had been trying their best to push up onto the bank and to our doom the whole way. As a way of compensation, nature bestowed a magnificent full moon that arced above the starlit prairie.

We suddenly heard the discharge of the rifles and saw the white smoke of gunpowder erupt from the brush along the river. The sound of several thwacks hit the pilothouse walls, and one ball shattered a pane of glass. We three instantly ducked under the windows with the assurance the iron plate would protect us. In my mind, I was briefly back on the Cumberland. At this close range, any Confederate sharpshooter would have plugged us but good. A fusillade of gunfire erupted from the boiler and main decks in reply. We couldn't tell if the settlers hit anything, but the Indians must now be lying low or skedaddling.

"That Trapper J fellow said this morning we were now in Crow country. The Indians in these parts are supposed to be friendly. They and the Sioux despise each other cordially."

"How does he spell that, Captain? Is that Jay as in j-a-y, or j-a-y with an *e*, or just the letter *J*?"

"He answers to all three, Mr. Olsson."

That question sounded rather foolish when he asked it.

"Well, if those were friendly Indians, Captain, I don't want to meet an uncongenial one."

Mr. Swanson had a point.

We passed through the Tobacco Bottoms and eventually came upon the mouth of the Yellowstone River. It was a wet dreary day, and the length of the journey was bearing down on everyone.

"There's the Yellowstone, Captain. Do you think that Foley fellow went up there?"

"Might have. We don't have the time or energy to pursue him if he did. That river doesn't look very inviting for this boat anyway. There's not enough water."

"They say upriver somewhere, steam shoots out of the ground. That would be a sight to see."

"Sounds like a tall tale, Mr. Swanson. I am beginning to feel the need to see things before I believe them in these parts."

Olsson said not a word but looked relieved to find I had no intention to go up the Yellowstone. When I was his age, I would have chomped at the bit to try a new river. Entering the years of midlife at thirty, it was me who was feeling the trepidation of this voyage. I felt old and ashamed. Maybe I could find that spark again.

The last few hundred miles of river passed through unsettled plains and what was called the Missouri Breaks. When water was low, the boats were forced to stop at the mouth of Cow Creek. There the boats would deposit their cargoes and rely on ox teams to carry the freight the 124 miles to Fort Benton. I was greatly relieved we passed Jones Island and Cow Creek with only a little difficulty. Although the sand dumped at the mouth was notorious for stopping boats, we were able to run a hawser to a clump of cottonwood trees and haul the boat across the bar. The sand did the hull no favors, and no doubt we would need at least a new coat of paint after our return to St. Louis. The engines needed full power to perform the maneuver, and we went through much wood to make that happen.

Eighteen miles upriver began a series of over twenty-seven rapids. These occur when there is a sudden drop in elevation. Actually, it is a sudden rise in gradient from our perspective of heading upstream. The charts were mostly useless in describing the composition of the riverbed, but it probably was mostly rock. As water flowed over and around the rocks, air bubbles mixed in with it, and portions of the surface acquire a white color, forming what is called *whitewater*. They should be easy to spot.

The water was high enough to navigate most of the rapids with ease. This ease is only in the case of navigating. The traversing of these cursed stretches of river required all the power the boilers could provide. The cottonwood fuel may not be up to the task.

The voice tube bell rang. I flipped the lid and called, "Ahoy!"

"This is Weatherby, Captain. It appeared you needed more power than the wood would provide. You are running on coal now. You have about six hours of it if we keep burning it pure. The Bourdon gauge is at 160 pounds, and I wouldn't want to push it any further."

"Bless my soul, Mr. Weatherby. You earned your pay for the week. I will buy you a drink and a Daniel Webster cigar if we make it through."

"It's a deal, Captain."

All my doubts about Mr. Weatherby went up the stacks and into the atmosphere. That cunning Hoosier hoarded some coal for this moment. With its judicious use, we just might power through all these rapids. It was a burly lesson for me and one to remember if we ever returned.

I was roused from my sleep from Mr. Olsson, who reported Mr. Swanson requested my immediate presence in the pilothouse. There I found the boat maintaining its position at the foot of Dauphin's Rapids.

"Captain! We are thwarted here. We have the power to push through, but the water is six inches too shallow. There are no trees or boulders to tie a hawser to, and we would rip the bottom out even if we tried to pull the boat through."

"Damnation. I cannot believe God himself brought us all the way to be stopped like this. Six inches, do you say? Hmm. Drift down and land on the west bank there. We will put ashore our passengers and as much cargo as needed to lighten the boat. Once we make the run-through, they will portage the cargo up to the boat, and we will be on our merry way. Labor omnia vincit!"

"What on earth does that mean? Are you speaking German again?"

"Hardly. It is a Latin phrase meaning 'work conquers all.'"

"Aye, Captain. As you say. Still sounded German to me."

I went below to speak with Messrs. Voight and Weatherby about our predicament. The first mate would organize the passengers while the engineer prepared to get the boilers up to full steam. The passengers were hesitant to leave the boat, fearing we would continue onward and abandon them. Although I thought to myself that leaving behind a few troublemakers might be a good idea I explained to them all the crewmen not on shift would be joining them. That seemed to alleviate their fears.

It took two hours, but enough freight was taken off to lighten the boat sufficiently. We left the bulky crates aboard as they would prove difficult to haul across the land by hand. With a skeleton crew, the boat surged forward. It took a pachyderm effort, but the boat made it through. The hull incurred more beating though, and we lost several planks on the paddle wheels. We could not hear the cheers behind us but saw the waving of arms and hats tossed into the air.

I landed the boat in an eddy that would facilitate loading. We would wait here until we retrieved our passengers and freight. The men nervously readied the boat's rifles and scanned for Indians. Those left behind were a good half-mile distant, and it would take hours to complete the task. We couldn't possibly leave until well into tomorrow. In the meantime, Mr. Weatherby and his crew saw to the machinery.

Two steamboats arrived below the falls, the *Amelia Poe* and the *Peter Balen*. The *Amelia Poe* is a sternwheel mountain boat captained by Thomas Townsend, a gentleman I met at the New Year's party. He pushed his boat up into the rapids without unloading but fell back downriver. She drew too much water, or her freight was too heavy for her little boilers. The *Peter Balen* is a side-wheeler almost big as us and had no hope of passing the rapids with disgorging some weight. Both them landed and started to unload cargo and passengers.

It was well past noon the next day when we departed. I was pleased to hear all the freight was accounted for. It would have been easy to mix up the cargoes from three boats at the landing below or to suffer from outright theft. Thank the Lord we did not have to portage again on this trip, and that our supply of coal held out for running through the remaining rapids.

We were all treated to the spectacular sight of the fabled Northern Lights for three evenings. The glowing waves of green, pink, green, yellow, blue, and violet are truly a marvel. Some of those on board had to be assured they were harmless, even though the cause of their formation is a mystery. I wanted to think God was giving his promise as he did with Noah after the flood.

"It looks to be a good day. It ain't got no rain."

"So what's a bad day then, Captain?"

"A bad day's when I lie in bed and think of things that might have been."

"Been doing any of that lately, Captain?"

"No more than usual."

There were more stops for wood and the cleaning of the machinery. Names on the charts, such as Sugarloaf Rock, Dark Butte, Hole in the Wall, and Fort McKenzie became real places for us. Coal Banks Landing was a welcome site as the miners there harvested the dark layer of lignite coal that passes through all the hillsides in the area. We took a hundred bushels on board with the promise of returning in a few days for more. We would normally not buy such a poor brown coal, but it was better than that awful cottonwood.

Mountains in the distance became monuments up closer. Until now I never could imagine the size and glory of these peaks. These made me embarrassed to think the hills downriver were formidable. Eagles soared, their screech a call to arms. It was no wonder these birds became the symbol of strength and freedom. Down here on the lowly earth, I felt trapped on this wretched river. It felt sad to see the grand peaks shrink into the distance and become rolling prairie yet again.

We finally rounded Evans Bend on Saturday May 26 and caught the first glimpse of Fort Benton. It looked to be a dusty and filthy place. The trading fort now owned by the Northwest Fur Company dominated the collection of clapboard and the calsomined adobe buildings that were built along the one main street running parallel to the river. Maybe a thousand people lived here. Mr. Olsson pealed the boat's "Hip, hip, hooray!" and almost got it right. The cheering from the decks below was unmatched during this journey, and I thought the stomping of feet would shake the boat apart.

The trip took seven weeks, and we did not set any speed records. The water had been the highest on record and the current strong, but that allowed us to cross over the countless sandbars with ease. We only had to contend with a couple dozen or so bars and shoals, and that cursed Dauphin's Rapids. We were on record though as being the largest boat to make Fort Benton to date. It was a great relief to feel the boat nudge up to the landing, and all the passengers cheered with gusto. They had made their destination. We still had a long way to return home, but that will come soon enough.

Fort Benton is an old trading post of the now defunct American Fur Company, and the first steamboat did not even venture here until the *Chippewa* in 1860. But streams of hopeful prospectors migrated to Fort Benton two years ago when gold was found at the Alder Gulch. More than thirty-five thousand people now lived within ten miles of the discovery site, and they all need their goods and sundries. But boats could go no further than here. So the Diamond R Transportation Company uses a system of ox trains to bring goods from Fort Benton to the even more remote locations. The company was run by a notorious trickster by the name of John J. Roe. If my suspicious were correct, that scoundrel Foley would ally himself with Ford. Birds of a feather flock together. Freight sent to the nearest town, Walla Walla, required animals and wagons to traverse six hundred miles of rugged and hostile territory along the Mullan Road. From there, cargo was freighted down the Columbia River to the Pacific coast.

Fort Benton completely relies on the steamboats to bring goods in the spring and late summer. Huge amounts of everything imaginable are brought upriver, but each winter there were shortages. This last winter, tobacco floor sweepings from the cigar stores were bought eagerly at a dollar to fill one pipe. Another item in shortage appears to be religion. There were no schools or churches to be seen. Catholic missionaries the locals call "black robes" come and stay for a few months during the summers. Their efforts seem to have been in vain so far. I doubt the entire "communion of saints" could do any better.

An odd assortment of people roamed the dusty streets of the town. There are some people of means, and the balance of the generally honest folk are those in the fur trade, merchants, wood hawks, and a few soldiers. There are some women and children here and about, but not many. The rest are scoundrels and killers, gamblers, and draft evaders. A handful of Indians are in town too, toting in furs to trade for goods and liquor.

The locals have taken to calling Fort Benton the "Chicago of the Plains." I had never been to Chicago, but the city on the lake is certainly was not an odd collection of adobe buildings made from the mud of the river. Fort Benton did have an impressive number of saloons. I also found the improbable sight of a hurdy-gurdy house. Hard to believe, but there it was in the spyglass. These are hands-off establishments befitting a large city. The sign out front was emblazoned with "A skirt is a skirt and must be respected as such!" I wonder if they got much business. Olsson should stick to those places.

The real money here came from the gold mines located over one hundred miles to the north. One was named the Confederate Mine. Many of the folks in these parts hailed from Old Dixie and still held dear their old habits. Miners dug and panned all year in their one loop outfits and brought their findings here to town to either cash in or take downriver. Quartz mining was on the rise as well. Gold dust was the currency, here and each establishment had their own weighing scales at the ready.

The steamboat *Marcella* was here with boilers cold. There was no need to rush over to her as she probably arrived here days ago. Foley could be anywhere by now, so I will make inquiries about that fugitive after my business here is finished. The other boats at the landing were the *St. Johns*, the *Waverly*, and the *Big Horn*. If my information in St. Louis was correct, Fort Benton could expect twenty-five more boats to land this season. The town, though, was missing out on significant revenue by not charging landing fees. It would be larceny if they did. There have been no improvements here whatsoever. Not even a "Welcome to Fort Benton" sign.

The passengers were offloaded first, and they needed no urging. There was almost a stampede as ragamuffin men, women, and children departed with their worldly goods with the utmost haste. Trapper J departed the boat with "See you around the haberdasher" and a satchel bag. What an interesting character.

I instructed Bosun Joe to pay the crewmen five dollars in coin after the cargo was unloaded and the new freight loaded so they could amuse themselves for a time. I suspected the five dollars would not go far here, and maybe most of them would stay out of trouble. If they had their own money to spend, well, that was on them. They were reminded that Fort Benton is a notoriously lawless place and to mind their manners. When the boat's signal was given in two days, they were to hightail it back to the boat.

I watched the unloading of the boat, glad to see the passengers disembark and the heavy cargo moved ashore. The work was slow and steady. My guess was the men were ready to move their limbs freely, and the work did that. Light was fading, but there was enough to see. Bosun Joe was down on the landing, entering bills of lading into his book and collecting payment. Beyond the landing, a man watching the boat caught my attention. He was dressed as a businessman, but his clothes had seen some wear. Our eyes met in recognition, and he fled down the street. It was Foley himself! The same man I remembered from that fateful conference in St. Louis. The villain we thought to be perished on the old *Kaw Nation*.

I was glad to have strapped on the Paterson earlier and felt confident to go after him before he escaped to the prairie or out to the mines. After a leap to the bank, the chase was on. I caught up with him within two blocks behind a new building with the sign of "Isaac and George Baker Mercantile and Grocer." We both stopped, winded from the sprint. Businessmen and steamboat captains were not known for their running prowess. We were but six paces apart and no one in sight to witness our confrontation.

"Foley! Stand where you are! You are a wanted man in St. Louis. I mean to return you there for justice!"

Foley came to the wilderness to escape his past, and now it caught up with him. In his current state of affairs, he sported an exceedingly unprepossessing appearance. He looked like the best man at a ten-dollar wedding. Gone were his gold vest and finery. This was a rascal at the end of his rope. His eyes were deep, sunken, and his look unsteady. He was still a dangerous hotspur, though, as Foley is a man that combines the cunning of a fanatic with a total lack of moral principles. I should have unholstered the revolver by now and cursed myself for being such a novice.

"My good captain, if you press this issue, my boys will take you out a ways and then put a bullet through your thick head!"

"That would be murder, Foley."

"I clerked law for a time in Jacksonville, Illinois. Of course, it's murder. But up here, no one would even bat an eye over it. Especially for a dead Yankee."

Before I could form a reply, he went for his revolver. Thomas Geldstein was right. This man was left-handed. I had been foolishly watching his right hand for danger. He had the drop on me, and there was no way in heaven I could withdraw the lengthy Paterson out of its holster in time. Instead, I reached under my coat for the diminutive Root revolver. I hoped Samuel Colt's workmanship held up to his name.

I fumbled and groped to pull back the hammer and get off at least one shot. Sensing my troubles, Foley slowed his efforts to watch in amusement. The weapon fired, but it was a clean miss. The Root was notorious in firing high, and the bullet may have scared some birds somewhere off in the distance. The thought occurred to me that I should have just rushed him.

Foley was not the sporting type and would not allow me a second try. He leveled his revolver at my chest.

"See you in hell, captain."

I heard the loud report of a pistol but felt no pain. Amazed, I opened my eyes to see Foley sprawled on the muddy street. Someone ran up beside me and put his hand on my shoulder.

"What a monumental shot, Captain! I thought he had you dead to rights."

"Huh, what? Bosun Joe? What are you doing here? For land's sakes, I missed him completely."

"Looks like a clean shot to me. There lies the man, slain by young Romeo. If Shakespeare were still around, he would be writing a legendary play of your daring and marksmanship."

"Romeo and Juliet, Act 3, I believe. Confound it! You didn't answer me. What are you doing here?"

"I just came ashore to tell you the freight is almost all deposited on the landing, and we will start loading cargo in the morning. We made quite a hefty sum on the way up. Our strongbox may not be big enough to hold it all."

My head was reeling from the encounter, and I had no words for the man who passed as a sheriff here. Bosun Joe did all the talking for me.

"That man flopped over there is a notorious criminal wanted on several serious charges in St. Louis. When the good captain here tried to take him into custody, the cad there produced his revolver. The captain was quicker on the draw and was defending himself. It was a sight to see!"

The latent lawman was apparently satisfied with the explanation and figured the Montana Vigilantes would have caught up with Foley someday anyway. It was probably the best reason for killing anyone he had heard lately. The few gold pieces found on Foley would cover any burial expenses and his saloon tab, so everyone was satisfied. I was not even asked to write an account of the event.

"Come along, Captain. You don't look well. Let's get you back to the boat and your cabin. Things get confused in gunfights. Let us leave it at that. You did a brave thing back there. Not bad for a Yankee."

"Bosun Joe, I have what may be a strange request. Permit me examine your revolver."

"Why, certainly, Captain. Please be careful as it is loaded."

The revolver was a common Colt navy model. All six cylinders were loaded. And the gun was clean. I was perplexed.

"Is this the only revolver you own and carry?"

"It is indeed, sir. The only one I both own and carry. Is there something amiss, Captain?"

"Yes, but this revolver is not the cause. Thank you."

That Bosun Joe could not have made that shot and reloaded was an undeniable fact. There wasn't enough time or opportunity to reload it in secrecy. We returned to the boat and found my legs unsteady during the walk up the stage. We found the crew in silence and staring at me in curiosity. Bosun Joe called out for the men's attention. I tried to shush him, but he went ahead anyway.

"You won't believe it, men! The captain here singlehandedly ran down that villain Foley and bested him in a stand-up gunfight! Plugged him dead with just one shot from his trusty Paterson revolver!"

I stammered, "But it wasn't the Paterson…" My words were not heard over the cheering and huzzahs of the crew.

Bosun Joe excused himself as he needed to finish making entries into his books.

Mr. Voight took over the duties of seeing me to the cabin. The congratulatory crewmen patted my back and delayed my progress to the hurricane deck. I felt irritated, confused, and at a loss to say anything about the encounter. All I wanted was some silence to ponder what had transpired. My left hand throbbed, and my knees were weak. This killing business was getting to be too routine. Maybe a drink will settle the nerves. Yes, there was a bottle on the table where I had left it. I asked my first mate to have someone wake me in the morning. It would be a long night, and it was.

I was awakened by the shouts and cursing of Mr. Voight and his mates down below. They were loading the buffalo-hide robes. The sun was just coming up. I only had a snort of whiskey last night but felt as if I had downed the whole bottle. After a quick washup, I was out through the cabin door and down to the main deck.

"Mornin', Captain. I was just about to send a man to awaken you. Sleep well?"

"As well as to be expected, Mr. Voight."

"We'll handle this here. Why don't you go ashore, Captain? Have a fine outing this time around. We would like it if you and Swanson were fresh as daisies when we shove off.

"Very well. I wonder what they have for cigars here. I may not have enough to make it back."

The steamboat landing was filling up with new arrivals. The morning sun revealed the *Cora*, *Ontario*, *Amelia Poe*, and others. The *Ontario* had rigged up gangway stage to extend out from her bow while underway. It was unorthodox but seemed handy. It would only take a few men to handle and free up some deck space. Our jack staff was not robust enough to run the ropes up like that and support the weight, but it might be something to consider at the next refit. The *Miner* had arrived sometime after I retired last night. I hailed my acquaintance Captain Porter from the landing. He said he had a load of over one thousand railroad ties for the Union Pacific Railroad. He didn't feel too bad about it as the railroad paid well, and work would not commence for months or even years. That was small comfort for the steamboat business. I did not envy him in hauling such a flammable cargo. It wouldn't take much to ignite those wood ties treated in creosote.

I quickly found cigars of any quality were sold at astronomical prices. I made a deal with a proprietor to trade a bottle of fine Wellers and Sons whiskey for two large boxes. He still got the better end of the deal.

Our primary cargo to deliver downstream was several thousand buffalo-hide robes. The hides had been pressed hair-side out, and each folded into a packet three-feet square. Twelve hides were twined together to make a 150-pound bundle that two men could carry. We ended up with five hundred bales of buffalo robes, forty-five of wolf, twenty of elk, and twelve of antelope. It wasn't considered a heavy boatload, but it would be bulky indeed. Fifty miners and their gold were the other cargo heading downstream. More miners wanted to head to St. Louis but were not yet in town and might not be for days or weeks. The going fare was 5 percent of the gold they were carrying, including what was in their pockets. We offered the miners passage at 4.8 percent to attract their business. Bosun Joe had his scales polished up and balanced in preparation.

Homeward Bound

Although the boat was loaded yesterday, I decided to steam this morning, Wednesday the thirtieth of May. The year 1866 would be half over in another month. Leaving now would allow us to make it further down the river before requiring a stop. The boat's signal produced some friendly waves from the landing and from the other boats. No crewmen were reported missing or seriously injured. That was a surprise blessing. We should be home in about two weeks if all went well. I filled my tankard with coffee and took a deep pull. I may have to start rationing it until we got back to civilization.

"What is ailing you, Mr. Olsson? Are your guts in arrears again? You look upset."

"Captain, I was just thinking again of what transpired to that Mr. Foley fellow at your hand. I know it was a fair fight, but I hate it when anybody dies, even when it is someone like him. I'm sure he probably wasn't a bad sort at heart. Maybe he was even a Christian."

"Well, when you subtract the murder, attempted murder, trying blow the boat to smithereens with all hands and cargo, shooting up the company office, and Lord knows what else, what have you got left? Just a sweet fellow with a social problem. Take the wheel, Mr. Swanson, and start us home. I am going below for my rounds."

If I didn't know any better, I would think the boy was from Massachusetts or something. His mother back in Jacksonville must have held off trousering him until well beyond the age to do so.

I had composed a letter here to my parents but did not place it in the mail. Chances foretold we would end up carrying it back with us to St. Louis anyway. I would add it to my next one.

The habit of meeting with the boat officers had faded away sometime during our voyage north. I reinstituted the practice the first evening out of Fort Benton. It was good again to hear from all the leaders of the boat, and they gained appreciation of the peers from hearing of their trials and tribulations. Mr. Weatherby surprised me with a potentially good idea. I was embarrassed to not think of it myself.

"Captain, do you and Mr. Swanson here really need full power on this downward run? If you can get by on two boilers, we won't burn so much fuel. It would save money and maybe some time."

"I have no objections if Mr. Swanson does not. Does this make sense to you?"

"I suppose it does. It is not as if we are charging on downstream with all these twists and turns. There are some stretches ahead that we should have full power, but we can signal Mr. Weatherby in plenty of time to light the other boilers."

"Well, there's the answer. Make it so, Mr. Weatherby. My hat is off to you for that suggestion."

The result of running on two boilers was a welcome success. We burned less of the remnants of that filthy lignite coal and corrupting cottonwood, thus saving money and time for refueling. The engineer's men did not have to clean the chimney stacks as often. God be praised. We did not have to stop at Fort Randall, but we did so briefly to pick up their mail. I had made the promise and meant to keep it.

We saw even more wildlife on journey south. There were deer, elk, and antelopes in every direction feeding on the hills and plains. They must all show up after the buffalo had passed. The pronghorns, in particular, clipped across the plains at an amazing speed. The fastest critters I ever saw. Foxes, coyotes, and wolves were in abundance, as well as soaring eagles, hawks, and buzzards.

On our travels, we also came upon little fleets of mackinaw and bullboats. Some of our offers to take aboard passengers were accepted, but they still had to pay up five percent of their gold. No special bargains out here. One miner tried to cheat us, claiming he possessed less gold than he did. Bosun Joe spotted an odd bulge on the man's leg, and he was walking queerly. Turns out the miner had tied a handkerchief about his thigh under his trousers with over one hundred dollars' worth of gold dust. The new passengers came mostly from the little bullboats. Those invested in the mackinaws were reluctant to give up on them. We came across a group that Indians shot up two days ago, and these men had had enough. The next day, we encountered a mackinaw hung up on a bar and towed it off for the nice sum of five hundred dollars in gold dust. That is the going rate in these parts.

The miners were a surprising quiet lot and seldom set up games of chance. Checkers seemed to be the game of choice when they played anything. I suppose that after all the work put in, they did not want to lose their winnings on a game of chance. They were all quite happy to leave the territory and showed it with their general good spirits. One fiddle player, though, was noted for his execrable results on his instrument. A fiddle played well is a joy to behold, but one played poorly was torture. The strained notes set most people's teeth on edge. After a few days, the miner found the nerves and goodwill of his colleagues eroded away. The threats of the destruction of his fiddle and bodily harm finally ended the misery. Good times resumed, but it was an odd sound with a dozen or more harmonicas playing different tunes at once throughout the boat.

The boat made it through all the rapids, and I was grateful to the Lord Almighty we did not have to unload and portage the cargo at the Dauphin Rapids. Special prayers were needed at Holmes Rapids near the mouth of the Judith River. We did not make it through unscathed though. The rocks gave the hull some rough treatment. Mr. Voight discovered the leaks quickly enough and put our negro carpenters on the job. The white crewmen bristled when give instructions by them, but the emergency was great enough that they complied. The water was bailed out and the cargo hatches left open to help dry out the buffalo robes stored below.

It was clear to me the Missouri River needs extensive work to be a viable river for commerce for the future against the railroads. This will require a massive investment by the government to remove snags, straighten the river, ad dredge it out. That will take decades and hundreds of thousands of dollars. The railroads will reach out here before that happens. Steamboats will reign out here until that time, but that time is coming.

One of the passengers we picked up at Fort Benton was an Englishman, of all things. He had come south across the British line of the Northwest Possessions and apparently found his fortune or was just tired of the wilderness. It is strange how the British accent allows even the feeble-minded of their kind to appear intelligent. It often took people some time to overcome this notion. I had met only a few Englishmen, but they were even worse in their worldviews than the cosseting Easterners who felt they knew best how to manage things out here in the West. While waiting in line for grub, I overheard one conversation where a miner was having none of it.

"I'm not terribly impressed with your American experiment in republicanism. A monarchy is much more stable. We no longer have civil wars and such, you know."

"You might take note that our army could probably best yours."

"Ah, but the men are mostly discharged and back on their farms."

"All we must do is ring the dinner bell, and they will all form ranks."

After one officer meeting my first mate made what I thought at first was a strange request, upon reflection, it was a very prudent one in these waters.

"Captain, we have fewer men on the boat now. While coming upriver, I figured all those around me were armed enough to keep the hostile Injuns at bay. I'm feeling a bit exposed now. May I borrow that Savage revolver of yours for a spell?"

"Why, certainly, Mr. Voight. It was loaded with fresh powder and caps not too long ago. I recommend you use the holster this time instead of sticking it through a waistbelt."

We went to my cabin and retrieved the pistol from the trunk. I handed to him, and he refamiliarized himself with its queer mechanism.

"Uh, Captain, there are only five rounds loaded. Could I trouble you for the sixth?"

"What the devil? I had loaded it fully with six rounds. I am sure of it. Huh. There are burn marks, and the percussion cap has been struck. This weapon has been fired!"

There were no holes in the contents or side of the trunk. It must have been taken by someone and then returned.

"Mr. Voight. This may be a strange question, but have any of our men been shot in the past two weeks?"

"No, Captain. Do you have any suspicions of who did this?"

"None that would stand up in court. Now let's get this fully loaded for you."

Along the way, we encountered the *Only Chance, Favorite, Helena*, and *David Watts* heading upstream. I was gladdened that we all rendered and gave heed to the established signals. There were no collisions or even a threat of one. Back on New Year's, Captain Joseph Johnson of the *Watts* exclaimed to those who would hear that he would make the trek to Fort Benton in seventy days or better. If it could be done, safe money was on his stout little stern-wheeler. The captain of the *Helena* called over to us as we passed. His boat had been shot up by an Indian band, and two men were wounded. That was two days ago, and the red devils could be anywhere.

One night, a crewman on the dogwatch fired blindly into the dark and sent the boat scrambling for their weapons. I arrived on the boiler deck in my shirtsleeves and my shoes untied. The second mate was already their giving his admonishment with the miners chiming in with agreement. They all surely wanted to slap the foolish lad about a bit.

"Oh, hey, Captain. I thought I saw an Injun out there."

"You might have or might not. They are a sneaky bunch. Do not shoot unless you have a clear shot and certain of a hit. All you have done is advertise you are scared and a poor marksman. That could give them the courage to attack in earnest."

I went back to my cabin and tried to pretend there were no Indians lurking about, but I knew they were out there watching and probably having a grand time of it. My guess was no one got much sleep that night.

We had to battle winds on our northward voyage but found the return trip even more troublesome. The bulky upper works acted as a sail, and it took great effort to keep from grounding on the eastern bank. My frustration and fear for the boat was such I was about to order the dismantling of the Texas cabin atop the boat to lessen the effects. The scrapped wood would also burn hotter than the green cottonwood we had on board. Before the demolition took place, our prayers were answered with a few days of relative calm. The winds did pick up again, but not with such intensity.

"Welcome back, Captain. The coffee is ready on the stove there."

"Thank you. Why are you slowing? This is one of the few straight lengths in this whole river."

"There is a big cottonwood tree in the river running alongside us. It is giving me a headache."

A cottonwood trunk in such a position was a problem, but not a big one if taken care of. If the tree got the notion, though, it could stove in our side. We needed to slow and let it go on or overtake it. If it were earlier in the day, I would try to leave it in our wake; but if we slowed for any reason up ahead, it could overtake us and smash the rudder or worse. With only four hours of light left, the engines were called to slow. Perhaps the tiresome trunk would ground itself during the night or at least get enough distance that we would not overtake it anytime soon.

As always, we anchored the boat in the middle of the river to avoid hostile wildlife and Indians. This now required spinning the boat about to point upstream. When the fires were ignited in the morning, the boat cruised up a short distance, turned about, and went on her way downstream. In darkness, the crew lit lanterns on the main deck to warn boats of our presence. We refrained from using lanterns higher in the boat so as not to attract Indians. But all the men struck lucifer matches throughout the evening to light pipes and cigars. Those could be seen for miles.

One morning, we were aroused by the whooping of Indians on both banks of the river. As before, there was a line of mounted braves fore and aft of the boat and along the banks. They displayed the copper hue of their race, with long black hair and dark-brown eyes. The channel again was too deep for the horses, and the warriors unintentionally marked it for us. The boiler fires were not lit though, and it would take a good hour to build up steam. We weren't going anywhere this time. Indians might be superstitious, but they were not stupid. I strapped on the gun belt and went to the forecastle. Along the way, I shouted to all the men to hold their fire until I gave the command or if we were fired upon first. The miners and crewmen used the bales of buffalo robes for cover.

Mr. Voight was at the forecastle and introduced me to a miner who claimed to speak the Sioux tongue. He was a dirty little man with spectacles. He looked perfect for his profession.

"Reverdy 'Bushwhack' Johnson? That is a fanciful moniker. Where did you get it?"

"I rode with Quantrill's Raiders during the 'late unpleasantness,' Captain."

This man may be a murderer of men, women, and children, but he might be useful. The Bible says Jesus ate with sinners. All I had to do is make use of what this man might have to offer and never converse with him again.

"Very well, what do you make of this situation, Mr. Johnson?"

"The banks are too far away to attempt a burning of the boat, and they haven't shot at you yet. They probably want you to pay up with robes for safe passage."

"That will not be happening. Look there! That Indian is walking his horse toward us."

"That would be the chief of this band. He is showing his warriors he has courage."

"What an eccentric performance. He doesn't frighten me with his knees-bent advancing behavior. Besides, the Indian chief statues in front of cigar stores all have a headdress full of feathers flowing all the way down their backs. This one has only and handful of feathers."

"Those are reserved for the big chiefs, Captain. All the little bands have their own chief who pays allegiance to the big boss-man only when they agree with him. Just because you make peace with the leader of the whole Sioux Nation doesn't mean one of these bands is obligated to make you feel welcome with flowers. He may not sport a headdress, but he earned every one of those quills."

"That makes it rather difficult or hard to make peace with them then."

"Indeed, and their ways of becoming men doesn't help. I've heard that each brave must steal three horses, kill three of the enemy, and lead a successful war party to be considered a full warrior. No squaw would marry him elsewise. Could you imagine us Jews doing all that for a bar mitzvah? Oy vey!"

The leader rode forward just the other did on our journey upstream, but this one came much closer. He was within easy pistol range. He looked us over and called out in that language of theirs. Naturally, he used hand motions as well.

"That can't be right. He's asking if you are *Napa Lute*, Captain."

"Tell him I am. I will prove it."

I removed my left glove and held it aloft. There was a murmur of shock among the braves, and their hands flailed in the air, making their sign language.

The leader rode up to within feet of the boat. He could reach out and touch the gunwale if he cared to. He then gave some sort of command. He yelled it loud enough for his men to hear.

"Johnson, what did he say?"

"He says he has heard of you and wants a closer look at the man who joined with the hand of *Wakíŋyaŋ*. I don't see any harm. There must be fifty guns trained on him."

I knew these people valued pride above all else, so I knelt closer to his level and held my hand forward with all the nerve in my possession. That wasn't very much in these circumstances. After a few moments of looking over my parboiled hand, the ornery Indian suddenly hit it with a decorated stick and whooped like an animal. Although surprised, I managed not to yelp or show undue surprise. He spun his horse around and galloped back to his band. Together the Indians rode out of the water and off to the east. Thank God none of the crew or miners fired. We would have been in a running gunfight for hundreds of miles. My guess was, the miners suspected what was going to happen. The crewmen with arms had dutifully waited for my order to fire, which did not come.

"Tarnation, Reverdy 'Bushwhack' Johnson! What was the meaning of that? That cussed heathen nearly broke my hand! It already has enough troubles."

"That, my good captain, was the practice they call *counting coup*. Instead of killing you, he hit you with that special stick. In their minds, it was just as good as killing you or even better. He will probably get another feather for defeating the chief of a fire canoe. You see, Indians generally don't care to kill each other off, just drive each other away. Warriors stay on the move, attack quickly, and then draw back. If a battle turns against them, they skedaddle. There's no need to stick it out and die. They preferred to return another day and fight again."

"I still don't fully understand."

"It's simple, Captain. If the Indians killed every time they met, there wouldn't be any more Indians, especially since many of them now have firearms. Counting coup allows them to win in battle without killing off too many of each other. If he thinks you held hands with a thunderbird, then maybe he figures you are part Indian. Maybe he just figured to count a coup without getting shot in the process. Either one works for him."

"That, Mr. Johnson, is the most outlandish thing I ever heard."

Return to Civilization

The city of St. Joseph came into view off in the distance when we passed by Worthwine Island. It was a joyful sight. Glad to be back in civilization, I fully realized the frontier had an allure of beauty and adventure that I would remember for years. I wasn't ready to go right back but would do so again if called upon. We have learned a trick or two, and the next time would be easier. In celebration, I allowed the crew to go ashore in shifts and had Bosun Joe pay them each five dollars. I suspected we would lose more than the usual four or five men during this port call. The men had been cooped up together and needed to blow off some steam. The local police and the hoosegow will be busy.

"They have plenty of coal for sale, Captain. What do you want us to do with the cottonwood we still have on board?"

"Sell it if you can, Mr. Voight. Give it away if you can't. Toss it in the river if that fails."

No telegram from the company awaited us at St. Joseph. That was unusual, but not alarming. I had expected a list of consignments to pick up along the river. We could carry the weight, but the issue was that of room. All the hides we carried occupied almost all the available space.

While seated on the hurricane deck with a cigar, a new boat, the *Luella*, pulled alongside and stuck her prow onto the landing. She is a stern-wheel mountain boat that looked about 240 tons. A friendly wave alerted me that the captain was Grant Marsh, whom I had met at the New Year's party in St. Louis. This was his first season as a captain.

"Are you going up or coming back?"

"Heading to St. Louis, Marsh. It was a good run. Watch out for Indians, though. They are getting fidgety waiting for the annuities. Unless they received some satisfaction, in the meantime by now, I would regard them as hostile. Glad to see you got that new boat. How is she holding up?"

"Just dandy so far. I will work on the river upstream all summer but hope to get in another full run from St. Louis after this one. Maybe try to set a new speed record in the process."

"Well, good luck with that, Marsh. See you in St. Louis."

That Grant Marsh is known to be a good, steady pilot. My only issue with him is that he feels compelled to tell everyone. The braggarts get the status of being legendary. At this rate, he will someday achieve that distinction. He still had that spark for the life on the rivers, and I momentarily envied him.

It felt as though I had lost some Christianity on this season. It was a good sign, though, that I recognized this. It's back to church once we reach St. Louis. Maybe a sermon along the way if a preacher shows up at a landing downstream.

I procured copies of the *St. Joseph Morning Herald* and the *Western Journal of Commerce* from the City of Kansas. Over in Europe, Austria and Prussia are at war with no end in sight. Such wars had the bad habit of drawing in other nations and disrupting trade. There was some economic panic concerning the Bank of England as well. The ill effects of such things are often felt here. If there was happy news from overseas, it was Princess Helena of England got hitched to Prince Christian of Schleswig-Holstein. Ironically, that province was being fought over right now by Prussia and Austria. I suppose the happy couple would not be honeymooning there.

With coal to burn and speed desired, Mr. Weatherby lit all four boilers. We had to watch for carelessness as we became more anxious to reach St. Louis. We only needed to stop in Booneville for fuel.

We completed our triumphant voyage on Thursday, June 14. I must admit we pushed the boat faster on the last leg than we would normally, but we were anxious to return and not do so on a Friday. Such superstitions were silly, but many of the men had faith in them. I humored them when convenient. We steamed on through the last two nights to make that happen. There was no moon in the heavens, but the stars shone brightly. The city of St. Louis was a welcome sight, and the riverfront was bustling.

Swanson noticed something was odd before I did. My eyes had been on an errant steamer that displayed a potential of becoming a hazard.

"Look there, Captain. All those boats yonder belong to the company, and none have any activity aboard at all."

He was correct. There were too many company boats at the landing. Most of them should be still underway at this time. The company banners were even missing from the jack staffs. Something was amiss here.

"I suppose we will find out upon landing. Take us in if you please, and well done on this run. Give Mr. Olsson an opportunity to take the wheel if you wish. He has worked hard enough for the honor. After another season or two, you might consider scheduling his pilot examination."

I went below to finish packing my trunks. Only one bottle of whiskey and half a box of cigars remained. That was cutting it close. My shooting days were over, so the vaunted Paterson went into a trunk to join the Savage revolver Mr. Voight returned at St. Joseph. Delivery will be arranged to the Barnum Hotel. The boat nudged gently onto the landing, and the shouts and orders meant the men were securing the hawsers to the stone bollards ashore.

Going below to the main deck, I observed Mr. Voight set the crewmen and hired roustabouts to work unloading the boat. Mr. Weatherby's men got to work on the machinery. Swanson already had his pilot reports prepared and headed straight away to the company office. He left Olsson up in the pilot house to clean the stove and sweep up.

Bosun Joe was on the landing collecting up his bills of lading and payments and was issuing receipts. He would then head to the company office to balance and adjudicate the accounts. The company will pay off the men once the boat is unloaded and cleaned. Many of them would receive the most money they had ever seen at one time. I was disappointed to hear the Negroes were greatly surprised they were to be paid as promised. My word on the matter was not taken seriously.

The company office seemed nearly deserted. The accounting office was active, but that was all. Before going down to see Mr. Geldstein, I wanted to check the lounge for Captain Sulloway. He was there, but Thomas Geldstein was present as well. They sat alone at the table with the padded seats. No one else was here. Even the barkeep was gone. Captain Sulloway looked worried, and Thomas looked ill. My old mentor spotted me and beckoned.

"Well, look what the cat dragged in. Your man Swanson was just here and submitted a ream of paper he called his pilot report. His wrist must be sore. Come on in and have a seat. Oh, grab a glass and another bottle from behind the bar first."

"Greetings from the great American frontier, gentlemen. Don't bother to remark on my odor. The essence of the prairie is strong enough to smell myself. What is going on here? Looks like our whole fleet is in port. Where is everyone around here?"

"No use beating around the bush. In your absence, I decided to liquidate all the assets of the Geldstein empire. I am retiring."

"You are selling the company, Thomas? Why?"

"Indeed, I am. You see, the West is not yet ready for a large transportation conglomerate. Too many hardheaded fools stuck in the past and obsessed with petty rivalries."

"So? Just continue as before. This company was doing quite well before you effected the changes last year."

"My good captain, word got out how well we treat the Negroes. Commercial business in the South was bad already but got worse. No one south of Cairo will ship with us. And all the white crewmen chafed at equal pay with the blacks and demanded an increase in wages that I won't pay. We have been operating at a loss all season with no hope of reversing the labor dispute."

"You have overcome worse than that, Thomas. Just cut back on the Negroes' pay. They were astounded to get white man's pay anyway."

"What's done is done. There is no going back. I have some investors interested in the shipping company, but they do not want the boats. The Memphis and St. Louis Packet Line is expanding and desires much of the fleet. They are a good outfit, as you know. The balance will be put up at auction. I will need to know in a few days what you decide to do. I will sell your boat to you at a fair price if you want to keep her. Otherwise, she will go to Memphis."

"I'm not buying this story, Thomas. There is something more to this. You haven't given up like this before."

"'Tis true, and the fact of the matter is, I am dying. The opium derivatives and laudanum I have used over the years to treat the burn contractures and pain have caught up with me. I feel weak, can't sleep, and the pain just will not go away. The physicians say my body just can't take it anymore and is shutting down. They say there may also be a cancer at work. The medicines have simply damaged my body beyond economic repair and affected my thoughts. There is a growing darkness in them, and I no longer feel myself. It is time to let go and maybe find some enjoyment with the time I have."

"I am so sorry, Thomas. I am at a loss for words. I owe you and your late father so much. You too, Captain Sulloway."

"Oh, enough about me. I'm not quite gone yet. There are things to be done first. By the way, you look almost as poorly as me. You lost weight, your eyes are sunken, and you're sporting more gray hair. You feel all right?"

"Just dog-tired. That felt like the longest run I was ever on."

"Well, you're no spring chicken anymore. Tell us about your grand adventure into the wild frontier."

These were stretches of the Missouri River both these men had never seen. Tales of the river and its hazards, wood camps, majestic scenery, isolated forts, and wild Indians flowed. I tried to explain the Indians but realized I knew only a fraction of what there was to learn about them. What I was told about them before the trek was mostly wrong. I sensed a bit of envy from Captain Sulloway, but he wanted every detail. No doubt he would claim some of these feats as his own at the next party.

"Tell us more of the encounter with Foley, Captain. Is he truly dead?"

"That evening was such a blur. I am finding it difficult to recollect just how things transpired. I was not prepared to fire, and Foley did have the drop on me. He ended up shot in the chest dead and his living spirit removed. I cannot account for it or my survival. But he is surely dead, as a half hitch on a kevel."

"Foley was a man of occasionally generous impulses, princely in his dealings with his friends, and implacable to his enemies. Altogether, though, he was one whom few cared to deal with. He was shunned by his own associates, as such men usually are. Life can be mighty long without friends and be cut short by enemies."

Mr. Geldstein looked at his watch and rose to depart. "That was a fitting epitaph, Sulloway. I did not realize so much time had lapsed. We will talk more, Captain. I have another meeting I must attend."

Thomas rose painfully from his chair and hobbled from the room. He was using crutches for the first time I ever saw. My mentor cleared his throat softly to keep me from staring.

"Captain Sulloway, it appears we truly are in a new era. With the boats gone, what do you plan to do?"

"Me? Huh. I cashed in. Everything. Even the house up on the hill. It is past time for me to retire. My property is crated, and the shipment will be made next week."

"Where are you going? What will you do?"

"I found a nice house on a quarter section of land. Fields and woods with a good creek running through it. The deal will be final once I take a good look at it, but all indications are it will more than meet my needs. Its location is in Henry, Illinois, and it has a fine view of the river."

"On the Illinois? I thought you had no respect for that river."

"Oh, it is a feeble river to steam upon, but there is great beauty in the fields and hills. The people there are fixing to build a lock and dam, and I can watch the boats in detail as they pass through."

"That was your aspiration you mentioned some months ago. I remember."

"What might you do, lad? You can buy up controlling shares of your boat or sell yours off for a tidy sum. The new Miami Packet Company is organizing across the river in East St. Louis and needs boats and pilots. Maybe even captains. You can throw your lot in with them. They are making the big move toward barges, though. If not them, there are plenty of others."

"If I find a change in profession, I may need to purchase a new hat."

"You are the poorest rich man I ever met."

"Do you have word from Captain Bemis? I have wondered what became of that one-legged bandit."

"I do, and I don't know how you will take it. He partnered in opening a bank down in Cape Girardeau, and it appears to be doing well."

"That is wonderful news."

"Well, the snag is that he sent for your lady friend Ann from Beardstown. His letter said they were married, and I figure the beatific event occurred about the time you were up in St. Paul. It was a scandalous affair being so sudden and without her family in the know, but they both seemed to revel in that."

"Well, that is surprising news, but I wish them both well. They will either bring happiness to each other, or we may read of a double murder in Cape Girardeau someday."

"Ha! Either one would not surprise me. But, uh, let us keep our fingers crossed on the former and not the latter."

With that, we both clinked our glasses and downed the contents. I still felt the burn of whiskey. He tossed his down the hatch as one would seltzer water.

"Please excuse me, Captain Sulloway. I must go to the boat to see to things. I want also to make sure the company flag is preserved."

I found the cargo unloaded and the crewmen gone by the time of my return. The men must have moved with an alacrity never witnessed by me. Messrs. Voight and Weatherby had unceremoniously disappeared. With pause, I lowered the company flag from the jack staff and folded it. I momentarily thought of my time on the navy gunboat during the war. The lowering of a flag would have merited a ceremony.

Checking Swanson's cabin showed he had not yet returned for his belongings. The clerk's office was locked tight. I would have to return to the office to confirm that Bosun Joe had removed all the papers and items of value. In my cabin, my trunks were already gone. It then occurred to me that my possibles bag was still in the pilot-house. I would not want to leave behind the handy odds and ends, my tankard, and of course, my trusty spyglass. Closing the door to my cabin, I then made my way up the causeway.

To my surprise, I found Mr. Olsson still aboard. His back was toward me, and his right hand was on the wheel. My guess was he was having a whimsical moment of dreaming of becoming a full pilot one day. But when he turned, his face was reddened from crying. Tears still streamed down his face.

"What ails you, Mr. Olsson? What is troubling you?"

Without a word, he lifted his left hand. I was looking down the barrel of a derringer. I had been in this predicament with this very pistol before, and I did not care for it. Dang southpaw. It's hard to predict what a man is going to do when he uses the wrong hand. Olsson cocked the piece with his right hand. He was shaking, but his aim was true. Just like that cad Foley. I had a sudden realization.

"Olsson, before you pull that trigger, I ask that you explain yourself. This action perplexes me. You have professed to hate killing, and yet here you are prepared to do so. I suspect you have been putting on airs. Foley was your kin, wasn't he? You don't look anything like him, but you both favor the left hand. You both hailed from Jacksonville, and you had some sort of connection with the *Kaw Nation*. That was always an unhappy boat."

Olsson's voice was harsh whisper. "Yes, he was my uncle."

"I suppose then it was you who orchestrated placing the incendiaries in our coal bunker and the assault upon Captain Doyle of the *Piankeshaw* back in New Orleans. It is remiss of me not piecing all this together sooner. Did it ever occur to you that the detonation of the boilers would have killed most everyone on board and you as well? You really are all sorts of stupid, aren't you?"

"The extent of the explosion was not explained to me. You really don't fear death, do you, Captain?"

"There you go being stupid again. Of course, I do. Fear of death has kept me alive up to this point. A pilot faces death every day he is on one of these boats. You cope by getting close to God and try to stay there. After a year on board, I would have thought you had figured that out by now. I've heard all I care to from you. If you are really going to pull that trigger, get on with it."

To my surprise, he really did it. The hammer fell squarely on the firing cap with a bang. Within the enclosed pilothouse, the noise was deafening. It would have been louder if the powder ignited. He was bedeviled with a misfire! Bewildered, Olsson collapsed on his knees and began to sob again. He was catawamptiously chewed up. Defeated.

I withdrew the Root revolver and aimed at his head. At this range, it could not miss. After some consideration, I simply kicked him in the jaw, sprawling him backward. He was out cold. Within moments, Swanson stomped up the stairs and entered the door.

"Captain! Are you out of your mind? Why did you shoot Olsson?"

I told him I did no such thing and filled him in on what just transpired. My fully loaded little revolver confirmed the fact. Curiously, the derringer wasn't loaded at all. The powder and ball were found in the possibles bag where I had kept it. The bullet had rolled out of the barrel weeks ago and dumped the powder.

"Gott sei gelobt!"

"Was that German again, Captain? I haven't heard you say any all season."

"I thought it fitting for the situation."

"I heard the shot in my cabin and came soonest. Frankly, I fully expected you to be the cause of the discharge and not the recipient. Had I been armed, I might have shot you before you could explain. I'm surprised you just didn't kill him."

"I don't enjoy killing, and he isn't worth the bullet, Swanson. Those cost five cents apiece."

"You want to press charges, Captain?"

"No, just get him off my boat. Remove his hat and frock coat. Those are company property. No need to be gentle about it. His days on the river are through, if I have anything to say about it. I will contact the Boatman's Association to see to that. By the way, where are you from? You never brought it up before."

"Portsmouth, Ohio, Captain."

"That's fine by me. I always figured you for a Buckeye. Good people."

"Oh, I just came from the company office. Mr. Geldstein wants me to round up a small crew in the next few days and take the boat down to Carondelet for repairs on the hull. Part of the yard burned in our absence, but they can still do the job."

"Very well, Mr. Swanson. Such command responsibility completed well is a good way to make captain. Good luck."

I was given my usual room at the Barnum Hotel. My attitude improved immensely with a bath and haircut. It was improved even more with a meal at Schwoob's on Adam's Street. Its advert claimed to serve delicacies of the season served in the most approved style. Who could pass that by? When I got around to opening my mail, my parents in Beardstown had some momentous news. They had sold the farm to the Bockmeier brothers and declared themselves retired. They still retained the house and garden but sold the barn, animals, and tools. The proceeds should sustain them through their golden years, and of course, I would not let them want for anything. They had no word on my brother. I then perused a stack of newspapers.

We were gone for only ten weeks or so, which was not unusual in a busy season on our familiar rivers. But the voyage to Fort Benton felt like a year of isolation, and the world passed us by in the meantime. While we were away, the Carondelet and Marine Railways Docks and the steamer *Jeanie Deans* moored there were destroyed by fire. Here in St. Louis, the *Ida Handy*, *James Raymond*, *Bostona*, and *Magnolia* were destroyed by fire. The *Magnolia* was a fine boat worth $150,000. In national news, President Johnson vetoed the Civil Rights Act of 1866, and the moderate Republicans are now convinced there was no hope of working with him on Reconstruction. Without any safeguards for the Negro freedmen, the president's habit of restoring states to the Union by executive fiat was in deep trouble. Johnson simply refused to grant the Negroes any rights beyond legal freedom. The building rebellion in Congress was for the best as Johnson was letting off the old Confederate states off too easily.

In other news, the United States Treasury began issuing a half dime called a "nickel." I wonder what they will look like and how useful they would be.

Along with these troubles, the cholera outbreak we left behind erupted and, so far, has taken over three thousand lives. It appears to be slowing. The city of St. Louis has established a board of health to help solve this and to prevent them in the future. Good luck with that. I don't have faith in these so-called physicians to even tie their shoes correctly.

Thomas would soon need my decision. I took an omnibus out to Lindell's Grove to think things through. While approaching the vehicle, I was nearly run over by a drayman and his horse team. My new hat parted my company and landed in the dust. At least this time, it was not damaged. Upon arriving at the park, I found a cornet band playing lively tunes on the gazebo. The music compelled even the straitlaced Congregationalists, Methodists, and Baptists tap their toes. I strolled some distance away to ponder things.

I did love my boat and position, and I had worked long and hard to obtain both. It is a good life that gives back what you put in and more. Steamboats will be on the river for decades, but the business has changed. Barges and established packet lines will become the norm. There would be no shame in returning to just piloting. Lots of fellows do that. A fancy showboat with a calliope would be a hoot, but I might have to contend with heathen drunken riotous crowds. If I retired from the river, I could not imagine what I would do productively to pass the time. There was no interest in politics, and giving sermons was not my forte. I don't care to farm and learned to hate it while growing up. Perhaps I should take a season to think things over and find my wayward brother. The frontier is wide open and full of opportunities. The Great Lakes has shipping, but I know nothing about navigating on the open waters. Maybe just take up a slower routine, like a regular packet run. No more tramping over the whole continent. I suppose then I could finally meet a respectable woman with mutual toleration. Maybe someone who takes an occasional snort of whiskey and might smoke a cigar on Sundays. Stranger things have happened.

I slept on the matter one more night and had a breakfast at the hotel. I walked the distance to the company office instead of using the omnibus line. It gave me time to think one last time. I found Thomas in his office.

"I naturally heard about that incident with your cub pilot, Olsson. How did he miss you at that close distance?"

"He didn't, or at least he wouldn't have if the derringer worked properly. It was a misfire. Improper loading was the cause. I failed to use a patch, and the ball rolled out the barrel at some point. I had not tended to it in months. Never had a need for it."

"There's no use for an unloaded pistol. They just get you into trouble. Why didn't you have him placed under arrest? You were entitled. You could have killed him them and there, and no one would have held it against you."

"I probably just fell for his act."

"If that don't cap the climax. My good captain, if that derringer had fired, I doubt you would be so magnanimous. I have some news about Olsson that will be comforting. You will not be needing to sleep at night with your revolver."

"Olsson? He's harmless. He's not worth more than a squirrel load of powder."

"He certainly poses no danger now. His body was fished from the river. Someone plugged him with a .36 caliber bullet at close range. The wound was quite ghastly."

"A Colt navy revolver fires that caliber, Thomas."

Mr. Geldstein's eyes narrowed. I was close to crossing a line of some sort. It was time to push forward or back off.

"I surely don't know what you are insinuating, Captain. Remington and Starr make .36 caliber weapons too. Your old Paterson is a .36. It is a very common round of ammunition for thousands of pistols out there. The police say it was probably the result of an act of robbery. No money was found on him. Happens all the time on the riverfront."

I did not point it out, but it was unlikely Olsson had any money on him as he had not been paid off. I did not have the courage to push across the line. I suppose I should be thankful that Olsson was gone. On the other hand, I had no idea what other kinfolk might lurk out there. So far, no one has even suggested I killed him. I had the opportunity to do so legally if I had wanted. But having a reputation as a gunman has disadvantages. Every prairie punk with a gun will try to test you. Always looking over your shoulder is a gritty way to live. I did not want that.

"Thomas, I should check to see how Bosun Joe is doing with reconciling the accounts."

"I just received an update before your arrival. He and the accountants should be finished soon. The rough numbers show the boat took in receipts for about $110,000. Subtracting operating costs, pay, and estimated repairs, there should be a profit of just over $80,000. It's not a record for that run, but well done. You can be proud of that entire feat. Come by tomorrow, and we will have your banknote ready. It will be a tidy sum indeed."

"What will happen to Bosun Joe with the folding of the company? I have heard Voight and Weatherby will move on to other boats in other companies."

"I have retained good ol' Bosun Joe to be one of my special assistants. He will be helping me with the books and the tying up of loose ends. He has proven to be quite handy. The question is, what do you plan to do?"

"I can't imagine what I would do off the rivers. I would probably end up in a lumberyard."

"What is the matter with lumberyards? I happen to own two of them."

"I notice you don't spend much time in either one."

"I'm not precisely sure where they are. Besides, that's what mangers are for."

"Just like first mates, I suppose."

"Exactly. I still have some bits and pieces of various businesses left. Would you be interested in chicken farms? There is also a substantial herd of Chester County White hogs and some cattle too. I believe there is another economic panic coming on. Not right away, but it will manifest itself in a few years. Too many people are throwing money at bad investments. Own land, my boy. It always holds its value. In any case, I need your decision now. What will it be?"

"Cash me out, Thomas. I am going my own direction beholden to no one. I hope there are no hard feelings."

"Absolutely none!" he said with a smile. "We have been through much together over the years, and I am out of the steamboat business as you know. Have you ever thought of working for a railroad? I still have some goodwill there, and they may have just the position for you. Railroads are the future."

Before I could answer, we were interrupted by the bells and whistles of a departing boat on the landing. We both instantly recognized my old boat. Thomas stiffly drew the curtain open for us to watch her go. Swanson was in the pilothouse and was taking her to Carondelet for repairs. The paddle wheels stopped their backward turns, hung motionless, and then churned forward. The proud boat with the proud namesake was beginning her new life under a new banner.

"Thomas, about my decision. This America and I have the means to undertake a host of opportunities. I believe I know what I am going to do."

My parboiled but dangerous old friend smiled that devilish grin that could only come from his scarred face. He placed a hand on my shoulder in anticipation, but I was interrupted by the boat's peal.

"Hip, hip, hooray!"

About the Author

K endall D. Gott is a retired army officer a retired senior historian of the Combat Studies Institute at Fort Leavenworth, Kansas. He is the author of several studies on American military history and the book *Where the South Lost the War: An Analysis of the Fort Henry Fort Donelson Campaign February 1862*. In addition, he is the author of *Ride to Oblivion: The Sterling Price Raid into Missouri, 1864*. Mr. Gott resides in Leavenworth County with his high school sweetheart, Julia, and his dachshund, Stevie.

CPSIA information can be obtained
at www.ICGtesting.com
Printed in the USA
BVHW022136220322
632165BV00021B/258